Praise for *Oscar Wilde and a Death of No Importance*

"One of the most intelligent, amusing and entertaining books of the year. If Oscar Wilde himself had been asked to write this book he could not have done it any better." —Alexander McCall Smith

"Wilde has sprung back to life in this thrilling and richly atmospheric new novel. . . . The perfect topography for crime and mystery . . . magnificent . . . an unforgettable shocker about sex and vice, love and death." —*Sunday Express*

"Gyles Brandreth and Oscar Wilde seem made for one another . . . There is much here to enjoy . . . the complex and nicely structured plot zips along." —*The Daily Telegraph*

"Brandreth has poured his considerable familiarity with London into a witty fin-de-siècle entertainment, and the rattlingly elegant dialogue is peppered with witticisms uttered by Wilde well before he ever thought of putting them into his plays." —*The Sunday Times*

"Fabulous . . . The plot races along like a carriage pulled by thorough-breds . . . So enjoyably plausible." —*The Scotsman*

"Both a romp through fin-de-siècle London . . . and a carefully re-searched portrait of Oscar Wilde. . . . Very entertaining." —*Literary Review*

"Brandreth has the Wildean lingo down pat and the narrative is dusted with piquant social observations. A sparkling treat for fans of Wilde and Sherlock Holmes alike." —*Easy Living*

"A lively, amusing, and clever murder mystery starring Oscar Wilde— larger than life, brilliant, generous, luxurious—with a new trait: he is now a master sleuth not unlike Sherlock Holmes. . . . Brandreth is steeped in the lore of Wilde, but this doesn't oppress the story which is a cleverly plotted thriller through London's demi-monde. . . . Highly entertaining." —*The Dubliner*

"This is not only a good piece of detective fiction in its own right, it is highly entertaining, spiced as it is with Wildean sayings, both real and invented and the imagined conversations and intellectual sparring between Wilde and Conan Doyle. Future tales in the series are something to look forward to."
— *Leicester Mercury*

"Excellent . . . I'd be staggered if, by the end of the year, you'd read many better whodunnits. Brandreth demonstrates supremely measured skill as a story-teller."
— *Nottingham Evening Post*

"Wilde as detective is thoroughly convincing. . . . The period, and the two or three worlds in which Wilde himself moved, are richly evoked. . . . This is an excellent detective story."
— *The District Messenger,* newsletter of the Sherlock Holmes Society of London

"Brandreth knows his Wilde. . . . He knows his Holmes too. . . . The plot is devilishly clever, the characters are fully fleshed, the mystery is engrossing, and the solution is perfectly fair. I love it."
— *The Sherlock Holmes Journal*

"A skilful and erudite piece of writing and one well worth reading, not only for the plot but for much information about Wilde and his friends at that period."
— Tangled Web

"It works quite brilliantly. This is the first of a series. You'll want to start the next the day after finishing this one."
— *The Diplomat*

"A witty and gripping portrait of corruption in late-Victorian London, and one of which Oscar Wilde and Arthur Conan Doyle would be proud."
— *Livewire*

"A wow of a history mystery . . . a first-class stunner."
— *Booklist*

"Beautifully clear prose . . . We tend to be wary of books that use real-life characters as their protagonists, but we were completely enchanted with this one."
— *The Denver Post*

"Wilde beguiles those inside the novel and out. . . . Brandreth writes breezily, effortlessly blending fiction and historical facts in a way that keeps the novel moving."   —*The Atlanta Journal-Constitution*

"An intriguing tightrope walk . . . engaging, ingenious."   —*Newsday*

"Immensely enjoyable, one of the best in the canon of literary mysteries."
—*The Philadelphia Inquirer*

Praise for *Oscar Wilde and a Game Called Murder*

"The second in this wickedly imagined and highly entertaining series . . . an intelligent, jaunty, and hilarious mystery."
—*The Good Book Guide*

"Hugely enjoyable."   —*Daily Mail*

"A cast of historical characters to die for."   —*The Sunday Times*

"A carnival of cliff-hangers and fiendish twists and turns . . . The joy of the book, as with its predecessor, is the rounded and compelling presentation of the character of Wilde. The imaginary and the factual are woven together with devilish ingenuity. Brandreth also gives his hero speeches of great beauty and wisdom and humanity."
—*Sunday Express*

"Wilde really has to prove himself against Bram Stoker and Arthur Conan Doyle when a murder ruins their Sunday Supper Club. But Brandreth's invention—that of Wilde as detective—is more than up to the challenge. With plenty of wit, too."   —*The Daily Mirror*

"Gyles Brandreth's entertainment is an amusing and satisfactorily unlikely story featuring Bram Stoker, Arthur Conan Doyle, a locked room, and Oscar Wilde in the role of the series detective."
—*Literary Review*

"The plot speeds to an exciting climax. . . . Richly atmospheric. Very entertaining."
—*Woman & Home*

"Sparkling dialogue, mystery piled deliciously on mystery, a plot with pace and panache, and a London backdrop that would grace any Victorian theatre."
—*The Northern Echo*

"The acid test for any writer who has enjoyed first-time success is that all-important second novel. Gyles Brandreth, I am happy to report, has sailed through the ordeal with flying colours. . . . Irresistible . . . Elegant . . . Rich . . . Enjoyable . . . A classic Agatha Christie–style whodunit involving some particularly inventive murders with a few well-placed red herrings."
—*Yorkshire Evening Post*

"As much imaginative biography as murder mystery . . . Terrifically well researched, it whizzes along."
—*Scotland on Sunday*

"What raises this book several notches above most mysteries is the authentic historical detail and the engaging portrait of Wilde . . . sparkling."
—The Historical Novel Society

"Terrific period atmosphere, crisp writing style, and the flamboyant Wilde make this series pitch-perfect. Great entertainment." —*Booklist*

"[*Oscar Wilde and a Game Called Murder*] is the eagerly awaited second volume in Gyles Brandreth's series of detective stories and it doesn't disappoint."
—*The District Messenger,* newsletter of the Sherlock Holmes Society of London

"I can't wait until the next one."
—*The Scotsman*

Praise for *Oscar Wilde and the Dead Man's Smile*

"One of the most consistently entertaining historical series starring a real-life sleuth."
—*Booklist*

"The murders begin. Highly theatrical ones . . . An entertaining and meticulously researched piece of pop fiction about Wilde and his circle."
—The Washington Post

"Through his excellent writing Brandreth has brought to life 1880s Europe and his descriptions evoke all the senses as if you were there following Oscar. It is a fun book that introduces you to many interesting characters. . . . A light-hearted and entertaining murder mystery."
—The Irish Post

"Gyles Brandreth began his Oscar Wilde murder mysteries in grand style. The second book was actually better than the first, and the third consolidates and improves on that achievement. An exceptionally good detective story, it's also a fascinating historical novel."
—The District Messenger, newsletter of the
Sherlock Holmes Society of London

"A cleverly plotted, intelligent, and thoroughly diverting murder mystery. This novel is an educated page-turner, a feast of intriguing and light-hearted entertainment."
—The Good Book Guide

"An entertaining yarn, easy and pleasing to read—with an extensive set of vivid characters."
—Gay Times

"Very funny."
—The Independent on Sunday

"For me this whole series is a guilty pleasure: Brandreth's portrait of Oscar Wilde is entirely plausible; plots are ingenious; and the historical background is fascinating."
—The Scotsman

Praise for *Oscar Wilde and the Vampire Murders*

"Inventive . . . Brilliant . . . Marvelous . . . Glittering . . . Graceful . . . Intricate . . . Enthralling."
—Booklist

ALSO BY GYLES BRANDRETH

THE OSCAR WILDE MYSTERIES

Oscar Wilde and a Death of No Importance
Oscar Wilde and a Game Called Murder
Oscar Wilde and the Dead Man's Smile
Oscar Wilde and the Vampire Murders

BIOGRAPHY

The Funniest Man on Earth: The Story of Dan Leno
John Gielgud: An Actor's Life
Brief Encounters: Meetings with Remarkable People
Philip and Elizabeth: Portrait of a Royal Marriage
Charles & Camilla: Portrait of a Love Affair

AUTOBIOGRAPHY AND DIARIES

Under the Jumper: Autobiographical Excursions
Breaking the Code: Westminster Diaries
Something Sensational to Read in the Train:
The Diary of a Lifetime

NOVELS

Who Is Nick Saint?
Venice Midnight

SELECTED NONFICTION

Created in Captivity
I Scream for Ice Cream: Pearls from the Pantomime
Yarooh!: A Feast of Frank Richards
The Joy of Lex
More Joy of Lex
Great Theatrical Disasters

OSCAR WILDE

AND THE

VATICAN MURDERS

—◆—

GYLES BRANDRETH

A TOUCHSTONE BOOK
Published by Simon & Schuster
New York   London   Toronto   Sydney   New Delhi

Touchstone
A Division of Simon & Schuster, Inc.
1230 Avenue of the Americas
New York, NY 10020

First Touchstone hardcover edition May 2012

TOUCHSTONE and colophon are registered trademarks of Simon & Schuster, Inc.

For information about special discounts for bulk purchases, please contact
Simon & Schuster Special Sales at 1-866-506-1949 or
business@simonandschuster.com.

The Simon & Schuster Speakers Bureau can bring authors to your live event. For more
information or to book an event contact the Simon & Schuster Speakers Bureau at
1-866-248-3049 or visit our website at www.simonspeakers.com.

Manufactured in the United States of America

10 9 8 7 6 5 4 3 2 1

Library of Congress Cataloging-in-Publication Data
Brandreth, Gyles Daubeney, 1948–
    Oscar Wilde and the Vatican murders / Gyles Brandreth.
        p.   cm.
    "A Touchstone Book."
    1. Wilde, Oscar, 1854–1900—Fiction.   2. Doyle, Arthur Conan, Sir,
1859–1930—Fiction.   3. Vatican City—Fiction.   4. Murder—
Investigation—Fiction.   I. Title.
    PR6052.R2645O77   2012
    823'.914—dc22   2011038380

MAY 16 2012

ISBN 978-1-4391-5374-1
ISBN 978-1-4391-7230-8 (ebook)

For Michèle
from first to last

Oscar Wilde and the Vatican Murders

Drawn from the previously unpublished memoirs of
Sir Arthur Conan Doyle (1859–1930), creator of
Sherlock Holmes and friend of Oscar Wilde

Principal characters in the narrative

Oscar Wilde, Irish poet and playwright

Dr. Arthur Conan Doyle, Scottish author and physician

Dr. Axel Munthe, Swedish author and physician

The British community in Rome

The Reverend Martin Sadler, Anglican chaplain

Irene Sadler

James Rennell Rodd, First Secretary, British Embassy

At the Vatican

Cesare Verdi, sacristan at the Sistine Chapel

Chaplains-in-residence to His Holiness Pope Leo XIII:

Monsignor Francesco Felici,
Pontifical Master of Ceremonies

Father Joachim Bechetti

Monsignor Nicholas Breakspear SJ, Grand Penitentiary

Brother Matteo Gentili, Capuchin friar

Monsignor Luigi Tuminello, papal exorcist

You know a conjurer gets no credit when once he has explained his trick; and if I show you too much of my method of working, you will come to the conclusion that I am a very ordinary individual after all.

SHERLOCK HOLMES TO DR. JOHN WATSON,
A STUDY IN SCARLET, 1887

OSCAR WILDE
AND THE
VATICAN MURDERS

Rome, Italy, April 1877

Letter from Oscar Wilde, aged twenty-two, to his mother

Hotel d'Inghilterra

Darling Mama,

I am in Rome, city of saints and martyrs!

I have just come from the Protestant Cemetery where I prostrated myself before the grave of "A Young English Poet"—John Keats. He died here in Rome, not yet twenty-six, a martyr after his fashion, a priest of beauty slain before his time, a lovely Sebastian killed by the arrows of a lying and unjust tongue. I lay face-down upon the grass, amid the poppies, violets and daisies, and said a prayer for one who was taken from life while life and love were new. (Fear not, Mama, the grass was quite dry and the sun was shining. I will not catch a chill.) The grave is all simplicity—a hillock of green grass with a plain headstone bearing the epitaph Keats wrote for himself: "Here lies one whose name was writ in water." This is to me the holiest place in Rome.

*I say that despite having spent the morning at the Vatican!
Yes, Mama, earlier today Oscar Fingal O'Flahertie Wills
Wilde, your son, had the privilege of an audience with His
Holiness Pope Pius IX. All here call him "Pio Nono" and say
that, in everything but name, he is a saint already. Certainly,
he must soon be with the angels. He has been pontiff for more
than thirty years. He is eighty-four and cannot be long for
this world. He is so frail. The English lady standing next to
me in the receiving line said that, in his white dress, the Holy
Father looks like a small child just put down to run alone. He is
diminished by age and he* totters.

*There were perhaps thirty of us admitted for the audience—
Irish, English, American, and French, as well as Italian.
Audiences like this take place in a grandiose corridor somewhere
between His Holiness's private apartments and the Sistine
Chapel. We arrived at noon and waited upwards of an hour
for the Holy Father to appear. I assumed that he was about his
devotions. The English lady assured me that he was attending
to his midday broth. "His mind may not be what it once was,"
she said, "but his appetite is undiminished, thank the Lord."
(Though an Anglican, the lady attends upon His Holiness as
often as she is able. The English community here is* devoted *to
the Pope.)*

*When, at last, the Holy Father appeared in our midst he was
surrounded by a fluttering retinue of priests and acolytes—old
and young, half a dozen of them at least. Slowly, the pontifical
party proceeded down the line, His Holiness giving each
pilgrim a moment in turn. With some he was quite chatty,
putting his hand to his ear to hear what was being said to him.
Naturally, his attendants laughed at all his little jokes. Pio*

Nono's body may be worn out, but his eye is beady and his voice still strong. To the Englishwoman next to me he remarked, "Inglese, no?"—and that was all. ("That's what he always says to me," she told me later, proudly.) When he reached me and I gazed directly upon his face, I was much moved. He has lost his teeth and his underlip protrudes, but there is great sweetness in his smile. I genuflected and kissed the third finger of his right hand. He placed his left hand upon my head and gave me his blessing.

I was almost the last in line. Beyond me were two Italians: a Capuchin father and a young girl, aged thirteen to fourteen. The girl's beauty was extraordinary—she had the face of a Madonna by Botticelli, with hair the colour of moonbeams and eyes the hue of cornflowers. She was dressed in a simple white smock and she fell to her knees the moment His Holiness entered the corridor. Clearly, the Holy Father knew her because, as soon as he reached her, he lifted her veil from her face and caressed her head and said warmly, "Dio ti benedica, figlia mia." He then took both her hands in his and raised her from her knees. She smiled shyly up at him. Beaming, he looked around at his attendants and back along the line of pilgrims, then, in Italian, told us: "Look on this child and give thanks. She is pure innocence. She is a lamb of God, surrounded by the seven deadly sins." He let go of the girl's hands and, laughing happily, went on his way.

I shall not forget this day.

Ever your newly blessed son,
Oscar

I.

Homburg, Germany, July 1892

From the unpublished memoirs
of Sir Arthur Conan Doyle

I am a details man. I can tell you that in 1892, my thirty-third year, I wrote a total of 214,000 words, all too many of them concerned with the adventures of Mr. Sherlock Holmes. My industry was well rewarded. My income for that year amounted to £2,729—a substantial sum, an *outrageous* sum, you may think, at a time when a schoolmaster was earning, at most, £150 per annum and a housemaid no more than £40.

On account of Sherlock Holmes I was prosperous. On account of Sherlock Holmes I was becoming famous. On account of Sherlock Holmes I was exhausted. The public could not get enough of "the world's foremost consulting detective": I was weary of his very name. Halfway through that year, at the start of July 1892, having completed seven Holmes stories in the space of six months, and having settled my wife and baby daughter in our new home in the London suburb of South Norwood, I decided to take a break. I wanted ten days (no more) of rest and recuperation. I needed, as the phrase now goes, to "get away from it all." I took myself off to the foothills of the Taunus Mountains, to the German spa town of Homburg. I went to catch up with a backlog of paperwork, undisturbed. I went in search of peace and quiet and solitude. As I arrived at my hotel on Kaiser-Friedrich-Promenade, I came face-to-face with Oscar Wilde.

Do not misunderstand me. In the hurly-burly of the metropolis, in the crush bar at the opera house, or a drawing room in Mayfair, there could be no better companion than Oscar Wilde. He set every room he ever entered on a roar. I never knew a wittier man, and he was wise as well as witty. And his wit sparkled and soared: it was never mean or cruel, never exercised at a lesser man's expense. But Oscar Wilde was not a quiet person. He was Irish and he would not—could not—stop talking. His was a talent to amuse, excite, delight, and stimulate, not to soothe. He had genius and charm, and in the years that I first knew him, before his terrible downfall, he was, at all times, a perfect gentleman. But he was not *restful* company.

Even as I came through the doors of the hotel, even before the hall porter had relieved me of my bags, I heard Oscar's voice calling out to me.

"Arthur? Arthur Conan Doyle! Is that really you? Heaven be praised. Thank the Lord you are here."

My friend was bounding towards me. He appeared distraught. His pale-blue eyes were red-rimmed and shiny with tears. His puttylike features were flecked with beads of perspiration. He did not look well.

He offered me no formal greeting, but simply cried: "I

need cigarettes. Do you have some, Arthur? Turkish for preference. Or Algerian. American, even. Anything will do."

I gazed at him, bemused. "Cigarettes? What for?"

"To smoke, of course!" he expostulated.

"But you never travel without your cigarettes, Oscar."

"I arrived with a dozen tins," he wailed, "but I have exhausted my supplies and in this godforsaken town there's not a tobacconist to be found. They have been outlawed by the burgomaster."

I put down my cases and felt in my coat pocket. "I believe I have some pipe tobacco," I said, laughing.

He seized the tobacco pouch from my hands and kissed it reverently. "You are my salvation, Arthur. There's a Lutheran Bible in my room—a poor translation but printed on the most delicate rice paper. I shall use its pages to roll my own cigarettes."

"It's a rough tobacco," I warned him, apologetically.

"No matter, it's tobacco and I shan't overwhelm it. I shall begin with Hosea and confine myself entirely to the minor prophets." Bearlike, he put his arms around me. He was a big man: over six feet. "Thank you, Arthur. You are a good friend. Welcome to Bad Homburg. Dinner as my guest shall be your reward."

I looked about the cheerless hotel hallway. There were no pictures on the walls, no flowers in the pewter vase that stood on the heavy oak sideboard. "What on earth are you doing here, Oscar?" I asked.

"Suffering," he sighed. "And mostly in silence. The other guests are German. Conversation is limited. I find it is so exhausting not to talk."

I laughed. "Are you here for the cure?"

"Yes," he answered, bleakly, "and it is killing me. I go over to the spa every day and drink the waters. The taste is utterly repellent. It takes a bottle and a half of hock to recover from it. I have never felt so unwell in my life." He grinned and waved my tobacco pouch in the air. "But your shag will set me right, Arthur. And over dinner you'll tell me why you're here."

"I'm escaping Sherlock Holmes," I said.

"You'll never do that, Arthur. You cannot deny your destiny. No man can. Besides, we may need Holmes's counsel over dinner. We must discuss the sorry business of the murder of the pastry chef."

I stood amazed. "The hotel's pastry chef has been murdered?"

"Not yet," smiled Oscar, holding the tobacco pouch above his head as he made his way towards the stairs, "but it is quite inevitable. When you see the dessert trolley you will know why. *A tout à l'heure, mon ami.* We'll meet in the dining room at eight."

I settled myself into my room on the hotel's top floor, but at the back of the building, low-ceilinged, airless, and sparsely furnished. My narrow window overlooked the hotel's kitchen yard. My narrow bed faced a whitewashed wall adorned with the room's only piece of decoration: a heavy crucifix carved from Black Forest oak. As soon as I had unpacked my bags, I changed for dinner and lay on the bed, disconsolate, gazing alternately at the crucifix and my pocket watch, willing the minutes to pass. As I reflected on the austerity of my surroundings, the prospect of dinner with Oscar seemed ever more enticing.

My friend did not disappoint. On the stroke of eight, I made my way into the hotel dining room. The room (oak-panelled and candlelit) was filled with diners, yet felt deserted. At every table, mature couples sat face-to-face in accustomed silence.

"You notice," whispered Oscar, as I sat down before him, "how they study their plates and their water glasses and the vacant middle distance just beyond their spouse's left or right shoulder. Will it be like this for us in years to come?"

"No," I said, smiling, "we are both happily married men. We can look our wives in the eye with a clear conscience. We talk to them and they talk to us. We are blessed." I gazed about the room as the waiter unfurled my napkin and, with a heavy hand, laid it across my lap. "Is there anything worse than a loveless marriage?" I pondered.

"Oh, yes," said Oscar. "A marriage in which there is love, but on one side only."

Despite the Lenten surroundings, my friend entertained me royally that night. Oscar Wilde was, as another Irishman observed, the greatest talker of his time—perhaps of all time—but he was not a monologue man. He was a conversationalist: he listened attentively before he spoke. He took as well as gave, and what he gave was unique. He had a curious precision of statement, a delicate flavour of humour, and a trick of small gestures to illustrate his meaning, which were peculiar to himself.

We had first met three years before, in London, introduced

to one another by an American publisher who sought from each of us "a murder mystery" for a monthly magazine. I had obliged with my second Sherlock Holmes adventure. Oscar had written *The Picture of Dorian Gray*. As writers we were very different. As men we were dissimilar, too, in age (Oscar was five years my senior), appearance (he was taller, stouter, and not a man for a moustache), and outlook (Oscar was an aesthete: I was a medical and a military man), but from that first encounter we were immediately in sympathy. Ultimately, I believe it was an arrogance akin to madness that brought him low, but in the heyday of our friendship Oscar seemed to me to be among the best of men. I liked him and admired him. I was awed by his high intelligence, intrigued by his fascination with detective fiction, and amused by his fondness for aping Sherlock Holmes at every possible opportunity.

When the waiter had served us our turtle soup and poured us each a glass of excellent Moselle wine, Oscar remarked: "I feel sorry for the fellow, don't you? He's unhappily married, as you can see, and it must be humbling for a once-proud Bavarian officer to be reduced to this."

"Are you talking about our waiter?" I asked.

"I am."

I smiled. "Has he confessed all this to you, Oscar, or have you deduced it?"

"You know my methods, Arthur," answered my friend, playfully tapping the side of his nose with his index finger. "We can tell that he's unhappily married because, though he wears a wedding ring, there is a button missing on his jacket and his waistcoat is both stained and poorly pressed.

His wife no longer cares for him. He was evidently a soldier because of his bearing. He is stiff and heavy-handed. And his accent tells us he is Bavarian."

"What tells us that he is a 'once-proud officer'?"

"His cuff-links and the duelling scar on his left cheek. The cuff-links bear the black and yellow badge of the German Imperial Army. As he poured your wine, you could clearly read the motto on the Imperial Cross: *Gott Mit Uns.*"

"I noticed the cuff-links," I said, "but not the duelling scar."

"It's dark in here. They keep it deliberately crepuscular to prevent you from seeing too precisely what's on your plate."

I laughed and looked once more around the gloomy dining room. "Why on earth are you here, Oscar?"

"It was my darling wife's idea. Constance wishes me to lose weight. I have put on two stone in two years. Here at Bad Homburg, I am advised, I can lose two stone in two weeks."

He said this with a mouthful of bread and butter, as the soup was being cleared away and a dish of turbot in mushroom sauce was being laid before us. Wiener schnitzel, boiled potatoes, and sauerkraut were to follow, then cheese, then blancmange, then fruit and nuts.

"I am on the strictest regimen," he declared. "Morning and afternoon, religiously, I cross the road to the bathhouse and take the repellent waters. At the end of the day a remarkable specimen of humanity named Hans Schroeder comes to my room. He has the body of a Greek god and the hands of a Teutonic prize-fighter. He is my personal masseur and he knows me better than I know myself. For an hour each evening he pushes, pummels, and pulverises me, without remission. He is ruthless, remorseless—and in the pay of the hotel. His ministrations leave me so enfeebled that I haven't the strength to venture out to find a decent restaurant. I am forced to rebuild my strength as best I can in this dismal dining room." He drained his wineglass, shook his head, sighed, and closed his eyes.

"The wine is very good," I said.

He opened his eyes and grinned. "I agree. It's exceptional. I think we need another bottle right away." He waved towards our waiter. "We must toast your arrival, Arthur. You have heard my sorry tale. Now it's your turn. Why are you here? You don't need to lose weight."

"I've come to clear my head," I said. "And to clear my desk."

Oscar raised an eyebrow. "You've brought your *desk* with you?"

"I have brought a portmanteau of paperwork with me, yes. I am overwhelmed with correspondence, Oscar. No one told me this was the author's lot. I have hundreds of letters demanding a response."

My friend looked alarmed. "Are these from creditors, Arthur? Are you in trouble?"

"These are from readers, Oscar."

"You get *hundreds* of letters from your readers?" Oscar sat back wide-eyed in amazement and, I sensed, a little in envy.

"No," I reassured him. "I get only a handful, fewer than you do, I'm sure. It is Sherlock Holmes who gets hundreds of letters—thousands, even."

"But Holmes is a figment of your imagination."

"He is, but the letters aren't. The letters are all too real and my publishers insist that I at least *glance* at each and every one. Most can be dealt with by means of a printed postcard of acknowledgement, of course, but simply opening, scanning, and sorting it all takes time—and gets in the way of my real work."

"Cannot your wife serve as your secretary?"

"My precious Touie does not enjoy the best of health, as I think you know. She has a weak chest and a small daughter and a new house. She is frail. She cannot take on anything more. No, I must clear the correspondence that has accumulated and then stay on top of it. It can be done."

"It will be done," said Oscar, emphatically, as the waiter arrived with the fresh bottle of Moselle. "And I shall assist you. Do not protest. We shall start work tomorrow—immediately after breakfast. I shall forgo my morning cure to be at your service." He raised his hand and shook his head. "Do not protest, Arthur," he repeated. "I insist."

I did not protest. I merely smiled. I was accustomed to Oscar's sudden enthusiasms. I had no doubt that his offer was sincere, but equally I had no doubt that once the novelty of the enterprise had worn off, I would be working my way through Holmes's correspondence alone.

"Thank you," I said. "And thank you for dinner. This wine really is outstanding and, for all that he's an old soldier down on his luck, I'd say our waiter is looking after us rather well."

"He is," my friend conceded, smiling as he sipped at his wine.

"But just now, Oscar," I continued, "as he was serving us, I studied his face quite closely. I saw no duelling scar."

Oscar raised his glass to me once more and narrowed his eyes. "You must allow a fellow writer a little licence, Arthur."

The following morning, at ten o'clock, as agreed, we gathered in the hotel lounge to begin our work. When I arrived, Oscar was already in place, seated alone at a card table by the window overlooking the promenade. He was heavily built and massive, with a suggestion of uncouth physical inertia in his figure, but above his unwieldy frame perched a head so masterful in its broad brow, so alert in its blue-grey, deep-set eyes, so full in its lips, and so subtle in its play of expression that after the first glance one forgot the gross body and remembered only the dominant mind—and the outrageous garb. He was dressed in a bottle-green linen suit, sporting a pale-grey shirt and an elaborate daffodil-yellow tie that exactly matched the toe caps on his leather ankle boots. His overlong hair was swept back over his large head. He was freshly shaved; his cheeks were pink and his eyes sparkled.

"You've clearly breakfasted well," I said, by way of greeting.

"I am breakfasting now," he replied, indicating the small hand-rolled cigarette that he held between the middle and the ring finger of his left hand. "And never better. And I've ordered a bottle of iced champagne to help ease us into our labours: Perrier-Jouët '86. I adore simple pleasures, don't you? They are the last refuge of the complex."

"Are you going to be saying clever things all morning?"

I asked, opening up my portmanteau and placing four bundles of correspondence on the table.

"I hope so," he replied, pulling one of the bundles towards him. "Are we opening these at random? May I start?"

"We are," I said, "and you may." I looked about the empty lounge as I took up my place facing Oscar across the card table. "Our fellow residents are all over at the bathhouse taking the waters, I presume?"

"Yes," he answered, drawing languorously on his little cigarette. "We shall have nothing to disturb us now, except this correspondence and our consciences."

"Does your conscience trouble you, Oscar?" I enquired, untying the bundle of letters before me.

"Insufficiently, I fear. Life's aim, if it has one, is to be always looking for temptations—and there are not nearly enough of them, I find. I sometimes pass the whole day without coming across a single one. It makes one so nervous about the future."

I smiled. "You're on form today, my friend."

"I am hungry for excitement," he answered, waving his first opened letter towards me. His eyes scanned the paper and he sighed. "However, it seems I am not destined to find it here." He drew more impatiently on his cigarette. "Listen to this. 'Dear Mr. Holmes, I am secretary of the Godalming Gardening Society. During the winter months, when gardening is not possible, we run a series of lecture evenings and trust that you may be able to accept our invitation to address us on either 3 November or 1 December next at seven o'clock. We meet on the first Thursday of the month. We expect a talk of sixty minutes in duration, followed by questions from the floor. We are not able to offer a fee, but will cover all reasonable expenses and provide refreshment on the night. Our hope would be to hear something about the cases of yours that have not yet been reported in *The Strand Magazine*. We look for *originality* in all our speakers. I look forward to hearing from you at your earliest convenience. Yours most sincerely, Edith Laban (Miss).'" Oscar let the letter fall from his grasp. "Even the woman's name is banal."

I smiled. "A postcard simply saying 'Mr. Holmes regrets he cannot oblige' will suffice, Oscar."

He picked up the letter again. "She has underlined the word 'originality,' Arthur. The impertinence of the woman, the effrontery . . ."

"Just scribble a note of regret on a postcard and be done with it, Oscar."

"I'm not sure we should reply at all—or perhaps I should reply on Holmes's behalf and explain that he is unavailable but that I am willing to come in his stead. Yes, I think that Oscar Wilde should address the Godalming Gardening Society on 3 November. I am ready to be entirely original. I have things to tell the members of the Godalming Gardening Society that they are certain never to have heard before!"

I laughed. "Give me the letter, Oscar. I shall reply."

My friend passed me the letter with a despairing snort and began to sort through the remainder of the pile in front of him.

"Be warned," I said, "it'll mostly be requests for autographs, photographs, and the recipe for Mrs. Hudson's apple pie."

"Ah," cried Oscar, holding aloft a small packet, about eight inches long and four inches wide. "This looks more promising."

"Do not get too excited. It is probably a book of sentimental poetry—a gift from the author. Sherlock Holmes has many female admirers."

"This comes from Italy," said Oscar, inspecting the package more closely. He studied the postmark. "From Rome. And the address is written out in capital letters. I think it's more likely to be from a man. It does not feel like a book. It's more malleable. Unbound proofs, perhaps."

He tore open the brown wrapping paper. Inside the package was a large unsealed envelope. Oscar shook the contents onto the table. What fell from the envelope appeared to be a human hand, severed at the wrist.

2.

The Tell-tale Hand

Oscar recoiled in horror and pushed his chair back from the table. "This is grotesque," he hissed.

"It's certainly a surprise," I said.

"Don't touch it, Arthur," cried Oscar.

"It's only a hand," I reassured him. "It won't bite. And we've known worse. As I recall, when we were investigating the case of the death of no importance, a severed head was delivered to your front door."

"I remember," he said, flinching at the recollection.

I took out my pocket handkerchief and, using it, picked up the dismembered limb, holding it towards the window light to examine it. The skin was dark, the hand small; for a moment I thought it might have been the paw of a gorilla or an orang-utan.

"It is a human hand?" asked Oscar, as if reading my thoughts.

"Yes," I said, inspecting it more closely.

"It's not made of wax or India rubber?"

"It's the real thing, I'm afraid—flesh and bone. It's a right hand, quite small, quite smooth—almost delicate. I'd say it was a woman's hand but for the rough cut and shaping of the fingernails. Look."

I held the hand out towards Oscar. My friend summoned up his courage and, through gimlet eyes, keeping his distance, inspected the severed limb. "Yes," he whispered. "It is quite delicate, I see."

"And look at the wrist. Look at the bone, look at the stump. It's a clean cut, but brutally done. It's the work of a butcher's cleaver rather than a surgeon's knife."

"And the black marks below the knuckles?" enquired Oscar, peering closer.

"Mottling, I'd say, nothing more, signs of age. And yet the palm is smooth, almost unlined. The hand looks young . . ."

"It's not diseased?"

"I don't think so." Oscar winced as I brought the hand to my nostrils. "It's been pickled, I reckon, or embalmed. That would explain the dark pigmentation of the skin—and the quality of the preservation. It's a dead hand, but, apart from its colour, it has all the appearance of a living one."

I was about to lay the hand back on the table when heavy breathing and the clink of glasses alerted me to the arrival in the lounge of our Bavarian waiter from the night before. Rapidly I wrapped the dismembered limb in my handkerchief and thrust it into my jacket pocket.

"Guten Morgen, mein Herr," cried Oscar, a touch overexuberantly.

Ponderously, in silence, the waiter opened the Perrier-Jouët and poured us each a glass. With an utterly irrelevant quotation from Goethe (something about the land where the lemon trees grow!), Oscar pressed an English florin into the man's hand, explaining that it was the only coin he had about him but, as it bore a portrait of Kaiser Wilhelm's grandmother Queen Victoria, he trusted it would be acceptable as a modest token of our appreciation. The waiter said nothing. When he had gone, Oscar raised his glass and drank down his champagne in a single gulp. He poured himself a second glass and said quietly: "Arthur, you sit there with a dead man's hand in your pocket. What does it mean? Why has it been sent to you?"

"It's not been sent to me. It's been sent to Sherlock Holmes."

"Care of your publishers."

"No. Look at the label on the wrapping. It was sent to Holmes at 221B Baker Street, London. There's no such address, of course. Baker Street runs up only to number 100. The post office covering the Marylebone district kindly collects the letters and forwards them to my publisher."

Oscar examined the brown wrapping paper. I looked at the envelope that had contained the hand itself. "It's a sturdy envelope," I observed, "and made of quality paper."

"Is there a watermark?"

I held the envelope up to the window. "No, not that I can see. It's thick paper—card almost. It's the sort of envelope that a lawyer might use to store deeds in, or a will."

"The envelope is unmarked?"

"Quite."

"There's no note inside? No message of any kind?"

I looked inside the envelope. "No, there's nothing." I put down the envelope and took a sip of the iced champagne. It was strange to taste champagne so early in the day. "Nothing at all."

"The hand is the message," mused Oscar, still studying the brown wrapping. "But what does it signify? Is it a cry for help?"

"Or a warning?"

"Or a threat?"

"Or an act of madness?" I put down my glass and smiled. "Is it simply a practical joke? An English admirer of Edgar Allan Poe once sent Holmes a dead raven."

Oscar looked up at me and pursed his lips. "Yes, well, we know an Englishman's idea of ready wit is a bucket of water perched on top of a half-opened door—but this isn't an Englishman's work. This hand was sent to Holmes from Italy."

"Is the handwriting on the label Italian?"

"Impossible to tell." Oscar scrutinised the wrapping once more. "The stamps are. The postmark is. 'Roma, 8 marzo 1892.'"

"*Marzo?* That's March, Oscar. It's now July. The package was sent four months ago."

"Is that significant?"

"It may be. If this was a cry for help and it has gone unheeded, there may be others, yet more desperate." I turned to my portmanteau on the floor beside my chair and pulled out four more bundles of correspondence. "We must go through all this, I'm afraid, every item."

"How far back do these letters and packages go?" asked Oscar, pushing his glass and ashtray to one side and taking a bundle from me.

"To the beginning of the year. I have let it all accumulate since Christmas. I've been ignoring it because I find it so oppressive. I'm a doctor, Oscar. I'm a writer. I have no wish to be correspondence secretary to an imaginary detective. I'm not interested. I haven't the time."

"Calm yourself, Arthur," my friend said, soothingly. "These letters are the fruits of your success. Take pride in the fact that you have created a character so vivid, so real, so *tangible* that strangers turn to him in their hour of need." Oscar was now rifling through a substantial handful of the correspondence, noting the postmark on every letter. "London, London, London, Chester, Plymouth, London, Glasgow, New York, Babbacombe, Leeds, London, Milwaukee, Moscow, the Isle of Wight . . ." He paused and looked up at me. "Holmes has conquered the *world*, Arthur. Be happy."

"I have a dead man's hand in my pocket, Oscar," I said.

"And between my thumb and forefinger," cried my friend exultantly, holding up a small cream-coloured envelope and waving it towards me, "I have another letter from Rome—look! 'Roma, 22 gennaio 1892.'"

"That's January—open it, open it!"

Oscar tore open the envelope and peered inside.

"What is it?" I asked. "A note this time?"

"No," he said. "It is a lock of hair." Oscar tipped the contents of the envelope onto his open palm. It was indeed a lock of hair, a thick loop about an inch in diameter and two inches in length. "It is hair the colour of honey," he said, gazing down at it.

"It's a brackish yellow, Oscar."

"It is golden," he persisted. "It's the colour of a leaf in early autumn. It's beautiful. Look at the shape. It might be a kiss-curl from a young boy's forehead."

I lifted the lock of hair from his palm. It was surprisingly rough to the touch. "Or it might be a ringlet cut from an old lady's wig," I suggested. "The hair feels very coarse." I held it to my nostrils. "It smells musty. It smells of overripe apples."

"There you are," said Oscar, raising his glass to me. "The very smell of it evokes Keats's season of mists and mellow fruitfulness."

I laughed out loud. "Three glasses of champagne in lieu of breakfast, Oscar, and you'll say anything."

"But isn't it possible?" he asked, earnestly, putting down his glass and leaning across the table towards me. "This lock of hair, the severed hand in your pocket: they could have been cut from the butchered body of some poor Italian youth . . ."

"Yes," I replied. "Or the hair could have come from a wig—that's what it feels like. And the hand could have been cut from a legitimate cadaver, in the dissecting room of a hospital or in a respectable mortuary."

"Then why send them to Sherlock Holmes?"

"As a hoax? As an unpleasant joke?"

"Or as evidence of a terrible crime. You must concede that is at least a possibility, Arthur?" Quickly, he lit another of his home-rolled cigarettes and, sucking on it urgently to draw the smoke, he continued to rifle through the piles of correspondence on the table. I joined him in the task. "We must look at every envelope," he said. "There may be more from Rome."

There was. Among the last batch of letters we inspected—it was, in fact, the batch that had contained the original package with the severed hand—I came across a third, and final, envelope bearing Italian stamps. The postmark read: "Roma, 15 maggio 1892."

Oscar raised his glass to me, as if in triumph. "Is the handwriting the same as before?" he asked.

"It appears to be. With capital letters it's difficult to tell. But the address is written in black ink, as before, and in a steady hand. It's a different envelope, smaller than the first, larger than the second. But it's evidently from the same source."

"Open it up," commanded Oscar. "What will it be this time?"

"A photograph of the sender, I hope, with a detailed letter of explanation—preferably in English." I opened the envelope. There was no letter. I saw at once what was inside and tipped the contents onto the littered table.

"Ah," cried Oscar, narrowing his eyes, "just what I've been wanting: a small cigar."

"I think not, Oscar," I said. "You really have drunk too much. Look at it, man. It's a finger—a human finger—an index finger, I'd say, severed at the knuckle."

Oscar peered down at the table suspiciously. "It looks like a small Havana to me. Look, there's the cigar band."

"That's a ring, Oscar." I shook my head and sighed, unable to decide whether my friend was being playful or perverse. "May I borrow your handkerchief?" I asked.

"If you must," he said, fishing into his top left-hand coat pocket and handing me an apricot-coloured square of silk.

Carefully, I laid out the finger on Oscar's handkerchief and, from my own pocket, produced the severed hand, laying it, palm down, alongside the severed digit. "What do you think?" I asked.

"I think the members of the Godalming Gardening Society would be in for a treat if one took these along as exhibits."

"Don't you see, Oscar?" I said, somewhat impatiently. "Concentrate, would you? Focus."

"What don't I see?" he asked, pouring himself yet more champagne. "It's plain enough, alas. I see a dead man's hand and a dead man's finger."

"But you don't," I said. "Or, at least, not necessarily so. Who is to say these limbs belong to a man?"

"Do they belong to a beast?" he cried, melodramatically.

"No, but the hand might be a woman's. It is small and smooth. We must not make assumptions, Oscar. We must consider the evidence." My friend sipped his wine, gazing steadily at the hand and finger that lay on the table before him. When I sensed that I had his full attention once more, I went on: "These limbs do not come from the same person, Oscar."

"Do they not? How can you tell? Their colour is identical."

"They have been preserved in the same way, pickled in the same fashion. But look at the hand: it is a complete right hand. And look at the finger. From the shape of the joint and the curvature of the nail and the tip, you can see that it is a finger from a right hand also, and an altogether larger hand than the other. The hand and the finger come from different bodies."

"Good God," murmured Oscar, putting down his glass. "A double murder."

I laughed. "Or no murder at all. These could simply be limbs cut from two people who have died of natural causes. Or, alternatively, limbs cut from individuals who are still living."

"Is that possible?"

"Quite possible," I said. "Have you heard of the Mafia?"

"Is it a restaurant?"

"It is a secret criminal society based in Sicily, Oscar. Members of the Mafia are sophisticated bandits whose power and influence grow by the day. They hold sway far beyond the toe of Italy. They are brutal and they are fearless. Cross them, betray them, and they will exact their revenge in barbaric ways."

Oscar gazed wide-eyed at the severed limbs laid out on the handkerchiefs before him. "I am beginning to warm to the Godalming Gardening Society. Dismemberment has never been a feature of everyday life in Surrey."

"But, of course," I added, "this horror may have nothing whatsoever to do with the Mafia. The Mafia simply sprang to mind because I have been considering involving them in one of Holmes's yarns."

"Have you told anyone of this?"

"No one. No one at all. That's what makes it so curious." I glanced towards the bottle of Perrier-Jouët. "Is there any left? I think I'm ready for a drink now."

"I'll order more," cried Oscar, as he poured the remains of the champagne into my glass.

"No more, thank you. This will be enough. We must

keep our heads clear. We must think. And think carefully."

"No, Arthur, we must act. And act recklessly. We must pack our bags. We must order our tickets. We must be on our way."

"What do you mean, 'on our way'? I have only just arrived."

"Yes, but you can't wait to leave and neither can I." He looked around the deserted hotel lounge. Outside, the sun was shining; within the room, there was a settled gloom. "We don't belong here, Arthur. This ghastly place is for the old and the decrepit—"

"Some of the guests are younger than you are, Oscar."

"They are older in spirit, all of them. They don't drink, they won't smoke, they can't talk—why do they bother to breathe?" He threw back his head, expanded his chest, raised his broad shoulders, and drew deeply on his little cigarette. Turning towards the window, he looked out onto the road leading to the spa. "These sad folk, look at them, with their dreary faces and their ludicrous lederhosen, 'taking the cure,' 'drinking the waters'—they don't live. They exist. And then they die." He turned back towards me, tears in his eyes. He raised his glass and bumped it gently against mine. "That's not our way, Arthur. Whatever our age, we are to be young. Here's to us! Here's to Life!"

"Here's to you, Oscar," I said, oddly moved by his sudden outburst. He was thirty-seven years of age, but, in truth, because of his bulk and his crooked teeth, with his blotchy complexion and his red-rimmed eyes, he looked older. "Where do you want us to go, my friend?"

"Is it not obvious?"

"To the police, I suppose. We should. We should indeed. But what would the police make of this? Are they going to scour the streets of Rome in search of a man with a missing finger and a woman who has lost her hand? Why should they?"

"We are not going to the police, Arthur. You are right: there would be no point. But we are going to Rome, Arthur, this very afternoon. We must. We are going to solve this mystery, you and I."

"Why?"

"Because it'll do us good! It'll be an adventure—and that's the only 'cure' we need." He looked down at the littered card table and touched the brown wrapping paper and the envelopes that had contained the severed limbs and the lock of hair. "Besides, for whatever reason, someone has sought to make contact with Sherlock Holmes. Holmes is your creation, Arthur. You need to discover what is going on."

"I need to be back in London in ten days."

"You will be, I promise you, and when you get there, what a story you'll have to tell. And if you don't get there— if the Mafia get to you first—what a way to go! The obituary writers will have a field day."

"Oscar, you have drunk too much."

"On the contrary, I have drunk too little." He pushed back his chair and beamed at me. "I can see the headlines, Arthur: 'Scottish author cut down in prime. Creator of Sherlock Holmes slain by Sicilian bandits.'"

"Oscar, you are drunk and you are absurd."

"Nevertheless I am taking you to Rome to unravel the

mystery, to unmask the murderer!" He clapped his hands in glee.

"Who is to say there's been a murder, Oscar?"

My friend looked down at the table and indicated the hand and finger lying there before us. "There's clearly been a murder, Arthur, and, by the look of it, more than one."

"This is not evidence of murder, Oscar."

"It's evidence of mutilation, at the very least." He pushed his chair further from the table and got to his feet. "Kindly wrap up the exhibits. As you're the medical man, we will leave them in your care. Have a special regard for the honey-coloured lock of hair and the finger. I shall enquire about the train. You go and pack your bags. Rome calls."

I began to move, reluctantly. "It'll be a wild-goose chase, Oscar."

"And when we get there, we'll be searching for a needle in a haystack. I know, Arthur. But at least, thanks to the ring, we'll have somewhere to start."

"Thanks to the ring?" I repeated.

"Ah," he said, smirking. "Can it be that Oscar Wilde, even when intoxicated, has noticed the tell-tale clue that the creator of Sherlock Holmes, entirely sober, has missed? Examine the ring, Arthur."

Oscar had removed the ring from the finger. He handed it to me. "It's a simple gold band," I said.

"Rose-gold," said Oscar. "The colour is distinctive."

"Rose-gold," I agreed, "but otherwise unremarkable." I turned over the ring in the palm of my hand. "A little scratched on the inside, perhaps."

"Examine the scratch marks carefully, Arthur."

I peered closely at the ring. "This is where I need Holmes's magnifying glass," I said.

"Or Wilde's eagle eye," my friend countered. "Do you not see a shape in the scratch marks?"

Screwing up my eyes, I saw something. "The outline of a key?" I suggested.

"Exactly."

"Two keys, in fact, lying end to end, overlapping."

"Crossed, I think," said Oscar. "The keys of St. Peter, I suggest. The symbol of His Holiness the Pope. When we get to Rome, Arthur, we will start our investigations in the Vatican City. We will begin at the Basilica of St. Peter's. The key to the mystery lies in the keys. The game's afoot, my friend."

3.
The Train to Rome

*T*he soul is born old but grows young. That is the comedy of life. And the body is born young and grows old. That is life's tragedy."

On the little local train that took us from Homburg to Mainz, Oscar was in a philosophical frame of mind. He resisted all my attempts to get him to talk seriously about the practicalities of the assignment we had embarked upon. Instead, gazing dreamily out of the window at the passing mountain scenery, he offered up epigram after epigram— some, no doubt, original; others, I suspect, borrowed from Montaigne or Mark Twain. (Oscar maintained that he had an arrangement with Mark Twain: on their respective sides of the Atlantic they could appropriate one another's quips with impunity and without acknowledgement. Oscar liked to say that plagiarism is the privilege of the appreciative man.)

At the railway station in Mainz, Oscar bought cigarettes, salami, bread, cheese, and a small cask of red wine. For a man who worshipped youth and beauty above all else, he most surely did not treat his own body as a temple. From Mainz to Zurich, we had no choice but to travel third-class, sitting on a wooden bench, side by side, awkwardly, in the corner of a crowded and airless compartment, consoling ourselves with our picnic and our cigarettes, and talking in whispers. None of our fellow travellers (six dour-faced working men in blue overalls) looked in the least likely to be English-speakers, but nevertheless I felt uneasy with Oscar's line of conversation. He had moved from philosophy to religion.

"It is curious how the love of God can lead to acts of unspeakable cruelty," he said, chewing on a piece of cheese. "You were brought up by Jesuit priests, Arthur. Were they unspeakably cruel?"

"I was brought up by my mother, Oscar, but I went to a school run by Jesuit priests, yes. It was a boarding school and the regime was Spartan. Everything in every way was plain to the point of austerity. Dry bread and well-watered milk were all we had for breakfast. The life was harsh, but the priests were not cruel."

"Did they beat you?"

"All the time." I laughed at the recollection. "And I was beaten more than most. The corporal punishment at Stony-hurst was severe, I grant you that."

I gave Oscar a sidelong glance. He was studying me with disconcerting intensity. "Go on," he said.

"It was peculiar, too, administered with an instrument of torture imported from Holland, as I recall."

"An instrument of torture," he repeated.

I lowered my voice further. "It was called a 'tolley'—I don't know why. It was a piece of India rubber the size and shape of a thick boot sole. One blow of this 'tolley,' delivered with intent, would cause the palm of your hand to swell up and change colour. Nine blows to each hand was the customary punishment, and, once you'd taken it, you'd not be able to turn the handle of the door to get out of the room. To take twice nine on a cold day was about the extremity of human endurance."

"And why were you, Arthur Conan Doyle, beaten more than most?"

"Because I was mischievous. Because, deliberately, I broke the rules. Because I wanted to show them that I would not be cowed."

"Bravo, Arthur."

I returned Oscar's gaze. "In the end, I think the beatings may have done us good, because it was a point of honour among us boys to show that we were not hurt. And that's a useful training for a hard life."

Oscar took a swig of the red wine. Now he looked at me with gently mocking eyes. "So you emerged from Stonyhurst upright and uncowed, bruised but unbroken."

I smiled. "I like to think so."

"And well educated?"

"The curriculum, like the school, was medieval but sound."

"And chaste?"

"That's a curious question, Oscar."

"I'm a curious fellow, Arthur."

I lowered my voice still further. "Since you ask, the answer is 'yes.' Jesuits have no trust in human nature. Perhaps they are justified. At Stonyhurst we were never allowed for an instant to be alone with each other and I think that in consequence the immorality that is rife in other schools was at a minimum. In our games and in our walks the priests always took part and a master perambulated the dormitories at night—all night. Such a system may weaken self-respect and self-reliance, but it at least minimises temptation and scandal."

Oscar exhaled a thin plume of blue-green cigarette smoke and murmured: "What is the point of life without temptation and scandal?"

At Zurich we changed trains once more. For the penultimate leg of our journey—overnight from Zurich to Milan, via the Gotthard railway tunnel—Oscar had succeeded in securing us a second-class sleeping berth. For the first time since leaving Homburg, we had some privacy. At midnight, as the train departed and we stood together alone in the narrow galley adjacent to our bunk beds, Oscar suggested we "inspect the evidence" once more before retiring. I still had the hand and finger, wrapped in their respective white and apricot shrouds, hidden about my person. Oscar had placed the lock of hair in its envelope inside his wallet. We laid out the specimens on the upper bunk, immediately beneath the Pintsch lighting gasolier, and stood, shoulder to shoulder, staring down at them.

"What do you think?" asked Oscar.

"We have indeed embarked on a wild-goose chase," I said. "I don't know how I've allowed you to cajole me into this."

Oscar rubbed his knuckles against his chin. "Has a murderer sent these to Holmes as a challenge?" he mused.

"It is an extraordinary act of hubris if he has."

"Or is it a witness to murder who has sent them? That's more likely."

I shook my head. "I think this is the work of a rival author bent on distracting me from my proper labours."

Oscar laughed. "Your rival must be exceedingly jealous to go to so much trouble to keep you from your desk, Arthur. This is a human hand, this is a human finger, this is human hair."

"The hair does not feel like real hair to me," I said.

"And what about the ring? You'll concede that the ring tells us something."

Using Oscar's handkerchief, I lifted the finger to examine the gold band once more. With my own finger, I touched it. The ring moved easily. "It's loose," I said.

"Remove it," said Oscar.

I obeyed his instruction and handed my friend the rose-gold band. He took it between his thumb and forefinger and held it up to the gas lamp to examine. "These are the crossed keys of St. Peter, without doubt, but there's nothing else. There's no inscription and no other marks on the inside of the ring."

"And there is no mark on the finger, either," I said, inspecting the digit more closely now that it was unadorned. "There's no indentation where the ring was resting. It seems that the ring and the finger do not belong together."

"The ring was placed on the finger after the finger was severed?"

"And after it was embalmed. Look at the colour of the finger: it's consistent along its whole length."

"This ring is a sign," cried Oscar, "and intended as such. It must be."

"It is certainly all we've got, but if the Pope had been murdered I rather think we'd have heard, don't you?"

"Sarcasm ill becomes you, Arthur," Oscar snapped. "This isn't the papal ring, I know that. The papal ring depicts St. Peter the fisherman casting his net in the Sea of Galilee. I have kissed the papal ring. I know what it looks like."

"I know," I said. "You have told me often enough."

"This ring is not the papal ring, but it does feature the keys of St. Peter. It was sent for a reason, and, mock as you may, Arthur, popes *have* been murdered—poisoned, strangled, *mutilated*. Leo XIII is not the beloved figure Pio Nono was. He may be in mortal danger."

"Don't be absurd, Oscar. It's a thousand years since a pope was murdered. Let's get some sleep. We're both exhausted."

I wrapped up the severed limbs and returned them to my pocket; Oscar placed the gold band and the lock of hair inside his wallet. We loosened our collars and took off our boots, then turned down the gasolier and clambered onto our bunks. Oscar lay above me, breathing noisily in the dark. I knew he was not asleep. Eventually, in a low whisper, he said: "Yes, it is nine hundred years since the murder of Pope John XII. He was a notorious debauchee, you'll recall, killed by an irate husband whom he had cuckolded. But, though some dispute it, I am almost certain that Benedict XI was poisoned by a rival as recently as 1304."

I laughed. "Good night, Oscar," I said. "I believe we have had enough excitement for one day."

He lay silent for a minute or two, then, through the darkness, he spoke again. "Did you send Touie the telegram from Zurich?"

"I did."

"And what did you tell her?"

"The truth."

"Oh, Arthur, that was a mistake. When a husband starts telling his wife the truth the marriage is as good as over. Certainly, the mystery's all gone."

"Good night, Oscar."

"Good night, Arthur." He fell silent once more, but not for long. "What was it called, Arthur, that instrument of torture? A 'tolley,' did you say?"

I made no reply.

He went on: "There's never been a Jesuit pope, you know."

I said nothing. Minutes passed. I listened to his breathing. Gradually, it quietened; eventually, it slowed. Lulled by the steady lurch of the train, we both slept till dawn.

In Milan, we changed trains for the final time. At the station hotel, we washed and shaved, changed our linen, and took breakfast. We each bought a newspaper to read with our coffee and brioches.

"I see the Pope is alive and well," I said, mischievously, looking up from my paper. "There is a photograph of His Holiness here. He appears to be in remarkably good health for a man of eighty-two."

"I'm pleased to hear it," said Oscar, tersely. "Your paper is evidently more diverting than mine."

I pressed home my advantage. "It seems the Holy Father

is on his way to his summer retreat." I took a sip of my coffee and muttered: "Remind me, Oscar. Why are we going to Rome?"

My friend lowered his newspaper and looked me in the eye. "I will not be discomfited by you, Arthur. I don't know why we're going to Rome—except that all roads lead there and there is the most wonderful tobacconist's shop in a corner of the Piazza del Popolo. It stocks cigarettes from four continents, while in Bad Homburg they don't stock cigarettes at all." He put down his coffee cup so dramatically that it rattled in its saucer. "We are going to Rome to get away from Homburg, the dullest place in Christendom. Even the Germans find it dreary. We are going to Rome in search of adventure and to escape dullness. Could there be a better reason?" He waved at the waiter for our bill. "Dullness is the coming-of-age of seriousness. It is our duty to avoid it. Throw away your newspaper, Arthur. I am throwing away mine. It's dull, dull, dull." He tossed his paper onto the floor beside the table. "Even the typeface is dull. When I am editor of *The Times,* the commas will be sunflowers and the semicolons pomegranates."

Suddenly he was crackling with energy. He paid the bill (with English money—he did it so charmingly, the young waiter seemed not to mind at all); he confiscated my newspaper (throwing it onto the floor next to his own); he tucked his arm into mine and led us from the hotel back onto the station concourse.

"We shall find our train and if our porter has lost our luggage, so much the better. We can each buy a new wardrobe at the tailors in Via del Corso. They dressed John

Keats, you know." He looked down at me and winced. "You are wearing *tweeds,* Arthur, in July, in Italy. No wonder the Pope is leaving town."

When we found our carriage—Oscar had booked us first-class on the ten o'clock Milano–Roma *diretto*—we found that we were not alone. Already ensconced in the window seats, with hats, cane, and parasol, their bags and baggage on the seats immediately beside them, were a man of about forty and a young woman, seemingly a dozen years his junior. I sensed at once that they were English and I saw at once that she was very pretty. As we stepped into the compartment, she looked up at me and smiled. She had round brown eyes, a small, pointed nose, a small, happy mouth, and the hint of a dimple in her chin. Her face was boyish, but her figure was not. She was wonderfully alluring, dressed in a cornflower-blue pleated skirt and white silk blouse. As her eye caught mine, she held out her hand.

"Irene Sadler," she said.

"Arthur Conan Doyle," I replied.

As we shook hands and I caught the scent of lily of the valley in her perfume, the book she had been reading fell from her lap onto the floor. I bent forward to retrieve it.

"Ah," I said, returning the volume, "*Lays of Ancient Rome.* I've never read it."

Oscar loomed over my shoulder. "A classic is something everybody wants to have read and nobody wants to read."

"I'm enjoying it," said the young woman, smiling. "Very much."

Oscar lifted my portmanteau onto the luggage rack above us and intoned:

"Then out spake brave Horatius,
The Captain of the gate:
'To every man upon this earth
Death cometh soon or late.
And how can man die better
Than facing fearful odds,
For the ashes of his fathers,
And the temples of his Gods.'"

He looked down and extended his hand to our fellow traveller. "Oscar Fingal O'Flahertie Wills Wilde," he said. "I'm Dr. Conan Doyle's gentleman."

"No, he's not," I burst out, embarrassed. "He's—"

"I know who you both are," interposed Irene Sadler, laughing. "You're celebrated. Mr. Doyle is the creator of Sherlock Holmes, and Mr. Wilde is a poet and a better poet even than Lord Macaulay, in my estimation." She gently tapped her copy of *Lays of Ancient Rome* and tucked the book under the straw hat on the seat next to her.

"Man is the only creature who blushes—or needs to," said Oscar, bowing towards the lady.

The man seated opposite her lowered his newspaper and nodded briefly to each of us in turn. "Martin Sadler," he said, curtly, and uttered nothing more.

He was taller, leaner, darker than the lady. His eyes were large and brown like hers, his hair was curly. On second glance, he was not as old as I had first reckoned. He was thirty-seven, perhaps, but his features had a weary, malcontent quality to them that added to his years. Apart from a cream-coloured shirt and brown shoes, he was dressed all in black.

"Martin is shy," said the young lady. "He doesn't mean to be boorish. It's just his way."

The man grimaced, grunted, and disappeared once more behind his newspaper.

"I understand entirely," said Oscar. "In this I am with Mr. Sadler completely." My friend seated himself in the corner of the compartment, by the door, and indicated that I should take my place opposite him. "Let us be seated, Arthur, and let us be quiet." He looked from me to the young lady. "You two have books to read and I have a sonnet to compose. Hush now. Not a word before Bologna." He closed his eyes and rested his head against the antimacassar.

"Are we going via Bologna?" I asked, seating myself with a small sigh. The train was moving now and the sun streamed into our compartment; I felt that a congenial conversation with Irene Sadler was something that would make the final leg of our long journey most agreeable.

"Hush, Arthur. Not a word before Florence, then. Not a word."

"Nonsense, gentlemen. Pay no attention to Martin. He's an old curmudgeon. Of course we must talk. I am so excited to meet you both. I want to learn all about you. What brings you to Italy? Why are you here? Where are you going?" She turned towards me and stretched out her hand, across her hat and book and the bags and parcels on the seat next to her. "What are you writing now, Mr. Doyle? Are you here undertaking research? I am sure you are. Do tell."

"Well . . ." I hesitated. "Yes and no."

"It's *Dr.* Conan Doyle," said Oscar, opening one eye and

turning his head towards the lady. "Customarily, he's quite particular about it. He's a medical man, a physician, as well as an author."

"Oh," said Irene Sadler, blushing prettily. "I hadn't realised." She looked at me with wide-open eyes. "You'll think me very foolish, Dr. Doyle, but somehow I thought you were a detective."

It was my turn to grunt. "People do think that," I said. "It's an occupational hazard, I suppose." I brushed imaginary crumbs from my trouser legs. "Sherlock Holmes is the detective. But he's a fictitious character, of course."

"He's so real I supposed you had to be a detective also."

"No, it's all imagination." I looked over towards Oscar, hoping that he might come to my rescue. "My friend Wilde here is more of a detective than I am."

"Am I?" he said, unhelpfully, opening one eye.

"You are. You know you are. You're observant. Though normally you never stop talking, you know how to listen, too. Your parents taught you. It's a good discipline. And you're a poet, so you can make the imaginative leap when necessary."

"The 'imaginative leap,'" repeated Oscar, both eyes open now. "I like that."

"You know what I mean, Oscar. You dare to think things that Lestrade and the other plodders at Scotland Yard would never dare. And you're a gentleman, in your way, so you can mix and mingle among all sorts. Your ordinary detective has to come in through the servants' entrance, but you can walk in through the front door."

"So you're the detective, Mr. Wilde," said Irene Sadler,

turning her gaze on Oscar. "How wonderful." She leant forward, eagerly. "Tell me, what does your detective's eye tell you about me?"

Oscar sat up. "That you are young, pretty, highly intelligent, and wonderfully well read," he said.

"I could have told you as much," I protested. "Anyone could."

Oscar ignored me and continued to look steadily at our beautiful companion. "What more can I say?"

"Anything that occurs to you, Mr. Wilde. This is marvellously amusing."

"Well, then," said Oscar, "I can tell you that you like to be amused, that you have secrets, and that you are impressively protective of your older brother."

"I have secrets, Mr. Wilde?"

"We all have secrets," said Oscar.

I turned to Irene Sadler. "You have a brother?" I enquired.

Oscar intervened. "The gentleman sitting opposite Miss Sadler is her brother. Our companions are brother and sister, Arthur, not husband and wife."

"Is that so?" I asked, confused. The young lady nodded, smiling. "I assumed . . ."

"Never make assumptions, Arthur. It's the golden rule."

I turned to Oscar. "Brother and sister. How on earth did you know?"

"Well, it was fairly obvious, Arthur, even before we learnt their names. The couple are sitting face-to-face. They might have been married, except for the fact that Miss Sadler is not wearing a wedding ring. They could have been sweethearts, except that then we would have expected to see them sitting side by side. When we discovered that they shared a surname, I thought for a moment they might be cousins, except that Miss Sadler's easy familiarity with Mr. Sadler—a familiarity bordering almost on impertinence: she called him boorish and curmudgeonly—suggested a much closer kinship. The age difference does not allow them to be father and daughter, ergo they must be brother and sister."

"Well done, Mr. Wilde."

"Yes, Oscar, congratulations. A tour de force."

"And I'll hazard two more thoughts while I'm about it. Miss Sadler and her brother are orphans—and Mr. Sadler is not all that he seems."

4.

Brown Shoes

*M*artin Sadler lowered his newspaper and turned his head towards Oscar, his stare cold and unamused. He spoke in a low voice, slowly, emphasising each word in turn. "And how, sir, do you know that I am not all that I seem?"

"Because of the brown shoes that you are wearing," replied Oscar, lightly.

Sadler glanced down at his elegantly shod feet. He was wearing two-tone ankle boots in chestnut and tan. "Is there something amiss in my 'brown shoes'?" he asked. Again he spoke slowly, emphatically, without emotion.

"No," said Oscar, quickly, "nothing at all. Far from it. I have a pair quite like them myself, bought—like yours, I think—from John Lobb of St. James's."

There was an awkward pause. "Yes," said Sadler, eventually, looking up from his boots to return Oscar's gaze. "And what of that?"

"They are beautiful brown shoes, Mr. Sadler," answered Oscar, smoothly, "but I cannot help noticing that you are wearing them with black socks."

"Ah," grunted Sadler, folding his newspaper and placing

it carefully on the seat at his side. "I see. A faux pas—literally." He did not smile. He folded his arms and studied Oscar. "I have read about you, Mr. Wilde," he said. "I know that you are a man of fashion, noted as an 'aesthete.' I apologise for my sartorial lapse. But explain to me, please, if you can, how it leads you to believe that I am not entirely what I seem?"

"It's not just the socks and the shoes, Mr. Sadler. Your elegant cream silk shirt is equally at odds with the black serge suit that you are wearing. You are sporting the shirt *de luxe* and the handmade shoes of a man-about-town—a gay blade. But in all other respects you are dressed in the unseasonable and sombre garb of a clergyman. You are a clergyman, are you not?"

"I am," he answered, dryly.

"Well done, Mr. Wilde," exclaimed Irene Sadler, clapping her hands together with delight.

"It was hardly a miracle of deduction, dear lady. Since we boarded the train, until just now, Mr. Sadler has been lurking behind a copy of the *Church Times*. I observed his eyes while he was looking at the paper. He was reading it, column by column, page after page, most assiduously. Only a clergyman would do that."

Martin Sadler said nothing. His sister leant forward and touched him on the knee, playfully. "You see, brother dear, Mr. Wilde has found you out. You shouldn't pretend not to be what you are—even on holiday."

"Oh, I don't know about that," said Oscar, pleasantly. "I love acting. It is so much more real than life."

Mr. Sadler looked at him coldly. Miss Sadler laughed

and patted her brother's knee reprovingly. She glanced in my direction and smiled at me, then turned back to Oscar. "And how do you know that we are orphans, Mr. Wilde? You are correct, of course. Our parents died many years ago."

"I am sorry to hear it," said Oscar. "I sensed you might be orphans, that was all. It was a guess, nothing more."

"The 'imaginative leap,'" she said.

"If you like." I followed my friend's look as he glanced between the brother and sister—one so cold and forbidding, the other so warm and tender—and continued boldly: "Forgive my impertinence for saying so, Miss Sadler, but I sensed your shared isolation. I sensed it was just the two of you against the world."

Her smile softened. "There is no impertinence, Mr. Wilde. It was I who invited you to tell us what you could see with your detective's eye. I confess I'm a little startled that you have seen so much so quickly." She gave a small sigh and looked down at her delicate hands, now resting, folded, in her lap. "Martin is the Anglican chaplain in Rome—newly appointed. He has been in post only three months. It is not altogether easy."

"Change is never easy," said Oscar. "And perhaps Mr. Sadler is fonder of incense than some of his flock?"

"How do you know all this, Mr. Wilde?"

"I am just playing imaginative leapfrog, Miss Sadler. The *Church Times* is an Anglo-Catholic newspaper. I imagine your brother's parishioners, being expatriates in the main, are wedded to the tea-and-muffins Anglicanism of the old school. There will be tensions."

"There are tensions, Mr. Wilde."

Sadler, who had been staring out of the window at the passing countryside, turned back to look at Oscar. "Pay no heed to my sister," he said, quietly. "I am quite content with my lot."

"I am happy to hear it," said Oscar.

"But Mr. Wilde speaks true," protested Irene, gently. She looked at Oscar once more. "My brother's predecessor was the Anglican chaplain in Rome for many years. He was much loved."

"He was a spiritual husk," said Sadler, tartly.

"Nevertheless, he was much loved."

"And I am not."

"You are respected, Martin, I am sure of that. And love will come—in time."

"The scriptures tell us that we must love our God, I know that, but I am not sure where it says in the Gospels that Our Lord tells us that we must love our clergy. And I am not sure, either, that we need trouble complete strangers with the trivial difficulties of the Anglican chaplaincy at Rome."

"Quite right, brother mine. We do not." Irene Sadler sat back in her seat and rearranged the pleats of her skirt. She did not seem unduly abashed by her brother's reproof. After a moment's silence, she looked up once more and smiled. "Enough about us," she declared. "Tell us about you." Her small teeth were pearly white and there was something delightfully mischievous about the sparkle in her eye. She turned towards me. "You are coming to Rome to undertake some research, did you say?"

As I was forming my reply, I heard Oscar boom, "Yes!

Yes indeed. Conan Doyle is writing a new mystery. It has an intriguing title: *Sherlock Holmes and the Vatican Murders.*"

"Oh, my," exclaimed Miss Sadler, delightedly. "*Murders?* There is to be more than one?"

"Oh, yes," Oscar swept on. "His American readers expect that. His American publishers demand that. He is almost paid by the murder nowadays, you know."

I intervened. "This is nonsense, Miss Sadler. Ignore my friend, please—though he is correct, to an extent. We are engaged upon research of a kind and we are going to Rome and, once there, we are hoping to visit the Vatican . . ." My train of words ran out of steam as, suddenly, in my mind's eye I pictured the severed finger, the severed hand, and the lock of hair that had been sent to me care of Mr. Sherlock Holmes.

Oscar came to my rescue. "I have been to Rome before," he announced, con brio, "fifteen years ago, in younger and happier days. When I was just twenty-two, I had the honour of a private audience with Pope Pius IX—Pio Nono."

"How wonderful, Mr. Wilde," said Irene Sadler, warmly. "What was he like?"

"Very old. Very frail. He was an epileptic, they say, though I saw no sign of it. It was the year before his death. He gave me his blessing, which I shall treasure always. And I sensed his goodness. He had the sweetest smile."

"He is fondly remembered still. Apparently, on hot days he would send out for ice creams for the cardinals."

Martin Sadler shifted in his seat. "I imagine he would rather be remembered for defining the dogma of the immaculate conception of the Blessed Virgin Mary."

"Almost certainly," said Oscar, "but none of us can choose how history will come to view us, alas."

"How is Leo XIII viewed?" I asked, recovering my concentration.

"He is seen as more austere," replied Martin Sadler, looking at me directly for the first time, "more disciplined. He is said to be more of an intellectual, though quite as devoted to the Marian cause as his predecessor."

"We have not yet had an audience," added his sister. "We are hoping to arrange one later in the year, but it is not easy—as you will know, Mr. Wilde."

"As I recall, it's a matter of whom you know or how much you can pay. I was fortunate," said Oscar. "I had a Catholic friend with the right connections."

"We are doing our best to cultivate those," said Miss Sadler, with an impish smile. "We have our summer fundraiser at All Saints' tomorrow evening to which we have invited the Pontifical Master of Ceremonies as a guest of honour—and he has accepted."

"We have a new Anglican church in Rome," explained Martin Sadler. "It has been ten years in the building." He sighed before muttering, somewhat sourly, "The fundraising never stops."

"It is necessary, Martin, you know that, and the evening will be enjoyable. Even you would enjoy it if you approached it in the right spirit." She turned to Oscar and to me. "You would enjoy it, gentlemen—I know you would. There will be sherry and Italian cheeses."

"In the church itself?" I enquired.

"In the nave," she said. "You must come."

"In the nave?" said Oscar. "That's very bold."

"It's a new building," explained Martin Sadler, "not yet consecrated."

Irene Sadler looked towards us and held out her hands imploringly. "You will come, won't you?" She turned to her brother. "We would love them to come, wouldn't we, Martin?"

The Reverend Sadler half closed his eyes and tilted his head to one side. "Some come to church in search of spiritual sustenance; others come for sherry and Italian cheeses. By all means, join us, gentlemen. Everyone will be there, my sister tells me, so I am sure you will feel quite at home. I had wanted the event cancelled, under the circumstances, but Irene would have none of it."

"'Under the circumstances'?" repeated Oscar.

"One of the carpenters lost his life, working up in the rafters, above the nave."

"It was an accident, Martin, and it was months ago."

"Yes. He was a North African. And the wretched man had been drinking, by all accounts."

"It was a dreadful accident."

"He was working alone up in the roof. He chopped off his own hand and fell from the scaffolding onto the marble floor forty feet below. Unconscious, he bled to death in the nave—on the very spot where tomorrow night we'll be enjoying the sherry and Italian cheeses."

"Life goes on," said Irene Sadler, simply. "It must."

"Ah, yes," added the clergyman, " 'In the midst of life we are in death.' Perhaps that should be my text when I welcome everyone tomorrow night. Do you know how the line runs on?"

"I do," said Oscar. " 'Of whom may we seek for succour, but of Thee, O Lord, who for our sins art justly displeased?' "

"We don't want a homily from you tomorrow night, Martin. We just need the briefest word of welcome."

Sadler ignored his sister and, casting his eyes upwards as if to heaven, continued sonorously, " 'Yet, O Lord God most holy, O Lord most mighty, O holy and most merciful Saviour, deliver us not into the bitter pains of eternal death.' "

"Stop it, Martin. Stop now." Irene Sadler leant towards her brother and put her hands over his as they rested on his knees. She held them there as she turned towards us and said as brightly as she could: "Will you both come tomorrow night and, when Martin has welcomed everybody, will you both read for us? That would be a most wonderful surprise for everybody. Will you read one of your stories for us, Dr. Doyle? Will you recite one of your poems for us, Mr. Wilde?"

I hesitated, but Oscar had no doubts. "We shall be honoured, Miss Sadler," he said at once. "At what time will you want us on parade?"

"Eight o'clock at All Saints' on the Via del Babuino."

"I know the street," said Oscar, happily. "Our hotel is at one end of it. This was meant to be. And have no fear, dear lady. I shall choose one of my shorter poems."

She laughed and turned to me, apparently surprised to find that I was not laughing also. "You look pale, Dr. Doyle. Are you unwell?"

"I am quite well, thank you," I said, somewhat unconvincingly. As I spoke, with my right hand I felt the outline of the severed hand that was wrapped in my handkerchief and hidden in my jacket pocket.

Oscar came to my rescue once more. "My friend has a sensitive soul, Miss Sadler—notwithstanding his ferocious handshake and bristling moustache. I am going to hazard a guess that Dr. Conan Doyle is pale because he is still contemplating the death of the unfortunate workman who fell from the scaffold, having inadvertently chopped off his own hand. Am I correct, Arthur?"

"You are."

"Dr. Conan Doyle trained as a surgeon, you know. And, as he likes to say, he's a details man. I am sure he is pondering which hand it was the poor wretch cut off."

"I believe it was his right hand," said Martin Sadler.

"His right hand," repeated Oscar. "Are you certain of that?"

"I think so. I can't recall. The hand itself was never found, despite an extensive search. It's still missing. Curious, that. Perhaps it will turn up tomorrow night, amid the sherry and Italian cheeses. If it does, it'll put a dampener on the fund-raising, don't you think?"

5.

Via del Babuino

*T*he train journey to Rome lasted more than seven hours. We passed the time without difficulty, talking, smoking, reading our books, dozing, or gazing out of the window at the sun-drenched Tuscan countryside.

By the time we had reached Bologna, Oscar had succeeded in establishing a rapport with the Reverend Martin Sadler. I did not listen intently to their conversation (I gave my attention to Miss Sadler), but I overheard, in passing, a spirited exchange on the visions of St. Teresa of Avila and the names of Thomas Aquinas, Augustine of Hippo, and Martin Luther, as well as those of Apollo, Aphrodite, Artemis, and assorted popes from St. Pius to Leo XIII.

At Florence, where the train stopped for twenty minutes, Oscar and Sadler went together in search of bread and Parma ham, fresh and dried fruit, and bottles of wine and water. As they climbed back aboard with their supplies, the clergyman said, "It is the most beautiful day, don't you agree, Mr. Wilde?" and Oscar replied, "Whenever people talk to me about the weather, I always feel certain they mean something else." We all laughed.

The many charms of Irene Sadler quickly made me

forget the horror of the severed hand lurking in my jacket pocket. Of course, the young lady's simple, unaffected beauty was a delightful distraction in itself, but what really drew me to her was her warmth of spirit. She had a sunny disposition and a generous soul. She was also keenly intelligent and widely read. Could one ask for more in a travelling companion? While Oscar and Martin Sadler talked of theology and theosophy, I told her of my adventures as a student in Edinburgh, of my explorations in West Africa, and of my time whaling in the Arctic Ocean. She told me of her "mundane life" as her brother's housekeeper and of her twin passions—for painting and for poetry. She had much poetry by heart. As our train neared Rome, she recited for me three of her favourite poems by Mrs. Browning. On the Milano–Roma *diretto* on that long, hot day in late July 1892, I sensed that I had found a friend for life.

It was early evening when finally we arrived in Rome. The city was dry and dusty, the streets crowded with carts and carriages, cattle and oxen, horses, mules, and donkeys. Together with our new friends, we took a pony-and-trap from the railway station to the Via del Babuino. On our route we passed the ancient Colosseum, where Oscar commanded our driver to halt his trap so that we might pause and wonder at the "vast and wondrous monument."

"A ruin," cried Oscar, "yet what a ruin!"

"Gladiators fought one another to the death here," observed the Reverend Sadler. "And those that showed insufficient courage in combat would have their hands cut off when the day was done."

"How horrible," cried his sister. "Can that be true?"

"It was the price they paid for lack of valour."

Oscar was shading his eyes and scanning the stone walls of the ancient amphitheatre. "This place has changed since I was last here," he muttered. "The flora has all gone. The mosses, flowers, plants, bushes that adorned the ruins—they've been stripped away. Nature has been usurped. The place has been 'restored.' And those people over there—they are not a motley band of beggars as I supposed. They are tourists!" He sank back in his seat and sighed despairingly. "It's true what I say: in this century we know the price of everything and the value of nothing. *Avanti! Forza! Drive on!*"

The Via del Babuino was a long and narrow street at the heart of the Eternal City's English and artistic quarter. It was cobbled and shaded, as well as noticeably cooler and less dusty than the streets and squares nearby. It had an unexpected grandeur and boasted a fine pedigree. Rubens came here to die. Poussin painted here in his prime—in a studio that now provided a spacious apartment for the British chargé d'affaires. As well as residences for diplomats and studios for more successful artists, the street also housed two grand hotels, any number of *pensiones,* an English tearoom, a variety of *caffè* and restaurants, a photographic studio, an assortment of shops selling confectionery, stationery, artists' materials, and ladies' fashions, in addition to two churches—a late sixteenth-century Catholic church built for Rome's Greek community and, ten doors down from it, exactly halfway along the street, the newly built Anglican church of All Saints.

"Ah," cried Oscar, as our pony-and-trap drew up outside

it, "a little touch of St. Pancras a stone's throw from St. Pe-ter's. I am very fond of red brick."

"It's beautiful inside," said Irene Sadler. "Let us show you."

"No, dear lady, not tonight. We're all exhausted." As I helped Miss Sadler down from the trap, her brother as-sisted Oscar. "Travel may improve the mind," said my friend, "but it does terrible things to the body. I need a brandy, a bath, and bed."

"Your hotel is at the end of the street," said Martin Sadler, extending a civil hand to each of us. "It's no more than a hundred yards, if that."

"I know," answered Oscar. "And these lads will carry our bags for us." He gave a handful of small coins and some pieces of dried fruit to a pair of barefoot urchins who were hovering close by. The lads pocketed their booty and sa-luted him smartly. "Which of you is Romulus and which Remus, I wonder?" They looked up at him with grubby faces and grinned, uncomprehending. I gave the boys our cases, while Oscar and Sadler settled up with the driver.

I said good-bye to Irene Sadler and felt—or imagined I felt—a special pressure in her fingers as she took my hand.

"Good night, Dr. Conan Doyle," she said. "Until eight o'clock tomorrow evening, then. And you must read us one of your stories, I insist."

I bowed and clicked my heels as the Sadlers stepped up to the front door of the church and took their leave of us. "We have a set of rooms behind the vestry," explained the clergyman, unlocking the door. "In time, we shall be given proper accommodation, I daresay. Good night, gentlemen."

"Good night."

When they had gone, we turned and made our way down the street, our urchin bag-carriers at our heels. Oscar, so weary as he had clambered out of the trap a few minutes before, now seemed possessed of boundless energy.

"What did you make of our travelling companions?" he demanded, lighting a cigarette and looking sideways at me with mischief in his eyes.

"Miss Sadler is enchanting," I said.

"She is an enchantress, certainly." He laughed. "She had you spellbound from the off. I thought quoting Mrs. Browning at a first encounter was possibly overstepping the mark, but let that pass. She knows her business." I began to protest, but Oscar swept on. "And what about the brother, Arthur? What did you make of him?"

"I did not care for him—to begin with. He is a puzzle."

"A mask tells us so much more than a face," said Oscar, putting a hand on my shoulder. It was one of his favourite lines. "This will prove a three-pipe problem, Arthur, make no mistake." He paused. *"Helloa!"* His right arm was in the air and he was waving a raucous greeting across the street. *"Helloa!"*

"Who's that?" I asked.

"The fellow in the straw hat—I know him."

As I turned to look, a horse and carriage trotted by. When it had passed, all I could see on the pavement opposite us were a pair of pale-faced priests wearing birettas and a young washerwoman carrying a basket of laundry on her head.

"He's gone," muttered Oscar, disconcerted. "Perhaps I was mistaken."

"Who was it?"

"A friend from Oxford. I'm sure he caught my eye."

"And now he's gone?"

"If he was ever there." He stood for a moment, gazing across the roadway and drawing on his cigarette. "Perhaps it was a vision."

"It was a man in a straw hat, you said, Oscar, not the Virgin Mary."

"God moves in a mysterious way, Arthur. And we are in Rome . . ." He threw his cigarette into the gutter. "But you're right, my friend. I'm seeing things. It's the heat." He pulled a piece of dried fruit from the paper bag in his pocket, tore it in two, turned around, and pushed a portion into each of the gaping mouths of our young bag-carriers. "And we're all faint with hunger. We need to find somewhere to eat."

"We need to find our hotel," I said.

"Well, we won't find it here," exclaimed Oscar. "We've come the wrong way."

We had reached the end of the Via del Babuino but the wrong end. The narrow street we had come down had opened suddenly onto a wide square dominated by a curious fountain built in the form of a sinking ship.

"This is the Piazza di Spagna," cried Oscar, raising his arms in the air as if in exultation. He stopped in his tracks and turned to beam at me. The two urchins, sensing his delight, set down the bags and started to applaud and cheer.

"Shouldn't we retrace our steps?" I asked, bemused by this unexpected frenzy of excitement.

"No, Arthur, never go back. Always press on. That's the rule."

"But isn't our hotel at the other end of the street?"

"It is. It was. But we're not staying there."

"Where are we staying, then?"

"Here." He turned and pointed dramatically across the square. "Look, beyond the fountain, by the steps, behind the flower stall, the pink house . . ."

He began striding purposefully across the piazza. The boys picked up our bags and ran alongside him. I followed, hot in my tweeds, irritable in my exhaustion. "But why, Oscar, when we're booked in elsewhere?"

We had reached the pink building. I stopped and, sighing wearily, looked up at it. It was an elegant four-storeyed town house, built, I imagine, in the middle of the previous century. The stucco was peeling here and there, but the shutters appeared freshly painted and red geraniums in flowerpots were neatly arranged on all the window ledges. It looked to be a quiet and respectable establishment.

"This," said Oscar, sonorously, rapping at the front door as he spoke, "is where John Keats spent the last three months of his short life. This is where we shall live while we are in Rome."

"Is it a *pensione?*" I asked.

"It was in Keats's day. It will be still. Nothing changes here. This is the Eternal City." He beat on the door once more, then looked around for a bell and turned to me with a radiant smile. "I have long wanted to visit this house, Arthur. This was meant to be." He stepped back and looked up at the building. "Have we got a stone we can throw up at the windows?" He cupped his hands around his mouth and hollered: "*Helloa!* Is anyone there?"

The two boys set down the luggage and began shouting, too.

"This is madness, Oscar."

"And why not? There is nothing stable in the world, Arthur—uproar's your only music."

He stepped up to the front door again and raised his fist to beat on it once more. As he did so, we heard the faint rattle of a chain within and the sharp crack of a key turning in the lock.

The door was opened by a dark-haired, sallow-skinned man in his midthirties. He wore a white linen suit, a white shirt, and a black tie knotted loosely at the neck. His hair was cropped, his full beard and moustache were neatly trimmed, and he peered up at Oscar through a pair of round, thick, wire-framed spectacles. He looked like a professor disturbed at his studies.

"*Si?*" he said, impatiently.

"*Buonasera, signore,*" Oscar replied smoothly. He spoke good Italian. "My name is Oscar Wilde. I am a poor Irish poet devoted to the immortal memory of the great John Keats. My companion and I are newly arrived in Rome and need a place to stay—for a week, no more. Two rooms for preference, but one will suffice. My friend will sleep on a divan, if need be. We pay cash, of course."

"This is not an hotel," said the man at the door, blinking in the evening sunlight. "I am a doctor. Are you sick?" He spoke in perfect English, but with the trace of an accent. I took it to be German or Swiss: it turned out to be Swedish.

"I am sick at heart," answered Oscar, with a theatrical flourish. "Aren't we all?" The news that the house was not a *pensione* after all seemed not to perturb him in the least. He turned and beckoned to me to come forward. "Although we may not be able to stay under this roof, might we trespass on your hospitality for a moment nonetheless? You see, this is a wonderful coincidence, for my friend is a doctor, also." He held his left arm out towards me and his right towards the bewildered figure standing in the doorway. "May I present Dr. Arthur Conan Doyle? You may have heard of him."

The bearded doctor turned his head towards me and narrowed his eyes. "I have," he said. "I know exactly who he is."

6.

"Dr. Death"

*D*r. Axel Munthe was a Swedish doctor resident in Rome. He was, we quickly discovered, Roman high society's most sought-after personal physician. His patients included royalty and cardinals, persons of wealth and distinction, men of letters and women of leisure—and more of the latter than the former, he explained to us, because leisure is an enemy to health.

"We need work: we need purpose. Too many of my patients are intelligent women locked in loveless marriages, leading useless lives. They lie in bed all day, eating too much or too little, feeling sick and sorry for themselves and not knowing why. I cure them by telling them to take up good works and long walks. It is not a complicated form of medicine, but I find it rewarding."

Dr. Munthe never presented a bill to anyone who consulted him. He allowed them to pay him whatever they wished and could afford. One grateful person gave him a yacht, another a sculpture by Canova. Of his poorest patients he expected nothing at all and many more of those who sought his help were poor than rich. He spent much of his time in the filthiest corners of the vilest slums of Rome.

"I specialise in the ailments of the idle rich and the worthless poor," he said. His first claim to fame was his published account of his work in the streets of Naples during the deadly cholera epidemic of 1884, when, as he told us, "Fourteen thousand souls lost their lives and I ran frantically among them, doing what little I could."

He was a physician and he was a writer—and it was because he was a writer that he knew of me. As he stepped out of the doorway of number 26 Piazza di Spagna to shake my hand, he smiled and said, "We are literary bedfellows, Dr. Conan Doyle. We have appeared together, side by side, in the pages of *Blackwood's Magazine*. I forget which story of mine it was, but I remember yours distinctly. It was called 'A Physiologist's Wife' and dealt with the conflict between romance and reason. It was a fine tale, beautifully told. I was very taken with it. I am honoured to meet you."

That he made no mention of Sherlock Holmes charmed me very much. That he immediately invited us into the house to inspect the room in which Keats had died charmed Oscar equally. He told us to leave our luggage with the boys on the doorstep—"I know those two," he said; "you may trust them, after a fashion"—and to follow him. As we climbed the narrow wooden staircase to the second floor, over his shoulder he said, "Fear not, Mr. Wilde, I recognised your name, also—though, I confess, I have not read your work."

"There is no need," said Oscar, pausing on the stairs to catch his breath.

"Perhaps not," replied the Swedish doctor. "I think already I understand your style."

Keats's bedroom was at the front of the house, overlooking the piazza. It was a small room, rectangular in shape, sparsely furnished, with a red-tiled floor and bare, white-washed walls. A simple, single iron bedstead faced the window.

"This is where he died," said Dr. Munthe, "and this is where I sleep. I sleep well. This is a peaceful room, a good room in which to die."

Oscar said nothing.

"You are interested in death?" I asked, as we stepped out of the bedroom into what appeared to be the doctor's study cum consulting room. It was a much larger chamber, windowless and candlelit, the walls lined with crowded bookshelves, the floor covered with Persian rugs and piles of books and papers. Above the fireplace, in the centre of the mantelpiece, between two amber-coloured candles, stood a human skull. A second skull sat perched on top of a chest of drawers. A third served as a paperweight on the doctor's desk.

"Death is inevitable," he said, smiling. "It fascinates me—of course it does. But I have seen so much of it that it holds no terror for me. Sometimes it is my enemy; sometimes it is my friend." From a shallow metal tray that rested next to the skull on the chest of drawers he picked up a small syringe and held it up close to his face. "This morning, for example, I welcomed death. My patient was suffering too much and to no purpose."

"You assist your patients to die?" I asked.

"On occasion, when appropriate. I know it is not your way, Doctor, but it is mine. I make no secret of it. And because of it, in certain circles I am known, they tell me, as 'Dr. Death.'"

"You do not object to the title?"

"On the contrary," he replied, returning the syringe to its tray, "I wear it as a badge of honour."

Oscar had stepped into the room and was now standing at one end of the mantelpiece, scrutinising what appeared to be the bones of a human hand. The hand was cupped, the fingers upturned.

"Does this serve as an ashtray?" Oscar asked.

"It does," answered Munthe, revealing his teeth in an impish grin. "Feel free to use it, Mr. Wilde."

"It is the skeleton of a dead man's hand," I said, quite shocked.

"It is the skeleton of a lady's hand, in fact, Doctor. I keep it as a reminder of what always lies beneath those soft caresses."

As he said this and Oscar, lighting a cigarette, began to laugh, from just outside the room we heard the muffled sound of pots and pans cascading onto a stone floor. We both looked towards the corner from whence the noise had emanated and saw that there was a heavy brocaded curtain separating the study from a room beyond—presumably the kitchen. The curtain twitched and then fell still.

"I do not live alone," said Dr. Munthe. "You will meet my companion another time."

"I look forward to it," I said.

There was a further clatter of pans from beyond the curtain. Dr. Munthe smiled awkwardly. "I fear that too much drink may have been taken."

"If your dinner here is spoilt," said Oscar, drawing on his cigarette, "perhaps you would care to dine with us?"

"I should like that very much," said Dr. Munthe. "It would be good to get out of the house for a while. Thank you." He brought his hands together in a salaam. "Where are you staying, gentlemen? You must have a hotel. May I join you there in an hour?"

Our faithful urchin bag-carriers were waiting for us beside the boat-shaped marble fountain. We led them back along the Via del Babuino, past the ancient church of Sant'Atanasio dei Greci and the bright new edifice of All Saints', to the Hôtel de Russie, at the far end of the street, on the corner of the Piazza del Popolo. Oscar paid off the boys with all the change in his pocket and the remainder of his supplies of dried fruit. I told him he was being far too generous and that we'd now find the boys at our heels night and day.

"I hope we do," he said. "We may need them. We can call them 'The Rome Irregulars.'"

At the hotel, we were expected and welcomed with oppressive obsequiousness. The hotel manager turned out to be an admirer of my Baker Street sagas and found it almost impossible to release from his grasp the hand that had held the pen that had written *Sherlock Holmes e il segno dei Quattro*. Eventually, having plied us with French champagne and Tuscan cheese straws, he showed us to our rooms—the finest in all Rome, he assured us—and, at last, having personally supervised the unpacking of our bags, he left us in peace to bathe and shave and change for dinner.

"I'm too tired to send Touie a wire tonight, Oscar," I called to my friend through the open door that connected our two rooms. "Remind me to send one in the morning, will you? I mustn't forget."

"I'll remind you," he replied. "And will you still be telling her the whole truth?" he added, laughing.

He was in high spirits that night.

When we were both dressed, he came into my room and looked me up and down appraisingly. "And the finger? And the severed hand?" he asked, an eyebrow raised. "Have you moved them from one set of clothes to the next?"

I touched my jacket pocket. "I have," I said.

"Good. We must keep the 'evidence' about us at all times. Leave a stray limb in the room and the next thing you know the hotel manager will have purloined it as a Sherlockian souvenir."

It was a little after nine o'clock when we reached the dining room. Dr. Munthe was already at table. He had not changed for dinner. As we joined him he noticed that I had noticed this and, as I took my seat, he said, touching my arm lightly, "I hope my day clothes do not offend you, Doctor. I live by my own rules. Whether it is arrogance or individuality, or a mixture of the two, who is to say? I am who I am. I do not expect to change."

"I am certain that you won't, Doctor," said Oscar, pleasantly. "In my experience there is no such thing as changing one's life. One merely wanders round and round within the circle of one's personality."

Munthe raised his glass to Oscar. "I salute you, Mr. Wilde." He turned to me. "And I salute you, dear Doctor. I am so happy to meet you."

The wine waiter was hovering at our elbows with a decanter. "I have taken the liberty of ordering the wine," said Munthe, smiling. "Another solecism, I fear."

Oscar looked at the decanter in dismay. "It is red," he whispered.

"It is from the Piedmont," said Munthe, "inexpensive yet extraordinary. Please try."

The wine waiter poured a small libation. Oscar sniffed at it suspiciously. "I suppose the danger is half the excitement," he murmured. He took a sip and then a gulp. He drained the glass. "It is a blood-red sunset turned to wine," he declared. "We'll have a second bottle right away."

I laughed.

"Shall we drink to the memory of John Keats?" suggested Dr. Munthe. "Will you propose the toast, Mr. Wilde?"

"With pleasure," said my friend, "and a breaking heart." The waiter charged our glasses and Oscar raised his towards Dr. Munthe. "You sleep in the room where he died, Doctor—that godlike boy, the real Adonis of our age. Let us drink to him now who knew the silver-footed messages of the moon, and the secret of the morning, who heard in Hyperion's vale the large utterance of the early gods, and from the beechen plot the light-winged Dryad, who saw Madeline at the painted window, and Lamia in the house at Corinth, and Endymion ankle-deep in lilies of the vale, who drubbed the butcher's boy for being a bully, and drank confusion to Isaac Newton for having analysed the rainbow. In my heaven he walks eternally with Shakespeare and the Greeks, and it may be that someday he will lift his hymeneal curls from out his amber gleaming wine, and with ambrosial lips will kiss my forehead, clasp the hand of noble love in mine."

"Steady on, old man," I said. "It's only a toast."

He smiled and set down his glass. There were tears in his eyes.

"You have a way with words, Mr. Wilde," said Axel Munthe.

"And you have a way with people, Doctor," said Oscar, wiping his eyes with his handkerchief and reaching for the menu. "And people are what count. As Keats taught us, 'Scenery is fine, but human nature is finer.' When we have ordered, you must tell us your story. I will speak no more. I have said enough."

"On the contrary, Mr. Wilde, I sense you've scarcely begun. And I want to talk to Dr. Conan Doyle about his writing."

"Food first," cried Oscar. "I insist."

"And when you insist, you get your way?" asked the Swedish doctor.

"Invariably."

"And yet you are never satisfied? Every gift, however great, is a minor disappointment—another broken toy on the withered Christmas tree of Nature's most favoured child."

"You are very perceptive, Doctor," said Oscar, smiling.

"And I am very hungry." He raised his hand to summon a waiter. "I think it'll be the swordfish, the turtle soup, and the suckling pig for me. Dr. Munthe can choose the wines."

We ate well and drank liberally. And, as we did so, Oscar was almost true to his word: he said very little. Dr. Munthe enquired about my work, both my writing and my special interest in ophthalmology. His own sight was poor and failing.

"My spirit likes the sunshine," he said. "My eyes do not." He told us something of his story—of his childhood in Sweden, of his medical training in Paris (under the notorious Professor Charcot at the Hôpital Pitié-Salpêtrière*), of his journey south, first to Naples and then to the island of Capri. "Capri is my heaven-on-earth," he said. "I say that, even though I lived there with my first wife and our marriage was not a happy one. It did not last. We parted company four years ago."

"I am sorry to hear that," I said.

"Do not be. I should never have married her. From the beginning there was the sense of an ending. Her name was Ultima."

Oscar smiled. *"Nomen est omen,"* he said. "The name is everything."

"Indeed, Mr. Wilde. And what is your wife called?"

"Constance."

Munthe smiled. "Congratulations. I trust you count your blessings, sir. I count mine—and being free of my wife is one of them. Knowing the island of Capri is

---

* For the story of my own association with Professor Charcot, see *Oscar Wilde and the Vampire Murders.*

another. I shall return there one day, when I have made my fortune. Meanwhile, I am here in Rome, where work is plentiful and I know everyone. I like to know the best people." He raised his glass to both of us once more. "Now I can boast that I know even Mr. Oscar Wilde and Dr. Arthur Conan Doyle."

Towards the end of our meal, as we lingered over our cheese and wine, our conversation slowed. I filled a silence in looking about the room: the restaurant had emptied and all but two of the waiters had gone home. I felt for my pipe. As I stirred, Oscar roused himself and, to light his cigarette, leant forward, towards the guttering candle that stood at the centre of the table. He glanced up at me as he did so, and his oyster eyes sparkled in the candlelight.

"You trust Dr. Munthe, Arthur," he said, softly. "I can see that. Show him what is in your pocket."

"What do you mean?" I asked, momentarily confused.

"Show him the 'evidence,' Arthur. Show him what has brought us to Rome."

I hesitated, but Oscar was insistent. I set down my pipe and, diffidently, glancing furtively about the room, I produced the handkerchief parcel from my jacket pocket and, pushing aside plates and cutlery, placed it tentatively on the table.

Slowly, I unwrapped it.

"Good God," exclaimed Dr. Munthe, peering down at the severed hand that now lay before him. "What's this?"

"That's what we were hoping you might be able to tell us, Doctor," said Oscar, quietly.

Dr. Munthe turned to me. "Is this yours, Doctor? Is this

something from your dissecting room? Or a hideous trophy from your travels in Africa?"

"It is mine," I said, "in the sense that it was sent to me—or, rather, it was sent *care of me* to Mr. Sherlock Holmes. But why it was sent, and from whom, I have no idea."

"It came by post? In a parcel?"

"Yes."

"How bizarre." Munthe screwed up his eyes and lowered his face closer to the hand. "May I touch it?"

I looked towards the waiters standing idly at the entrance to the restaurant. They were deep in conversation. "By all means," I said.

Dr. Munthe lifted the dead hand and sniffed at it and turned it over and, with his nose and spectacles no more than an inch or two from it, examined it minutely. He spent some time considering the fingernails and then the stump.

He replaced the hand on the table. "What do you want to know that you don't already? I'd say it's a man's right hand severed with a single blow. It's not been cut from the wrist with any skill. It's not the work of a surgeon or a doctor."

"Could it be the work of the Mafia?" asked Oscar.

Munthe chuckled. "Yes, I, too, have read the stories, Mr. Wilde. These Mafia men are partial to dismemberment, we're told. They might present you with a severed hand by way of threat or warning, but I doubt that they'd trouble to embalm it first." He looked down at the one that lay before us. "This hand is mummified, as you can see. It has been preserved in formaldehyde and cut off after death. The severing was brutally done, but the embalming looks to be the work of an expert. This is not the Mafia's style—at least, not as I understand it. Was it sent to you from Sicily?"

"No," I answered. "It was posted from Rome."

"And was there no note with the hand? No message in the parcel?"

"None whatsoever," said Oscar. "But there were other packages, apparently from the same source—with content almost as surprising."

From his pocket Oscar produced his wallet and opened it. He looked to me. "Arthur, show the doctor the finger."

"The finger!" exclaimed Munthe, shaking his head in amused amazement. "This is Grand Guignol."

"You are right, Doctor," said Oscar, carefully laying the lock of hair and the ring next to the dead hand on the table. "It is all very theatrical."

I took Oscar's apricot handkerchief from my pocket and unwrapped the finger.

"There you have it," said Oscar, sitting back in his chair and drawing slowly on his cigarette. "A hand, a finger, a lock of hair, a tell-tale ring—that's all the evidence we have."

Dr. Munthe surveyed the table. "But it's enough," he said.

"What do you mean, 'it's enough'?" I asked.

"It's done its business. It's brought you to Rome—to do what the police here would never do: to investigate further." Dr. Munthe looked at me and smiled. "In this country, no one trusts the police, no one at all. The local police—the *vigili*—are fools, to a man. And they can all be bought."

"And the *carabinieri*?" asked Oscar. "They look tremendous in their uniforms."

Munthe laughed. "And quite magnificent on horseback. They guard the king—and look after their own. They may be cannier than the *vigili,* but they are just as corrupt, and considerably more expensive. The police in this country don't combat crime: they promote it. I can well understand why anyone who knew of his existence might turn to Sherlock Holmes in desperation."

"And this 'evidence,'" said Oscar, waving his cigarette in circles above the table like a witch conjuring spirits from a cauldron, "does it smack of desperation?"

"I think it does."

"And these 'clues,' what do they tell us?"

"I don't know," said Munthe, gazing at the table. "The finger is self-evidently from a different hand—and from a different person."

"And the lock of hair?" asked Oscar. "What do you make of that?"

Munthe picked up the curl and held it close to his eyes. He rubbed it between his fingers. He put it to his nose. "This isn't human hair," he said. "This is lamb's wool."

"Are you certain?" asked Oscar, sitting forward and consigning the butt of his cigarette to his water glass.

I laughed. "Oscar took it to be a golden kiss-curl from a young man's forehead."

"It is lamb's wool," repeated Munthe, handing it to me to examine. "Feel it."

"And the gold ring?" enquired Oscar. "What do you make of that? Don't tell me it's nothing more than a gewgaw from one of Tom Smith's Christmas crackers." The Swedish doctor removed the ring from the finger and peered closely at it. He turned it carefully between his own fingers. Gently he bit on it. He put it onto the palm of his hand and held it out for us all to see.

"The ring is made of gold, to be sure. And inside the ring I see what you must have seen—the crossed keys of St. Peter."

"And what do you make of the ring, Doctor? What does it tell us?"

"I am not sure what it tells us," said Munthe, "but I have seen the ring before, just a year or two ago, on the bedside table of a dying woman."

"Was it her ring?"

"No. It belonged to the priest who had come to administer the last rites to her. At the time I did wonder whether he might not have murdered her."

7.

The Pyramid of Cestius

*A*nd had he murdered her?" asked Oscar.

Munthe did not answer directly. He held the ring towards the candlelight as he spoke and studied it intently. "He was her lover, of course. That I do know."

"Why do you say 'of course'?" I asked. "He was a priest."

"These things happen, Dr. Conan Doyle—all the time."

"How do you know that he was her lover?" asked Oscar.

"She told me and I believed her. She was dying of tuberculosis. She had no reason to lie. He was her lover and she was expecting his child."

"Ah," murmured Oscar.

"Yes, he had motive, means, and opportunity. He was with her at the end, alone. She was very weak. He could have killed her simply by holding a pillow across her face."

"But why would he murder her if she was already dying?" I asked.

"Because he feared a deathbed confession. She carried his child—and his secret. So long as there was breath in her body it was a secret she might share."

"And this notion that he'd murdered her: when did that come to you?"

"As I entered her room. He'd sent for me. His message said that she was fading and that I should hurry. As I arrived, I saw at once that she was dead. She was dead and he was kneeling at the foot of her bed in prayer."

"He was a priest," I said.

"He was also her lover. I would have expected him to have been at her side."

"The picture was too perfect," said Oscar.

"Exactly, Mr. Wilde. She lay in peace, with her arms folded across her heart and her eyes closed. He knelt silently at her feet in prayer. The scene was contrived."

"And the ring?" asked Oscar, taking it from Munthe's fingers and holding it up to the candlelight between his own.

"I saw it on the bedside table, next to the girl's rosary."

"What of that?" I asked.

Dr. Munthe turned to me and smiled. "Why had he removed it, Dr. Conan Doyle?"

Oscar answered, "Because it was a priest's ring, a sign of his calling. He removed the ring while he committed the mortal sin of murder."

"Exactly so, Mr. Wilde. As I entered the room and approached the bed, I saw the ring on the bedside table. I noticed it because of its colour—rose-gold—and because of its size. It was clearly a man's ring. Moments later, it had gone. I next saw it on the priest's hand. While I attended to my patient, he had retrieved the ring and slipped it back onto his finger."

I tugged at my moustache. "It's a fine story," I said.

"You should write it up, Doctor—it would appeal to the readers of *Blackwood's Magazine*."

"Do you think that your priest *was* a murderer?" asked Oscar.

"No," said Munthe, sitting back and folding his napkin carefully.

Oscar laughed. "And why do you say that, just as you've convinced me otherwise?"

"Because of his demeanour in the months since the young woman's death."

"Has it changed?"

"No, not at all. I know the man quite well. He is a patient, also. And since the woman's death, he has appeared to me to be exactly as he was before. You would expect murder to leave its mark upon a man, would you not?"

"Not if the man was in the habit of murder," said Oscar. "Not then."

"Now who is being fanciful?" I asked.

Oscar laughed and dropped the ring onto the apricot-coloured handkerchief that lay on the table before him. "Isn't it time for a glass of grappa, gentlemen?"

We packed away the "evidence" (as Oscar termed it) and adjourned to a far corner of the hotel's candlelit lounge, where one of the waiters brought us our drinks and we sat, in semidarkness, talking of mortality, late into the night. Dr. Munthe spoke of death with a fascination bordering on reverence.

"Death is not a god," said Oscar. "Death is only the servant of the gods."

"What can any of us know of death as mere observers?" asked Munthe. "As your hero Keats says, 'Nothing ever becomes real till it is experienced.'"

It was gone three when we saw our new friend out into the Via del Babuino once more. The street was deserted. The air was still and warm. In the sky there was already the hint of dawn. Dr. Munthe bowed quite formally to each of us as he shook our hands and took his leave. "I have had a most memorable evening, gentlemen," he said. "Thank you."

"We shall see you again very soon, I hope," said Oscar. "And you must introduce us to your friend, the priest—the one with the ring."

"He is a patient more than a friend," said Munthe, "and no ordinary priest. But I will do what I can for you. I want Dr. Conan Doyle to write up the story for *Blackwood's Magazine*."

Oscar and I retired at once to our rooms and I slept more soundly than I had done for many months. It was one o'clock in the afternoon before I awoke. As I opened my eyes, I found Oscar standing at my bedside, looking down at me. His huge head was at its most leonine: his hair was newly washed, his cheeks were pink, his eyes were shining.

"We've missed breakfast," he hissed. "Now we're missing lunch!" He was dressed all in black, with a black silk tie held in place with a diamond tiepin.

"What's happening?" I asked, still half asleep.

"You are sending your telegram and I am meeting you in the piazza in half an hour."

"You are dressed in mourning," I said, sitting up.

"We are visiting the dead," he replied.

He had drawn back the curtains: warm sunshine was flooding the room. I threw off the bedclothes and dressed hurriedly, wording the wire to my wife in my head as I did so. I limited myself to twenty words. I wanted to keep the message simple: NOW WITH OSCAR WILDE IN ROME RESEARCHING NEW STORY FOR BLACKWOOD'S. ALL WELL. MISSING YOU AND OUR PRECIOUS DAUGHTER. ACD.

Within the half hour, I had joined my friend in the Piazza del Popolo. I found him waiting at the cab rank, engaged in earnest conversation with the two street urchins we had encountered the night before.

"I warned you this would happen, Oscar," I said.

"These boys are natural philosophers, Arthur," he replied. "They know that generosity is the essence of friendship."

"I can see what you are giving them," I said, shaking my head as Oscar handed each of the grinning ragamuffins another silver coin. "What are they giving you?"

"Devotion!" he answered, triumphantly. "I do not ask for anything more."

"Or less," I said, with a gentle jeer, as we climbed aboard the *carrozzina*. "Where are we going?"

"To the gates of Rome—to the Porta San Paolo. We are making a pilgrimage to the Protestant Cemetery."

"Are your disciples coming, too?"

"They live close by, apparently."

The journey took half an hour. Barefoot, bare-chested, the broken-toothed, olive-skinned boys ran behind our carriage all the way, along narrow side streets, across wide-open piazzas, down dusty lanes to the southern edge of the city. At first, as they ran the boys chatted to one another and called out to Oscar, but as the pounding got harder they fell silent and concentrated on their running.

Oscar gazed upon them lovingly. "What wonderful lives they lead!"

"Do you think so?" I asked.

"They know freedom, Arthur."

"They know poverty, Oscar. The sunshine and their youth mitigate the worst of it, perhaps, but they are dressed in rags all the same. They're beggars."

"It is safer to beg than to take," he declared, grandiloquently, waving the midges away from his face, "but it is finer to take than to beg. Don't you agree?"

"That's too deep for me, my friend. I am just a general practitioner from South Norwood."

"You're the man who created Sherlock Holmes," he cried. "You're set to join the immortals!"

As he said this, our carriage came sharply round a bend in the road and, with a jolt, we were confronted by the most remarkable sight: a mighty pyramid set immediately alongside the highway. Oscar called out to our driver, "*Basta! Basta!* Whoa!" and put out his arm to stop me from falling forward as the *carrozzina* juddered to a halt.

"This is extraordinary," I gasped.

"This is the tomb of Gaius Cestius," said Oscar. "He's joined the immortals, too—thanks to this."

The pyramid stood a hundred feet tall at least. It was faced in pale-grey marble, but the early-afternoon sun shone upon it so brilliantly its surface shimmered like gold. We clambered down from the carriage and stood gazing across the road towards the ancient monument.

"Gaius Cestius." I repeated the name. It meant nothing to me. "Who was he?"

"A Roman, from not long before the time of Christ. A tribune of the people. As I recollect from the inscription on the tomb, a member of the college of priests known as the Septemviri Epulones. They organised the great religious ceremonies, the feast days, public banquets, and the like. Cestius was an impresario. He had flair, as you can tell from his creation. He built it in anticipation of his own demise— in just three hundred and thirty days. He was very proud of that."

"And his claim to fame?"

"The pyramid, nothing else. But it's enough, don't you think?"

I stood marvelling at the scale and grandeur of the edifice and reflecting on the vanity of a man who could create such a monument to himself.

"And young Romulus and Remus live hereabouts—so they say."

The two street urchins stood on the far side of the road, at the foot of the pyramid. They were panting from their exertions and their torsos glistened with sweat. Seeing us look towards them, they waved and beckoned us to follow them.

"Let's inspect their living quarters," said Oscar. "Let's see if they're as poor as you think."

"Aren't we on our way to the Protestant Cemetery?" I asked.

"It's only a hundred yards further on. Let's follow the boys for a moment, since we've come this far."

Oscar gave instructions to our driver to wait and then, urging me to "stop dawdling and keep up," strode purposefully across the road towards the urchins.

"You're not normally one for a country hike," I remarked.

He paid no attention. "Youth is the one thing worth having," he said, his eyes fixed on the two street boys. "Youth is everything."

The boys ran ahead of us, along the eastern side of the pyramid, towards a stone wall that abutted the monument and separated the bank alongside the roadway from a field and woodland beyond. We followed them.

"This is the old city wall," said Oscar. "There are steps, of a sort."

The boys scampered up the rough stone steps that jutted out from the wall and disappeared over the top. Laboriously, now sweating profusely ourselves, we followed on.

"Where are we going?" I asked.

"I have no idea," said Oscar, gasping for breath, "but it's an adventure—there's no denying that."

The boys were now running across a short expanse of scrubland, away from the pyramid and out of the sunlight, towards a clump of trees at the edge of the wood. There they stopped and turned towards us, grinning, arms outstretched.

As we came close, the scene became less charming and more sinister.

Immediately beneath the trees, in the shade where the boys were standing, was a wooden shelter, about fifteen feet long and ten feet deep, but no more than six feet high. It was a ramshackle affair, insubstantial, dilapidated, open to the elements, with a sloping roof and a back wall, but no sides or front or floor. It might have been a refuge for sheep or a pigsty. On the ground within the shelter, strewn about, were three worn-out mattresses, filthy blankets, torn sheets, piles of newspapers and rags, and the detritus of the beggar's life: broken bottles, old tin cans, and the remains of scavenged meals. At the far end of the shelter, by a small, low-burning fire, was a mound of bones, and alongside the bones, lying on the ground, was the curled-up figure of an old man. His body was shrouded in a blanket. His face, clearly visible, was vicious. He had the sallow skin and the beaklike nose of a corpse, and I might have taken him for dead but for his beady, watchful eyes.

Oscar did not appear to see any of this. He was looking steadily at the two boys who stood before us smiling.

"God save us," he muttered. "I spy entertainment."

"What do you mean?" I asked.

"I see the leer of invitation," he said.

The boys looked at us and laughed and pulled down their ragged trousers to reveal their nakedness.

8.

All Saints'

We fled the scene at once.

"This is not what I had expected," murmured Oscar as we paced across the scrubland, back towards the pyramid.

"It's appalling," I said. "It's perverse, unnatural."

"Unexpected, certainly." He laughed. "Your tweeds, your moustache, your military bearing, Arthur: they appear to attract a different kind of attention in these southern climes."

I ignored his ribbing. "I suppose the sick old man is their beggar-master," I said. "The hapless boys are obliged to do his bidding."

"The 'hapless boys' looked happy enough to me—willing enough, too."

"It's a filthy trade."

"And not their only one. Did you see the pile of bones next to the old man?"

"I did. To sell old bones for glue-making is one thing. To sell young bodies for base gratification, quite another. It's immoral—it's *sinful*."

"Is sinfulness so very dreadful, Arthur?" he asked, looking back at me over his shoulder as he clambered gingerly onto the jagged stone steps that jutted from the city wall. "The body sins once, and has done with its sin, for action is a mode of purification. Nothing remains then but the recollection of a pleasure, or the luxury of a regret."

"I don't believe you know what you're saying, Oscar," I replied. On occasion, I felt my friend's verbosity overwhelmed his innate good sense.

We reached the roadway and found our horse and carriage waiting where we had left them. The driver, wearing a tattered straw hat and sucking on a little clay pipe, looked down at us with ill-concealed contempt. I sensed a wicked quip forming itself on Oscar's lips. I intervened and hushed my friend, urging him to keep his counsel and climb aboard.

"The man won't speak English, Arthur. Besides, I imagine he knows exactly what goes on behind the pyramid. He probably brings English milords out here on a regular basis. I hate to think of the size of tip the wretch will be expecting."

"Inversion is a sickness, Oscar," I hissed under my breath. "It is not something to make jokes about." I looked at him sternly. "This is no laughing matter."

He returned my gaze with a smile in his eyes. " 'Our sincerest laughter with some pain is fraught; our sweetest songs are those that tell of saddest thought.'"

"Keats?"

"Shelley. He came here, too—to see the pyramid and to visit Keats's grave." Oscar called up to the driver, coldly: *"Cimitero, avanti!"*

"Shouldn't we return to the hotel?" I asked.

The heat of the afternoon was dry but nonetheless

oppressive. I had no hat and my clothing was entirely un-seasonable. As a consequence of our exertions, I was soaked in perspiration.

"We'll see the cemetery first. We're almost there. It's a beautiful spot. It will refresh you."

It was. And it did. It was an oasis, only a few hundred yards beyond the pyramid, discreetly tucked beneath the ancient city walls, wonderfully cool, surrounded by pine trees, shaded by tall cypresses. As Oscar led me in through the wrought-iron gate he said, "When Shelley came to this cemetery for the first time, he wrote, 'It might make one in love with death, to think that one should be buried in so sweet a place.'"

I said nothing. Did Shelley write those words, I asked myself, or has Oscar just invented them?

"Shelley's heart is buried here," he continued. "His body was burnt on the beach at the mouth of the river Arno, near where he was drowned. His flesh and bones were cremated there, where he was washed ashore—something to do with the quarantine laws at the time. But his heart rests here: 'the heart of all hearts.'"

As we stood inspecting the plaque in Shelley's memory, Oscar turned to me: "The bones we saw behind the pyramid, where the old man lay, were they human bones?"

"No," I reassured him. "Sheep and cattle, I'd say. And mules and donkeys." I looked at him. "Yes, I had wondered for a moment, too."

We paid our respects to Shelley's heart—interred at the base of a tower in the cemetery's outer wall—and then found the grave of John Keats. I had feared my friend might prostrate himself on the grass or give way to hysterical sobbing. In fact, he remained quite calm: more Holmes, less Wilde. As we stood, looking down at the poet's simple tombstone, he remarked, "Keats marvelled that men could be martyred for their religion—and then he discovered love and declared that he, too, could be martyred for his religion. 'Love is my religion,' he said. 'I could die for that.'" Oscar put his hand lightly on my shoulder. "Love will be at the heart of our murder mystery, Arthur. I think we can be sure of that."

"You are convinced, then, that we are dealing with a mystery that involves *murder*?"

"Oh, yes," he said, "murder most foul. And I am convinced, too, that Dr. Munthe's patient—the priest, but 'no ordinary priest'—holds the key. We shall meet him soon enough."

We met him that very evening.

We did not linger among the graves and our return to our hotel was uneventful. As we drove back past the tomb of Cestius, we looked beyond the pyramid to the scrubland where we had left the wretched street boys. There was no sign of them and, from the roadway, the view of their hovel at the edge of the wood was obscured by an elderly shepherd and his unruly flock.

"Perhaps our mystery lock of hair comes from one of those sheep?" mused Oscar.

"They are goats, Oscar," I said.

Back at the Hôtel de Russie, we took tea (Ceylon tea with Madeira cake), talked of Keats and Shelley (Oscar talked: I listened), and retired to our rooms to bathe and change. Then, while Oscar dozed on his bed, I spent an hour or so working through my seemingly bottomless portmanteau of letters from the admirers of Sherlock Holmes. At seven-thirty, Oscar awoke. At eight o'clock we set off together for the short walk along the Via del Babuino to the newly built Anglican church. We arrived at All Saints' to find Dr. Axel Munthe—still dressed, it seemed, in the exact costume he had worn the night before—assisting a stout and halting clergyman up the front steps to the church door. As the doctor and the priest paused in the doorway, we joined them.

Munthe smiled. "This is the reverend gentleman of whom I spoke last night," he said.

I nodded by way of acknowledgement. Oscar bowed low and bent forward to kiss the clergyman's ring.

"I am not a bishop," protested the priest, laughing. His voice was sonorous: rich and deep. He spoke good English with a pronounced Italian accent.

"But you are a magnificent monsignor," breathed Oscar, unctuously.

The priest, a mountain of a man, was impressively garbed in a black cassock edged in purple silk, with a broad purple sash swathing his mighty girth. He had a toad's face, full and fat, with sensuous lips. His head was bald. His bulging eyes shone. His jowls shook as he addressed us.

"I take it you are Oscar Wilde," he rumbled. Moisture spilt onto his lips as he spoke, but his manner was entirely genial. He turned to me and his bulbous eyes widened further. "And this must be Arthur Conan Doyle. Munthe has just been telling me all about you—but he did not need to, because I knew all about you already."

"May I present Monsignor Francesco Felici," said Axel Munthe, "*Maestro delle Celebrazioni Liturgiche Pontificie.*"

"By all that's wonderful," cried Oscar, "you are Master of Ceremonies to His Holiness."

The priest heaved his shoulders and offered a theatrical, self-deprecating shrug. "One does one's humble best."

"And yet you are here among the Anglicans," continued Oscar.

"Missionary work," said the Monsignor, with a throaty chuckle. "The Holy Father is on his summer retreat, so I am permitted to stray from the confines of St. Peter's. I come here in the hope of converts—and to see my English friends."

I said, "Your English is exceptional, Monsignor."

"I am learning. We have a small *circolo inglese* at the Vatican. And one of the ways in which we learn your language, Mr. Conan Doyle, is to read your work—out loud to one another, in the sacristy, behind the Sistine Chapel, after Mass."

"Good Lord," I murmured.

"We all admire the great Sherlock Holmes."

"Dr. Conan Doyle is going to be reading to us tonight," said Oscar.

"A new Holmes adventure?" enquired the Monsignor, eagerly.

"No," I said, a touch too sharply. The portly priest appeared quite startled. I lowered my eyes. "I am sorry to disappoint you."

"You won't disappoint us, Dr. Doyle," said a gentle voice at my shoulder, "I am certain of that."

I turned. It was Irene Sadler. She looked much younger than she had done the day before—less travel-stained, I suppose, more rested.

"Whatever you have brought to read to us will give huge pleasure, I know," she went on. "We are simply delighted that you are here. And grateful. Thank you." She looked about our little group gathered on the doorstep. "Welcome, gentlemen. Monsignor, Dr. Munthe, Mr. Wilde—welcome." She bobbed a curtsey to the priest and shook Oscar and Axel Munthe by the hand. She touched my elbow and led us into the church. "It's very crowded, I'm afraid. We may run out of refreshments and everyone has to talk at the top of their voices because the acoustics are so peculiar."

"Are we late?" asked Dr. Munthe.

"No, everybody else is early. The English ladies have been arriving since seven o'clock."

We had passed through a narrow vestibule and now stood on the threshold of the church, in a side aisle, looking out across a sea of bobbing heads. Some of them were male (and grey and balding in the main), but most of them were female and sporting an extraordinary array of head apparel: hats large and small, feathered and veiled, scarves, toques, bonnets, berets, and tam-o'shanters. There must have been a hundred women, at least, clustered in the echoing nave of All Saints'.

"It sounds like the monkey house at the zoo," said Irene Sadler, laughing.

"Every Englishwoman in Rome must be here," observed Monsignor Felici.

"Of a certain age," added Axel Munthe.

Head held high, Oscar was scanning the scene. "Never trust a woman who wears mauve, whatever her age may be, or a woman over thirty-five who is fond of pink ribbons. She will always have a history."

"Very droll, Mr. Wilde," said the Monsignor, "but I think you'll find the ladies here are of a different order. They wear brown and grey when they are not wearing black and they come with 'hope' rather than 'history.' They are of riper years, even the young ones."

"But they love a clergyman," said Oscar, amused.

"Even a Catholic priest," said the Monsignor.

"*Especially* a Catholic priest. They know he's dangerous, yet they feel quite safe with him."

"In that case, I had better throw myself among them. Come, Munthe, let us mingle with the Englishwomen of Rome. I imagine many of them are your patients already and those that aren't soon will be."

"We will catch up with you later," said Oscar.

"Of course," replied the Monsignor. "I must introduce you both to Father Bechetti. He's very frail, but he's here tonight. He's a great Anglophile. He speaks perfect English—when he speaks. He will want to meet you, I know. We will see you anon and you must come up to the Vatican. We take English afternoon tea in the sacristy, you know, with cucumber sandwiches."

With benign smiles, Monsignor Felici and Dr. Munthe

took their leave of us and moved towards the nave to join the milling throng.

"I must find Martin," said Irene Sadler. "He'll be hiding in the vestry." She touched each of us lightly on the arm. "Wait here, would you? I don't want to lose you. I think we should do the readings sooner rather than later. You are reading first, Mr. Wilde—from the pulpit. I thought you wouldn't mind."

"I am always at home in a pulpit," said Oscar.

"And I must find you some sherry—if there's any left."

"And some Italian cheese, I hope," added Oscar.

Miss Sadler looked across the church and shook her head. "It's all got a little out of hand. We invited everybody and everybody's come." She laughed and raised her eyes to heaven as she moved away. As she went, she turned and waved to us with her fingers.

"She's smitten, Arthur," whispered Oscar, grinning at me wickedly. "Congratulations, man."

"Don't be absurd, Oscar."

"And you're a little in love, too. Don't deny it."

"I do deny it, absolutely."

"When one is in love, one begins by deceiving oneself. And ends by deceiving others."

"That's not my way, Oscar," I protested. "I am wholly faithful to my wife and you know it."

"I am sorry to hear it, Arthur. Faithfulness is to the emotional life what consistency is to the life of the intellect—simply a confession of failure."

"You are preposterous."

"I am in earnest."

"Then I do not like your philosophy. And, most certainly, I do not share it."

Oscar smiled and looked around the crowded church. It was well lit, both by candles and by electric light. "Do you share my estimation of Munthe's friend, the bonhomous Monsignor?"

"That he's no murderer?"

"He's too stout for murder. But he holds the key, don't you think? He wears the ring."

"Yes, I saw a rose-gold band on his finger. But if he's *wearing* the ring, it cannot be the ring that was sent to Sherlock Holmes on the severed finger. That's in your wallet, Oscar."

"It is a ring exactly like it."

"There could be scores of rings exactly like it."

"Possibly, but I doubt it. By the pricking of my thumbs, something tells me His Holiness's Master of Ceremonies is the man to lead us to the heart of the mystery."

"I hope so," I said, touching the side pocket of my jacket. "This dead hand weighs on me heavily."

Oscar smiled. "I am glad you are keeping it about you, Arthur—it's wise to do so." He touched the pocket of his own jacket. "Since sherry is being served in church, would it be bad form to smoke, do you think?"

"Most certainly."

"They're eating cheese in the transept and I'm sure I can smell incense burning somewhere," he said, looking about him as he pulled a silver cigarette case from his pocket.

"Put your cigarettes away, Oscar," I said firmly. "Remember where you are."

"You know I smoked a cigarette on the stage of the St. James's at the opening of *Lady Windermere's Fan*."

"For your curtain speech—you told me. You wore a green carnation in your buttonhole and held a lit cigarette in your mauve-gloved hand. I remember."

"My enemies were not amused."

I smiled. "Do you have enemies, Oscar?"

"Yes," he said, snapping shut the cigarette case and slipping it back into his pocket, "and I have just seen one of them on the far side of the nave."

I turned quickly to look in the direction indicated by my friend. I saw no one I recognised, except for the Reverend Martin Sadler pushing his way to the edge of the crowd.

"My apologies," he called out as he came towards us. "I am an appalling host."

"You have your flock to attend to," said Oscar, pleasantly. "They must be entertained."

"They are entertaining themselves. Listen to them. The House of God has been turned into a house of gossip. I cannot hear myself think above the hubbub. The sherry's all gone."

"And the cheese?" asked Oscar.

"They've gobbled the lot." The clergyman shook his head despairingly. "It's our moment to take to the stage—if you can face it, gentlemen."

"We are at your service," said Oscar.

"A poem from you, Mr. Wilde? And a Sherlock Holmes story from you, Dr. Doyle: is that correct?"

"I had something else in mind," I said, crisply.

"Oh. No matter. We are very grateful. Come this way,

please." He led us from the side aisle towards the pulpit steps. "I'll say a few words—very few—then introduce you as our surprise guests." He looked at us both with troubled eyes. "It is not easy for me here. Thank you for agreeing to this, gentlemen. I am very grateful. Tonight the ladies can talk about you, instead of me. It will make a pleasant change."

Anxiously, he shook each of us by the hand. I was clutching the manuscript of the story I proposed to read: it was a Highland adventure, as yet unpublished.

"I wonder if this will be too lengthy?" I asked.

"If it was about Sherlock Holmes," said Oscar, playfully, "they'd think it not nearly lengthy enough."

"Do you have your poem, Mr. Wilde?" enquired the clergyman.

"I have it by heart," said Oscar. "It is by John Keats."

"Ah," said the Reverend Sadler, widening his eyes, "very good." He took a long, deep breath. "Let us do what we must."

He turned and made the sign of the cross and, with a steady step, climbed the narrow stone stairway to the pulpit. As he went, Oscar pointed approvingly at his well-polished black boots.

"Your friend looks after her brother well," he whispered.

From the pulpit, the vicar called the multitude to order. "Good evening, ladies and gentlemen, may I have your attention for a moment?"

The tentative, seemingly troubled soul that had left us a moment before now appeared in full command of himself and his congregation. His voice was clear and resonant: the people fell silent almost as he spoke. Peering round from our vantage point behind the pulpit, we could see half the nave.

"What do those faces tell us?" asked Oscar.

"It is difficult to say," I replied.

"Exactly," whispered Oscar. "They do not know what to make of their man—and neither do I."

The only joyful face that I could see belonged to Monsignor Felici. He stood no more than ten feet from us, in pride of place, at the front of the crowd, surrounded by a cluster of English ladies of riper years. The Pontifical Master of Ceremonies beamed beatifically as he gazed up at the Anglican vicar of All Saints'.

"He exudes the complacency of the righteous, does he not?" whispered Oscar. "How I envy his certainty."

Dr. Munthe stood on the Monsignor's right hand and an elderly priest, wearing a black cloak and black biretta, stood on his left. The old man was tall and thin, but his pallid face was wizened and his body bent like a weeping willow. He wore round spectacles with darkened lenses.

"Is that Father Bechetti?" I asked.

"Is he blind?" asked Oscar.

The old priest held on to the Monsignor's arm with one hand. With the other he held out his empty sherry glass as if he were about to propose a toast.

"Is he simple?" I wondered.

"Is he our murderer?" asked Oscar, laughing softly as he spoke. "Look at his fingers, Arthur. Look carefully."

"I see nothing."

"Neither do I. Father Bechetti wears no rings."

"In the name of the Father, the Son, and the Holy Spirit," declared the Reverend Sadler from the head of the pulpit, "welcome to the soon-to-be-consecrated church of All Saints, our new and beautiful Anglican parish church here in the heart of Rome—the Eternal City. Let us stand where we are, humbly before God, recalling the eternal verities and bowing our heads in prayer."

Sadler spoke with an unassuming authority and the assembly did as it was bidden. The brief prayers done, he thanked those gathered before him for their prompt attendance and their generosity, "some of it already manifested, much of it still eagerly anticipated." (This pleasantry was met with silence. The congregation gazed up at Sadler quite impassively.) When he went on to welcome "our honoured guests," notably the First Secretary from the British Embassy, representing His Excellency the British ambassador, and "our friends and neighbours" from the Vatican, there was a murmur of apparent approval, but news of "the surprise presence in our midst of one of the most dazzling literary personalities of our time, Mr. Oscar Wilde" provoked no response at all.

There was an eerie silence as Sadler climbed down the pulpit steps and, slowly, Oscar mounted them. I felt for my friend as he reached the summit and surveyed the sea of sullen faces that gazed up at him.

"I have been asked to share a poem with you tonight," he began, lightly. "I am honoured to do so. It is one of the most beautiful poems ever penned—yet, you may be surprised to learn, it is not one of mine."

Dr. Munthe smiled. Monsignor Felici laughed. I heard

an English voice close to the pulpit hiss, "The man's beyond the pale."

Oscar glanced behind him and smiled. "Nevertheless, here is the poem . . . It is called 'The Eve of St. Agnes.'"

St. Agnes' Eve—Ah, bitter chill it was!
The owl, for all his feathers, was a-cold;
The hare limp'd trembling through the frozen grass,
And silent was the flock in woolly fold:
Numb were the Beadsman's fingers while he told
His rosary, and while his frosted breath,
Like pious incense from a censer old,
Seem'd taking flight for heaven without a death,
Past the sweet Virgin's picture, while his prayer he saith.

He spoke the poem beautifully, liltingly, the words flowing from him like music played upon a cello. Almost at once—before he had spoken even four lines—he held the assembly in his thrall. I watched the fat Monsignor looking up at him, smiling in admiration.

But as Oscar embarked on the second stanza of the poem and reached the end of the line "His prayer he saith, this patient, holy man," the old priest standing next to the Monsignor suddenly lurched forward, throwing down his sherry glass so that it smashed violently on the ground. The old man cried out as if in agony, "No, no!" and then he fell, pathetically, in a heap, onto the marble church floor.

9.

"The Wilde effect"

*T*his is what I call the 'Oscar Wilde effect.' The man exerts an unhealthy influence on all who come too close to him."

"Is that intended as a joke, sir?" I murmured, through clenched teeth.

"It is the truth, sir. At least, it reflects my experience of Mr. Wilde."

Four of us carried the body of the old priest from the foot of the pulpit of All Saints' to the dimly lit church vestry. I was one of the four, the others being Martin Sadler, the Anglican chaplain; Axel Munthe, the Swedish doctor; and the gentleman who uttered this gratuitous slander at the expense of my friend Wilde.

"Who are you, sir?" I demanded, angrily.

"Mr. Rennell Rodd is First Secretary at the British Embassy," said the Reverend Sadler, "and, consequently, our principal guest of honour this evening."

"His remarks do his office no credit," I said.

"Please, gentlemen," cried Axel Munthe, "desist! I have a patient to attend to."

"I apologise," I said, without conviction, as we lowered

the frail body of the old man onto a leather chaise beneath the vestry window. He was alive. His face was as white as a surplice, his toothless mouth hung open, his grey tongue lolled loosely over his lower lip.

"I apologise, also," said the so-called diplomat, now standing upright and nodding his head towards me.

He was in his early thirties, tall and slender, immaculately dressed (he wore a Balliol College tie), impeccably groomed, with thick auburn hair swept back from a broad, smooth brow, and a luxuriant moustache, waxed at the tips. His appearance struck me at once as being too good to be true, but he had high cheekbones, a distinguished nose (in the Wellington tradition), and piercing blue eyes. He was undeniably handsome.

"I spoke out of turn," he said, "in the heat of the moment."

"Please," insisted Dr. Munthe, "don't speak at all." He lifted the old priest's right arm, took hold of his wrist, and searched for his pulse. He then rested his head on the old man's chest and pressed his ear against his heart. "Doyle," he instructed, "loosen his collar, straighten his head."

I did as Munthe told me and, as I did so, the old man started to breathe noisily, gasping first, then wheezing like the bellows on a chapel organ.

"Is that the death rattle?" enquired the Reverend Sadler anxiously.

Munthe raised his head and laughed. "No, it's an old man snoring. Leave him to us, gentlemen." He looked at Martin Sadler. "Return to your flock, Padre. I imagine the ladies will be in quite a state. You can tell them that all's well."

The vicar and the diplomat took their leave. "I think

we'll have to forgo your story, Dr. Doyle," Sadler said. "The night has proved unruly."

"Good evening, gentlemen," said Rennell Rodd. He bowed to us and accompanied Sadler to the vestry door.

When they had departed, Munthe returned his attention to the old priest stretched out before us on the chaise. "His breathing has calmed considerably," he said. "He looks quite peaceful." He removed the old man's spectacles and, with thumb and forefinger, carefully raised each eyelid in turn. "And look at his eyes . . ." They were those of an old man: swollen, yellow, and cloudy.

I bent down to look into them closely. "Beyond the cataracts, I see nothing out of the ordinary."

"We are agreed, then?" said Munthe.

"It was not a stroke."

"Nor a heart attack."

"What was it?"

I replayed the scene in my mind's eye. "His head was held up, as though he were listening to Oscar's recitation, listening intently. Then, suddenly, he lurched forward and cried out, 'No, no!' and then he threw his glass onto the ground."

"He threw the glass—deliberately?"

"I think so."

"It did not simply fall from his grasp?"

"No, he threw it, violently. And then he collapsed. His body simply gave way."

"He fainted." Munthe looked down at the priest once more. "There was a sudden outburst of anger—or distress—and then he lost consciousness. And now he sleeps, like a baby."

I looked down at the old man. "Who is he?" I asked.

"Joachim Bechetti, a papal chaplain and a good man, by all accounts. He's been at the Vatican for years, since Pio Nono's time. He was an artist in his day—a painter and a fine one, too. I've seen his work."

"Will he live?" asked a voice from the shadows.

We looked towards the vestry door. Two clerics stood there, one of whom was Monsignor Felici. He came into the room slowly, reverentially, as if solemnly approaching a deathbed, holding the old priest's biretta.

"Will he live?" he repeated.

Munthe looked at Monsignor Felici with an amused eye. "He will outlive you, my friend, unless you lose some weight."

"He appears to have fainted," I said. "That's all."

"He was standing too long," said Munthe, "the crowd was too great, he had perhaps drunk too much—he was overwhelmed."

"I am relieved," said Felici, laying the old priest's biretta on the chaise.

"What is happening in the church?" I asked.

Felici smiled. "Mr. Oscar Wilde is the hero of the hour. He finished his recitation and now he is moving slowly among the ladies so that they may shake his hand and touch his garb. The commotion by the pulpit went unnoticed by most, but word has since spread—so there's excitement in the air."

"It will be dampened somewhat when they discover there hasn't been a death, after all."

It was Felici's companion who spoke, in a rasping voice

and with the distinctive accent of an English aristocrat from a bygone era.

"Good evening, Munthe." He nodded towards the Swedish doctor, then extended his hand towards me. "Good evening, Arthur *Conan* Doyle."

I shook his hand. At once, I noticed the rose-gold ring upon his finger. I noticed, too, the unnatural softness of his skin and the weakness of his grasp. He was dressed in robes identical to Felici's—his cassock was edged with purple silk; he wore a purple sash—but he was younger than Felici, around forty years of age, and, though reasonably well fleshed, not a fat man. He was broad-shouldered, sturdily built, with a round and ruddy countryman's face. He had thick, bushy eyebrows and tightly curled, iron-grey hair. His whole manner and appearance belied the feebleness of his handshake.

"You don't remember me?" he said. "I am surprised."

In the dim vestry light, I peered at his face closely. I felt not the least glimmer of recognition.

"I am disappointed," he continued, "hurt, even. It's not that long ago, surely?"

"You have the advantage of me, sir," I said, awkwardly.

"We were at school together, Conan Doyle. At Stony-hurst. I thought one always remembered the older boys. Apparently not." He laughed. It was a hard, guttural laugh. "I remember you," he went on, looking at me appraisingly. "I remember you vividly—the insistence that you were called *Conan* Doyle. You were a cocky little fellow, very full of yourself. We had to beat you regularly." He looked at me and raised his bushy eyebrows. "You must remember the tolley?"

"I remember the tolley," I said.

"It was the Stonyhurst instrument of retribution," he explained to the others. "Where lesser schools used the cane, we used the tolley."

The priest looked at me and grinned. His white teeth were small and even. "I distinctly recollect the last time I had to thrash you. It was on 22 May 1872. It was my birthday."

"I don't remember," I said. "It was a long time ago."

"You were thirteen—and very wicked. I was eighteen—and very good." He laughed.

"And now?" enquired Axel Munthe.

"Arthur *Conan* Doyle is an author of international renown and I carry the sins of the world upon my shoulders."

"Monsignor Breakspear has recently been appointed Grand Penitentiary at St. Peter's," explained Monsignor Felici. "He hears our confessions. He knows all our secrets."

"And shares them only with Almighty God," said the Englishman, smiling.

"He is the Pope's confessor," Felici continued. "He will be a cardinal before long."

"I am honoured to make your reacquaintance," I said. "Forgive me for not recollecting our last encounter. Perhaps I do recollect the name, now I think of it, but I don't remember the beating. I don't often think of my school days."

"Don't look back," said Axel Munthe. "It's a good rule."

The old priest lying before us on the chaise began to cough.

"What are we to do with him?" asked Monsignor Felici.

"I will look after him tonight," said Axel Munthe, leaning down to replace the spectacles on the old priest's nose.

"Oh, no," protested Monsignor Breakspear, with a barking laugh. "We want poor Bechetti to live a little longer." The Monsignor reached out and, for a moment, rested his soft fingers on my hand. "We call Dr. Munthe 'Dr. Death,'" he said, with a disconcerting smile. 'When he gets the opportunity, he likes to ease his older, weaker patients from this world to the next. He admits it. Indeed, he boasts of it. We do not approve."

"Father Bechetti is not in mortal danger," said Munthe.

"Good," said Breakspear, "then we'll take him back to the Vatican now. I have a carriage waiting."

"He needs bed rest, plenty of fluids—water and milk—and regular meals, but the simplest diet: pasta and vegetables. His pulse is steady, his heart quite strong. I think he was probably overwhelmed by the heat and the numbers in the church, that's all."

Father Bechetti began to stir. His thin hands twitched at his side.

"Brother Matteo will nurse him back to health," said Breakspear. He glanced towards me. "Brother Matteo is a Capuchin friar and our Florence Nightingale."

"He is the best of men," said Monsignor Felici.

"Very good," said Munthe. "Let's get Father Bechetti to your carriage now. I'll call on him tomorrow."

"And bring Conan Doyle with you," said Breakspear. "And Mr. Wilde, too. I missed his recitation. I would like to meet him—very much." He turned and looked directly at me, smiling and resting both his hands on mine. I felt the smoothness of his fingers on my knuckles. "You must come for tea in the sacristy—join our little English circle. There are just five of us: Monsignor Felici and myself, Father Bechetti, Brother Matteo, and Monsignor Tuminello. He is the papal exorcist. Few can resist him." He laughed and released my hands. "Come at four o'clock—sharp. Munthe will show you the way. We have cucumber sandwiches. It will be home from home. And bring one of your stories to read to us, won't you? We all love Sherlock Holmes."

The nearby clock of Sant'Atanasio dei Greci was striking ten as Munthe and I escorted the three Catholic priests to their carriage. The toothless old father had recovered sufficiently from his fainting fit to totter down the vestry steps supported on my and Monsignor Breakspear's arms. Munthe assisted the corpulent Monsignor Felici. We bade the trio good night with a firm promise to attend them on the morrow.

"At four o'clock," repeated Breakspear through the carriage window, "sharp."

"He will be obeyed," said Munthe as we stood in the moonlit street watching the *carrozza* trundle away from us over the cobblestones.

"He has a commanding presence," I said.

"A natural authority—and a name to reckon with."

"Breakspear?"

"Nicholas Breakspear. *Nomen est omen,* as your friend Wilde likes to say. Nicholas Breakspear was also the name of the last English pope, was it not?"

"That was seven hundred and fifty years ago," I said.

Munthe gazed steadily after the churchmen's carriage as it disappeared into the darkness of the Piazza del Popolo.

"Nevertheless . . ." He smiled. "In the fullness of time, your old schoolfellow expects to ascend the throne of St. Peter. I am certain of that."

"That's absurd."

"Ambition often is absurd."

"He's English."

"That is a problem nowadays, I grant you. And he's a Jesuit. That may be the greater disadvantage. No Jesuit has ever become pope. The other cardinals don't trust them."

"Are you Monsignor Breakspear's doctor?" I asked, as we turned to go back into the church.

"No, Monsignor Breakspear has no need of a doctor. He is wonderfully robust—as you saw. He has the constitution of an ox."

"He has very delicate fingers."

"He has a farmer's build, but a priest's hands."

"I did not care for the softness of his handshake," I said.

"But you noticed the ring?"

"Yes," I said, "I noticed the ring."

It was well after eleven o'clock when finally we left All Saints' that night. It took time to draw Oscar from his audience. The Anglican ladies of Rome had greeted him in silence, but having seen him and heard him and felt the charm of his personality, they were now reluctant to let him go until they had held his hand in theirs and implored him to take tea with them or play whist with them or open their forthcoming bazaar.

"Being adored is such a nuisance," he declared as we untangled him from the final knot of female admirers.

"Women treat us just as humanity treats its gods. They worship us and are always asking us to do something for them."

"We all need to be needed," said Axel Munthe. "We need that more than anything."

"I need a nightcap," said Oscar. "I need that more than anything."

We were among the last to leave the church. As we departed, the Reverend Martin Sadler and his sister were effusive in their thanks.

Sadler shook Oscar warmly by the hand: "You transformed what would have been the dreariest of fund-raisers into a memorable theatrical event, Mr. Wilde. I am grateful."

His sister held out her hands to Munthe and to me: "You doctors saved the evening—saved it! We would have been lost without you. We are so in your debt."

While Oscar and Munthe stepped out into the street, I lingered for a moment in the church vestibule.

"Will you read me your story very soon?" Irene Sadler asked—and she kissed me gently on the cheek as she bade me farewell.

The white moon was full and Oscar stood on the pavement gazing up at it, his vigour magically restored. "It's time for cigarettes and brandy, gentlemen, don't you agree?"

I felt that it was time for bed and shut-eye, but Oscar's sudden exuberance was not to be gainsaid.

"If you have the cigarettes," volunteered Axel Munthe, "I have the brandy. Come!"

Amused by Oscar's unashamed appetite for pleasure, the Swedish doctor marched us along the deserted Via del

Babuino to his house by the Spanish Steps. As he put his latchkey to the door, he whispered, "Please be very quiet as we climb the stairs. We must not disturb the neighbours."

"Will your companion be about?" asked Oscar.

"I hope not," said Munthe. "We have had enough excitement for one evening." He picked up the oil lamp that stood on the hallway table and checked his pocket watch. "It's late, long past her bedtime. She'll be asleep, I trust."

"Ah," exclaimed Oscar, "your companion is a lady? I had assumed otherwise . . ."

Munthe seemed unperturbed by Oscar's impertinence. He laughed softly. "She is no lady, I assure you. You'll meet her soon enough—but not tonight, I hope. She's quite a handful."

"Italian?" Oscar persisted.

"Egyptian," said Munthe.

Happily, Oscar now seemed lost for words. He said nothing further until we were ensconced in low leather chairs around the empty fireplace in Dr. Munthe's study. As our host poured us generous glasses of Italian brandy, Oscar drew languorously on his first cigarette of the night. He threw back his head and, closing his eyes, murmured, "A woman's life revolves in curves of emotion. It is upon lines of intellect that a man's life progresses. Is that not your experience, Doctor?"

"Let me reflect on that for a moment," said Munthe quietly, moving about the room and turning up the oil lamps that stood on his desk and mantelpiece.

"That's rather deep for this time of night, Oscar," I observed.

My friend tilted his head towards me and opened one eye. "I am trying to raise my game, Arthur—in keeping with the surroundings. Keats died in the room next door, remember. His ghost may be listening."

"Let us raise our glasses to Keats's memory," said Axel Munthe. "Your reading of his poem was clearly the making of tonight's event."

"It was a *recitation,* my dear Doctor, not a reading. I have 'The Eve of St. Agnes' by heart—all forty-two stanzas."

"The Anglican ladies were much taken with it, clearly."

"It's a tale of virginity dramatically lost and of love ecstatically found. I thought it might hold their attention."

I laughed. "It brought the old priest to his knees quickly enough."

Oscar sat up abruptly. "The old priest!" he exclaimed. "I forgot him altogether. How is he, poor old man?"

"Recovered," said Munthe. "I shall see him tomorrow. He will live a while longer."

"What was it? His heart?"

"I think he was simply overwhelmed," said Munthe. "The nave was very crowded. He'd been standing a long while."

"I thought I saw him throw his glass to the ground. For a moment I feared it was something I had said. I watched him fall, but I decided it was best not to stop the recitation. The congregation as a whole appeared not to notice the commotion."

"You held them in your thrall," said Munthe.

"And I carried on because I saw you all rush forward to the rescue. I even noticed James Rennell Rodd springing from the shadows at the critical moment."

"He's the rising man at the British Embassy here," said Munthe.

"I can believe it," said Oscar.

"He lives across the piazza," continued Munthe.

"Ah," said Oscar, sitting back in the leather chair once more and drawing on his cigarette. "I thought I caught sight of him in the street yesterday—wearing a straw hat."

"Do you know the man?" I asked.

Oscar smiled at me, widened his eyes, and picked a trace of tobacco off his lower lip. "Do I know James Rennell Rodd? Yes, Arthur, I know him well. I know him very well indeed. Did he not mention it?"

"No," I lied.

"I am surprised," said Oscar, gazing at me steadily.

"We were very preoccupied with the old priest. He was still unconscious."

"Of course," answered Oscar, turning his eyes towards his brandy glass and contemplating it. "Rennell Rodd and I were close friends once upon a time—none closer. We are enemies now. I know because he wrote to tell me so. He has the soul of a bureaucrat. He must put everything in writing. Our 'falling-out,' as he termed it, is official and destined to be life-long. Friends, of course, do make the best enemies. They know what they're about."

"What caused this 'falling-out'?" asked Munthe.

"We were at Oxford together. I won the Newdigate Prize for poetry and, two years later, Rennell Rodd won it also. We revelled in one another's success. And when it came to our final examinations and I secured a First, it was expected by one and all that Rennell Rodd would do the same. Alas, it was not to be. Rennell Rodd got a Second. He tried too hard. It's his besetting sin."

"Is that it?" I asked.

"It's enough, isn't it?" He laughed and took a swig of brandy. "But you are right, Arthur. There was more to it than that. About ten years ago, I did young Rennell Rodd a kindness—at his behest. I wrote the foreword to his first book of poems. There are some men who can never forgive a kindness done to them. Obligation turns to enmity." My friend sat up once more, holding the lit butt of his cigarette in the air. "Do you have a dead man's hand that I might use as an ashtray, Doctor?"

Munthe picked up from his desk what appeared to be a large black mummified hand, its fingers stiffly erect. He passed it to Oscar.

"It's surprisingly light," said Oscar, cupping the hand in his own. He looked at Munthe and smiled. "Is this, by any chance, the severed hand of the unfortunate workman who fell to his death from the rafters of All Saints'?"

"It is," replied Munthe, lightly. "I was called to the scene at the time of the accident. I found the hand at the foot of the pulpit. I knew the poor man would have no further use for it, so I kept it—as a souvenir."

"And you embalmed it?" said Oscar, examining the hand more closely.

"Yes," said Munthe. "Your cigarette can't harm it now."

10.

The Sacristy

On the morning of the next day I sent a telegram to my wife, Touie, and allowed Oscar to take me to Keats's tailor in the Via del Corso. I asked for something "not too Italian." Oscar and the tailor assured me they would have something *"che va bene"* ready by lunchtime.

In the afternoon, at three o'clock, Munthe joined us at the Hôtel de Russie. The Swedish doctor was dressed precisely as he had been the night before, but his beard appeared freshly trimmed and his thick, round spectacles gleamed in the sunlight. He carried with him a small, somewhat battered black leather medical bag. Together, by carriage, from the door of the hotel, the three of us proceeded to the Vatican. As we crossed the Piazza del Popolo the overfamiliar urchin boys once again ran after our *carrozza*. As they called up to us, waving and laughing, I looked away. Oscar turned towards them, smiled, and threw them some change.

"Don't encourage them, unless you want to," said Axel Munthe. "They're notorious. Rome is full of feral children—waifs and strays who sleep outside the city walls and eke out a living by preying on kind-hearted tourists—but those two stand out from the crowd. I know them. They hunt as a pair and once they've latched on to you, they won't let you go."

The sun was high; the air was dry; there was no breeze; the streets were dusty. Self-conscious as I felt at my appearance, I was grateful to be wearing the light linen suit that Oscar had chosen for me.

"And the straw hat becomes you, Arthur," said my friend, teasingly. "We'll make a Roman of you yet."

Door to door, the journey took less than half an hour. As we crossed the blue-brown river Tiber, Oscar looked down at a ragged knot of beggars sheltering from the sun beneath the abutment of the bridge.

"The evolution of man is slow," he said. "The injustice of men is great." As we turned in to the tree-lined Borgo Santo Spirito and caught our first glimpse of the mighty Basilica of St. Peter's ahead of us, Oscar declared, "From Constantine's foundations and Caligula's obelisk to Bernini's façade and Michelangelo's dome, all beautiful things, I find, belong to the same age."

As names, allusions, and sententious turns of phrase tumbled out of him, I listened—intrigued, amused, impressed, but also conscious that my friend's manner (and his learning) might well infuriate those who did not realise how essentially good-hearted he was.

The Piazza San Pietro was crowded with pedestrians: pilgrims, priests, friars, nuns, beggars, tourists, street vendors, young men in boaters, old women in veils. Boldly, instructed by Munthe, our driver steered our carriage through the crowd, across the square itself, past the flower sellers and rosary pedlars, past the fountains, past a colossal, newly erected statue of St. Paul, to a gate at the right-hand end of a colonnade of Doric columns. As the carriage pulled up before the gate, four or five members of the Papal Swiss Guard, helmets gleaming, halberds in hand, stepped briskly forward. They looked resplendent in their red, blue, and yellow striped uniforms, but not welcoming.

"Are we expected?" I asked.

"Have no fear," said Munthe, stepping down from the carriage lightly. "Follow me."

The moment the Swiss Guards recognised Munthe, they moved aside to let our party pass.

"It is the little black bag that does it," said Munthe. "It is a doctor's passe-partout. It allows you to go safely anywhere."

"Where are we going?" bleated Oscar, eyeing the wide stone stairway that stretched up before us beyond the gate.

"To the Sistine Chapel. It is no more than a hundred steps."

"No wonder the Pope insists on being carried everywhere," cried Oscar, plaintively. "How on earth does Monsignor Felici manage?"

"With difficulty," said Munthe. "I believe he has acolytes to help him. The Swiss Guard carry the old priest to and fro."

"Acolytes and guardsmen," murmured Oscar. "It's the only way."

"More exercise, my friend," countered Munthe. "That's the only way."

Oscar said nothing more. He could not. His breath was all used up in climbing the steps.

When we reached the summit, Munthe did not pause. "This way," he said, leading us now along a wide, high-ceilinged, and marbled outdoor corridor, lined with ancient Greek and Roman statuary. "Prepare to adjust your eyes, gentlemen," he instructed as we arrived at a small, un-marked doorway cut into a high, whitewashed wall. With a heave, he pulled open the door and indicated that we should step through the narrow aperture ahead of him. I entered first. Oscar, breathing heavily, followed. Munthe's warning was well given. From golden sunlight we were plunged into inky gloom.

As Munthe pulled the door close to behind us, I asked, "Is this the Sistine Chapel?"

"Yes," said Munthe. "This is the private entrance."

"We have come to the most beautifully decorated space on the face of the earth," cried Oscar, "and we cannot see a thing!"

"Well, you're not 'ere for the frescoes, are you, Mr. Wilde?"

The question came out of the darkness in a cheery cockney accent. It was followed almost at once by the appearance of a cheery cockney face, lit by a single wax candle held up before it in a brass candlestick. Hold-ing the candlestick was the owner of the face, a sturdy, middle-sized fellow, some forty years of age, clean-shaven and sallow-skinned, with shiny black curly hair and shiny black merry eyes.

"Good God," exclaimed Oscar. "It's Gus Green!"

"It ain't, Mr. Wilde. It's 'is brother: Cesare Verdi."

Oscar turned to me, laughing. "This is Gus Green,

Arthur—maître d'hôtel at Willis's restaurant in King Street, St. James's, and my particular friend."

"No, Mr. Wilde. It's Cesare Verdi, sacristan at the Sistine Chapel, St. Peter's, Rome. You think I'm my brother, but I'm not."

"You *are* Gus," insisted Oscar, peering at the man. "You must be. I can see the devil in your eye."

"Two peas from the same pod, Mr. Wilde—but I'm the older, by a good hour, and I'm Italian. *Si, è vero.* I'm my father's son. Augustus is the English one. 'E's 'is mother's boy. 'E's the one with the devil in 'is eye. I've got the Archangel Gabriel in mine."

Oscar laughed. "By all that's wonderful, can this be true? You're telling me that you and Gussy are twins?" Oscar gazed intently at the man behind the flickering candle. "But I'm sure I've met you. You seem *so* familiar."

"You 'ave met me, Mr. Wilde—at Willis's. I come over to London now and then, to see Augustus and our mother, just for a little 'oliday, you know. I 'elps out at Willis's when I can. I've 'ad the honour of serving you once or twice, sir, and I've 'eard all about you from Augustus. 'E's partial to you, Mr. Wilde."

"And I'm partial to him. He's a good man."

"And what 'e does for you gents in London, I do for my priests 'ere in Rome. Augustus gets to look after Mr. Oscar Wilde. I gets to look after 'is 'oliness Pope Leo XIII."

"Is that so?" Oscar laughed.

The man laughed, too. "But we'll all be one in paradise, Mr. Wilde. I'm counting on that."

"You are the sacristan here?" I asked.

"Yes," he replied, winking at me. (It was a genial wink, not furtive or conspiratorial.) "As my father was before me. And as 'is father was before that. It runs in the family." He held his candlestick up above his head and turned to indicate the vastness of the chapel all about us. "Welcome to my world," he said.

My eyes were gradually becoming accustomed to the gloom. I now saw that we were standing in a corner of the chapel, immediately adjacent to the High Altar. Michelangelo's triumphal *Second Coming on the Day of Judgement* was just discernible above us.

"Come through to the sacristy," said Cesare Verdi, still chuckling. "We'll get you some tea."

"And cucumber sandwiches?" asked Oscar.

"Not today, Mr. Wilde. We do an English tea 'ere—muffins, crumpets, anchovy toast, and all—but not on a Friday."

"I believe Monsignor Breakspear is expecting us."

"Not today, Mr. Wilde. 'E's not 'ere."

"But he said . . ."

Cesare Verdi cocked his head to one side and looked at Oscar with an amused air. "Monsignor Breakspear is a Jesuit, Mr. Wilde. And a Jesuit doesn't always *mean* what 'e *says*."

Oscar did not rise to this sally. "Where is Monsignor Breakspear, then?" he asked.

"With the 'oly Father. The Monsignor is 'earing the Pope's confession. It's 'is day for it."

"I thought the Holy Father was on his summer retreat," I ventured, somewhat confused.

"'E is, in the summerhouse at the far end of the Vatican gardens. The Pope does not leave the 'oly City—ever."

"He chooses to be a prisoner here," explained Axel Munthe. "It is part of the Vatican's ongoing struggle with the Italian state. It's a territorial dispute."

"Is 'oliness will win in the end," said Cesare Verdi. "'E 'as God on 'is side."

"I like your lively sense of humour, too, Signor Verdi," said Oscar.

"It's 'Cesare,' Mr. Wilde, and you'll like my tea, too, sir. Darjeeling from Fortnum and Mason. Served in cups lately bequeathed us by Cardinal Newman. Fortified with a little Italian brandy, should you be so inclined. We aim for the best of both worlds 'ere."

The curly-headed cockney turned and led us just a few steps towards another unmarked door, as narrow and obscure as the one we had entered by. He opened it and we stepped back into the afternoon sunlight.

"This is the sacristy," he said. "This is my domain."

We had entered the first of what appeared to be a series of simple stone-built chambers located immediately behind the High Altar of the Sistine Chapel. To our left was a wide window overlooking the rooftops of the Basilica of St. Peter's; to our right were two separate sets of stone steps leading up to the rooms beyond. The walls of this first chamber were lined with dark-red damask. On the wall immediately facing us was a simply framed depiction of the Last Supper, painted in startlingly bright colours in something like the early style of Edward Burne-Jones. Below the painting, ranged against the wall, stood an elegant gilt chaise longue covered in deep-red velvet.

"That is the Seat of Tears," said our host.

"The Seat of Tears?" repeated Oscar, looking down at it.

"The Sacred College of Cardinals meets in conclave to elect a new pope in the Sistine Chapel. That much you know. The Sistine Chapel was built by Sixtus IV for the purpose."

"That much we know, also," said Oscar.

"But you may not know this, Mr. Wilde. When the new pope's been chosen—the *moment* 'e's chosen—even as the ballot papers are being burnt and before 'is name is given to the world, 'e comes in 'ere, alone. 'E sits on that chaise, alone, and 'e weeps. Alone. 'E weeps for the world—and for 'isself. Some is so miserable, they say they weeps tears of blood. Look there, you can see the mark—the stigmata."

The man pointed to a small brown smudge on the deep-red velvet. It was no larger than a thumbprint.

"It's a responsibility," I said, "becoming pope."

"And that's why I gives 'im a nip of brandy and then 'e gets 'is change of clothes. Out of the cardinal red, into the pontifical white. Of course, we don't know for certain beforehand who's going to be elected so we 'as to prepare papal robes in assorted sizes. Popes tend to go fat, thin, fat, thin—that's the general rule, but you can't depend on it. Pio Nono and Pope Leo were both pretty scrawny."

"Were you here for Pope Leo's election?"

"I was, Mr. Wilde. My father was sacristan, but I was 'ere. And, God willing, I'll be on 'and to see the next one in, too. Pope Leo is an old man, but it'll be a few years yet. Monsignor Breakspear is in with a chance—not much of a chance, not as much of a chance as 'e thinks, God bless 'im, but a chance all the same. 'E'll be a cardinal soon, that we can be sure of."

"How is Father Bechetti?" asked Axel Munthe. The Swedish doctor was standing behind us, looking over our shoulders, studying the painting of the Last Supper.

"Much as usual, Doctor. Brother Matteo's with 'im. 'E's in 'is cell. They're expecting you."

"I'll go and see him now," said Munthe. "I know the way."

With precise steps, the doctor, still clutching his black bag, slipped quietly out of the chamber up the right-hand set of stairs.

"Is this one of Father Bechetti's paintings?" asked Oscar, indicating the Last Supper.

"It is," said Cesare Verdi. "We've got 'is paintings everywhere. Look." He turned and pointed to another large canvas on the wall behind us. It was a double portrait of an old man and a young girl. "Pio Nono and the Blessed Virgin Mary. What do you make of that?"

"It is only an auctioneer who can equally and impartially admire all schools of art," said Oscar.

"I'd 'ave thought the bright colours would've been to your liking, Mr. Wilde—the *vibrancy*, if you knows what I mean."

"I know what you mean, Cesare," replied Oscar, as he considered the picture.

"Your English is remarkable, sir," I added, looking at our curly-headed host. The man's black eyes and oily hair suggested a Venetian fisherman painted by Bellini, but his way of speaking was pure billingsgate.

He laughed. "Remarkable—for an Italian."

"Are you Italian?" asked Oscar.

"*Completamente,*" replied the sacristan. His Italian accent was as impeccable as his cockney. "But I was born by London Bridge, within the sound of Bow Bells. And I lived in London until I was eleven. My mother's a cockney—and a cook."

"And the best of both, I'm sure," said Oscar, ingratiatingly.

"She met my father just nine months before I was born."

"Your father was Italian?"

"*Assolutamente, del tutto*—'e was Roman, to the core."

"And why was he in England?"

"'E was sent there with Cardinal Wiseman, in 1850, when the Roman 'ierarchy was reestablished and the cardinal was appointed first Archbishop of Westminster. My dad was part of the retinue—deputy sacristan in charge of vestments and the silver and gold plate. 'E'd never been abroad. 'E was in London only for a week or two, but it was long enough. 'E was young and 'ot-blooded."

"And Italian."

"Yes, Mr. Wilde. By all accounts my conception was merry, if not immaculate, and my old dad, if not exactly a gentleman, did have the decency to give my mother 'is name and address—and when 'e 'eard about 'er babies 'e sent 'er a few lire when 'e could. And when I was eleven, and '*is* dad died, and '*e* became sacristan 'ere, 'e came to London to fetch me to join 'im."

"And did your mother not object?" enquired Oscar.

"She 'ad Augustus. Augustus was always 'er favourite.

And because we're twins and we look alike, she says it doesn't matter so much. When she sees Augustus, she sees me, too. That's what she says."

"She is a philosopher," said Oscar.

"Does she still live by London Bridge?" I asked.

"No, she's moved up west. She 'elps out in the kitchens at Willis's most nights—not for the money, but because she likes it. She's 'appiest in a kitchen. She lives in Bloomsbury now, so she can walk 'ome. She's got a nice 'ouse, two up, two down. I've done my best to look after 'er. It's what Italian sons are supposed to do, you know—look after their mothers."

He clapped his hands noiselessly and rubbed them together with filial satisfaction. As he did so, I noticed for the first time that he was wearing the rose-gold ring.

"Tea, gentlemen?" he said suddenly, as if rousing himself from a reverie. He smiled, showing small, very white teeth, and widened his shiny olive-black eyes. "With a nip of brandy?"

He went to the left-hand stairway and we followed him up the few steps, under a stone arch, to the adjacent chamber. It was a larger room than the first, windowless, with a flagstone floor and dark wood panelling on the walls. There were gas lamps on each wall and between each pair of brass gasoliers hung one of Father Bechetti's colourful paintings. The most striking of these was a life-sized portrait of a young girl. She was seated on a rock, dressed all in white, holding a prayer book and a rosary in her lap. Her golden hair fell in tresses to her shoulders. Her skin was as pale as snow (whiter than her dress), though her lips were red and her cheeks were tinged with pink. Her eyebrows were dark and strong, her eyes cast down. She was not smiling, nor was she sad. She was simply seated, lost in thought, upon the rock. Around her head there was the shadow of a halo.

In the centre of the room was a large, round dining table, made of polished oak, with six chairs arranged around it.

"This is our little refectory," said Cesare Verdi. "This is where we take tea. This is where we dine. We dine well. Monsignor Felici makes sure of that."

"You say 'we'?" asked Oscar.

"Quite right, Mr. Wilde. I don't dine with my priests. I serve them first and I dine afterwards—but at the same table. It's my table, my sacristy."

"And they're 'your' priests."

"That's how I thinks of them. There are just five of them living 'ere—in the cells upstairs. They're papal chaplains and I looks after them. They prays for me and I skivvies for them."

"I've no doubt you do them proud—in the Willis's tradition."

"They don't do so badly. Brother Matteo is a Capuchin, of course, so he eats pretty frugally: bread and water, vegetables and fruit, no meat, no cheese. And poor old Father Bechetti lost his appetite when he lost his teeth. So it's really the three Monsignors who do the feasting. Take a seat, gentlemen."

We did as we were told, while Cesare Verdi went over to a sideboard on the far side of the room and busied himself, preparing a tray of cups and saucers and lighting a gas burner under a large black kettle that began to wheeze and whistle almost at once.

"Monsignor Felici and Monsignor Breakspear we've met," said Oscar.

"You'll like Monsignor Tuminello," said the sacristan, spooning leaves from a tea caddy into a handsome Royal Crown Derby porcelain teapot. "'E's interesting. 'E's the papal exorcist."

"So he, too, sees the devil in your eye, Cesare," said Oscar.

"'E sees the devil *everywhere*," said the sacristan, laughing and bringing the boiling water to the teapot.

"What's this?" I asked, indicating the large circular pewter dish that stood in the centre of the dining table. It was piled high with what at first glance I had taken to be an arrangement of crystallised fruit, but I now realised, on closer inspection, was an assortment of precious stones wrapped in what appeared to be a fur stole. "Is it a still life arranged for Father Bechetti?"

"No, 'e 'asn't painted a picture in ten years. 'Is eyes 'ave gone, along with 'is teeth. Those are jewels from papal crowns."

"And this," said Oscar, leaning across the table and lifting up a dark-green stone the size of a plover's egg, "is the emerald from Pope Julius II's fabled tiara?"

"It is indeed," replied the sacristan. "She's a beauty, ain't she? I'm giving 'er a little polish. Pope Leo 'as a mind to wear the crown at 'is next pontifical Mass. 'Is 'oliness is partial to 'is triple tiaras. 'E's one for 'is dignity—and why not?"

"Papa tantae est dignitatis et cesitudinis, ut non sit simplex

homo, sed quasi Deus, et Dei vicarius," said Oscar, replacing the emerald among the other gems.

"Hinc Papa triplici corona coronatur, tanquam rex coeli, et terre et infernoram,"† responded the sacristan. "You'll want to see the tiaras, then, Mr. Wilde. We've got 'undreds, 'undreds. All 'ere in the sacristy. I'll take you on the tour later. And your friend, of course." The sacristan turned his bright black eyes towards me and revealed again his small white teeth. "I never caught your name, sir."

"Conan Doyle," I said. "Arthur Conan Doyle. Doctor."

"Ah," he chuckled, holding the teapot by its handle and spout and swirling it vigorously. "The Sherlock 'olmes man. My priests just loves their Sherlock 'olmes."

"I'm gratified," I said.

"And this?" asked Oscar, still concentrating on the pewter dish in the centre of the table and pointing to the roll of fur that surrounded the pile of jewels. "Is it ermine? It looks more like a lady's wrap than a papal stole."

"It's a weasel," announced the sacristan, with a laugh.

He put down the teapot on the sideboard, stepped over to the table, and lifted the bundle of fur from the dish. As it unfurled, the hapless creature's face and paws swung round towards us.

"Oh, my God," cried Oscar, flinching away from the table. "It's hideous."

---

* "The Pope is of so great dignity and so exalted, that he is not mere man, but as it were God, and the vicar of God."

† "Hence the Pope is crowned with a triple crown, as king of heaven and of earth and of the lower regions."

Cesare Verdi held the animal by the scruff of the neck. Its body was long and thin: it must have been three feet in length, including its tail. The wretched animal's pointed face appeared to be grinning at us grotesquely; its eyes were wide open and staring, its teeth were bared and clenched.

"Why is it here?" I asked.

"For dinner," replied the sacristan. "We are going to eat it."

"In God's name, why?" hissed Oscar.

"Because my brother in Christ, Monsignor Breakspear, is determined to eat his way through the animal kingdom. He is doing it wilfully, to assert the primacy of man and to upset me."

This observation was made in Italian. I did not understand it at the time: Oscar translated it for me later. But I realised at once that the person making it was Brother Matteo.

The Capuchin friar stood beneath the stone arch at the top of the steps leading into the dining room. He was a man of about sixty, tall and spare, bearded but pale. He was dressed in the coffee-coloured habit of his order. His cowl was thrown back; his head was held high; a thin piece of rough cord hung about his neck; his hair was snow-white and sparse. I looked down at his feet. They were bare and callused. I looked at his hands. They were a workman's hands: he wore no rings. I did not understand what he was saying, but from the glint in his grey eyes and the gentleness of his manner I took it to be something amusing.

I got to my feet. Oscar did likewise. Axel Munthe, who stood just behind the Capuchin, introduced us. Handshakes

were exchanged and pleasantries murmured. I did not follow what was said, but I recognised the name Sherlock
Holmes more than once and nodded in acknowledgement
of it, doing my best to disguise my irritation.

The sacristan laid the dead weasel to rest on the sideboard and brought his tea tray to the dining table.

"*Tè pomeridiano?*" he said.

"*Sì, grazie,*" said the Friar, inviting us to take our seats
once more and joining us at the table. "Tea from Darjeeling
prepared in the English way, with boiling water brought to
the pot, is one of my favourite drinks. And a full English
tea is undoubtedly my favourite repast. It's such a civilised
meal. Even a Capuchin is permitted a cucumber sandwich.
Monsignor Breakspear is a barbarian—a savage. He does
not believe he has eaten unless he has tasted blood, and
recently he has come up with this ludicrous notion that it is
his Christian duty to eat of the flesh of every one of God's
creatures, from the antelope to the zebra."

"Is he making his progress through the animal kingdom
alphabetically?" asked Oscar, in Italian.

"There is no order to his thinking, merely self-indulgence.
This isn't science. This is greed—and perversity. There are
some wild boys who live in the woods here, by the pyramid.
They scavenge and hunt for Monsignor Breakspear, and
for every new creature they bring to the pot he gives them
money. It's absurd. It's obscene."

Oscar translated the essence of what the Friar was saying
into English and I shook my head in amazement. "Can this
be true?" I asked.

"*Si, è vero,*" said the sacristan. "'Oney buzzard and ibis, frog, bat, vole, mole—flesh and fowl, all creatures great and small." He opened a drawer in the sideboard and from it produced a small silver hammer, about ten inches in length, holding it up for us to see. "We uses this to crack open the crustaceans. We had spider crab last week. Whatever the lads turn up with, if we've not tried it before, we give it a go. That's the Monsignor's rule. If you eat wild boar, why not wild wolf? Some of what we've 'ad 'as proved surprisingly tasty. Porcupine meat is very tender." He returned the hammer to the drawer.

The Friar laughed. "And Breakspear will soon be a cardinal. We all know that. God moves in a mysterious way."

As the sacristan poured us our cups of tea, another priestly figure appeared on the threshold. He stood silently in the archway, studying the group seated at the table. I was the first to see him. As his eye caught mine, I sensed a flicker of recognition—or uncertainty. He appeared puzzled by our presence, perturbed, even. From his sash and his biretta, it was evident that this was the third Monsignor—a man similar in age and build to the Capuchin, but beardless, hairless, sallow-skinned, and sorrowful in demeanour. His eyes were sunken and heavily hooded. His forehead and cheeks were deeply lined. He had a smoker's complexion and a drinker's nose. Once we registered his presence, Axel Munthe, Oscar, and I rose quickly to our feet and bowed towards the priest.

"Monsignor Tuminello," said Munthe pleasantly, "may I present two distinguished newcomers to Rome: Mr. Oscar

Wilde, the poet and playwright, and Dr. Arthur Conan Doyle, the celebrated creator of Sherlock Holmes."

As the Monsignor extended his hand to shake mine, I noticed the rose-gold ring on his finger. As he released my hand from his cold, tight grasp, his eyes flickered upwards, violently, his head jerked backwards, and, without uttering a sound, he fell in a heap to the floor.

Something in the Air

The air in Rome is notoriously foul. These are old men. They do not lead healthy lives. I do not believe that we can regard Monsignor Tuminello's collapse as in any way suspicious. He fainted, he recovered. There's an end on it."

This was Axel Munthe's considered verdict, delivered for the third time over the third bottle of champagne at the end of that night's dinner at the Hôtel de Russie. Oscar had insisted on ordering our food—"it will be all simplicity": wild asparagus, wild boar cooked with raisins and pine seeds, *zabaione* with fresh raspberries—and on selecting our wines—"wholly unpretentious": Italian Barolo and French champagne—and on paying for everything—"with a little help from my dear friend, Lady Windermere."

"Is she your mistress or your patroness?" asked Axel Munthe.

"She was one and is now the other," said Oscar, darkly.

"Ah," murmured Munthe, evidently impressed. "Customarily, it is the other way around."

I intervened. "Lady Windermere is the principal character in a play of Oscar's," I explained. "*Lady Windermere's Fan.* It's a comedy. It's delightful. And a huge success. It's been running in London since February. The critics were not sure about it, but the public is."

"It is the will of God that we must have critics and we will bear the burden," said Oscar, skewering a raspberry with his fork and dipping the fruit into his champagne. "Lady Windermere earns my keep night after night and I am grateful to her."

"Congratulations," said Munthe, raising his glass to Oscar. "Are you resting on your laurels now or planning something new?"

"Both."

Munthe laughed. "Another comedy?"

"No," said Oscar, swallowing the raspberry and leaning forward earnestly. "A murder mystery. It's a collaborative venture. I'm writing it with my friend Conan Doyle here. We're calling it *Sherlock Holmes and the Case of the Papal Chaplains*. It will run for years."

"You are ridiculous, Oscar," I said.

Oscar turned his head towards Axel Munthe and widened his now glistening eyes. "What do you think, Doctor?"

Munthe smiled and set down his glass. "I think you have a problem with your 'murder mystery,' my friend."

"And what is the problem, pray?"

"Very simple. You have a mystery of sorts, to be sure, but, so far as I can tell, no murder."

"We have a dead man's hand!" exclaimed Oscar, beating the table with his fork. "We have a dead man's finger!"

"Yes," said Munthe, now laughing, "and a locket of lamb's wool. But where's the murder?"

"We have death stalking in the wings!" cried Oscar.

"You have two elderly clergymen collapsing in the heat of a Roman summer. You don't have murder."

"It is only a matter of time. Arthur and I have been here for only three days and already we have been drawn into the circle of death."

I raised my hand in protest. "Steady on, old man."

Munthe shook his head and sipped his wine. He tilted his head to one side and peered at Oscar through his heavy spectacles. "And who is in this 'circle' of yours, Mr. Wilde?"

"The men who wear the ring," said Oscar, calmly, "the ring that has lured us to Rome."

"And who are they?" asked Munthe.

"To begin with, Monsignor Felici—your patient, Doctor. The man you thought might well have been a murderer on the night you first saw the rose-gold ring, on the night his mistress died. And Monsignor Breakspear, Arthur's old schoolfriend, the boy-beater, the would-be cardinal who is busy eating his way through the animal kingdom. He wears the ring. And Monsignor Tuminello, the third Monsignor, the sere-and-yellow papal exorcist. Another of your patients, Doctor—they're a sickly band up at the Sistine Chapel. He wears the ring, also."

Munthe shrugged. "Three Monsignors, three papal chaplains: they wear the same ring. Is it so surprising?"

"Cesare Verdi, the sacristan, a layman—he wears it, too," I said.

"But Joachim Bechetti, the aged artist, and Brother Matteo, the good Capuchin—they don't," said Oscar. He sat up at the table and spread his fingers out on the tablecloth in front of him. "Why not? They're papal chaplains, also.

They, too, live above the sacristy. Why are they not wearing the rose-gold ring?"

"Because they don't belong to your 'circle of death'?" asked Munthe.

"Or because one or other of them has sent his ring to Sherlock Holmes," I suggested, "as a coded summons."

"As a cry for help," said Oscar, closing his eyes momentarily. "Exactly, Arthur." He let out a deep sigh, opened his eyes again, and looked around the table, smiling. "A grappa in the lounge, gentlemen—and then bed, I think, don't you?"

I slept well that night. My bed at the Hôtel de Russie was blessed with silent springs, a firm mattress, and crisp white bed linen that was both cool and soothing. When I awoke, it was nine in the morning. In the distance I heard the clock of Sant'Atanasio dei Greci striking the hour. I rose, opened my window, and pushed back the shutters: a wave of warm sunshine flooded over me.

To my surprise, I found that Oscar was not in his room, nor in the dining room, so I breakfasted alone, contentedly, on coffee, a boiled egg, and black bread. (Why are continental cooks incapable of making toast?) As I drank and ate, I leafed through a ten-day-old copy of *The Times* and learnt of floods in Switzerland, fires in Newfoundland, and Mr. Gladstone's imminent return to office—at the age of eighty-two. *Plus ça change* . . . (Why do I read the newspapers? Oscar doesn't. He says the news is predictable and the leaders even more so. He is right.)

Breakfast done, I made my way to the front desk, thinking there might be a wire from home. There was none (unlike

Oscar, my darling wife is not one for the extravagance of telegrams when there is nothing urgent to report), but there was a note from Oscar telling me to join him in the café in the piazza by the Porta del Popolo. I collected my straw hat (I removed the blue bandanna) and, at ten o'clock, went out to find my friend.

As I stepped out of the hotel and turned to my right, I recognised, coming along the Via del Babuino towards me, the elegant figure of Mr. James Rennell Rodd, attaché at the British Embassy and Oscar's so-called enemy. Our eyes met. Mine held his and, to my surprise, Rennell Rodd did not look away. Indeed, as he approached he touched his hat to me and smiled quite pleasantly. As we passed on the pavement, he paused briefly and, raising the waxed tips of his moustache lightly with the backs of his fingertips, said, "*Buongiorno,* Dr. Doyle. This is the kind of day that makes me grateful for the posting."

"Good day, sir," I said.

"And how is that priest?" he enquired. "The old blind father from the Vatican? Is there any news?"

"He is recovered, I believe."

"I'm relieved to hear it. You can never be entirely sure when 'Dr. Death' is in attendance."

"You mean Dr. Munthe?"

"I do, sir," answered Rennell Rodd, stroking his moustache. "He has quite a reputation—he *boasts* of 'putting down' elderly patients as though they were stray dogs. No one's actually complained, so far as I know, but if they're dead, I suppose they wouldn't." He laughed at his own joke. "I have no idea as to the truth of the matter."

"Dr. Munthe seems to know his business," I murmured.

"And have you met the creature he lives with? Extraordinary."

"No, I've not yet had the pleasure."

Rennell Rodd growled gently, sniffed the air, and with his index finger lightly brushed his eyelashes upwards. "I think the Swedes are even more inscrutable than the Chinese, don't you?"

I said nothing (I could not think what to say) and the English diplomat nodded, touched his hat once more, and went briskly on his way.

A minute or two later, I found Oscar, as promised, outside the café on the far side of the piazza by the Porta del Popolo. He was alone, seated at a table in the shade, dressed in a lime-coloured linen suit, nursing a long glass of Tokay and seltzer, and reading a book.

As I pulled up a chair to join him, he held the volume out towards me. "This was written for us, Arthur. It's called *The Innocents Abroad*."

I smiled. "I like the title," I said.

"You'll like the book. It's a traveller's tale: Mark Twain at the height of his powers—wry and perceptive. It starts here in Rome, among dead Capuchin friars. I'm gripped." He beamed at me. "Has your morning been instructive?"

"I've just seen Mr. Rennell Rodd," I told him.

"I saw him, too, here in the piazza."

"Did he speak to you?"

"No, he cut me—deliberately. He walked right past me and looked the other way."

"Are you sure that he saw you, Oscar?"

"He saw me and I saw him. He was with the Rome Irregulars."

I looked at him, not comprehending.

"Our boys," he smirked.

"'Our boys'? You mean the street urchins?"

"Yes. Romulus and Remus: Munthe's 'notorious pair'— Breakspear's little scavengers."

"Rennell Rodd was in conversation with those two . . ." I let the sentence trail away.

Oscar laughed at my embarrassment. "Yes, Arthur. *Deep* in conversation, over there, by the obelisk, in the very centre of the square."

"But he's a gentleman, he's First Secretary at the British Embassy. What possible business could he have with those wretched boys?"

"Perhaps he was ordering up a haunch of badger for the ambassador's table or making an assignation of a more personal nature for himself."

I looked at my friend. "What are you suggesting?" I asked.

"When we were at Oxford together, Rennell Rodd and I, we were disciples of the great art critic Walter Pater. Pater was our teacher and our guide. We read his *Studies in the History of the Renaissance*. It was from Pater that we first learnt of the beauty of 'brilliant sins.' It was Pater who taught us that a person of cultivation must seek out every exquisite experience that he can—taste all the fruits of all the trees in all the gardens of the world. Rennell Rodd may simply have been enquiring of the boys what sweet delights are currently on offer in the wild orchards behind the pyramid."

"What you are suggesting is appalling, Oscar," I said with great seriousness, "and slanderous."

"They are good-looking lads," said Oscar, wickedly, "and I'm sure I saw Rennell Rodd twirling his moustaches."

"The boys are no more than fourteen or fifteen years of age," I protested.

"In ancient Greece—" Oscar began, smiling.

"We are in modern Rome, Oscar," I countered sternly. "I want to hear no more of this."

"Well," said my friend, lighting a cigarette and blowing out the match, "let us assume, then, that he was merely after a weasel or a stoat in the Breakspear tradition."

A waiter had appeared at our table. I ordered a glass of grenadine and soda.

"What do you make of Monsignor Breakspear?" I asked, after a moment's pause, grateful for the opportunity to change the subject. "I thought it odd that he invited us to tea so pressingly and then failed to appear himself."

Oscar drew on his cigarette. "Ill-mannered, I agree," he said. "But, worse than that," he added, "I sense that Monsignor Breakspear is not an original thinker, which is surprising, given he's a Jesuit."

"What do you mean?"

"I mean that Breakspear borrows other men's ideas. This notion of eating his way through the animal kingdom, for example . . ."

"Tasting all the fruits of all the trees . . ."

"It's not original. Far from it. Dr. Buckland, palaeontologist, Canon of Christ Church, Dean of Westminster, was doing it before Breakspear was born. Panther, crocodile, bluebottle, louse: Dr. Buckland ate the lot. He was truly omnivorous. Once he came across the preserved heart of Louis XIV of France in a reliquary, declared, 'I have eaten many strange things in my time, but never the heart of a king,' and, before anyone could stop him, swallowed the precious relic whole. Buckland's son, Frank, whom I knew, carried on the family tradition, hosting extraordinary feasts at Willis's—with sea-slugs, kangaroo, elephant trunk, and mole pie on the menu. The Bucklands were the genuine article. There is something about Breakspear that doesn't ring true."

"These eccentric banquets were held at Willis's Rooms in St. James's?"

"Yes, at Willis's—the same Willis's where the sacristan's mother helps out in the kitchens and his twin brother is the maître d'hôtel, Gus Green."

"Your particular friend."

"A good maître d'hôtel is a gentleman's truest friend. I know Gus Green. I trust him. But there's something about Cesare Verdi that I don't trust."

"He seemed a decent sort to me."

"Did you notice what he was wearing?"

"Not especially. He seemed well dressed."

"Exactly. He was wearing a silk shirt. With cufflinks."

"Is that suspect?"

"In a sacristan, it's certainly surprising."

Oscar stubbed out the remains of his cigarette in the ashtray on the café table and drained his glass. He breathed in deeply, expanding his chest and raising and turning his head to gaze about the piazza. "We shall learn more hereafter," he announced. "This very afternoon, in fact." He sat back and produced from his pocket a small envelope, which he handed to me. "Note the crossed keys embossed on the back of the envelope. It's a missive from Monsignor Felici, delivered to our hotel before breakfast. He apologises for yesterday's botched tea party and invites us to a proper one today. The Holy See's *circolo inglese* will be taking English tea at five o'clock this afternoon and requests the pleasure of our company." He looked me in the eye. "This is what we've come for, Arthur. The mystery is going to start to unravel now, I'm certain of it. And I think we will find it darker than you dare imagine."

"Why do you say that?"

"Because a severed finger and a severed hand have brought us here—and whoever sent them did so in desperation." He waved to the waiter, summoning our bill, pushed back his chair, and rose from the table.

"And between now and then," I said, "what other avenues should we be exploring?"

"None," he declared roundly. "We have secured our entrée to the Vatican. That's all we need."

"Then I'd best get on with ploughing through that portmanteau of correspondence," I said, with a sigh. "That's why I came to the continent, after all."

"Forget your correspondence, Arthur. The Godalming Gardening Society can wait." He put a hand on my shoulder. "It's a beautiful day, my friend. We should take the air." He looked at me conspiratorially. "Follow me, Arthur. I have a surprise in store for you."

12.

"*A* sandbag!"

*A*s we left the shade of the café and made our way into the heat of the open piazza, I felt apprehensive.

"We are not going anywhere near those wretched boys, I trust."

Oscar laughed. "Nowhere near. The 'wretched boys' have cut and run. Rennell Rodd seems to have frightened them away."

"I am glad to hear it. So where are we going? Are we taking a carriage?" My friend was walking us towards the *carrozza* stand in the northeastern corner of the piazza, by the church of Santa Maria del Popolo.

"Of a kind—but first we are climbing a hill."

We reached the church and went beyond it, past the *carrozza* stand, out of the piazza, up some stone steps and onto a narrow, sandy path that led through trees and bushes to a steep incline. It was most unlike Oscar to seek a hill to climb.

"Where *are* we going?" I asked again.

"In search of romance," he replied. "We are in Rome, after all. And I promised you adventure."

"You are making me anxious, Oscar."

"I want to make you happy," he answered, leading the way up the slope. "'They do not sin at all who sin for love.'"

"You are making me *very* anxious. Is that Keats or Shelley?"

"It's Wilde—*The Duchess of Padua*. Though I flatter myself that both Keats and Shelley would have been content with the line. Keats and Shelley both climbed this path in their day, you know." He paused and unbuttoned his jacket. "I am taking you to the Pincio Gardens, Arthur—the *collis hortulorum* of the emperors of Rome. This is where Nero fiddled of a summer evening and where Keats came to flirt with Napoleon's sister Pauline Borghese." His pace had slowed as we clambered upwards. "This is supposed to be the shortcut, recommended to me by the boot-boy at the hotel. I hope you'll think it worth the effort when we get there."

It was well worth the effort. When we reached the summit of the hill and emerged from the trees and undergrowth, we found ourselves in a veritable garden paradise: acres of green and pleasant parkland, with terraces and parterres, ornate bubbling fountains and overflowing flower beds, broad avenues and shaded pathways, stretching as far as the eye could see.

We were not alone: it was a Saturday and, by routes less rigorous and obscure than the one recommended by the hotel boot-boy, fashionable Rome had made its way to the Pincio to promenade along the *passeggiata*. Clearly, we could have come by carriage: gigs and ponies, dog carts and phaetons were trundling along the driveways. There were nurses with perambulators, children on tricycles, and a young priest trying to look nonchalant on a high-seated penny-farthing.

"This is charming, Oscar," I exclaimed.

"And it's blessedly cool after the heat of the piazza. This way," he said, pointing in the direction of a bandstand on which a picturesque assortment of musicians in comic-opera uniforms were playing tunes by Rossini and Berlioz. "We're aiming for the meadow."

"All human life is here," I said as we passed a pair of old soldiers hobbling along arm in arm (they had just two legs and two crutches between them), followed by a trio of young nuns (giggling and eating ice cream) and a lone African beggar with a ring through his nose and a parrot on his shoulder.

"Quite," said Oscar, lifting his head into the breeze. "There may even be a murderer in our midst."

"By all that's wonderful!" I exclaimed.

We had gone beyond the bandstand, reached the highest point on the hill, and come to what, for all the world, looked exactly like an English village green. It was a small rectangular field covered in lush grass, spotted with wildflowers and surrounded by a well-kept gravel path. In the centre of this field, tethered to the ground by sturdy ropes tied to iron pegs, was a wicker basket—no bigger than a sauna-bath in a gentlemen's club—surmounted by a gorgeous, multicoloured hot-air balloon fifteen feet high. It was like a picture from a child's storybook, but it was prettier than a picture, because standing by the basket, just a few feet from it, and looking lovelier than ever, was Irene Sadler. She was wearing a cornflower-blue and white striped dress, with navy ribbons at her waist and on her hat. She seemed not the least surprised to see me.

"Hello, Dr. Conan Doyle," she said, extending her hand, not to shake mine, it transpired, but to draw me closer. "You're just in time."

"By all that's wonderful!" I said again. "Why are you here?"

"It was Mr. Wilde's idea," she said, still holding on to me.

"It was the Reverend Sadler's idea," said Oscar. "I met him in the piazza this morning and he told me about the balloon trip. I gave him money and here we are."

"And here we go," said Miss Sadler, tugging at my arm. "We *must* go. I've kept everybody waiting for you."

"Is your brother joining us?" I asked.

"No, it's just us."

She turned and pulled me with her towards the balloon-basket. It was a small affair, seven feet square at most, with sides to it no more than four feet in height. On one of the sides there was a narrow gate for access. Ten to a dozen passengers were already crowded on board, standing expectantly, shoulder to shoulder, around the basket's perimeter, each with one hand, or both, holding on to one of the taut ropes that ran from the basket's sides to the air-filled balloon above. Standing just inside the basket's gate, holding it open and gesticulating towards us, was a small, fat man, black-haired and middle-aged. He turned out to be the captain of the vessel. He wore the costume of a Venetian gondolier—striped blue vest and crimson neckerchief— but his blackened hands and sweating face—swarthy and scarred, with a black patch over one eye—suggested a pirate from a pantomime.

"Robert Louis Stevenson *must* have come here on holiday," muttered Oscar as we approached.

"Scusi, comandante," said Miss Sadler, apologetically, as we climbed aboard.

The pirate captain pulled shut the wicker gate and bolted it—with a single wooden peg.

"Do you think he knows his business?" I whispered.

"In the kingdom of the blind . . . ," murmured Oscar, squeezing himself into a corner of the basket.

One of the unexpected features of my friend Oscar Wilde was that, overweight, indolent aesthete that he was, he did not lack physical courage. He was a big man who knew how to stand his ground and use his fists. He did not court danger nor, as a rule, physical adventure of any kind, but when he found himself facing the one or having to endure the other, he took the challenge in his stride and displayed no lack of spunk or nerve.

With the gate shut, our captain moved to the centre of his craft, where, on the floor, a brazier the size of a dustbin was burning fiercely. He bent over what was, in essence, the engine of his ship—the brazier and its concomitant parts—and, with ungloved hands, twisted valves and levered open airways, so that the powerful flow of hot air, already rising upwards from the fire, turned into a roaring torrent. He then made his way to each of the four corners of the basket and, in near-incomprehensible Italian, instructed two of the male passengers standing there to lift from the floor a sack of ballast and hold it between them in their arms. In our corner of the craft, Oscar and I were chosen as his lieutenants.

"What's this we've got to hoist aloft?" shouted Oscar, above the roar.

"A sandbag," I called back.

Between us we lifted it into our arms. "A *sandbag!*" cried Oscar, in mock indignation, as if utterly outraged at the effrontery of the captain's request. "I booked for us to travel first class."

I laughed and, as I did so, the basket began to lurch from side to side and Miss Sadler, standing just behind me, grabbed hold of me anxiously. On the grass around the basket men were loosening the ropes that held the vessel tethered to the ground. As the basket lurched, we began to lift upwards into the air. We swung from side to side, buffeted by the breeze, and as we swung the balloon lifted us higher at alarming speed.

Almost immediately, we sensed that something was amiss. The basket was perilously lopsided. Our corner was tipping sharply downwards. Other passengers began to shout at us: one of the women began to scream. The captain pushed his way from the centre of the craft towards us, pulled Miss Sadler away from me abruptly, and, hissing *"Accidenti!"* heaved the sandbag we were still clutching out of our grasp and over the basket's edge.

The flying basket righted itself at once. "Good God," I cried, "we might have caused the accident."

Irene Sadler put her windswept face up towards mine and shouted, through her laughter, *"Accidenti!"* is a curse—the worst. It means, 'May you die in a fit without benefit of clergy!'"

Oscar began laughing, too. "This flying game is not as easy as it seems. No wonder Icarus came to grief."

Our balloon swept us higher and higher. Gradually, as we rose in the sky, our ears became accustomed to the burning engine's roar, and our eyes turned to marvel at the view: the clouds above us and the earth below.

"No wonder the gods like it up here," said Oscar, "the people down there look so small." He was in high spirits. He called out something in Italian to the captain, and the captain, laughing derisively, shouted back.

"What is it?" I asked.

"I enquired whether we might float over the Vatican and catch sight of the Pope in his garden. Apparently not. We go up, we go down—the Vatican is out of bounds. *Proibito.*"

The pirate captain came over to us, talking as he came. In his right hand he carried a small brass telescope. With a flourish, he lifted it to his blind eye and, turning west towards the Vatican, directed Oscar's attention to St. Peter's Square. He handed Oscar the spyglass, jabbering good-humouredly as he did so.

"What is he showing you?" I asked.

"The line of *carabinieri* standing at the boundary of the Holy See. He says they are useless and corrupt, but they are the law nonetheless and they must be obeyed."

The captain went on jabbering and gesticulating, pointing both his finger and his telescope in the direction of St. Peter's.

"Now he is showing me the line of Swiss Guard and

telling me that the Pope's men are no better. There is corruption everywhere, he says, except here in his balloon, where we are closer to heaven, and where he and the Almighty—and no one besides—are in command of all our destinies."

Oscar bowed to the captain and found a silver coin in his pocket to give the man. The fellow took the money and indicated that Oscar should keep the telescope while he went back about his business. My friend lifted the glass to his eye once more and continued to gaze towards the Vatican.

"Our pirate king has solved the mystery for us, hasn't he, Arthur?" he said. "At least, in part."

I said nothing. I was conscious of Irene Sadler at my side, her arm pressed close to mine. Oscar appeared to read my mind.

"How rude of me, Miss Sadler," he declared suddenly. "I got carried away. Here, take the captain's spyglass and survey the scene. You must." He passed the telescope to the young lady and, as she lifted it to her eye, set about directing her attention. "Look below us, can you see your church? And along the street from it, Sant'Atanasio dei Greci? And there, further south, the Capuchin church that Mark Twain writes about. Do you know it?"

"I know Mark Twain's book," she said, "*The Innocents Abroad.* It is a favourite of mine. And I know the church you mean—where the Capuchin friars are all buried." She peered through the telescope. "But I cannot see it. There are so many churches down there. I can see the Pyramid of Cestius, however. And the Pantheon. And the Colosseum. And the slums."

"Nothing changes," said Oscar. "Two thousand years on and it is still the problem of slavery. We try to solve it by amusing the slaves."

Irene Sadler held the glass steadily to her eye and looked all about her. Her gaze moved from left to right, slowly, methodically. I followed her gaze, holding her elbow to keep her steady in the breeze. Oscar held on to the basket's edge with both hands and peered below.

"There it is, spread out for all to see: the glory of Rome—and the squalor."

She put the telescope into my hands and smiled at Oscar. "From here I think it all looks beautiful."

Oscar returned her smile. "They say distance lends enchantment."

"I am with Miss Sadler," I declared fervently. "It all looks quite wonderful to me."

"Yes," she said. "It's heaven."

"But even in heaven the novelty wears off." Oscar looked up at the sky and sighed. "When you have seen one cloud, you really have seen most of them. Wordsworth was always overrated."

We laughed and, with some difficulty, I persuaded my friend not to light a cigarette.

The balloon trip did not last long. Less than forty minutes after we had been swept in our basket up into the sky, we were back on terra firma.

"You can have a cigarette now," I said to Oscar as we disembarked and stood on the grass, somewhat unsteadily, adjusting once more to life on earth.

"I shall," he answered. "I shall have several. And they will both soothe and exhaust me, as they always do. And then I'll rest before we go up to St. Peter's for our English tea." He turned to our companion and proffered her his cigarette case. "Would you like a cigarette, Miss Sadler?"

"No, thank you, Mr. Wilde. I'd like an ice cream."

"I am relieved to hear it. Half the pretty women in London smoke cigarettes nowadays, but I very much prefer the other half."

"May I buy you an ice cream, Miss Sadler?" I asked.

"I should like that very much," she replied.

Oscar drew heavily on his cigarette and turned his head to look at us askance. "You two go and find your ice creams. I'll go and find my bed. I'll take a dogcart to the hotel." He pressed his hand upon my shoulder. "Come and find me at four, Arthur, no later. Munthe is joining us for the Vatican tea party." He bowed ceremoniously. "Miss Sadler, thank you for allowing us to join you on your journey to the heavens. Look after Arthur now—and answer any of his questions, won't you? I know he has a great deal he wants to ask you."

"You are impertinent, Oscar," I protested.

"But you know you have questions for Miss Sadler," he persisted. "Questions are never indiscreet. Answers sometimes are."

"I shall be happy to tell Dr. Conan Doyle anything he wishes to know," said Miss Sadler, lightly. "We are firm friends. We shall have no secrets. I shall tell him everything."

"Not quite everything, I'm sure. 'Heard melodies are sweet, but those unheard are sweeter.'"

Oscar laughed and, gaily waving his copy of *The Innocents Abroad* above his head as he departed, made his way towards the line of gigs and pony-traps that stood on the gravel path at the edge of the field.

When he had gone, and when, from a vendor by the bandstand, I had bought us each a strawberry ice (served in a biscuit cone—the latest fashion), Irene Sadler and I found a quiet and shady path to walk along. She told me it was not one that she had explored before.

"I know the gardens here quite well," she said. "I come here often."

"With your brother?"

"No, he is far too busy. And he prefers reading to walking. I come on my own."

"You don't have friends?" I glanced at her. "You don't have a special friend?"

"I am quite lonely, Dr. Conan Doyle."

"Will you tell me your story?" I asked, offering her my arm.

"It is not a happy one," she said, pressing her hand lightly on mine, "but it is easily told."

As we walked together, beneath fine oaks and umbrella pines, she told her tale without self-pity and with touching simplicity. Oscar had been correct in his surmise. Irene Sadler and her brother were orphans. Their parents, both dead before Irene was yet three, had been Anglican missionaries, servants of the Church Missionary Society stationed in Peshawar in northern India. Irene's father was an Anglican clergyman, passionate in his faith; her mother, the daughter of a missionary herself, had run the Peshawar mission school. It was in a fire at the schoolhouse—a bungalow built of wood—that both parents had died. Their bedroom was directly behind the schoolroom. It was a hot summer's night and, a little before daybreak, in a matter of minutes, the whole building had burnt to the ground. No one knew what had caused the fire. Was it the deadly work of rebellious Pashtun tribesmen come down from the hills—or just an accident? Irene and Martin, miraculously, escaped the blaze. On the hottest nights their parents would put them to sleep in a shared cot on the mission school's back veranda, just outside their bedroom door. The children were rescued by brave natives as their parents were engulfed in flames.

"What were your parents like?" I asked. "Do you remember them?"

"Not at all. And I have no record of them—no letters, no photographs, no mementoes of any kind. Everything was destroyed in the fire. We lost our past that night in Peshawar."

"And your future?"

"It was in the hands of the elders of the Church Missionary Society. We were babies, without parents, without *grand*parents (they were already dead), without uncles or aunts. I think our only friends were our parents' kitchen wallah and our ayah. They lived in a hut in the school's backyard—it was they who saved us from the fire. We had no family, no home, nowhere to go."

"But you were not brought up in India."

Irene Sadler paused in her tracks. She had finished her

ice cream. We had come to a turning along the pathway and were standing close together beneath a spreading ilex tree.

"Why do you say that?" she asked. "How do you know?"

"There is no singsong lilt to your voice," I replied, smiling down at her. "Anyone brought up from a baby in India—however English their origin—always has that Indian lilt. You can't escape it."

She returned my smile. "You *are* a detective, Dr. Conan Doyle. I must remember that." We resumed our walk and she pressed her hand over mine once more. "And you are correct," she said. "There was no future for us in Peshawar. We were sent to Canada to be put up for adoption."

"Why Canada?"

"Because one of the other missionaries was a Canadian and she was returning to Canada that summer in any event. Her passage was already booked. With the blessing of the British agent in Peshawar, and with a small grant from the Missionary Society, she took us with her."

"She did not adopt you herself?"

"No, she was an older lady. She took us with her as her Christian duty, but that was all. In the event, no one adopted us. We were taken in by one family after another, but never for very long. We were fostered by many, but adopted by none." She glanced up at me. "I fear we were not very lovable."

"That can't be true."

"I fear it is. And I can understand it. We were not rewarding children. We were too wrapped up in one another to give anything back to those who were caring for us. I see that now. Wherever we went, we were fed, we were clothed, we were sent to school, but we were not loved, we were not wanted. And when we were sent to live with families where there were other children—*proper* children, true sons and daughters of the house—we knew that, secretly, we were despised. We were the outsiders, the low-caste little Indian orphans. And when eventually, when Martin was fifteen, we ran away, we knew that, truly, we were not wanted because no one came to look for us. No one at all."

"How did you live?"

"Through God's mercy," she said, breaking away from me for a moment and running forward along the path to warm herself in a shaft of sunlight that had found its way through a gap in the trees. She stopped and turned her face to the sun and stretched out her arms at her side. "We were saved by the Lord!"

I laughed at her sudden burst of exuberance.

"I'm being serious," she insisted. "In our hour of need, the merciful Lord stretched out His hand and came to our rescue."

"What happened?"

"We met a priest in Etobicoke—in the street, near the market. It was only a few days after we had run away. We told him we were sleeping in ditches and living off scraps stolen from the market stalls. It was the truth. He offered us a cup of tea and a room for the night at the Anglican seminary in Toronto. We stayed there for seven years. I worked in the kitchens and the laundry, and Martin found his vocation and trained for the priesthood."

"Good God!" I exclaimed.

"Precisely so," said Irene Sadler, taking my arm again and pulling me back along the pathway.

"And since then you have lived happily ever after?"

"God gave us shelter and purpose—but we are still outsiders wherever we go. We did not belong in India. We did not belong in Canada. When Martin had finished his training, we thought that we would come 'home' to England, but we found that we were just as much outsiders there, too—perhaps more so. In England, everyone wants to know who you are and where you come from. 'Who is your family? Where do you live? What are your roots? Do tell.' Martin and I cannot even tell you on which days we were born."

"You don't know how old you are?" I said, amazed.

"Quite useful for a female of the species, don't you think?" She laughed. "But not helpful for a man. Brilliant though my brother is, he has found it very difficult to find work as an Anglican clergyman. He is a gentleman, as you can tell, but he cannot prove it. English parishes are not comfortable having a priest without a pedigree. He was very blessed when he secured the chaplaincy here. In Rome, he is an outsider among outsiders. Everyone here has run away from home."

"It's a good position," I said.

"That's why he took it. They were looking for a bachelor priest who could live on next to nothing. The chaplaincy here carries no salary. Martin's much-loved predecessor was a man of independent means."

"You have no income?" I asked, incredulous.

"What funds the church possesses are all committed. Building All Saints' has proved a costly enterprise. That's what the other evening was all about. The fund-raising never stops. But we must not complain, though Martin does. We have our board and lodging and I receive a modest wage as my brother's housekeeper. We should be content, we should be grateful, though we are poor."

"You have no money," I said, quietly.

"None to speak of," she replied.

"And yet . . ." I hesitated before I spoke. "And yet, when we met you on the train, when Oscar and I first introduced ourselves, were you not returning from holiday? Were you not travelling first-class?"

Irene Sadler stopped in her tracks once more. "Oh, Dr. Conan Doyle, you are a wonderful detective, that is clear, but you are no psychologist. Martin must have his holidays. Martin must have the best linen and tailor-made new suits. Martin must travel first-class. My dear brother has a foolish pride—and it has cost us dear." She put her arms about my shoulders and held me tight, as a child might cling to her father in a storm. "I am so lonely and we are as poor as church mice."

I held her close and told her that I would give her twenty pounds. She reached up and kissed me tenderly on the cheek and, as she did so, I breathed in the scent of lily of the valley on her neck.

13.

English Tea

*W*e were late for our tea with the *circolo inglese* at the Vatican.

I was late returning to the Hôtel de Russie from the Pincio Gardens. Oscar was late in rousing himself from his siesta. Axel Munthe was late because the patient he had been attending that afternoon had taken "so long to die."

"Did you despatch the poor unfortunate?" I asked, unamused, as I sat at the doctor's side in the pony-and-trap that jostled us at breakneck speed from the Piazza del Popolo to St. Peter's Square. Munthe was attempting to rearrange the contents of his medical bag as we were bumped and buffeted over the cobbles. A bottle of cocaine lotion fell from his hand onto my lap. I returned it to him. He thanked me, sniffed, and held the bottle up close to his thick spectacles.

"Yes," he muttered to himself, "there's sufficient should Father Bechetti be in pain." He returned the bottle to his bag and snapped the fastener shut, then turned his head towards me. "But, no," he said, smiling, "I did not 'despatch the poor unfortunate.' God did what He does so well, though He took his time about it. Had He kept my

suffering patient waiting longer, I might indeed have assisted in the process—out of the kindness of my heart. Either way, the outcome was inevitable."

"I could never be a doctor," said Oscar, drowsily. He was
seated on the banquette facing us, his eyes closed, his head
resting against our driver's back. "I can sympathise with
everything, except physical suffering. It is too ugly, too horrible, too distressing. There is something terribly morbid in
the modern sympathy with pain. One should sympathise
with the colour, the beauty, the *joy* of life."

He opened his eyes. We were passing the tiny twelfth-
century church of Santi Michele e Magno. A little girl in a
white pinafore was skipping up and down the church steps.
Oscar gestured towards her with a languid hand.

"I rest my case," he murmured, looking at us reprovingly
and then closing his eyes once more. "The less said about
life's sores, the better."

"We are not discussing medical details, Oscar," I said,
somewhat tetchily. "We are discussing medical ethics. A
doctor's duty is to save life, not extinguish it—whatever the
circumstances. Is what Munthe does *right*? Is it legal?"

Axel Munthe chuckled. "Don't leap onto your high
horse, Doctor." He leant his shoulder towards mine and
tapped his forefinger on my trouser knee. "Tell me something, Dr. Conan Doyle. Do you still have that severed
hand in your pocket? Is that sawn-off finger still hidden
about your person?"

"Yes," I said, hesitating, sensing the trap.

"Is *that* legal? No. Is *that* right? Who is to say?"

I wanted to protest, but words failed me. Oscar opened his eyes and stirred himself.

"Arthur's instinct was to take the horrid evidence sent to him directly to the police. I know my friend. He is one of Queen Victoria's most loyal and law-abiding subjects, and had all this occurred in South Norwood that is precisely what he would have done. But when in Bad Homburg it is not so simple. And when in Rome—"

Munthe completed his sentence for him: "And when in Rome, take the law into your own hands. It is the only way."

Our carriage had turned into St. Peter's Square and was now crossing the piazza, slowing down as it approached the main gate beyond the statue of St. Paul. Oscar sat forward, his strength returning, his spirits lifting.

"As I understand it from my new friend, the pirate captain of the Pincio Gardens' hot-air balloon, the police in these parts are, at best, incompetent; at worst, corrupt. Am I right, Doctor?"

"You are," said Munthe. "Everyone would acknowledge that, even, I suspect, the chief of police."

"And the reason we are investigating this mystery was reinforced this morning when I was up there in that basket in the clouds. If we don't, no one else will. The Pope's gendarmerie and the Roman *carabinieri* are incompetent, corrupt, and at daggers drawn."

Our carriage had now stopped. Oscar held up his hands to prevent us from moving while he finished his rhetorical rodomontade. As he spoke, he looked about him and surveyed the scene.

"This, gentlemen, is the no-man's-land between the city of Rome and the Holy See. Here are we, arriving at the Vatican—for English tea, with cucumber sandwiches, God save the mark!—and there are they, rival police forces, lined up on either side of an unmarked marble moat, hostile armies, encamped, face-to-face, just fifty yards apart."

He held one arm out towards the Swiss Guard standing sentinel at the Vatican gate and the other towards the band of *carabinieri* grouped around a pair of sentry boxes a few feet from where our trap had stopped. In truth, these men (most of whom were slouching, chatting, and smoking at their posts) did not seem like greyhounds in the slips straining upon the start, but the two forces were clearly set in opposition to one another—and neither looked as if it would inspire the least confidence in even the most naïve soul seeking assistance in a case of suspected murder.

"There you have them: Rome's rival representatives of law and order. They don't speak to one another and they cannot be trusted." Oscar rose to his feet and gazed down at us. "If one of the reverend gentlemen with whom we are taking tea this afternoon suspects foul play within the Vatican, or without, to whom is he to turn? Not to the police, either of church or state, that's for sure . . ."

"To God, then?" laughed Munthe.

"To the heavens, certainly," cried Oscar, handing money to the driver before clambering cumbersomely down from the trap. "In his hour of need our man decides his only hope is to summon a deus ex machina: a saviour who will float down from the skies to unravel the mystery and avenge the crime." Oscar held out a hand to assist me as

I climbed from the carriage after him. "There is no local help to be had—our man cannot trust the police, he cannot trust his friends—so, boldly, having nothing to lose and all to gain, he makes an imaginative leap, throws caution to the wind, and summons a stranger to his aid . . . but no ordinary stranger! He sends coded messages to the world's 'foremost consulting detective'! It is a wild gamble, improbable, absurd, and fraught with danger and uncertainty, but it pays off. The Lord be praised! Miracles *do* happen! For here we are, in loco Sherlock Holmes: Dr. Arthur Conan Doyle and party. *Avanti!*"

Munthe, much amused by Oscar's histrionics, jumped down from the trap without assistance and, holding his black bag prominently before him as his badge of office, led us, almost jauntily, past the sentry boxes to the Vatican gate.

"Well," he said, looking up at Oscar, "you have certainly convinced yourself that your journey was necessary and that you have arrived at the correct destination."

"I have," replied Oscar, his head held high.

"Well, I am less certain," I muttered.

"The rose-gold ring has led us here, Arthur—you must see that."

"And all your 'reverend gentlemen' will be gathered around the tea table to welcome you," said Munthe. "When you meet them, will you tell them why you have come to call?"

"Not for a moment. We must steal up on them unawares."

"This is life, Mr. Wilde. This isn't one of your penny-dreadful melodramas. Wouldn't it be simpler to be straightforward? As we say in Sweden: 'The best way out is through the door.'"

"This is a murder mystery, Doctor. I feel it in my bones. The straightforward has no place here. As we say in Ireland, *'Ní mar a shíltear a bhítear'*—'Nothing in life is as it seems.'"

"Will you at least ask which of them it was who summoned 'Sherlock Holmes' to the Vatican in this extraordinary way?"

"Oh, no," cried Oscar. "That might be fatal. Whoever it was who sent that lock of hair, and that severed hand, and that finger with the tell-tale ring to 'Sherlock Holmes' fears for his life. I am convinced of that. My instinct tells me there has been one murder at least—and there may be more. Whoever it was who sought the help of 'the most perfect reasoning and observing machine that the world has seen'—the phrase is Arthur's—believes he needs to hide behind a mask, or why not simply write Holmes a letter, giving his name and address in the usual way? Oh, no. This has been a secret summons from a desperate soul. For the time being, I have no doubt that we should respect our client's desire for anonymity."

Pausing at the foot of the long flight of steps leading to the Sistine Chapel, Munthe looked up at Oscar and smiled. "You call him your 'client'?"

Oscar shrugged. "Well, he has brought us here all the way from Germany. We are at his service, even if we are not in his pay."

Munthe turned to me and patted me warmly on the shoulder. "Congratulations, Dr. Conan Doyle. Mr. Wilde has definitely caught the Baker Street disease." He looked back at Oscar. "And do you have any idea who he might be, this 'client' of yours?"

"Of course," said Oscar, quietly.

"Of course?" I repeated, dumbfounded.

"Of course I know who he is," said Oscar. "Don't you?"

We climbed the stone steps in silence. I could not decide whether Oscar was simply being playful—he was a great spinner of yarns—or whether, in fact, he had truly deduced who it was had summoned Holmes to Rome and why.

As Axel Munthe was about to lead us through the small side-door that led to the chapel, I stayed his hand. "Forgive me, Doctor. Before we proceed further, I must speak to my friend."

I saw at once that I did not need to say a word. I could tell from Oscar's amused and kindly eyes that he understood my anxiety.

"I will take the lead this afternoon, Arthur," he said, "fear not. You may be the creator of Sherlock Holmes, but the great detective is a figment of your imagination, not your other self. I know that."

"Thank you, Oscar," I said. "I am relieved. The truth is, old friend, you seem to be certain of what's afoot, but, frankly, I'm baffled by the whole business. I'm quite lost. I can't see the wood for the trees."

He smiled. "Perhaps you have been distracted by your walk through the woods beneath the trees? Miss Sadler is most beguiling. Today she has commanded your entire attention. I understand. I am not surprised. The fair sex is your department. You can leave the clergymen to me."

He was as good as his word. Once Axel Munthe had taken us through the doorway and across the dark corner of the Sistine Chapel (heavy with the smell of incense and burning candles) to the near-invisible door to the sacristy, and the sacristan, Cesare Verdi, had admitted us to his domain, Oscar was in his element—and at his most effortlessly charming.

His urbanity and exuberance were matched only by those of Monsignor Felici, who welcomed us with the sign of the cross followed by an open-armed embrace. As we arrived, the portly Monsignor was waiting for us, perched awkwardly on the edge of the papal Seat of Tears. The moment the sacristan opened the door to us, the elderly cleric struggled to his feet and came forward, beaming. As one by one he took us in his arms, he explained, in his heavily accented English, that, as Pontifical Master of Ceremonies, he had the honour of being our official host.

"We are late," declared Oscar, bowing low before the priest, *"mea culpa!"*

"You are here," rejoined the Monsignor, taking Oscar in his arms, *"Deo gratias!* And the scones are still warm—and we are so happy to have you with us. Welcome to the *circolo inglese.* Tea is about to be served. Step this way."

With some effort he moved his huge bulk towards the left-hand stairway that led from the first chamber of the sacristy to the oak-panelled refectory we had visited the day before. Munthe took the Monsignor's arm. As we followed them up the steps, Oscar paused and breathed in deeply. "We pass from the odour of incense to the fragrance of fresh baking."

"It's all to the glory of God," rumbled the Monsignor. "Cesare has been busy. I took the four o'clock Mass, while our sacristan prepared our English tea."

The gasoliers in the refectory were turned up high. There were lit candles, too, upon the table. Apart from the lighting, the scene appeared to be drawn completely from *Alice's Adventures in Wonderland*. The long dining table was covered with a white linen cloth, set with cups and saucers and plates and cutlery for eight, and littered with cake-stands and salvers, dishes and trenchers, all piled high with sugary delights. This was the Mad Hatter's tea party. Even the life-sized portrait, on the wall above the sideboard, of the little girl in the white dress with the halo, seemed to echo Alice.

"There'll be savoury as well as sweet," announced the Monsignor reassuringly, "anchovy toast alongside the jam tarts."

"You can make toast?" I asked.

"Cesare can. He bakes his own bread—the English way."

"And cucumber sandwiches?" enquired Oscar, gleefully. (Neither of us had had lunch.)

"Oh, yes, as I promised you."

"Sorry, sir," piped up Cesare Verdi, who had skirted round us up the steps and was busying himself bringing a tray of scones to the table. "No cucumber sandwiches today."

"I ordered them especially," boomed Felici.

"There was no cucumbers in the market this morning, sir. I went down twice."

"No cucumbers? In Rome in July?"

"No, sir. Not even for ready money."

"And you always have plenty of that," snapped Felici.

The Monsignor turned, took Oscar's hands in his, and, closing his eyes, pressed them together as he might those of a grieving mother to whom he was offering consolation at her only child's graveside. "This is terrible, Mr. Wilde. I had promised you cucumber sandwiches."

"It's not in the least terrible. It's vastly amusing. This is an exquisite moment that I shall treasure forever."

"I feel your disappointment," condoled the Monsignor, "and I appreciate your understanding." Breaking away from Oscar, he turned to Munthe and me. "Now, gentlemen, *a tavola*! Sit where you please. I shall summon the others. They are, as you would say, waiting in the wings. Their cells are just above us."

He went to the sideboard and rang what appeared to be a sanctus bell. Its chimes sounded oddly in the oak-panelled dining room.

"This is extraordinary," purred Oscar, positioning himself at the end of the table but not taking a seat. He stood with his hands on the back of the chair, looking down at the table in wonder. Cesare Verdi was placing matching teapots on silver trivets in the remaining gaps between the dishes of teatime delicacies.

"This is the *circolo inglese*," said Felici, with a nonchalant shrug of his stooping shoulders.

"When did it start?"

"The *circolo*? Years ago."

"In Pio Nono's time?"

"Oh no, more recently than that. Pio Nono was not in

sympathy with the English. He used to say that he accepted Father Breakspear as one of his chaplains as a penance. It was his little joke. But when the possibility was raised of making John Henry Newman a cardinal, he considered that a joke too far. He wouldn't have it."

"It was I who founded the *circolo,* with Pope Leo's blessing, in May 1879, at the time of Father Newman's long-overdue elevation to the rank of cardinal."

Monsignor Breakspear had entered the room. He swept in briskly—brusquely, almost—and extended an immediate hand of greeting to each of us in turn. He murmured to me pleasantly, "Good to see you again, Conan Doyle. I apologise for not being on parade yesterday. I got my days mixed up."

I nodded and studied him in silence: the broad shoulders, the red face, the hard smile, the bushy eyebrows, the tightly curled iron-grey hair—I had no recollection of him whatsoever. Again, I wondered at his womanly handshake, so at odds with his robust manner. He did not acknowledge Felici or Cesare Verdi and gave Axel Munthe no more than a cursory smile. Having greeted me with the familiarity I have described, he addressed the rest of his remarks to Oscar.

"Cardinal Newman was our first guest. He sat at this very table just thirteen years ago. He chose to sit in the very seat that you appear to have chosen, Mr. Wilde. He always sat there. He took tea with us often—whenever he was in Rome, in fact. He was seventy-eight when he first came here. I was twenty-five. I loved him as a son should love a father—absolutely and without condition."

"We all loved him. He was the best of company and the best of men."

The doorway to the refectory was suddenly crowded. Three priests had arrived together. It was the sallow-skinned Monsignor Tuminello who spoke first. He had a smoker's voice, rough and dark, and weary, jaundiced eyes. In younger days, Munthe had told us, he had been a tutor at the English College in Rome. He spoke excellent English, with a natural authority, but appeared to be addressing no one in particular. (Indeed, the conversational style of the members of the *circolo inglese* put me in mind of the discourse at an Oxford high table, where the dons never catch your eye and speak to the world in general rather than to one another.)

"I come across Cardinal Newman from time to time and I always feel the aura of his sanctity."

"As the papal exorcist," explained Monsignor Felici, "Monsignor Tuminello regularly encounters the souls of the dear departed."

"I wrestle with the devil on a daily basis. It is hard, hard work—*molto duro*. But it has its compensations: easy access to the communion of saints being chief among them."

"You meet saints?" asked Oscar.

"I find myself in their presence, yes."

"You see them?"

"I *hear* them."

"On a regular basis?"

"All the time."

The Monsignor answered Oscar's questions without looking at him. On entering the dining room the priest had gone directly to the sideboard, and from a crystal decanter had poured himself a small glass of brown wine.

"The job of an exorcist is to free those who are possessed by evil spirits. The devil has entered their very being. My task is to confront the devil and his minions and drive them out. But, usually, by the time I come face-to-face with the unfortunate afflicted, I find that God, in His infinite mercy, has anticipated me and already sent in one of His favourite saints to begin the good work." He drank his wine in a single gulp and refilled the glass.

"You *hear* these saints, you say?" asked Oscar, gazing at the Monsignor with curiosity and delight.

"I meet the possessed and, usually, they are crying out in agony. I listen to the sounds of souls in torment. What is it I hear? Saints disputing with demons. It's as simple as that. The arguments are very violent, as you may imagine."

"And can you always tell who is speaking?" enquired Oscar.

"Not always, but as a rule saints are better-spoken than devils. They shout less and their vocabulary is more circumspect."

"And sometimes they talk to you directly? In what language?"

"In Latin in the main."

"And you respond?"

"I talk to the devil in Latin. He replies in French. When I am in conversation with Cardinal Newman we speak in English—always."

"He felt easy with us," said Monsignor Breakspear. "The Vatican was not Cardinal Newman's natural habitat, but in this room, at this table, I believe he felt at home."

"Cardinal Newman was very partial to cucumber sandwiches," said Monsignor Felici, casting a reproachful glance in the direction of Cesare Verdi.

The sacristan was at the corner of the table, with Brother Matteo, the Capuchin friar, assisting Father Bechetti to his place. The old priest's toothless mouth hung open; his sightless eyes stared vacantly ahead; with a trembling hand, repeatedly, he rubbed his temples and the side of his hawk-like nose: he looked more dead than alive.

"We are all partial to Cesare's cucumber sandwiches," said Monsignor Tuminello, once more downing his wine in a single draught. He pushed the decanter to the back of the sideboard and made his way around the table. "In the summer months, the cucumber sandwiches are virtually the *circolo inglese*'s sole raison d'être."

"Not today," said Monsignor Felici. "Today our raison d'être is to honour our distinguished guests."

"Illustri invitati," the Capuchin friar barked into Father Bechetti's ear. The old priest snorted derisively and struck the table with both hands.

"I shall sit between my patients, if I may," said Axel Munthe, placing his black bag on the floor by the sideboard and moving discreetly around the table. "Father Bechetti seems little improved since his fall. I am sorry."

"E arrabbiato e frustrato," replied the Capuchin, laying a kindly hand on the old priest's shoulder. With surprising force, Father Bechetti pushed the hand away.

Munthe smiled at Brother Matteo. "I will give him something to settle him before I leave."

The Capuchin shrugged and returned the doctor's smile. *"Come desidera."*

He appeared to understand English, but not to speak it. He made way for Dr. Munthe and, stepping round to the other side of the table, placed himself opposite Father Bechetti. Throughout the tea, I noticed, he continued to keep a watchful eye on the old man.

"But Monsignor Tuminello appears fully recovered," Munthe went on, "back to his old self."

The papal exorcist made the sign of the cross and then shook Munthe warmly by the hand. "Was it strychnine you gave me yesterday, Doctor? I think it was. It 'did the trick,' as the Americans say. I am grateful. God is grateful."

"I simply do my job," said Munthe.

"And in doing it you help me do mine—and *my* work is God's work. I'm sixty years of age. I'm not young anymore. Battling with Beelzebub takes it out of me. Yesterday my body gave way. I was utterly exhausted, broken, until you revived me, Doctor."

"With a dose of poison?" said Oscar, lightly. He was standing one place away from Munthe, at Tuminello's right hand.

The Swedish doctor smiled and shook his head. "Strychnine is a useful medicine, used in moderation."

"What is moderation?" asked Oscar. "Life should be lived excessively—or what's the point?"

"Ah," cried Monsignor Breakspear, exultantly. "What's the point indeed? We are to talk of the Meaning of Life. This is as it should be. I am glad you have assumed Cardinal

Newman's old seat, Mr. Wilde. You can lead our teatime colloquy."

"I shall be honoured. I am fond of my own voice. Is a 'colloquy' the usual form?"

"Only when we have guests. Otherwise we eat in silence—as we would in a Capuchin friary, with one of us reading out loud to the others."

"And you are the reader as a rule?" asked Oscar.

"This is the *circolo inglese*. The reading is always in English, so, yes, I am usually the reader."

"And what do you read? Sacred texts?"

"Of a kind. Recently we have been concentrating on the works of Arthur Conan Doyle! We are devotees of the great Sherlock Holmes. Look on the sideboard—there, alongside Cardinal Newman's *Apologia Pro Vita Sua*, signed by the author, you will find my copies of *A Study in Scarlet* and *The Sign of Four*, first editions, of course."

Breakspear bowed towards me unctuously. I felt even happier that I had positioned myself as far from him as possible.

We had all found our places around the table:

	Oscar Wilde
Monsignor Nicholas Breakspear SJ	Monsignor Luigi Tuminello
Monsignor Francesco Felici	Dr. Axel Munthe
Brother Matteo Gentili	Father Joachim Bechetti
	Dr. Arthur Conan Doyle

Cesare Verdi, standing by the sideboard, rang the Sanctus bell and the party fell silent. After a moment's pause, Monsignor Felici invited Monsignor Breakspear to say grace.

"Benedic, Domine, nos et haec tua dona quae de tua largitate sumus sumpturi. Per Christum Dominum nostrum. Ad coenam vitae aeternae perducat nos, Rex aeternae gloriae. Amen."

It was a grace I knew well, from my school days. Breakspear intoned it sonorously and offered me a knowing smile at its conclusion. All but Father Bechetti joined in the "Amen" and we took our seats.

I have to report that the feast spread out before us would have gladdened the heart of the greediest schoolboy.

"Help yourselves, gentlemen," said Felici jovially. "Don't stand on ceremony. The tea in the pots on the table is Darjeeling. If you prefer something lighter, Cesare will prepare you a special pot of Earl Grey."

Cesare Verdi stood hovering at my shoulder with a silver milk jug in his hand. "'Ome from 'ome, sir, eh?"

As he said those words, quite unexpectedly my mind's eye was suddenly filled with a vision of my darling wife, Touie. She was seated at the fireside in the front parlour of the little house we had lived in during the first months of our marriage. She was toasting muffins for me on the fire.

Felici roused me from my reverie. "Dr. Conan Doyle, we know you and your work. We all admire it. Father Bechetti understands English, and Brother Matteo, though he may not speak English as well as some of us, is learning the language—slowly. I know that both of them have sat at this table and listened to your stories with deep pleasure."

The bearded Capuchin, seated between me and Felici, nodded to each of us, benignly. He murmured, *"Si,"* and then returned his attention to buttering a scone for Father Bechetti.

"And Mr. Wilde," continued the Monsignor, "we know you and your reputation. We look forward to discovering your works in due course." Oscar smiled. "We are so delighted at the chance that has brought you both to our table. You are most welcome, gentlemen."

"We know you," echoed Monsignor Breakspear, looking from Oscar to me, "and, because we read the English newspapers, we feel that we know you quite well—but do you know us?" He looked directly at me and raised his heavy eyebrows. "Dr. Conan Doyle knows me, of course. We were at school together. But Mr. Wilde knows none of us." He turned towards Monsignor Felici on his right. "Perhaps, before our 'colloquy,' we should introduce ourselves?"

Oscar leant across the table and placed his hand on Breakspear's wrist. "There is no need, Monsignor. I know who you are." Oscar looked around the table and smiled, widening his shining eyes. "I know who you all are," he said, sitting upright and resting his elbows on the table's edge. He brought the tips of his fingers together and held them against his chin, as if in prayer. "Indeed, I realise now that I have met you before, every one of you. It was here, at St. Peter's, fifteen years ago. You may not recall the occasion, but I do. I was twenty-two and I had the privilege— the blessing—of an audience with Pope Pius IX. It was in one of the corridors close to the Sistine Chapel, only a few yards, I suppose, from where we are seated now. I remember how we stood in line, we pilgrims, waiting for the Holy Father. We waited for an hour, at least. And then he came. He was old and frail—it was not long before his death. He was not alone, of course. You were all in attendance. I can picture you now, hovering around him, anxiously, as he made his way along the line. I was at the end of the line, standing next to a garrulous Englishwoman and a young girl and a Capuchin friar."

I looked at Brother Matteo. He had put down his knife and was listening attentively, but his face betrayed no emotion.

"I remember the girl vividly," Oscar continued. "She was very beautiful, with hair the colour of moonbeams and eyes the colour of cornflowers. And I remember what Pio Nono said when he had blessed her and raised her from her knees and lifted her veil to see her face. I recollect his words exactly. He said: 'Look on this child and give thanks. She is pure innocence. She is a lamb of God, surrounded by the seven deadly sins.' I imagine that you, gentlemen, are the deadly sins and that she is the beautiful girl in that painting on the wall. Is her name Agnes? I am sure that it must be."

14.

The Seven Deadly Sins

*L*ife, I have found, is infinitely stranger than anything that the mind of man could invent. We would not dare to conceive the things that are really mere commonplaces of existence. If you and I, dear reader, could fly out of the window hand in hand, and hover over a great city, such as London or Rome, gently removing the roofs and peeping in at the queer things that are going on, the strange coincidences, the cross-purposes, the wonderful chains of events, working through generations, and leading to the most outré results, it would make all fiction with its conventionalities and foreseen conclusions most stale and unprofitable.

When Oscar had finished speaking, I sat marvelling at what he knew and how he had discerned it. The heavy silence that greeted his remarks suggested to me that my remarkable friend had been correct in each of his surmises.

I looked about the table. Brother Matteo had his eyes fixed on Father Bechetti opposite him. The old priest had his eyes closed and a curious smile upon his face. The three Monsignors gazed steadily into the middle distance.

Eventually, Cesare Verdi, standing by the sideboard, broke the silence. "More tea, gentlemen?"

"Thank you," said Oscar. "More tea would be delightful."

Monsignor Felici turned in his chair to look up at the painting of the girl that hung in a simple frame between the gasoliers on the wall behind him. "She is very beautiful, as you say, Mr. Wilde. It is some years since Father Bechetti painted her. It is some years since he painted anything. But it is a wonderful piece of work—possibly his finest. That is why we treasure it. The girl's face, of course, is the face of the Blessed Virgin in Michelangelo's *Pietà*. I am sure that is why people feel that they recognise her when they see her." The Monsignor turned back to look at Oscar. "We have the sculpture here, you know, in the basilica, in the first chapel on the right. It is the only work that Michelangelo ever signed—his masterpiece."

Oscar said nothing. Cesare Verdi passed around the table, pouring out fresh tea. In the hush that filled the dining room once more, Monsignor Felici chuckled softly to himself and contemplated the half-eaten custard tart that sat upon his plate. Then he raised his head and, narrowing his eyes and pursing his lips, lifted his replenished cup of tea and raised it to Oscar.

"And as for the seven deadly sins, Mr. Wilde, only five papal chaplains are ever allocated cells here in the sacristy. There's not room for more. There were just five of us here in Pio Nono's day. There are just five of us here now."

Oscar looked directly into the Monsignor's eyes. "With the sacristan it's six. And with Pio Nono himself it would have been seven."

"What are you suggesting, Mr. Wilde?"

"That the Holy Father was a humble man—with a sense

of humour. Even during my brief audience I recognised both those qualities in him. He would have acknowledged his own sinfulness. He counted himself as one of the 'seven deadly sins.'"

Angrily, Felici pushed his chair back from the table. His face had darkened and his jowls shook. "The Holy Father was human. He was not above the stain of sin—"

As he spoke, he began to struggle to his feet. Brother Matteo, seated on his right, put out a gentle hand to restrain him.

"Non affoga colui che cade in acqua, ma affoga chi male incappa."*

Breakspear, on Felici's left, also put out a restraining hand. He looked directly into his colleague's eyes. "We are unmasked, Francesco, but we are not undone. Mr. Wilde has uncovered our secret. Does it matter? It is a very small secret, after all."

"What business is it of his?"

"None, I'm sure, but since he has stumbled upon it, let us accept what has occurred with a good grace."

"It is an invasion of our privacy," protested Felici.

"Perhaps, but does it signify? We have nothing to hide."

Oscar sat upright at the head of the table. I noticed that the flush in his cheeks of a moment before had disappeared. His face had resumed its customary pallor and his eyes had lost their gleam. "I apologise, Monsignor," he said. "I intended no harm."

"And none has been done," answered Monsignor

---

* "He who falls in water does not drown, but he who falls badly will."

Breakspear. "Having shared our English tea, you now share our little secret. It is a very little secret."

"Explain it to him," said Monsignor Felici, calming himself. "It was a secret—that was its charm. But it contains no deep mystery."

"No mystery at all." Breakspear turned to Oscar. "It was, Mr. Wilde, rather as you suggest, a little joke of the Holy Father's. Among our duties as the papal chaplains-in-residence, we were—and are still—in attendance upon the Holy Father during his audiences. In the old days, before each and every audience, we would gather with His Holiness here in the sacristy."

The English Monsignor nodded in the direction of the steps leading down to the chamber with the red-damask wall hangings, and the Seat of Tears, and Father Bechetti's paintings of the Last Supper and Pio Nono and the Virgin Mary.

"Before processing through the Sistine Chapel to the audience corridor, we would stand together, clustered around the Holy Father, and say a prayer. One day, Pio Nono, laughing, looked around our little circle and remarked that there were seven of us—just seven." Breakspear put out a hand to indicate the sacristan, who stood at his post by the sideboard. "Cesare Verdi was always of our number. He would walk ahead of the procession, with his staff of office, opening the doors, clearing the way."

The sacristan nodded as if to confirm the accuracy of the Monsignor's account.

"As we stood in the circle that day, the Holy Father—laughing, as I say—suggested that we should think of ourselves as the 'seven deadly sins.' He said it would be a reminder to us all, himself included, that because we were the Pope's men it did not mean that we were above other men. We were as capable of the capital sins of the world as any other mortal."

Monsignor Felici wiped his mouth with his napkin. "So now you know, Mr. Wilde."

"But how do you know?" asked Monsignor Tuminello, pushing back his chair and reaching out towards the sideboard. Cesare Verdi, anticipating him, brought him a glass and filled it from the decanter. "How did you uncover our little secret?"

"I recognised the rose-gold rings you wear. I saw such a ring on Pio Nono's finger when I kissed his hand. It was such a simple ring for a Pope to wear. On the third finger of his right hand he wore the traditional papal ring, of course—the Fisherman's Ring of St. Peter. I kissed it, but as I kissed it, under it, half hidden beneath it, I noticed a second ring, a simple rose-gold band. It was the ring's simplicity that struck me. I saw that ring on Pio Nono's finger fifteen years ago. I see the same ring on your hands now."

Oscar looked around the table. Monsignor Breakspear followed his gaze. "Father Bechetti does not wear a ring," he said.

"So it seems," said Oscar.

"Nor does Brother Matteo."

"Not on his hand, perhaps," said Oscar. "He has a workman's hands, heavy and rough—not hands for jewellery. He does not wear the ring on his ring finger, but I suspect he wears it around his neck."

Brother Matteo smiled. He put both hands inside the top of his brown habit, pulled out the thin cord that hung about his neck, and displayed the rose-gold ring for all to see. *"Eccoti!"* he said, laughing.

"Pio Nono gave you the rings?"

"Yes, on the day of the special audience to mark the thirtieth anniversary of his papacy," said Breakspear. "Cesare Verdi had them made from a block of gold given to Pope Leo XI by an Ottoman sultan, as I recall."

"That's it, sir," confirmed the sacristan from the sideboard. He held up his hand to display the ring he wore.

"Does Pope Leo XIII know about this?" Oscar asked.

"No, he has never asked. He has not noticed the rings, I am sure. He is not close to us in the way that Pio Nono was. We are his chaplains, too, of course—but there is a difference. Pope Leo did not choose us. He inherited us. We serve him. We love him. We give him all obedience. He is the Holy Father, but we are not his children as we were the children of Pio Nono."

"Leo has other chaplains," said Felici, "personal chaplains of his own choosing. But we are the chaplains-in-residence. We remain here from the moment of our appointment until we die."

"Or become bishops or cardinals," added Tuminello, emptying his glass, and looking directly at Breakspear with amused and mocking eyes.

Breakspear shook his head and gazed down at the table.

"We are here until death," said Monsignor Felici, "or beyond, in Verdi's case. Our successors as chaplains-in-residence will be chosen by whoever is pope at the time of our demise, but the post of sacristan is a gift from God, handed down from father to son."

"How wonderful," said Oscar, smiling up at Cesare Verdi.

"Except I don't 'ave children, sir," said the sacristan. "Nor a wife."

"But you have time," said Oscar. "I have no doubt that both will be provided—in due course. God will provide. *C'est son métier.*"

Cesare Verdi said nothing. Monsignor Tuminello held up his empty glass and the sacristan fetched the decanter and poured the priest a further libation.

An awkward stillness filled the room once more.

"And Agnes?" asked Oscar, looking up at the painting on the wall. "Tell me about Agnes. Her uncanny resemblance to Michelangelo's Virgin notwithstanding, this was the girl that Pio Nono blessed that day—I am certain of that."

"No, sir," said Monsignor Felici, defiantly.

"*Sì,*" said Brother Matteo, gently, resting his hand on Felici's sleeve. *"La verità viene sempre a galla."*

"Yes indeed, we should not be frightened of the truth," said Monsignor Tuminello, leaning forward onto the table, pushing the tea things away from him and setting down his glass. "Yes, Mr. Wilde, the beautiful child in the painting is Agnes. She was named for Agnes of Rome, the virgin-martyr, the patron saint of chastity. We loved her dearly. We still do."

At my side, Father Bechetti stirred. His eyes remained closed, but his hands twitched. Brother Matteo leant forward and rested his hands on those of the old priest. "We all loved her," Tuminello went on. "I taught her to read and write. Father Bechetti painted her. Brother Matteo looked after her. But Pio Nono loved her most of all."

"Who was she?" asked Oscar, still gazing at the painting.

"A girl from the Vatican laundry—one of the waifs and strays taken in by the nuns. It was the nuns who named her. She would have become a nun herself in time. She had the vocation. Her faith was simple, but profound. Pio Nono saw that. She was his favourite. He delighted in her company. Who would not? She was all sweetness and light. She was, as he said, pure innocence—a lamb of God."

"And she is dead?" asked Oscar in a voice barely above a whisper.

"We do not know," said Monsignor Felici. "We have no idea."

"I know," said Monsignor Tuminello. He spread out his fingers on the table, on either side of his empty wineglass. "She is in heaven. She is with the angels. I have heard her voice. She is with God."

"The truth is, Mr. Wilde, we know nothing," said Monsignor Felici. He spoke with quiet deliberation now. "She may be alive. She may be dead. We simply do not know. She disappeared."

Oscar looked sharply at Felici. "Disappeared?"

"Yes, one day she was here, the next she was gone. It was as simple—and as final—as that."

"Did no one look for her?"

"We looked for her: all over the basilica, all over the Vatican City, all over Rome. She was nowhere to be found. The nuns looked for her, too. The Swiss Guard looked for her."

Tuminello interrupted angrily. "They did not. The Swiss Guard did nothing."

"They were preoccupied," said Monsignor Breakspear. "We were all preoccupied. The girl disappeared on 7 February 1878."

"Is the date significant?"

"It was the day of Pio Nono's death."

Another silence fell. I waited for Oscar to break it, but he said nothing. He sat facing me at the far end of the dining table, gazing fixedly up at the painting of the beautiful young girl.

"May I ask a question?" I said, eventually.

Monsignor Tuminello turned, smiled, and raised his empty glass towards me. "Ah," he said, "the voice of Sherlock Holmes."

"Could the girl have been kidnapped?" I asked.

"Yes," said Monsignor Felici, with a heavy sigh. "It happens all too frequently. Young girls are stolen from the streets and sold into slavery."

Oscar's eyes turned to Felici. "In Rome at the end of the nineteenth century? You surprise me, Monsignor."

"They are taken from Rome to Sicily and on to North Africa," explained Felici. "It is a terrible trade, cruel and brutish, but it thrives."

"She was not stolen from the streets and sold into slavery," said Tuminello. "She was not of the streets. She was an innocent child and she lived here, in safety. She slept in the dormitory above the laundry. The Reverend Sisters loved her as we did. This was her home."

"She may have run away," said Felici. "It is possible."

"Run away? Why should she run away?"

"She was a child, Tuminello. Perhaps she wanted the company of other children. Pio Nono taught her her catechism. You taught her to read and write. Perhaps she also wanted to do childish things—to *play* as well as pray. Have you considered that?"

"No," said Tuminello, shaking his head, and, turning to Cesare Verdi, he held out his empty glass. "That's not what happened."

"No one knows what happened," insisted Monsignor Felici. The Pontifical Master of Ceremonies had regained all his composure. He spoke once more with his accustomed authority, looking straight at me. "I fear that the poor child may have joined the band of feral children who live up on the hill beyond the pyramid. They are notorious."

"They are notorious now," cried Tuminello, slamming his hand upon the table. "There were none there then."

"There were Gypsies there then—a whole encampment."

"Look at her, Francesco. Agnes was not a Gypsy. She was an angel."

Felici turned in his chair once more to look up at the painting. "She was very beautiful," he said simply. "No one will deny that. And one day we lost her. She was here—then she was gone. She vanished into thin air. Where she went, or why, we do not know. It was a long time ago now and we do not speak of it because what purpose does it serve? It is idle speculation—and corrosive."

"She vanished into thin air . . ." Oscar repeated the phrase slowly, deliberately, folding his napkin carefully as he did so and laying it down next to his plate.

"That seems a little improbable," I added from my end of the table. " 'Vanishing into thin air' seems to me to be the least likely explanation."

Monsignor Tuminello, who was now quite drunk, looked at me with blazing eyes. "What does Sherlock Holmes tell Dr. Watson in *The Sign of Four*? You wrote it. We read it."

"It is just a story," I pleaded, "an inconsequential yarn."

"You will remember the line," insisted Tuminello. " 'How often have I said to you that when you have eliminated the impossible, whatever remains, however improbable, must be the truth?'"

"Yes, I recall the line," I said.

"Agnes vanished into thin air. She was assumed into heaven. There is precedence."

Monsignor Felici shifted his mighty bulk uneasily. "Verdi, what time is it?" he asked.

"Coming up to seven, sir."

"Evening prayer calls," announced the Monsignor. *"Agimus tibi gratias, omnipotens Deus, pro universis beneficiis tuis, qui vivis et regnas in saecula saeculorum,"* he murmured, closing his eyes and resting his fingertips on the edge of the table before him.

The other priests responded automatically: *"Deus det nobis suam pacem."*

"Et vitam aeternam," concluded Felici, pushing himself to his feet, his eyes still closed.

"Amen."

The Monsignor stepped away from the table, lifted his shoulders, and looked about the room, sniffing the air as a general might emerging from his tent on the day of battle. "I must be about my duties," he declared.

Axel Munthe, who had been seated facing him, got to his feet. "Thank you, Monsignor, for a memorable tea party." The doctor looked to either side of him and held out his hands. "Before I go, let me settle Monsignor Tuminello and Father Bechetti in their cells. Brother Matteo will assist me."

"Very good," said Felici, briskly, and nodded to Oscar and to me. "Thank you for your company, gentlemen." We rose to our feet and bowed towards the Monsignor. "At least we had tea—and a colloquy of sorts. It wasn't quite what Breakspear envisaged, but it had its lively moments. I think we can agree on that." He clapped his hands together. "Forgive me if I hasten away. God is my Saviour—and my timekeeper."

He considered which way to make his exit and settled on moving to the right, squeezing himself past Brother Matteo, resting his hands briefly on the Capuchin's shoulders as he did so. He paused to acknowledge the sacristan, who stood, head bowed, at the end of the sideboard.

"A fine English tea, Verdi. Thank you. Just a pity about the cucumber sandwiches."

As the Pontifical Master of Ceremonies swept out of the refectory, the candles on the dining table spluttered in a kind of genuflection.

15.

When a Pope Dies

Once Felici had gone, Cesare Verdi picked up Axel Munthe's medical bag and offered his arm to Monsignor Tuminello. The papal exorcist took it, gratefully. Verdi and Tuminello led the way; the Swedish doctor and the benevolent Capuchin followed on with the enfeebled Father Bechetti. Slowly, the five men shuffled and stumbled down the steps from the refectory and then up the immediately adjacent steps to the chaplains' cells. I volunteered to assist, but Munthe was adamant: "No, thank you, too many doctors spoil the diagnosis. We won't be long."

Oscar resumed his seat at the head of the table. Once the medical escort-party had departed, I took my cue from Oscar's lightly raised eyebrow and resumed mine. I noticed that Monsignor Breakspear had not moved. When Felici had got to his feet at the conclusion of the grace, Breakspear alone had remained seated at the table, gazing vacantly at the wall opposite.

Breakspear appeared to read my mind. "It was not bad form. I owe no deference to Felici. He and I and Tuminello are of equal standing. They are my senior in years—I am not yet forty: they are fifty and sixty or thereabouts—but our status is the same. There are fourteen grades of monsignor within the Catholic hierarchy, but, as it happens, we three are on precisely the same rung of the ecclesiastical ladder. The Pontifical Master of Ceremonies commands almost all he surveys within St. Peter's, I grant you that, but he outranks neither the Grand Penitentiary nor the papal exorcist. I do not need to stand in his presence."

"You are all equally exalted," said Oscar, inclining his head respectfully towards the Monsignor, "but I think you have reason to be the most exhausted. Listening to confessions day in, day out, must take it out of a man."

Breakspear laughed. "They give this job to the younger ones, you know, because we still have our hearing. In the confessional, the penitent is inclined to whisper. You have to strain your ears to catch the full horror of his sins. It *is* exhausting. And you end up with a crick in the neck." He pushed back his chair. "Shall we steal a glass of Tuminello's wine?"

"What is the wine?" asked Oscar. "It is a dull colour."

"And it has a deadening effect if drunk to the extent Tuminello drinks it. He imports it personally. We're doing him a favour if we drink some of it for him." He fetched glasses and the decanter from the sideboard and brought them to the table. "Come and sit down here, Conan Doyle. Let us pretend we're gentlemen and the ladies have left us to our port."

I moved to Tuminello's place, on Oscar's left, immediately facing Breakspear. The Grand Penitentiary poured out the wine. Oscar sniffed at it with nostrils superciliously flared. He took a tentative sip, and then another. "It's a Madeira," he declared, his face lighting up, "and it's utterly superb." He raised his glass to Breakspear. "Your health, Monsignor. 'Drink deep, or taste not the Pierian spring,' as Pope advises."

"Which pope is that?" asked Breakspear.

"Alexander Pope," said Oscar, "in his famous poem. 'A little learning is a dang'rous thing, drink deep,' et cetera. You must remember it from school."

"We didn't study Pope at Stonyhurst, did we, Conan Doyle?"

"I think we did," I said. "I'm sure we did."

"That's the wrong answer, boy!" cried Breakspear, laughing uproariously as he drained the decanter, filling each of our glasses to the brim. "More of that cheek and I'll take the tolley to you."

"I am glad I went to school in Ireland," said Oscar, smiling. "In England schoolboys appear to take pleasure in beating one another *relentlessly*. They make a ritual of it—a fetish, one might say. Very strange." He sucked the Madeira from the edge of his glass and rolled the wine around his tongue, considering Breakspear from beneath half-closed eyelids. "You've been in Rome how long, Monsignor?" he asked.

"I came here as soon as I left school. I trained for the priesthood at the English College here. Pio Nono chose me as one of his chaplains when I was not yet twenty-five. This is where I have been ever since."

"This is your world," said Oscar, raising his glass to the room.

"And these men are my family," replied Breakspear, looking at the empty chairs set around the dining table.

"And are they also your friends?" enquired Oscar. "Do you like them?"

Breakspear laughed. "Oh, no, I know them far too well for that. I love them. But I can't say I like them. Not at all."

"Do you trust them?"

"I am a Jesuit. The question is: do *they* trust *me*?" He turned in his seat to look up at the painting on the wall. "Father Bechetti trusted me. When I first came here he was my one true friend. He was already old and past ambition. He did not envy me my youth as the others did. He was not jealous of my promise. He treated me like a son. I miss him."

"He is still here," said Oscar, quietly.

Breakspear turned back from the painting. "But his mind has gone."

"Has it?" said Oscar. "He joined in the grace just now."

"You noticed?"

"He speaks . . ."

"When the spirit moves him."

"From the little I have seen of him, I would say that he understands something of what is happening around him."

"You are right. Now and then he does. But he is not the man he was. He has not been the same since Pio Nono died." Breakspear drank his wine and closed his eyes. For a moment he seemed lost in thought. "None of us is," he said.

"What happened on the day that Pio Nono died?" asked Oscar.

Breakspear sighed. "The world changed. Our world changed. Utterly." He opened his eyes and smiled at Oscar. "Pio Nono was pontiff for almost thirty-two years—for thirty-one years and two hundred and thirty-six days, to be precise. He was the longest-reigning pope in history. He was our Holy Father. He was Pope before I was born. He was my Holy Father."

"You were with him at the last?"

"We all were. It seemed all Italy was there—cardinals, bishops, chaplains, monks and nuns, members of the house-hold, members of the Swiss Guard, servants, diplomats, dignitaries. Towards the very end, half of Rome's aristocracy turned up. The king sent emissaries . . . The bedchamber was crammed to overflowing, like a marketplace, except for the silence. No one spoke. No one made a sound."

"There were no tears?"

"Now and then, at the back of the room, a Reverend Sister would begin to sob—and there were prayers, of course. But it is the silence I remember chiefly, the anxious stillness, as if, for hours on end, we all held our breath." Breakspear finished his wine and sat forward at the table. "When a pope dies, it is a moment in history."

"And you were there—in the room."

"I was there, kneeling at the bedside. For a time, on that last morning, I held his hand. He spoke to me—*to me. 'Nicholas, questa volta me ne vado davvero'*—'Nicholas, this time I am really going.' The poor man had been ill for months with bronchitis and fever. For weeks on end, he had teetered at death's door. He survived the worst of the winter and died on 7 February 1878. It was a Thursday. On the night before his death he slept quite well. He took quinine and a little broth, and he blessed us with the crucifix he kept beneath his pillow. All night we kept a vigil at his bedside. It was at a quarter to five in the morning that the terrible trembling in the limbs and the rapid breathing came on. But his mind remained clear to the end. When he received the viaticum—the final Eucharist—he repeated the prayers himself. He received extreme unction at nine. At one o'clock, Cardinal Bilio, as Secretary of the Supreme Sacred Congregation of the Holy Office, began the service for the dying. The Holy Father struggled with the responses, but once he had completed the act of contrition, with the words *'Col vostro santo aiuto,'* his strength seemed to return. He revived until about four, when the final agony began. Cardinal Bilio recited the *Proficiscere* to him: 'Go forth upon thy journey, Christian soul! Go from this world! Go, in the name of God . . .' He died at twenty to six."

From the first I had had my reservations about Breakspear. Instinctively, I had neither liked nor trusted him. But, I confess, I found this testament of his strangely moving. "And at the moment of the Pope's death," I asked, "how did you feel?"

"Bereft. Alone. Ashamed."

"Ashamed?"

"I knew that in that moment—of all moments—my thoughts should have been with the Holy Father, but the truth is: I thought only of myself. Pio Nono was dead and I felt sorry for *myself.* I felt close to despair." Breakspear rested his fingertips on his eyebrows and pressed the lengths of his fingers against his eyes. "Goodness, gentlemen, I am supposed to be the confessor and here I am telling you things I have not told anyone before."

"Please," said Oscar, leaning towards the Monsignor, "finish your story: complete the account of the day. What happened next?"

Breakspear looked at Oscar and appeared puzzled. "What happened next?" he repeated.

"Yes." Oscar urged him on. "You left the chamber?"

Breakspear took a deep breath and wiped his mouth with his hand. "Not at once. I stayed to witness the curious ceremony that marks the death of a pope. One of the cardinals stepped forward, holding a small silver hammer. You may have seen it. The sacristan keeps it here on the sideboard. The cardinal stood at Pio Nono's bedside and with the hammer he struck the Holy Father on the forehead, three times, sharply, calling him by his proper name, *'Giovanni Mastai, sei morto?'*—'Giovanni Mastai, art thou dead?' And when answer came there none, the cardinal turned to the room, raised his arms, and proclaimed to the world that Pio Nono was no more."

"And the girl?" Oscar cast his eyes towards the portrait hanging behind Breakspear on the refectory wall. "The beautiful child in the painting, Agnes?"

"What about her? She was not there."

"Where was she at the moment of Pio Nono's death?"

"In the laundry, I suppose. In her dormitory? Somewhere. I don't know. At prayer with the Reverend Sisters, perhaps."

"When, then, did she hear the news?"

"I have no idea. News of the death of a pope does not travel slowly. Within a few minutes of the Holy Father's passing she would have known. She would have heard almost at once, poor child. She was always somewhere nearby. She never left the Vatican. Apart from anything, from the bell tower she would have heard the death knell toll."

"But you saw her that night, Monsignor Breakspear. I feel sure that you did."

"Why do you say that?"

"Because when Monsignor Tuminello was talking about her just now—and talking about her so animatedly, with such passion and fondness—you said nothing, nothing at all. In my experience, when a clever man has a great deal to say, he says nothing."

"I have nothing to say about Agnes."

"Please tell me what happened, Monsignor."

Nicholas Breakspear placed his hands carefully on the table in front of him, one hand resting upon the other. Momentarily, he glanced towards me, as if looking for support; I looked down at his hands; he turned to Oscar and composed himself. He spoke quietly.

"Mr. Wilde, the death of a pope is a public event. I have described what I remember of the passing of Pio Nono to you to satisfy your curiosity. It was a moment in history—a moment of significance. I was privileged to be a witness and your interest is, in every way, legitimate. But the death of an unknown child is of no significance . . . that is something else."

"She is dead?"

Breakspear hesitated. "Why do you ask? I do not know. I think so. I believe so."

Oscar pressed on. "You saw her that night, Monsignor. Tell me what happened."

Breakspear sat back, bemused, exasperated. "What's this about, Mr. Wilde? How do you know anything about the girl? What's she to you?" Oscar stared at Breakspear with ungiving eyes. "*What's she to you*, Mr. Wilde?"

"Nothing," said Oscar, eventually, "nothing at all." He held the glass of Madeira in his right hand, cupped between his fingers. Slowly, he took a sip of the wine and looked up once more to consider the painting on the wall. "But there she is—the girl. She cannot be denied. Agnes . . . I see her beauty and I sense her innocence."

"How do you know her name?"

"Tuminello told me her name the other night."

"That is not possible," snapped Breakspear. "I do not believe you, Mr. Wilde."

"Tell me what happened," Oscar repeated. "Tell me. Please."

"Tell 'im, Monsignor." Cesare Verdi stood at the doorway to the dining room. His black eyes shone in the candlelight. "My brother 'as told me all about Mr. Wilde. You can trust 'im, Monsignor. If 'e wants to know, 'e'll have a reason."

"Thank you," murmured Oscar.

Breakspear looked up at the sacristan. "Are you alone?"

"Yes, Dr. Munthe is giving 'em their injections, working 'is magic."

Breakspear smiled. "Hastening their ends . . ."

Cesare Verdi remained, silhouetted in the doorway. "Brother Matteo is with 'em." He ran his hands through his curly head of hair and wiped them on the sides of his cassock. Apart from the absence of a clerical collar, he was dressed like a priest, but you knew even at a glance that he was not one. He folded his arms and nodded to Oscar.

Oscar picked up his cue. "What happened, Monsignor? You did see Agnes that night, after the death of Pio Nono?"

"Yes. I found her here in the sacristy at ten o'clock."

"She was alone?"

"Yes."

"Here? In this room?"

"No, down there." He pointed beyond Cesare Verdi, to the first chamber, the room with the red-damask walls. "I found her there. She was lying on the Seat of Tears."

"Asleep?"

"No. She was dead." He paused and took a small breath. He moved his empty wineglass towards the centre of the table. "At least, I think that she was dead. I assumed she was dead. She was as white as a surplice, as cold as a chalice."

"You touched her?"

"I touched her forehead. I held back her hair and searched for a pulse on her neck. I found none. There were tear stains on her cheeks. Her eyes were closed."

"She had been dead for some time?"

"I do not know."

Oscar had finished his wine. He, too, placed his empty glass near the centre of the table. He regarded Breakspear with kindly eyes. "She looked peaceful?"

"Yes. Her arms were folded across her chest. Her feet were resting on a pillow."

"Was there a smile on her lips?"

"Yes, Mr. Wilde, there was. How did you know?"

Oscar made no reply. I leant forward. "What did you do?"

"I did nothing. I did not know what to do. I knelt at the poor, dead child's side and I did nothing."

"You didn't call for help?"

"It was ten o'clock. Those who were not still at the Holy

Father's deathbed were at Compline. I knelt by the Seat of Tears and I shed my own."

"You wept," said Oscar, "and what did you think had happened? Why was she there? *Why* was she dead?"

Breakspear answered without hesitation: "I thought she had died of a broken heart."

"Is such a thing possible?" I asked.

"Oh, yes," murmured Oscar. "It happens all the time."

Nicholas Breakspear looked at me and smiled. "Agnes loved Pio Nono as I did. As we all did. But she loved him more. She had no father, no grandfather, no brothers, no uncles—but she had Pio Nono. And she was just a child, so her love for him was simple and selfless in a way that our love was not. And Pio Nono loved her deeply. He was fond of children. He was always easy with babies. He would make jokes with the altar boys, play little games with them, but Agnes was the only child he ever really knew. She was more than a daughter to him. She was his delight—the personi-fication of innocence. She brought pure joy to his declining years. She was his little lamb of God." Breakspear's eyes turned back to Oscar. "You ask me what I thought as I knelt by the Seat of Tears next to the lifeless body of this beautiful child? I thought, Pio Nono is dead and Agnes has gone with him to heaven. It is what they would both have wanted."

"Pio Nono was eighty-five when he died," said Oscar quietly. "Agnes was twelve or thirteen?"

"Thirteen or fourteen," said Breakspear, "something like that."

"A difficult age," said Oscar.

"So I have heard," said Breakspear. "But I have no sisters."

"What happened then?" asked Oscar.

"I left her where I found her. I got to my feet. I made the sign of the cross. I left the sacristy. I left the gas lamps high. I left the candles lit. I left the door unlocked. The outer door is always unlocked. I went to Compline. And during the service I had darker thoughts. As I knelt, I began to think that Agnes had taken her own life. As I prayed, I became convinced of it. In the face of Pio Nono's death, in her grief, in her despair, the poor child had gone to the Seat of Tears and killed herself."

"How?"

"I had no idea, but I was certain of it."

"And when the service ended . . . ?"

"And when the service ended, all the others returned to the Holy Father's deathbed to watch over his body through the night."

"And you?"

"I did nothing. I said nothing."

"Except to me," said Cesare Verdi, standing in the doorway.

"Yes," said Breakspear. "I found Verdi in the corridor that runs between the Sistine Chapel and the papal apartments. He was returning to the sacristy, so I knew I had no choice. I had to tell him. I swore him to secrecy and together, in silence, we came here."

"And what did you find?"

"Nothing," said Breakspear. "The Seat of Tears was empty. She'd gone. There was no sign of her. None at all."

"If she was ever there, she'd vanished," said Cesare Verdi, "into thin air."

16.

Lobsters and Lemon Mayonnaise

I have heard it said, and seen it written, that the character of my creation "Sherlock Holmes" is, in part, at least, modelled on the personality of my friend Oscar Wilde. Not so. I will concede this much—that both Holmes and Wilde were men of peculiar genius and eccentricity: intellectually brilliant, intuitive and observant, gifted as linguists, unique in their way of personal expression. Neither was much taken with the froufrou of skirts, but both were true to themselves—and to their friends. They shared many qualities, and had flaws in common, also. Each, at his worst, was self-regarding, self-indulgent, selfish, and self-absorbed, to a degree, I fear, that would be categorised in the modern psychoanalytical parlance as "narcissistic" and "egotistical." And each, too, had a strain in his nature that put him beyond the accepted mores of his times. In Holmes's case, this led to an unfortunate dependency on the use of the drug cocaine. In Wilde's case, it led to the gates of Reading Gaol. But these two remarkable contemporaries, so similar in so many ways, were nonetheless very different human beings. Holmes at heart was a man of science, a man of action, and a pragmatist. Oscar was a poet, a man of inaction, and a romantic. Besides, the one could not have been modelled on the other because I conjured up Mr. Sherlock Holmes some years before I met Mr. Oscar Wilde.

The character of *Mycroft* Holmes, on the other hand, is certainly indebted to my close acquaintance with Oscar Wilde. It was during our stay in Rome in July 1892, and on this particular Saturday night, I recall, that I decided to endow "the great Sherlock Holmes" with an older, taller, broader, stouter brother and make him yet more brilliant than his sibling. The moment the notion came into my head, I saw the figure fully formed. At once, without hesitation, I gave Holmes's brother Oscar's genius, his appearance, his indolence—and his appetite.

I have also heard it said that I modelled Dr. John H. Watson on one Dr. Arthur Conan Doyle. Again, I deny it absolutely but I will grant you this: that Holmes's friend and chronicler and I do have one characteristic in common. *We are regular in our habits.* For example, I like to breakfast at eight, to take luncheon at one, and to dine no later than at half past eight in the evening. Oscar, on the other hand, did not mind when he feasted, so long as it was frequently and well.

That evening we dined at midnight—in Axel Munthe's rooms in Keats's former lodgings—on cold lobster and lemon mayonnaise, fresh strawberries, and French champagne. Oscar picked up these supplies from the kitchens of the Hôtel de Russie at gone eleven o'clock, as we passed along the Via del Babuino on our way from the Vatican to the Piazza di Spagna. He brought them to Munthe's apartment in a picnic basket and laid them out before us on a low table in front of the fireplace. Having served the repast, he stood back to admire it.

"Much have I travelled in the realms of gold," he declared, with one hand resting decorously on the mantelpiece and the other waving a lobster claw aloft, "and many goodly states and kingdoms seen, but I don't believe I have laid eyes upon a midnight feast to rival this, gentlemen. Do you agree?"

I mumbled my assent, while thinking my friend's exuberance somewhat tiresome and wondering how long it would be before I could slip once more between the Hôtel de Russie's crisp white sheets. (I like to be in bed by midnight.) Munthe was more forthcoming. "This is indeed a treat, Oscar. Thank you. Our English tea notwithstanding, I'm surprisingly peckish."

"Of course you are," cried Oscar, dipping his lobster claw into the bowl of mayonnaise, "you were denied your cucumber sandwiches."

"No cucumbers in the market," chuckled Munthe, leaning forward from his armchair and, with his fingers, scooping out a morsel of lobster flesh from its shell.

"Not even for ready money!" hooted Oscar, happily.

"You are both in remarkably good humour," I said, a touch sourly, "given the lateness of the hour."

"Are you surprised? Munthe has tucked up two of his patients and left them sleeping like babies, and you and I, Arthur, have at last made real progress in unravelling the mystery of the beautiful child Agnes."

"Have we?" I enquired, incredulous. I sat back in the armchair facing Munthe's and folded my arms.

"You believe the girl was murdered?" asked Munthe.

"Well, I don't believe she was assumed into heaven on the wings of angels," answered Oscar. "Nor do I believe that she took her own life."

My friend stood posing by the fireplace. I watched him turn to the mantelpiece and notice the mummified hand of the unfortunate workman who had fallen to his death from the rafters of All Saints' Church.

He dropped the remains of his lobster claw into the open paw and continued: "Agnes was a waif and stray, an abandoned child taken in by the Reverend Sisters of the Holy See when she was just an infant. She was a happy little girl. Beautiful, wholesome, healthy. I know. I stood at her side at that audience with Pio Nono just ten months before his death, remember. She was loved—and then she was lost. One day she was there, the next she was not. How come? What happened? Did she disappear down a rabbit-hole? No. Did she vanish into thin air? No. She was either kidnapped or murdered or both."

"Couldn't she have run away?" suggested Munthe.

"She was thirteen or fourteen. It's possible, I suppose, but unlikely. Why run away? The Vatican laundry was her home and had been since she was a little girl. The nuns who worked there were her family. And the death of Pio Nono, though distressing, was not unexpected. He was an old man, and sick. The news of his demise will have upset the child, no doubt—it might even have 'broken her heart,' as Breakspear put it—but why should it have prompted her to run away? Running away makes no sense."

"But does murder make any more sense?" I asked, dryly.

"Couldn't Breakspear be right? Couldn't the girl have taken her own life?"

"From everything we know of her, it is clear that Agnes was a devout child. She was devoted to the Holy Father. I saw them together: I can vouch for that. The girl's faith was evident—simple, perhaps, but sincere. She will have known the Ten Commandments. 'Thou shalt not commit murder.' Self-murder is a mortal sin. Faithful Agnes would not have taken her own life."

Sitting back, blinking at us through his thick gig-lamps while carefully licking clean the tips of his fingers, Munthe summarised what we had reported to him of Breakspear's testimony.

"The Grand Penitentiary claims that he found the girl lying dead on the chaise in the sacristy. This was at ten o'clock. He observed her for a few minutes and then departed, leaving her body where it lay. He went directly from the sacristy to attend Compline and, as soon as the service was over, about half an hour later, he returned to the sacristy. On his return, he found the girl was gone."

"Exactly so."

"Nobody else saw her?"

"Apparently not. She was last seen by one of the nuns in the laundry at around five o'clock, when Pio Nono was still alive. At the time the Sister said that Agnes had seemed in every respect 'her usual self.' None of the nuns could understand her disappearance."

"And Monsignor Breakspear saw no one coming or going from the sacristy before or after he made his terrible discovery?"

"No one at all. The other chaplains-in-residence were either at Compline or in attendance at the deathbed of the Holy Father."

"And at the time Breakspear told no one about what he claims to have seen?"

"Only the sacristan, whom he encountered by chance returning from Compline. And he swore Verdi to secrecy on the night. And, according to both of them, neither has spoken a word of any of this to anyone since it occurred."

"Why not? Why the secrecy?"

"Because Verdi, of course, saw nothing—and Breakspear can't substantiate what he says he saw. He admits that he cannot even be certain that the girl was dead. He *believes* she took her own life, but he acknowledges that he has no proof. He maintains that the reason he has said nothing to anyone throughout the intervening years is because he cannot conceive what useful purpose it would serve."

Oscar paused and bent over the table to inspect the dish of lobsters. Carefully, he selected a second claw, fatter and pinker than the first. Then, from the inside breast pocket of his jacket, he produced a small silver hammer and with it proceeded to beat the shell of the claw until he had cracked it open.

"Do we believe him?"

"What do you mean?" I asked, leaning forward to look more closely at the silver hammer. I was sure it was the one we had seen on the sideboard in the sacristy. "What do you mean, 'Do we believe him?'"

"Do we accept Breakspear's testimony?" murmured Oscar, wiping the hammer with his handkerchief before slipping it back into his jacket pocket. "Did Breakspear *really* see Agnes lying dead upon the papal Seat of Tears?" He half closed his eyes and leant against the mantelpiece once more. "It's a poetic picture, to be sure, but is it too poetic to be true?"

"Are you suggesting it's all an elaborate lie, Oscar?" I asked, still sitting forward but now gazing down at the dish of lobsters, thinking I might have a bite to eat, after all.

"Why should he lie about such a thing?" asked Munthe, with a puzzled frown.

"For some men, lying is a way of life," answered Oscar. "Lying is what they do. It's how they are." My friend opened his eyes wide and looked down at me. "Arthur, do you think that Monsignor Breakspear is telling us the truth?"

I pulled a piece of lobster from its shell. "Yes," I said firmly. "I do."

"But I thought that you didn't like the man."

"I don't," I said, and dipped my lobster into the mayonnaise.

"I thought you did not trust him."

"I didn't, but I was moved by his account of the death of the Pope."

"Ah!" Oscar smiled. "The best confidence men are always the most convincing." He stood looking down at me, amused at the relish with which I was already dipping a second piece of lobster into the lemon mayonnaise. "Breakspear says that he was at school with you."

"I don't remember him," I answered, with my mouth now half full. "But why should I? When we were at school, he would have been several years my senior."

"Do you think that he *was* at school with you, Arthur?"

"Why on earth should he lie about such a thing?"

"Why indeed? But he hadn't heard of Alexander Pope—and Pope was on the syllabus at Stonyhurst, you say . . ." Oscar took a deep breath while his fingers hovered above the bowl of strawberries. "There is something about Monsignor Breakspear, gentlemen, that doesn't add up." He picked out a piece of fruit and held it up to the gasolier for closer inspection. "Take this business of eating his way through the animal kingdom—dining on weasels and stoats and porcupines. It's preposterous."

"Your friend Dr. Buckland did it."

"He did. And Breakspear has copied him. Breakspear lacks originality."

"Does that make him a murderer?" asked Munthe.

"Not necessarily, but it does make him *suspect* so far as I am concerned." Oscar bit into his strawberry and dropped the hull into the dead workman's upturned hand, mopping his mouth with his handkerchief. "And then there's his name—it's preposterous, too."

"Is it? Breakspear's an old name."

"Historic." Oscar felt in his pockets for his cigarette case. "Monsignor Nicholas Breakspear, who aspires to be the next English pope, has exactly the same name as the last English pope. It's absurd."

"It's a coincidence, certainly."

"Tomorrow, Arthur, when you send a telegram of reassurance to your wife—as I know you will—I would be obliged if you would also send a telegram to your old school. Make some enquiries about 'Nicholas Breakspear,' would you? Was he indeed your school-fellow or is he an impostor?"

"And if he *is* an impostor," asked Munthe, "does that also make him a murderer? Why should Monsignor Breakspear of all people kill an innocent child?"

"Because he could."

"Because he could?" Axel Munthe shook his head in disbelief.

"An assertion of 'self' is frequently the cause of murder," said Oscar, lighting his cigarette from the flame of one the candles on the mantelpiece.

Munthe muttered, "I'd be more convinced by a less abstract motive."

Oscar inspected the burning tip of his cigarette. "How does this suit you, then? In his quest for self-realisation, in his desire to taste every experience open to man, Monsignor Breakspear is not only eating his way through the entire animal kingdom, but, one by one, he is breaking each of the Ten Commandments . . ."

"Now that *is* preposterous," cried Munthe.

Oscar laughed. "Implausible, I agree."

I looked up at my friend and smiled. "I think we should stick to the known facts, Oscar, if we can."

"Agreed, Arthur. On 7 February 1878, as Pio Nono lay dead, mourned by the whole Catholic world, according to Monsignor Breakspear, someone stole the life of an innocent child. Someone is responsible for a young girl's disappearance. We shall garner all the facts and find out who it was." He drew slowly on his cigarette and blew a thin plume of pale-purple smoke into the air. "We must, for Agnes's sake."

I was contemplating the strawberries and thinking I might soak a couple in my glass of champagne. I looked up at my friend again. "I meant to ask you, Oscar: how the deuce did you discover the girl's name?"

"As I am sure you learnt at Stonyhurst, Arthur, *agnes* is Greek for 'pure' or 'holy,' and *agnus* is Latin for 'lamb.' Could there be a more fitting name for Pio's Nono's little lamb of God? When I saw Father Bechetti's painting of the girl, I guessed that her name would be Agnes. It was a guess, a leap of faith, albeit an educated one."

Munthe looked sharply up at Oscar. "You said Tuminello told you her name."

"He did—after a fashion."

"He can barely speak," said Munthe.

"He did not speak her name. He threw his glass to the ground and fell to the floor when I mentioned it. You were both there," said Oscar, sucking on his cigarette. "At the church of All Saints', at the fund-raiser, earlier in the week, when I climbed the steps of the pulpit and announced the poem that I was going to recite: 'The Eve of St. Agnes.' I think the title caught Father Bechetti's attention. He understands English. I think it was the reference to 'the sweet Virgin's picture' that tipped him over the edge."

"Is this possible?" murmured Munthe.

"Good Lord," I breathed, swallowing a crushed strawberry.

"Good God," cried Munthe, suddenly getting to his feet. "Who's that?"

From below us we heard the sound of heavy battering on the front door. When the hammering stopped, there were distant cries of *"Dottore! Dottore! Medico!"*

"You're wanted, Doctor," said Oscar, putting out his cigarette among the lobster claws in the dead workman's mummified hand. "While we're for our beds, *dottore*, for you duty calls."

The battering resumed below. I drank up my champagne and got to my feet. "I hope the noise doesn't wake your companion," I said, looking towards the curtained doorway in the corner of the room.

"It won't," said Munthe, moving into the hall and picking up his medical bag from his desk as he went. "Blow out the candles, would you? I'll clear up the rest when I return."

"Is she away? Your companion?"

"No," said Munthe. "She's sound asleep. I made sure of that."

"Did you drug her?" enquired Oscar, lightly, blowing out the candles on the mantelpiece as he spoke.

Munthe stood by the door to the apartment, holding it open for us. "As it happens, I did."

"Strychnine?"

"A touch of strychnine stimulates, Mr. Wilde. More than a touch can be fatal." The hammering on the door was growing louder. "I gave her phenacetin. She won't wake tonight."

17.

Unmasking

*T*he loud, insistent caller at the doctor's door was Cesare Verdi. The sacristan was no longer wearing the black cassock in which he had served us our tea: he was now dressed in a dishevelled trenchcoat, workman's trousers, and an open-necked linen shirt without a collar. Beneath a labourer's cap, his hair and forehead, his face and round cheeks glistened with perspiration. He held an oil lamp up close to his face and in the gleam of his eyes I detected excitement rather than alarm.

"Sorry to disturb you, Doctor," he said, breathlessly, speaking in English. "It's Father Bechetti."

"I feared it might be," said Munthe. "I'm ready." He pushed past Verdi and, half running, half walking, made his way rapidly to the pony-and-trap that stood waiting by the fountain in the middle of the piazza. "Come on," he called to Verdi. "Let us go."

As he made to follow, Verdi offered a cursory nod of acknowledgment to Oscar and to me. "It'll be the end, I think."

"In case you need to make sure," said Oscar, "here's this." From the inside pocket of his jacket Oscar produced the silver hammer he had used to crack open the lobster claw and handed it to Verdi. The sacristan took the slender object and looked at it, confused.

"I borrowed it without asking," said Oscar, with an apologetic shrug. "Forgive me. You have so many treasures . . ."

Verdi said nothing.

Munthe called from the pony-and-trap: "We must go." Verdi ran to join him.

"Shouldn't we go, too?" I asked.

"To be in at the kill?"

"That's not what I meant."

"To hear Father Bechetti's deathbed confession? I fear it's too late for that. Joachim Bechetti will take his secrets to the grave. I imagine that is what he would have wanted."

We watched the pony-and-trap trundle out of the piazza. Neither Cesare Verdi nor Axel Munthe looked back, though the doctor raised his hand in a farewell wave as the pair disappeared into the darkness along the Via del Babuino. Oscar gazed up at the blue-black night sky: there was no moon.

"It's time for bed, Arthur," he said. "It's been a long day."

"You think nothing's to be gained by going to the sacristy now?"

"Nothing at all. It's gone two o'clock: it's the dying time of night. Clearly, Bechetti is fading fast. If the poor man is not dead already, once Munthe arrives at the bedside it won't take long. The good doctor will despatch him pretty swiftly—and tomorrow, blithely, he will tell us that he did—because, in his view, his patient had suffered 'too much and to no purpose.' We don't need to witness a sad old priest's demise, Arthur. We won't be required at any inquest and a death is not a pretty sight."

"I have known peaceful deaths," I said. "Some, even, that might be called 'lovely.' Death is the gateway to a better world. I do believe that."

Slowly, side by side, in silence, we crossed the piazza towards the Via del Babuino. As we walked, I listened to the odd, echoing clack of our heels on the cobblestones. Oscar said nothing, but lit another cigarette. Eventually, as we were passing the old church of Sant'Atanasio dei Greci, I broke the silence.

"Munthe is a good man, don't you think?" I said.

Oscar laughed. "If you believe in 'mercy killing,' he's the best. If death is the gateway to a better world, Dr. Munthe certainly holds the key."

"He has some peculiar views, no doubt, but we shouldn't forget that he's a Swede."

Oscar looked sideways at me. "And what is that supposed to mean, Arthur?"

"Swedes are of a morbid disposition—it's well known."

"Have a care, Arthur. My godfather was king of Sweden."

"And of Norway. King Oscar I. I remember. Your father treated his cataracts."

"He removed them. He made a blind king see. My father was a miracle worker—and the devil incarnate, of course. He led my mother the most dreadful dance. He was both a good man and a sinner."

"We're all sinners, Oscar, but we're not all murderers."

"Death is central to the Swedish doctor's vocation, there's

no denying it. His study is awash with macabre memorabilia."

"That does not make him a murderer, does it?"

"I hope not. But, as we know, Arthur, when a medical man does go wrong he is the first of criminals. He has nerve and he has knowledge."

We had reached our hotel. Oscar peered through the glass-fronted door. The hotel hallway was in darkness. He rang the night bell.

"Perhaps, when we see Munthe tomorrow, we had better ask him where he was on 7 February 1878. You never know . . ."

He was about to ring the bell again when a bleary-eyed porter appeared and, muttering and grumbling, unlocked the door for us. Oscar appeased the man with a handful of coins.

As we stood in the corridor outside our rooms and bid each other good night, one last question sprang into my mind.

"Tell me one thing, Oscar. Why on earth did you steal the silver hammer from the sacristy this afternoon?"

"Because I could." He smiled at me as he opened his bedroom door. "Sleep well, Arthur. We're getting there."

In the morning, I breakfasted alone and at eight o'clock. I had slept for no more than five hours, but I am regular in my habits and, as a rule, the happier for it. I took my writer's notebook with me to the dining room and over breakfast (coffee, black bread, and Italian smoked ham) I made some preliminary notes for the Sherlock Holmes story that would introduce his brother, Mycroft. As a nod to Oscar's devotion to all things Hellenic, I decided to call the story "The Greek Interpreter." Despite my lack of sleep, my thoughts flowed freely. I was pleased with my endeavours.

I was less pleased, however, with the telegram that I drafted to send to my darling wife, Touie. I was not sure what progress in the case I could report. I could not be certain when I would be returning to London. In truth, I did not know what to say to her, so I simply said: STILL IN ROME WITH WILDE. ALL WELL BUT PLANS UNCERTAIN. TAKE CARE. ACD. I also drafted a brief wire addressed to the bursar at Stonyhurst College, Clitheroe, Lancashire.

At ten o'clock, as the dining room began to clear, I took my telegrams to the hotel's reception desk for despatch. There I found two notes awaiting me. One was from Oscar, advising me that he had gone out in search of cigarettes and hoped that I would join him shortly in the Piazza del Popolo for "a beaker—or two—full of the warm South." The other note was from Axel Munthe. It was written in English, in a doctor's spidery, near-indecipherable hand:

Arthur—

As a fellow medical man, you will understand this better than Wilde. When I arrived I saw at once there was no hope. The patient was sinking fast, but doing so in great discomfort: plucking at the sheets, crying out in distress. I had no choice. The old man had suffered too long and more than enough. I administered morphine—5 mg. He died in peace and I am glad for that.

The last rites were conducted by Msgr. Tuminello, with the other chaplains in attendance. Brother Matteo held Father Bechetti's hand to the end and will accompany the old priest's body on its final journey to the island of Capri. (Bechetti was born on the island and expressed a wish to be buried there. On Brother Matteo's behalf I have sent a telegram to Bechetti's family there. I may accompany the body, too. I know Capri and love it very much.)

I am going to my bed now, but please call on me this evening and we can talk further. Msgr. Tuminello asks especially to be remembered to you. He is conducting Mass in the Chapel of the Holy Sacrament today, at five o'clock, and hopes that you might attend. Tell Wilde I acted for the best. Had you found Bechetti as I did this night, I believe you would have done the same.

Yours,
Axel Munthe

"Methinks the doctor doth protest too much," said Oscar, tossing Munthe's note back across the café table to me. I returned it to my pocket and smiled at my friend.

I had found him seated in the shade at the far side of the piazza by the Porta del Popolo. He was dressed once more in his lime-coloured suit, wearing a matching tie and a shirt of daffodil yellow: he was quite unmissable. He was smoking a long, thin American cigarette and drinking a long, tall glass of Tokay and seltzer. His cheeks were pink, his eyes full of mischief. Two books lay open in front of him, propped up against a third.

"These were to have been my breakfast, Arthur—food for the mind. I was going to consume a page or two of

Twain's *Innocents Abroad* in lieu of porridge and then tuck into Butler's *Lives of the Saints* for my bacon and eggs, but I was rudely interrupted."

"By whom?"

"By James Rennell Rodd!"

"Good gracious!" I exclaimed. Oscar was gratified by my amazement. "You spoke to him?"

"He spoke to me."

"Was he civil?"

"Barely. He spoke to me only because he saw that I had seen him lurking by the obelisk and was embarrassed."

"Embarrassed?"

"I think so. Rennell Rodd and the Reverend Martin Sadler were together, thick as thieves, tucked behind the obelisk, deep in conference with Romulus and Remus, the urchin lads who dwell beyond the pyramid."

"What were they up to?"

"I hadn't yet breakfasted. I dared not think. The boys appeared to be in tears."

"If the Reverend Sadler was there, there will be an innocent explanation, I'm sure."

"Possibly," said Oscar, raising his glass to his lips, "possibly not." He took a sip of the wine and looked at me beadily. "All I can report is that Rennell Rodd caught sight of me catching sight of him and sent the lads scurrying at once, before wandering across the piazza with the Reverend Sadler to wish me good morning."

"'Good morning'? Was that all?"

"Rodd also asked how long I was planning to remain in Rome."

"What did you tell him?"

"The truth. I said that I did not know."

"And that was it?"

"Not quite. He saw my copy of Butler's *Lives of the Saints* and said that he was pleased to see me reading something of an 'edifying nature'—'for a change.' He had a book in his own hand. I asked what it was. It turned out to be a life of Pope Pius IX. He told me that he had been an admirer of Pio Nono's since his first visit to Rome, in 1878, when, as a young man, he had had the privilege of attending the Holy Father's funeral."

"Rennell Rodd was here in Rome at the time that Pio Nono died?"

"So it would seem."

"How extraordinary. Do you think he's somehow mixed up in all this?"

Oscar laughed. "I doubt it. He has too much ambition and too little courage for a life of crime. But you never know, there may be hidden shallows . . ."

I smiled and, taking off my straw hat, put it on the table alongside Oscar's books, then sat back, folded my arms, and surveyed the scene. The grand piazza was filled with brilliant sunshine, flower sellers, and a sudden flurry of worshippers in their "Sunday best," crisscrossing the square on their way to one of its three churches.

"This afternoon we are invited to Mass at St. Peter's," I said.

"Yes," said Oscar. "Munthe says so in his note. But I think it is *you* who are invited, Arthur. You are also invited to call on the Sadlers, by the way. The Reverend Sadler said his sister had something she particularly wished to ask you. I did not enquire further. I assured him I would pass on the message."

"Thank you," I said.

Oscar grinned at me—it was an impish grin. "Miss Sadler looks like a woman with a past. Most pretty women do."

"Her life has not been easy," I said.

"She has told you her story, then?"

"Some of it."

The waiter arrived with the coffee I had ordered and with a fresh Tokay and seltzer for Oscar. My friend offered me one of his American cigarettes.

"The tobacco is pale-yellow and absurdly bland," he said, apologetically.

"I have my pipe," I answered, feeling my jacket pockets to locate it.

"I'm glad. You may need it. This case could prove to be one of your 'three-pipe problems,' Arthur. It is turning out to be less tractable than I'd anticipated." I found my pipe. Oscar passed me his box of matches. "Do you still have the hand and the severed finger on you?" he asked.

"I do," I said.

"Good," he replied. "Keep them safe."

I held the lit lucifer to the bowl of the pipe and sucked hard on the stem. Through the matchstick's flickering flame I looked across at my friend as, languidly, he drew on his cigarette and slowly ran his little finger around the rim of his wineglass.

"What progress are we making, Oscar?" I asked, puffing

on my pipe. "This is a wild-goose chase, isn't it? We don't even yet know who brought us here."

My friend furrowed his brow and sat forward at the table. He laid down his cigarette, taking the saucer from beneath my coffee cup to use as an ashtray.

"Yesterday, I was certain that I knew whose cryptic 'cry for help' it was that brought us to Rome. Now I have my doubts. It's not Rennell Rodd."

I laughed. "Rennell Rodd is looking forward to our departure."

"To *my* departure, at any rate." Oscar smiled wanly. "It's not the Sadlers."

"Of course not."

"I don't know why you say 'Of course not,' Arthur. They were travelling on the same train as we were from Milan to Rome. They had reserved seats in the same compartment."

"Coincidence."

"Most likely. How were they to know what train we'd take? Nevertheless, we must consider every possibility— and we must face the fact that Miss Sadler has pressed her attentions on you, Arthur, in no uncertain terms."

"Don't be absurd, Oscar," I remonstrated.

"Love and gluttony justify everything."

"You do say the most ridiculous things at times, Oscar," I protested, unamused. "It seems likely from the items sent to Holmes—the severed hand, the finger, the ring, the lock of lamb's wool—that the 'cry for help' is connected in some way with the disappearance of this unfortunate girl, Agnes."

"You think so?"

"It must be."

"I thought so, too, but now I am having second thoughts."

"You amaze me, Oscar. I was confused to begin with, but I now see that the clues are as clear as daylight. The severed limbs point to foul play, obviously. The rose-gold ring with the crossed keys is what led us to the heart of the Vatican. It could lead nowhere else. It's the rose-gold ring that binds the chaplains and the sacristan and Pio Nono all together."

"And the lock of lamb's wool?"

I put down my pipe. "That's what completes the picture. It's the lamb's wool that leads us to Pio Nono's 'little lamb of God'—the little girl whose very name is Latin for 'lamb.'"

Oscar blew a cloud of smoke into the air. "I am now wondering whether it has anything to do with the girl at all."

"Don't be absurd, Oscar, it must have."

"There is no 'must' about it, Arthur. I am now thinking that the whole business may have nothing to do with Agnes and everything to do with Breakspear."

"With Breakspear?" I was dumbfounded.

"I am now wondering whether, in fact, it was not that mountain of flesh, Monsignor Felici—the Pontifical Master of Ceremonies and our official host—who sent those extraordinary parcels to Sherlock Holmes."

"Felici? To what end?"

"To lure you—*you*, Arthur Conan Doyle, the creator of Sherlock Holmes—to Rome, to the Vatican, for a specific purpose: to expose your alleged schoolfellow, the so-called Nicholas Breakspear."

"Why on earth should Felici want to do that?"

"Because Felici believes Breakspear is bogus but he can't prove it."

"But Breakspear has been a chaplain-in-residence at St. Peter's since Pio Nono's day. He is a Jesuit priest—clearly he is. He trained at the English College here. He knew Cardinal Newman."

"Of course, no doubt, all that may well be true. But before that, *before* he came to Rome, *before* he caught the late pope's eye, what was he then? *Who* was he then? Is his whole life built upon a lie? He claims to have been at school with you but you don't remember him, do you, Arthur?"

I hesitated. I was caught off balance by Oscar's maelstrom of words. "I am not sure."

"Exactly. *You are not sure.* The moment you set eyes upon the man, you did not trust him. And there is something about him that I do not trust, either. I have known him only three days. Felici has known him fifteen years and still doesn't trust him."

"If Monsignor Felici has had these doubts all these years, why has he acted now? Why not before?"

"Perhaps the doubts are new or perhaps they did not matter in the past. Or perhaps nothing is new, other than the circumstances. Here is Breakspear, ten years Felici's junior, suddenly on the brink of becoming a cardinal . . . It's too much to bear. Envy is a deadly sin, but Felici is only human: he is as guilty of it as he is of gluttony and pride. Felici will discover the truth about Breakspear. If Breakspear is a fraud, Felici will unmask him. It won't be easy, because Felici has no proof. He just has that uneasy feeling that you had when Breakspear greeted you with such over-familiarity this week—that uneasy feeling that I had when I heard that Breakspear was 'eating his way through the animal kingdom' and using those two boys from up the hill as his scavengers. Something about Breakspear doesn't ring true. Before it is too late—before young Monsignor Breakspear, the late pope's favourite, the new pope's confessor, receives his cardinal's hat—Felici is determined to find out all he can about the man . . . It may be nothing, it may be something."

"But why bring in Sherlock Holmes?"

"Who better to help him in such an endeavour? Felici can hardly go to the Swiss Guard or the Roman police. Why should they be interested? Besides, Felici does not necessarily suspect Breakspear of any criminal offence. He has accepted him as a fellow chaplain all these years. It's only now, when his junior looks set to overtake him on the canonical staircase, that his gorge rises. Breakspear is a mystery and an admirer of Sherlock Holmes. He even boasts that he was at school with Holmes's creator. Wouldn't it be perfect to engage Sherlock Holmes to uncover the truth about Nicholas Breakspear—to get one fiction to unmask another?"

"Oscar, this is so fanciful, and it ignores the most telling of all the clues parcelled up and sent to Holmes: that lock of lamb's wool. It is the lock of lamb's wool that leads us, inexorably, to Agnes."

Oscar moved his glass and my hat across the table. From beneath the two books that lay open before him, he picked out the third.

"Look what I have here, Arthur, as chance would have it." He inspected the spine of the slim volume. "It's *A Study in Scarlet* by one Arthur Conan Doyle. It is a first edition, published in July 1888 by Ward, Lock. You may recognise it."

"Where does this come from?" I asked.

"I borrowed it from the sacristy yesterday." He took in my reproving glance. "I will return it. I know I should have asked . . ."

I shook my head and clicked my tongue.

"I do hear your tut-tut of reproach, my friend," he continued, adopting an absurd little-boy-lost look. "But I think perhaps it was meant to be, because see this—on the fly-leaf, in pencil, the letters 'NB-O.' I take that to stand for 'Nota bene, Oscar.' And I do take note, Arthur." He flicked through the book's pages until he reached chapter seven, then put his finger on a particular line. "Now you take note of this, my friend. It's an aperçu from the great Sherlock Holmes. I came across it last night. It struck me as particularly pertinent. Read it out, would you?"

I took the book in my hand and read out the sentence he had indicated: "When a fact appears to be opposed to a long train of deductions it invariably proves to be capable of bearing some other interpretation."

I looked up at my friend. He was smiling. With his open wallet in his hand, he was removing from it the little envelope that contained the lock of lamb's wool.

"What are you trying to tell me, Oscar?"

"Encouraged by Holmes himself, no less, I am telling you that I am now looking in a different light at the clue that we have here. This may not be *lamb's wool* at all, Arthur. It may be *sheep's wool*—designed to point us not towards an innocent 'lamb of God,' but to 'the enemy within,' the false prophet of whom St. Matthew warns us: the ravening wolf who comes dressed in sheep's clothing."

18.

Tombs of the Popes

We lunched at the Hôtel de Russie. James Rennell Rodd was lunching there, also, but as we passed his table he made great play of studying the label on the wine that he was being served and so managed to avoid having to acknowledge us.

"He's cutting you," I said as the maître d'hôtel led us between leafy potted palms to a secluded alcove at the far end of the dining room.

"That's a relief," replied Oscar, collapsing onto a leather banquette and mopping his brow with his yellow handkerchief. The heat in the piazza had become quite oppressive. "James Rennell Rodd was charming once upon a time. He wrote bad poetry rather well. You might even have thought it had been translated from the French. Then he lost his looks and grew that moustache and joined the diplomatic service. Once we were friends. Once he was daring. Now he is dull, and I fear there is nothing to be done about it. He will certainly end up in the House of Lords. He has one of those terribly weak natures that are not susceptible to influence." Pleased with this sally, my friend grinned at me, widened his watery eyes, and said, "I think we should have an exceptional wine with our lunch today, Arthur. Lady Windermere can treat us."

I told Oscar that I would be happy to eat and drink whatever he cared to order. He told the waiter that, despite the weather, we wanted wild goose—"well roasted, with all the trimmings." The waiter apologised, but wild goose was not on the menu. Oscar insisted he must have it. "We have been chasing wild goose for days," he said, earnestly. He reiterated the line in English, French, German, and Italian, then declared that his father had been right: "One should never make jokes with waiters"—and ordered fresh asparagus followed by trout stuffed with sultanas, zucchini, garlic, chervil, and dill. He instructed the sommelier to bring us whatever wine he pleased and the wine the sommelier brought us pleased us very much indeed.

As we dined we talked about all manner of things, except the case in hand. "A serious meal calls for frivolous conversation," Oscar explained. He seemed especially eager to cross-examine me on the subject of the young ladies I had known in my life, "both before you met your darling wife—and after."

"There have been none after," I told him. "I do assure you of that."

"I am sorry to hear it," he said. "You have so much to offer, Arthur."

"You say wicked things, Oscar."

"I dare to speak the truth. There is only one real tragedy in a woman's life, you know. The fact that her past is always her lover, and her future invariably her husband."

After we had laughed (a great deal) and wined and dined

(if not wisely, certainly too well) and, through the foliage that surrounded our alcove, spied Rennell Rodd leaving the restaurant, Oscar announced that he would take to his bed for an hour to prepare himself for Mass in the Chapel of the Holy Sacrament. "I'll read Butler's *Lives of the Saints*."

"And I'll try to make some inroads on my correspondence," I said. "It is why I came away, after all. Touie will expect it."

"Don't do any work," cried Oscar. "Tuck yourself up with Mark Twain. Read his description of the Capuchin Church of the Immaculate Conception. We must go there. The burial crypt was a favourite haunt of the Marquis de Sade." He pressed the book on me. "Or read *The Sign of Four*—it's a rattling good yarn and rather deep at times." He riffled through the pages before passing the slim volume to me. " 'The chief proof of man's real greatness lies in his perception of his own smallness.' I am still mulling over that one."

While Oscar went to his room to take his siesta, I did not go to mine. I left the books he had put in my care with the hall porter and decided to venture along the Via del Babuino for a stroll. I thought I might wander as far as the fountain in the Piazza di Spagna, or even go beyond it up the Spanish Steps to the Pincio Gardens, but as I passed the Anglican church of All Saints I noticed that the main door was wide open and, on the spur of the moment, I decided to step inside.

It was three in the afternoon: across the street, the clock on the bell tower of Sant'Atanasio dei Greci was striking the hour. Outside, in the narrow Via del Babuino, it was baking hot; inside the darkened church, it was wonderfully cool. As I walked down the nave, looking up at the rafters and the stained-glass window above the altar, I breathed in the Anglican scent of beeswax polish and fading flowers, and was overwhelmed by a longing for home.

I found Irene Sadler and her brother standing close together at the foot of the pulpit. With her right hand she was soothing her brother's brow.

"Hello?" she said, turning at the sound of my footfall.

"Forgive me," I said.

"What for?" She smiled at me.

"The church is always open," said the Reverend Sadler, coughing to clear his throat before running his hands stiffly through his curly hair. "And I am always late—for something. I must go."

"You are never late for Evensong, brother."

"I will see you then," he said. He coughed again and, with a friendly grimace, nodded to me as he retreated towards the vestry door.

"Poor Martin." Irene Sadler sighed. Her face looked drawn. "His sermon was not to everybody's liking. His devotion to the Virgin Mary is a little too intense for Anglican tastes." She laughed sadly. "Thank you for coming to see me," she said, taking my hand.

"Your brother left a message . . ."

"I know."

"You wanted to see me?"

"Yes."

I said nothing.

"I wanted to see you," she continued, breaking away from me and walking towards the altar steps. "But for all the wrong reasons." She turned once more and looked me directly in the eyes. "I wanted a shoulder to cry on. I wanted someone sympathetic with whom I could share my woes."

I smiled, awkwardly. "Well, I'm here."

"Thank you," she said. She took a deep breath and spread her arms. "And I have work to do. I must rearrange the flowers. They have not met with approval, either—'far too fussy,' I'm told."

"May I help you?"

"You are a man, Dr. Conan Doyle. You can watch."

I watched as she rearranged the flowers. I assisted, too, when she would let me. And I listened to her woes. And heard of her hopes and fears. Her story touched me very much and, before I left, I gave her a cheque for forty pounds.

At five o'clock Oscar and I were seated in the basilica of St. Peter, at the west end of the great nave, at the back of the Chapel of the Holy Sacrament. We were not alone. It was a Sunday in summer and the pews were crowded with visitors and pilgrims, as well as what Monsignor Tuminello described to us as "the ever-faithful: the widowed and the very old." Tuminello, wearing a heavy chasuble of white and gold, his physical vigour seemingly all restored, conducted the Mass con brio. His theatrical style was more to Oscar's taste than mine. Though his skin was yellow and his face deeply lined, his voice was rich and resonant, his bearing impressive, and, when the Sanctus sounded and he raised the Sacrament on high, his eyes burnt with a frightening intensity. Oscar was much moved by the Monsignor's palpable faith, so unbending and implacable. I had my reservations.

They say, "Once a Catholic, always a Catholic." Not in my case, let me confess. I was reared by Jesuits—keen, clean-minded, earnest men, so far as I knew them, with a few black sheep among their number, but not many. I respect much that the Catholic Church has to offer: its traditions, its unbroken and solemn ritual, the beauty and truth of many of its observances, its poetical appeal to the emotions, the sensual charm of music, light, and incense, its power as an instrument of law and order. For the guidance of an unthinking and uneducated world it could in many ways hardly be surpassed . . . But I am neither unthinking nor uneducated: I am a man of science with a mind of my own. Blind faith is not for me. Faced with having to declare an unshakeable belief in the Immaculate Conception or transubstantiation, for example, my spirit rebels. Never will I accept anything that cannot be proved to me.

When the service was done and the faithful had departed, we remained seated at the back of the chapel. Oscar, who had changed his suiting from lime-green to olive-black, looked sideways at me, with thoughtful eyes.

"You have all this as your birthright, Arthur, and don't want it. I don't and I do. What a topsy-turvy world it is."

"Good afternoon, gentlemen," boomed Monsignor Tuminello, suddenly descending upon us and holding out both hands towards us. His yellow, weathered face was wreathed in smiles. "I am delighted to see you," he growled. He had divested himself of his chasuble and replaced it with a flowing white surplice that quite engulfed him and had the effect of making him look like a Nordic troll dressed as an angel. "Thank you for coming, Dr. Conan Doyle," he said, looking at me eagerly. "Thank you both for coming," he added.

We got to our feet. "If I am de trop . . ." murmured Oscar, apologetically.

"No, no," insisted the Monsignor. "You can both hear my story. Every Holmes must have his Watson. We all need scribes and acolytes. Where would Our Lord have been without the apostles? Please. Follow me."

His surplice billowing about him, he raised his left hand and, waving gaily at the sacristan, who passed us by carrying the communion plate back to the sacristy, led us out of the chapel through a side entrance. We followed him along a short corridor lined with the stumps of ancient marble columns, through a metal gateway, and down a flight of steep stone steps to what appeared to be another chapel—less ornate, it seemed, but larger and more cavernous than the Chapel of the Holy Sacrament above. Here there was no natural light. As Tuminello strode ahead we lost sight of him in the sepulchral gloom.

"We are in the old basilica now," he said from out of the darkness. "These are the Sacred Grottoes. This is where we house the Tombs of the Popes. As I am papal exorcist, they are my responsibility. Except on certain special days, we don't let the public come down here. We can talk freely. This is my domain. You may smoke."

He struck a match and, for a moment, his illuminated face leered out at us like a gruesome jack-o'-lantern at Hallowe'en. The Monsignor was lighting a small cigar. "The Almighty gave us tobacco to enjoy," he said.

"I am so pleased to hear it," said Oscar, reaching at once for his own cigarette case.

"And wine, too," continued Tuminello, cheerfully.

Gradually my eyes were adjusting to the obscurity. Tuminello was standing a yard or so from us, beneath a grey-stone arch, by a black-marble sarcophagus. His glowing cigar clenched between his teeth, he bent down and from a concealed niche cut low into the wall he produced a pair of golden chalices. He held them up triumphantly.

"Solid gold, rare rubies, and emeralds brought to Europe by Hernán Cortés himself. Pius VI drank from these. They are now surplus to requirements. We have *hundreds* more in the sacristy, just as exquisite. Cesare Verdi is very relaxed about what we may borrow."

"So I have noticed," said Oscar, taking one of the chalices and studying it admiringly. Tuminello handed me the other.

It was an object of extraordinary beauty and much lighter to hold than its appearance would have suggested. From the niche, Tuminello fetched a third chalice, for himself—again golden, again encrusted with precious stones—and a bottle of wine, already uncorked.

"Sacramental but unconsecrated. *Vitis vinifera ordinario,* I'm afraid, but it serves." He poured the wine into the chalices, sucking heavily on his cigar as he did so. I noticed that his hand trembled and the corner of his left eye twitched. He put down the wine bottle and raised his chalice. "To Joachim Bechetti," he said. "May he rest in peace."

"Amen," said Oscar, solemnly.

"Indeed," I muttered.

"He *will* rest in peace, of course. He was a good

man—brilliant in his day and brave in adversity. You have seen his work. He was a fine artist."

"I understand he is to be buried on Capri," I said.

"Yes," said Tuminello, from within a cloud of cigar smoke. "He was born there, but I don't think he'd been back in thirty years. Brother Matteo is accompanying the body, unembalmed."

"You don't approve?" asked Oscar.

"It's a mistake, given the heat. But Brother Matteo is a vegetarian with all that that implies. He maintains that embalming is 'unnatural.' He claims that St. Francis of Assisi spoke out against it. He didn't. But I'm too old and too tired to argue the point. And Brother Matteo took good care of Father Bechetti when he was alive. We must let him look after him as he thinks best now he's gone."

"Brother Matteo is a good man," said Oscar, reflectively.

"Undoubtedly," said Monsignor Tuminello. "Brother Matteo is the pattern of earthly goodness. *He* practises what *we* preach. He despises the sin, but goes out of his way to love the sinner. He gives the best of himself to the worst of us." The papal exorcist took a sip of wine. "Brother Matteo is almost a saint, I agree, but he is terribly naïve, as so many saints are. There is nothing wrong with embalming. I assisted at the embalming of Pio Nono. It was a beautiful experience, a privilege for all involved."

"Is Pio Nono here?" asked Oscar, peering around in the darkness.

"He was. But he's been moved to San Lorenzo fuori le Mura—St. Lawrence outside the Walls. Again a mistake, but it's what he wanted." Monsignor Tuminello spread his arms wide, his cigar in one hand, his chalice of wine in the other. "The popes should all be here, together, *safe,* close by St. Peter. This is where they belong."

"Who's this?" I asked, indicating the black sarcophagus.

"Gregory V," said Tuminello, dismissively. "German. We've had too many German popes." He smiled. "Too many Italians, too." He raised his chalice to us. "Not enough Englishmen."

"Just the one," said Oscar. "Nicholas Breakspear."

"Yes," said Tuminello, setting down his chalice on the floor and moving behind the black sarcophagus. "Hadrian IV."

He lit a second match and held it high above another tomb. In the flickering light before the flame died, I caught a glimpse of red porphyry and an ox's skull and two Medusa heads.

"He's in here, safe and sound, thanks to the embalmer's art. When we opened up the tomb, we found he was just a little man wearing tiny Turkish slippers and a huge emerald on a rose-gold ring. Cesare Verdi has promised to give Monsignor Breakspear the ring when he gets his cardinal's hat."

"Will Monsignor Breakspear be made a cardinal?" asked Oscar.

"Certainly and soon. We're due another English cardinal and Breakspear's the obvious choice. It would be cruel to deny him. He burns with ambition."

"And you, Monsignor Tuminello," asked Oscar, holding up his chalice as the old priest poured out more wine, "do you not burn with ambition?"

"I do," he said, "but not for myself, not any longer. I burn with ambition for another, one much more worthy. I burn with ambition for Agnes—our little lamb of God."

"You loved her?" I asked.

"All who knew her loved her. She was love made manifest."

"Who loved her most?" asked Oscar.

Tuminello laughed. "Pio Nono, without a doubt. He was Pope and no one in the world ever behaves entirely normally with the Pope . . . but Agnes did and the Holy Father loved her for that. They prayed together—they *played* together. He tottered along the corridor; she skipped along by his side. They were so easy in one another's company. It was a joy to behold them: the ancient pope, the old shepherd, and his little lamb of God."

"They were like father and daughter?"

"No, like grandfather and granddaughter, or great-grandfather, even. Pio Nono was *very* old. He was eighty-five when he died. Agnes was thirteen or fourteen. Father Bechetti was more like a father to her. He was the one who watched over her. He did not want her to be spoilt by all the petting she received. He worried that we paid her too much attention."

"And yet he painted her? Did that not feed her vanity?"

"Agnes was without vanity and Father Bechetti did not paint her from life. He painted her from memory. And his memory played tricks with him. It was when we lost her that Bechetti began to lose his mind. It happened very slowly. That painting in the sacristy—he began that about a year after she disappeared. It is not a good likeness, in my opinion. I think Felici is right. It looks more like the Blessed Virgin in Michelangelo's *Pietà* than like our little Agnes."

"Why did he paint her?"

"Because we asked him. We wanted something to remember her by. We *doted* on her. We all did: the chaplains, the cardinals, the Reverend Sisters in the laundry, the Lay Brothers who work in the gardens and in the builder's yard . . . Agnes was a free spirit; she could come and go as she pleased. Pio Nono allowed her a freedom within the Vatican enjoyed by no one else—no one at all. And she never took advantage of it. Everyone who knew her adored little Agnes."

"Brother Matteo?"

"He was like a brother to her. Breakspear, too. They were both younger men then. I taught Agnes to read and write, but Brother Matteo taught her about nature—about plants and flowers, about the birds and wild creatures—and Breakspear, bless his heart, tried to teach her English! He was very good with her. Very patient. He taught her English nursery rhymes."

"And what about Monsignor Felici?"

Tuminello paused and peered inside his now empty chalice. "I suppose if anyone loved her least, it was Felici. He loves very little beyond himself." The Monsignor looked up at us and grinned. "When Pio Nono teased us and named each of us after one of the seven mortal sins, he gave Felici the sin of sloth. He said Felici was too lazy to look beyond the looking glass. Felici has only ever really been concerned with himself."

Monsignor Tuminello chuckled, then frowned and shook

his head, casting his eyes down towards the chalice once again.

"May God forgive me," he muttered. "That was uncharitable—and wrong. Felici loved her, too. He prepared her for her first Communion. He was her confessor. He knew her well and loved her dearly. We all did."

The old priest returned to the niche in the wall and retrieved the bottle of wine.

"No more for me," I said. "Thank you." He divided the last of the bottle between himself and Oscar.

He looked at us, from one to the other, and his face was once more wreathed in smiles. "She wrought miracles, you know. Pio Nono suffered from epilepsy until little Agnes came into our lives. She cured him."

I raised an eyebrow.

"I know that she did," said Tuminello.

"Did she know that she did?" asked Oscar.

"No, she was just a child, no more than six or seven when she first arrived. She was utterly unself-conscious—all simplicity, all modesty. But she wrought miracles and she still does."

"And miracles are essential if little Agnes is to become a saint?"

"Two miracles are sufficient. Just two."

"And," said Oscar, casually, handing me his chalice to hold while he lit another cigarette, "it is with regard to the proposed canonisation of little Agnes that you seek the assistance of Mr. Sherlock Holmes . . ."

"Of Dr. Conan Doyle," replied Monsignor Tuminello, "yes."

He turned to me. I saw both supplication and excitement in his eyes. I did not know what to say.

"I am no expert on miracles," I began. "On the contrary, I—"

Oscar raised a hand to silence me and looked directly at Monsignor Tuminello. "You know for a certainty, do you, sir, that the child is dead?"

"Yes," replied the priest. "I know that she is dead. I have heard her voice—she is already at work among the angels."

"You know that she is dead because you have heard her voice from beyond the grave?" I asked.

"That is my profession, Dr. Conan Doyle. Yes, I have heard the voice of Agnes from beyond the grave."

Oscar raised his hand again to stop me from responding. "You know that Agnes is dead," he said to Tuminello, "but you did not witness her death yourself?"

"I did not see her on the day she died. I had not seen her for a day or so. I was in attendance on the Holy Father at the time. We all were. We knew that he was dying. I witnessed his death, but not hers. God took each of them on the same day—7 February 1878. He took them together."

"It was God's doing?" I asked, doubtfully.

"Everything is God's doing, Dr. Conan Doyle."

"You did not witness Agnes's death," Oscar persisted, "but did you see her body on the day that she died?"

"I did not," said Monsignor Tuminello, draining his chalice, "but I know that Monsignor Breakspear did. He found her body in the sacristy, laid out on the Seat of Tears."

"He told you that?" said Oscar, surprised. "Breakspear

swore to me that he had told Cesare Verdi what he saw and no one else."

"Breakspear did not tell me anything. I overheard him and Verdi talking about it once, years ago. It is not easy to keep secrets within the sacristy. The walls are thick, but there are no locks on any of the doors. I overheard Breakspear tell his story and I tried to question him about it, but he would tell me nothing further. He said no purpose would be served. He refuses absolutely to discuss the matter. I know that he believes that Agnes took her own life."

"And if she did take her own life—for whatever reason— she would not be eligible for canonisation. Is that correct?"

"That is correct, Mr. Wilde. The rules are strict. They have to be. A saint must die in a state of grace." He laughed. "Cardinal Bellarmine, you know, was well on his way to beatification when we opened his coffin and found that he had died with his finger in his mouth. It raised the question: had the unfortunate cardinal been buried alive? If he had been, who could tell what his final thoughts might have been! If you are to join the canon of saints, how you die is as important as how you lived."

"You are promoting Agnes's canonisation?"

"Yes, I will be her advocate. I am preparing the papers now. It has become my life's purpose."

"Who knows of this?" asked Oscar.

"No one, as yet—apart from you, gentlemen. I must have everything in order first or the cause is futile."

"Why are you doing this?" I asked.

"Because I loved her and I honour her memory. In God's

eyes, she is a saint already. I am merely doing God's work here on earth. In her cause I shall be God's advocate—*advocatus Dei.*"

"And when you have prepared your case, what happens?"

"I submit it to His Holiness for consideration. And His Holiness will then hand the papers to the office of the Promoter of the Faith, who will appoint a devil's advocate—*advocatus diaboli*—a canon lawyer who will test the case to exhaustion. He will require proof positive that Agnes lived and died in such an exemplary and holy way that she is now in heavenly glory."

"He will explore every aspect of her life?"

"Every aspect. The process can take years and the examination will be minute. A cause can stand or fall on the most trivial matter. There is a case being considered at the moment, that of Canonico del Bufalo, a missionary and a truly holy man. But the devil's advocate has found three things against him. Apparently, he ordered his servant to buy large fish at the market, his mother used to curl his hair, and he was fond of chocolate cream. His promoters can overcome the first two charges. Being in delicate health, he required good food. He needed his strength to do God's work. His mother curled his hair because, in his day, longer hair was the fashion for ecclesiastics and *not* to have allowed it to be curled would have been a sign of ostentation. But how to overcome the matter of the chocolate cream: that is the problem!"

Oscar and I joined in Tuminello's wheezy laughter—Oscar with delight, I with incredulity.

Oscar drew on his cigarette. "We can take it that little Agnes, though a child, was not unduly fond of chocolate cream."

"On hot days, when Pio Nono sent out for ice creams for the chaplains and the cardinals, Agnes always chose a chocolate ice and then gave hers to Monsignor Felici."

"Ah," said Oscar, "as ever, self-indulgence was Monsignor Felici's besetting sin, but it was not Agnes's."

"No one will accuse Agnes of self-indulgence. No one will question her goodness, her virtue, or her faith. I am sure of that."

"And the miracles?" I enquired.

"From his boyhood onwards Pio Nono suffered from epilepsy. It is well known. He had attacks all his life—they caused him much private distress and occasional public embarrassment. And then Agnes came among us . . . and, after her first Communion, Pio Nono and Agnes prayed together, side by side, and from that day the attacks stopped. He never had another."

"You have *proof* of this?" I asked.

"I have the Holy Father's medical records. I have his doctors' notes. Pio Nono suffered from epileptic fits for every year of his adult life until 1871, the year Agnes came to live in the Vatican. I have all the details. I have sufficient proof. Agnes cured a pope of epilepsy!"

"But you need two miracles," said Oscar.

"I have proof of a further miracle—and Dr. Munthe can vouch for this one."

"Munthe knew the girl Agnes?" I exclaimed.

"No, I don't believe so. Dr. Munthe has not been in Rome that long. But the man for whom Agnes performed her miracle is a patient of his."

"Who is he?" asked Oscar.

"Nobody special, a charity case—an old man who lives up on the hill, in the woods behind the pyramid. He collects bones from around the city and sells them to the glue-maker. In the old days, every Friday before dawn he used to come here with his cart to collect the bones from the Vatican kitchens. He knew Agnes. She gave him coffee and bread for his breakfast. He called her his 'little angel,' and when she disappeared he missed her sorely. When he realised that she must be dead, he began to pray to her."

"And the miracle?"

"The man was a cripple, born with a withered foot. He dragged his leg when he walked. I saw it with my own eyes. Then he prayed to little Agnes and she cured him. Dr. Munthe will attest to that."

Oscar finished his wine and returned the chalice to Monsignor Tuminello. The priest returned the empty vessels to the niche in the wall.

"I have all I need," he said, "except a clear understanding of how Agnes died."

I wanted the light of reason to cut through the miasma of "belief." "If she took her own life—" I began.

Tuminello interrupted me. "Then the case is hopeless, Dr. Conan Doyle." He looked directly at me. "But she did not take her own life—I am convinced of that."

"How can you be?" I persisted. "You say the girl was devoted to the Holy Father?"

"She was."

"And how old was she at the time of his death? Thirteen or fourteen? Girls of that age are the creatures of their emotions, Monsignor Tuminello. Any doctor will tell you that. They are at an age when changes are taking place within their bodies that lead to emotional volatility. It is well known. In such a state, Agnes's distress at the death of Pope Pius might have driven her to do something desperate."

Tuminello smiled at me. He had disposed of the end of his cigar and now clasped his hands together, holding them up almost as if in prayer.

"I hear what you say, Dr. Conan Doyle. And, yes, in the weeks before the Holy Father passed away, when he lay dying, Agnes came to visit him in his quarters, and she found those last visits deeply distressing. She kept her tears from the Holy Father, but she shed them."

"Did you talk to her about her distress?"

"No, I was not her confessor. That was Felici's role. He spent time with her—a great deal of time. I was surprised. Customarily, Monsignor Felici is quite self-absorbed. I think he took pity on the child. As the Holy Father's death approached, Felici heard her confession almost daily."

"And what did the girl confess?"

"The secrets of the confessional are sacred, Dr. Conan Doyle."

"You know that, Arthur," murmured Oscar, reprovingly.

"I do, Oscar," I said, quietly. "I also know, from all I have heard, that suicide in this case is undoubtedly a possibility. I think Monsignor Tuminello must accept that."

"I do accept that," cried the Monsignor, without rancour.

He smiled at me, almost seraphically. "Suicide is a possibility, but in this case not a likelihood. Agnes may have been troubled, but she was ever-faithful. Suicide is a sin. Despair is a sin. Agnes was without sin. I know it."

Oscar was now looking about, somewhat distractedly. He was wondering, I realised, if he dare stub out his cigarette on the tomb of Pope Gregory V. (Oscar was oddly fastidious: he never liked to drop a lit cigarette on the ground.) As he did the deed, over his shoulder he asked: "Could she have been murdered? Is that a possibility?"

"It would be a blessing," declared Tuminello, roundly.

"A blessing?" I expostulated.

"I understand," said Oscar, returning to us. "She might have died a martyr's death. That could assist her on the road to sainthood."

"But if all who knew her loved her," I said, shaking my head wearily, "who would murder the poor child—and why?"

"Exactly," said Tuminello. "She was universally adored."

"And yet," said Oscar, putting his face close to the priest's, "you have considered the possibility of murder, Monsignor, have you not?"

"I have."

"And why is that?"

"Because of something Agnes said, not long ago."

"Not long ago? *After* her death?"

"It was earlier this year. In January. I encountered her spirit at an exorcism."

"You know it was Agnes?" Oscar enquired.

"Oh, yes. She spoke her name quite distinctly."

"And she addressed you?"

"No, she was wrestling with a devil within the troubled soul of one of the Reverend Sisters who works in the laundry here."

"And what did the child say?"

"She spoke of the struggles of life and death. And she spoke of her own death—a violent death. She spoke of a hand at her throat and a single finger pressed against her mouth. She spoke of violence and of a secret she had not shared."

"And?"

"That was enough. It troubled me. It resolved me in my purpose. It was then, in January, that I knew I should not rest until I had discovered all I could about how Agnes died."

"Not only about how she died," said Oscar, "but also where she died, and what happened to her body."

"We know what we have learnt from Monsignor Breakspear," I said. "According to his testimony, her body was last seen at ten o'clock on the night of 7 February 1878. Less than an hour later, it was gone. Who took it? Where was it taken?"

"'Eliminate all other factors,'" said Monsignor Tuminello, "'and the one which remains must be the truth.' A favourite maxim of Mr. Sherlock Holmes, I think."

"I recognise the line," I said.

"I know the truth," said Tuminello, still gazing at me. "God took her body. Agnes was assumed into heaven."

I clasped my hands together and shut my eyes. "Forgive me, Monsignor," I sighed, "but that is preposterous."

"There is precedent," said the priest, lightly. "But the fate of Agnes's body does not worry me unduly. What concerns me—and what will concern the devil's advocate—is the nature of her death. I must discover the whole truth about that, and I need help to do so." Tuminello put a hand on my shoulder. "Frankly, I need the services of a good detective, however sceptical."

Oscar laughed. "And that is why you lured Dr. Conan Doyle to Rome, is it? You wanted the brains behind Sherlock Holmes to come to your aid in your hour of need."

The Monsignor laughed also but less comfortably. He cast his eyes downwards. "No," he protested weakly. "I am simply hoping to take advantage of Dr. Conan Doyle's being here. It's a happy chance that he has come to Rome and that we have met."

"It's not a happy chance, Monsignor. You planned it and planned it well. I must congratulate you." Oscar narrowed his eyes and peered about him into the gloom. "And to which of these late lamented popes did the finger and the hand you sent to Mr. Holmes belong? Before we leave, you must tell us that."

19.

Capri

*A*nd did he tell you?" asked Axel Munthe. With tightly clenched fists, the Swedish doctor was rubbing his eyes and stifling a yawn as he asked the question.

"He did!" replied Oscar, gleefully. "The hand belonged to Pope Leo XII and the finger to Pope Benedict XIV." Oscar paused dramatically. "Or was it the other way around?"

My friend, wide-eyed with excitement, looked to me for assistance—in vain. He turned back to Munthe and gave a histrionic shrug of his shoulders. "It matters not. According to Monsignor Tuminello, neither Holy Father had much to commend him beyond the fact that his mortal remains were easily accessible and epitomised the best of the ecclesiastical embalmer's art."

It was now ten o'clock at night and—as per Munthe's instruction in his note to me that morning—we had presented ourselves at Keats's house by the Spanish Steps. The doctor asked us up into his rooms but neither took our hats nor suggested we take a seat. Given that we had called on him at his invitation, he seemed oddly wary of us. He was self-evidently weary. He had removed his darkened spectacles: his weak, pale eyes had a hollow, haunted look.

Oscar appeared not to notice. "I told Monsignor Tuminello that I had first suspected that it was he who had summoned Sherlock Holmes to the Vatican on the afternoon that we first met, from the moment when the Monsignor arrived in the refectory at the sacristy, saw Conan Doyle, and immediately collapsed. It was the shock of recognition—the surprise of a wild dream realised."

Oscar's eyes flicked around the room: he glanced towards Munthe's desk, table, sideboard, chest of drawers. I was familiar with the signs: my friend was hoping for a drink. None was forthcoming. He reached into his pocket for his cigarette case.

"Then, foolishly," he went on, "I allowed myself to be distracted by the notion that it was *Felici* who had summoned Holmes, wanting someone to expose Breakspear!"

"Does Monsignor Breakspear need to be exposed?" asked Munthe, looking confused and stifling another yawn.

"He does and he will be. Conan Doyle is on the case."

Oscar took his cigarette to one of the candles on the mantelpiece above the fireplace. "I should not have allowed myself to be distracted," he said, putting his cigarette to his mouth and bending his face close to the candle flame. "Tuminello's story makes perfect sense."

"If you believe that a man can hear the voices of the dead," I said, sarcastically, "it does."

"Even if you don't, it does," rejoined Oscar, robustly. He was in no mood for argument. "Tuminello's actions are all of a piece. The Monsignor—the *exorcist*—is obsessed with Agnes. To him, she is a saint already. But to prove it to the world he needs to be able to answer the questions he knows the devil's advocate will ask. He needs to discover *precisely* how little Agnes died. At the time of her disappearance, extensive enquiries were made, but nothing of substance came to light. Breakspear says he saw her body, but he will say no more than that. What's Tuminello to do? For years he does nothing. He broods, he *believes*, he drinks, he smokes, but he *does* nothing. And then, on 21 January this year, he hears her voice! *Agnes speaks*—and she speaks of a violent death and of a secret, of a hand at her throat and a finger at her lips . . ."

"Did Tuminello say it was 21 January?" I asked, surprised. "He mentioned the month, but not the day."

"Well done, Arthur," said Oscar, drawing enthusiastically on his cigarette. "You have Holmes's ear for detail. The precise date is merely my surmise. Tuminello sent the first package to Sherlock Homes on 22 January this year—we know that: we have seen the postmark; you kept the packaging. I am guessing that he heard the voice on the day before, on 21 January, the feast of St. Agnes."

I smiled. "Clearly, I am going to have to get Holmes to pen a monograph on the uses of hagiography in the detection of murder." Oscar reached out his right arm and squeezed my shoulder happily.

Dr. Munthe looked on bleary-eyed. "Why on earth did he approach 'Sherlock Holmes' at all?"

"He was desperate. It was a shot in the dark. Through the winter, week in, week out, the Vatican's little *circolo inglese* had been enjoying the tales of the 'world's foremost consulting detective.' In his hour of need, Tuminello thought he might consult him, too. The book was there. He could copy out the Baker Street address. Tuminello—who speaks near-perfect English but claims to be able to read and write barely a word of the language—despatches his first clue. It is a simple tuft of lamb's wool." Oscar pointed his cigarette towards Munthe triumphantly. "You saw that at once, Doctor."

"Did I?" asked Munthe.

"You did," I laughed. "I seem to recall that Oscar was convinced it was a lock of hair plucked from the brow of a golden Adonis."

Oscar was too merrily on song to be put off his stride. "Eventually, of course, we recognised what we should have seen at once: that the lamb's wool symbolised Agnes, Pio Nono's little lamb of God." He turned to the mantel-piece and flicked ash from the tip of his cigarette into the upturned palm of the late builder from the church of All Saints. "The dead hand—not a woman's hand, as we first thought, but the small and delicate hand of a pontiff unfa-miliar with hard labour—was Tuminello's second clue, sent to Holmes in growing desperation six weeks after the first. As it transpired, it was the clue that we unwrapped first. It certainly caught our attention. The final clue, of course, was the finger. It was the finger that pointed us in the direction of the Holy See, thanks to the tell-tale rose-gold ring—"

"Stolen," I added, "by Monsignor Tuminello's own ad-mission, from the dead hand of Pope Pius IX. Tuminello attended the embalming of His Holiness and brought away Pio Nono's rose-gold ring as a souvenir."

"Yes," mused Oscar, twin plumes of cigarette smoke filtering from his nostrils, "of the seven rings once in the possession of Pio Nono's 'seven deadly sins,' the only ring not yet accounted for is the one that belonged to Father Bechetti. Where it's got to, heaven knows."

He stood erect, head held high, chest expanded, with his back to Munthe's fireplace. With his right hand he patted the outside of his breast pocket.

"I still have Pio Nono's ring in my wallet, as my souvenir, but before we left St. Peter's, we returned the severed limbs to their respective sarcophagi. Arthur generously gave them up, though Monsignor Tuminello said they'd not been missed. We said a prayer as we reunited hand and digit with their rightful owners."

"You have returned them?" Munthe smiled at Oscar. "I might have hoped to add them to my collection. Even a minor pope's hand is quite a novelty."

As we laughed, from behind the brocaded curtain in the corner of the room came the noise of cascading saucepans. Oscar turned eagerly. "Are we going to eat?" he asked.

"You may do as you please, gentlemen," said Munthe, putting on his spectacles. "I must calm my companion and then I am for my bed. I must be up at five. I have said that I will accompany Brother Matteo and Father Bechetti's coffin to Capri. We are taking the Naples train at a quarter to six."

"We shall join you," declared Oscar, jubilantly. "Capri in July will be glorious."

"We're accompanying a coffin, leaving at dawn and returning at dusk. It's not a seaside holiday."

"Nevertheless, we shall come, too, if you've no objection, Doctor?"

"None whatsoever," said Munthe, distractedly. He had moved to the chest of drawers on the far side of the room and, from on top of it, from a shallow metal tray that stood alongside a human skull, he had picked up a small syringe. He handled it with care.

"Which is it tonight," asked Oscar, "morphine or cocaine?"

Munthe raised his eyes languidly from the needle's point and gazed at Oscar. "It is cocaine," he said, "a seven-percent solution. Would you care to try it?"

"Thank you," said Oscar, "we'll have a sandwich and a bottle of Barbaresco at the hotel instead. You should eat something, too, Doctor. Won't you join us?"

"If you'll excuse me," he said, "I've eaten, but I have not slept all day." He stood facing us, syringe in hand. It was clear that our evening was at a close.

"I do apologise, Doctor," I said, hastily. "We would not have called, but in your note to me this morning you said you were going to rest during the day and suggested we come by this evening."

"I did, but as it turned out I got no rest. I've not slept since Friday night. As soon as I got in from Father Bechetti's deathbed this morning, I was called out again. Another case."

"Another day, another death," said Oscar, smiling.

"As it happens, yes," said Munthe, "but in this instance I arrived too late to be of any use. I had no involvement in the patient's death. The poor man killed himself—gradually, over many years."

"Ah," sighed Oscar, "the demon drink . . ."

"Yes. It broke him, slowly. He was a pathetic creature at the last. He lived up the hill, by the Protestant Cemetery, not far from where your hero Keats lies buried. His boys want him buried there."

"His boys?" asked Oscar, leaning forward earnestly. "This is the father of the two boys who come from the field behind the pyramid?"

"The immoral ones?" I added.

"The boys I warned you about—yes, those lads. Their father was a bone man and a drunkard. He'd been of little use to anyone for several years. Now he's dead. He passed away last night, according to the boys."

"How do you know?" asked Oscar, pressingly. "Have you spoken with them?"

"I have been with them for much of the day. They found his body this morning when they went to give him his breakfast. He was dead. They saw that at once. His body was rigid and stone-cold. They ran into town, encountered the Anglican chaplain and Rennell Rodd in the piazza, and told them what had occurred. Then they came here to find me. It's a sorry business, but the boys will be fine. Their father had not been a father to them for many years. He had only been a burden. Today they are saddened by their loss. Soon they will simply feel relieved."

From behind the brocaded curtain came the sharp clatter of tumbling kitchenware. Oscar started.

Munthe laughed. "Before you go, gentlemen, let me introduce you to my companion. She is not easy to live with, but I do love her so. Her name is Cleopatra. Around this time in the evening she gets hungry for attention—and for cocaine."

Dr. Munthe stepped across the room and slowly pulled back the brocaded curtain to reveal the kitchen beyond. There, on top of the unlit stove, cross-legged and rocking to and fro, sat a beautiful Arabian baboon.

At five-forty-five the following morning, Oscar Wilde and I scrambled aboard the Roma–Napoli *diretto* at the very moment of the train's departure. We had reached the railway station before five-thirty, but Oscar refused to proceed to our platform until he had equipped himself with coffee—and the station's coffee vendor was not a man to be hurried. (And his coffee, it turned out, was not coffee to be drunk. "It's cold and tastes of sour walnuts," croaked Oscar, bitterly. "It was sent to punish us. God does not approve of early risers.")

The murky liquid having been consigned instantly to the gutter, we rushed across the station concourse towards our train. Amid doors slamming, whistles blowing, and steam hissing, frantically we ran along the platform until, at last, we caught sight of Axel Munthe seated in the corner of a second-class compartment. As the train juddered to life and lurched ponderously forward, we heaved ourselves onto it. The Swedish doctor, dressed in his customary linen suit, wearing his usual hat, holding a handkerchief and polishing the lenses of his spectacles with fastidious fingers, squinted up at us as we stumbled, breathless, into the carriage and tumbled, panting, onto the seats opposite him.

"Ah, you're here, gentlemen," he said, smiling.

"We are," wheezed Oscar. "Just. How are you? How is your monkey?"

"I am well, and Cleopatra is a baboon, not a monkey, but thank you for asking. When I left, she was sleeping like a baby." The doctor put on his spectacles and tucked his handkerchief neatly into his pocket. "She's only eighteen months old, so, in fact, she isn't much more than a baby. Baboons can live to be forty-five years of age in captivity, you know. They thrive as pets in a way that's impossible in the wild. I much prefer animals to humans, don't you?"

"That's too deep a question to ask a man who's not yet had his morning coffee," murmured Oscar. He sniffed and looked sharply around the compartment, then turned back to study Munthe. "Where is your corpse?" he demanded.

"Father Bechetti's coffin is in the luggage van. Brother Matteo is there, too. He felt he should keep an eye on it. He's a good man."

"So everybody says," muttered Oscar.

His hooded eyes shifted their gaze from Dr. Munthe to the young lady seated next to him. I had already greeted her with a smile and a mouthed "Good morning." It was Irene Sadler, looking lovelier than ever, despite the ungodly hour. She was wearing a summer dress of the palest pink, with deep cuffs and a high collar of soft white silk. I was surprised to see her. Clearly, so was Oscar.

"Look at the state of us, Miss Sadler," he apologised. "We're a disgrace. I'm unshaven and unkempt." Oscar glanced towards me with a look of exaggerated disgust. "Arthur is probably unshaven, also—it's difficult to tell, given his absurd moustache. If we'd known we were to have the honour . . ." He half rose in his seat to bow to the lady.

"When I saw Dr. Munthe yesterday," she explained,

"he mentioned that he was coming to Capri and, as I have never been, I asked whether I might come, too. I shan't get in the way, I promise you. I'll be as quiet as a church mouse."

I smiled at her. She had a lovely way with words and a charming manner of speaking: the tone of her voice combined clarity and strength of character with intelligence and gentleness.

Oscar ran his eye over her rose-coloured costume. "You're not coming to the funeral?"

"None of us is," said Munthe, intervening, "unless, of course, you wish to stay on. I can't. The funeral won't be for a day or so. We're merely accompanying the coffin to the church. As I am the doctor who signed the death certificate, it simplifies matters with the paperwork at the harbour if I escort the deceased onto the island. If all goes well, we can return to Rome late tonight."

"I will keep in the background," said Irene Sadler, lowering her eyes. "I have brought my book."

Oscar raised an eyebrow. "*Lays of Ancient Rome*?"

"No," she answered, prettily. "*The Sign of Four* by Arthur Conan Doyle. I am fond of a good detective story."

Oscar sniffed again, stifling a sneeze. "Has Dr. Munthe told you about the case we are investigating?"

The young woman looked anxiously in the doctor's direction.

"I have told Miss Sadler everything," said Munthe, "without breaking a doctor's code of confidentiality, of course."

"Of course," said Oscar. "This is good. It means we

can speak freely. There is something I wanted to ask Dr. Munthe last night, but there was not time."

"We have time now," said the doctor, amiably.

Oscar pushed himself forward on his seat so that his face was close to Munthe's. He lowered his voice: we had to strain to hear him above the hiss and rumble of the train. "Is Monsignor Tuminello *mad*?" he asked.

"Mad?" repeated Munthe.

"This exorcism business—it's lunacy, isn't it?"

"I am not that sure it is," replied Munthe, carefully. He sat back in his seat, pulling his face away from Oscar's. "As Tuminello's physician, and friend, at his behest I have attended a number of his exorcisms. He certainly appears to bring peace to troubled souls. With nothing more than words and oil and holy water, he achieves what I can manage only with a syringe and a seven-per-cent solution."

"What happens?" I asked, turning to Munthe. "How does the act of exorcism work?"

"It's a ritual," said Munthe, "that's all."

I pressed him. "What takes place—exactly?" I asked.

He regarded me steadily. "It varies, but it always begins in the same way. The priest, holding up a crucifix, addresses the victim, the 'possessed one,' with the words *'Ecce crucem Domini'*—'Behold the cross of the Lord.' Then he touches them with the hem of his stole and rests his hand on their head. The object of the exercise, according to Tuminello, is to engage 'the demons within,' to take them on in personal combat and defeat them. It's a fight to the death."

"And these 'demons,'" enquired Oscar, "how do they manifest themselves?"

"They speak through the victim—usually they cry out loud. They declare themselves: 'I am Satan, I am Lucifer, I am Beelzebub.' Sometimes they emerge slowly, stealthily; more often in loud and sudden bursts. I was with Tuminello once when he performed an exorcism on a young boy of nine or ten. The child was uncontrollable. His language was vicious, utterly vile. The lad—he was a slip of a boy—had to be held down by four grown men. They struggled to subdue him. I watched amazed. Tuminello explained it very simply. He said the boy had 'the strength of the devil' inside him."

"Could there have been another explanation?" I asked.

"Possibly, but it's one not yet known to science."

Oscar sat back and considered Munthe. "And how does the exorcist defeat these diabolical forces?" he enquired.

"With difficulty—and determination. Tuminello is wonderfully condescending towards them. 'The secret is to find your demon's weak spot,' he says. Apparently, some demons cannot bear to have the sign of the cross traced with a stole on an aching part of the body; some cannot stand a simple puff of breath on the face; others resist with all their might a blessing with holy water. According to Monsignor Tuminello, 'relief' is always possible, but in certain cases to rid a person of his demons can take many exorcisms over many years. It seems that for a demon to leave a body and return to hell it has to die forever. I've heard one of these devils in its death throes crying out, 'I am dying, I am dying. You are killing me, Tuminello. All priests are murderers.'"

"Extraordinary," I murmured.

"Indeed," acknowledged Munthe. "Had I witnessed these goings-on just the once, I'd have dismissed them as trickery, but I am a man of science and, in Tuminello's company, I have attended exorcism after exorcism. There is more to it than hocus-pocus."

"Do you admire Monsignor Tuminello?" I asked.

"He brings relief to those who need it. I respect him. He is an unusual man." He looked engagingly from Oscar to me. "I like unusual men."

"Do you think he will achieve the canonisation of little Agnes?" asked Oscar.

Munthe laughed and removed his spectacles to polish them once more. "Is that his ambition? Tuminello wants to make the child a saint? I am sorry to hear it. Frankly, without a body and without a miracle, he's without a hope."

"He claims that the girl cured Pius IX of epilepsy," I said.

"Some say the old pope's final illness was *provoked* by an epileptic attack! The Holy Father's fits may have become less frenzied and less frequent as he grew older, but I don't think Pio Nono was ever completely cured."

"And what about the man who lived in the woods behind the pyramid," I asked, "your patient, the bone man?"

"He is dead," said Munthe.

"He was a cripple with a gammy leg," said Oscar, "until he prayed to Agnes."

Munthe smiled and shook his head. "The man was a drunkard and a wastrel. If he dragged his foot, it was to get pity. If he ceased to drag it, it was to draw attention to himself. Even if the poor wretch were still alive and half coherent, his testimony would be worthless."

Our journey to the harbour at Naples took three hours. We filled it with talk of monsignors and miracles. Munthe had respect for Luigi Tuminello ("He knows his business"), reservations about Nicholas Breakspear ("He asked me if he might *roast* my Cleopatra"), and what he called "a curious fondness" for Francesco Felici. "Felici lives in the moment, *for* the moment. I find his undisguised greed oddly disarming."

"Is it greed or a lust for life?" asked Oscar.

"God alone knows," said Axel Munthe, blinking endearingly from behind his darkened glasses.

On the tiny, iron-hulled steamship that took us from the harbour station across the Bay of Naples to the island of Capri, we agreed, nem con, that if anyone merited immediate beatification it was Brother Matteo. The Capuchin friar appeared to be the exemplification of saintly virtues. Tall and lean, bearded and handsome, with sparse snow-white hair and kindly dove-grey eyes, in his simple brown habit, with cowl thrown back, he looked every inch the part. The four of us had stood simply looking on as, with bare feet, grace, and good humour, the Capuchin friar had overseen the removal of Father Bechetti's coffin from the goods van of the train, found porters to convey it across the railway tracks to the dockside, and helped manhandle it onto the cargo deck of the waiting vessel. Brother Matteo was around sixty years of age. He did what he did with dignity and without fuss.

"No tips expected or forthcoming, I notice," Oscar whispered (with a touch of envy, I thought).

"He has natural authority," said Irene Sadler admiringly. "He commands respect."

"The monkish habit helps, no doubt," Oscar murmured, "and the presence of a coffin."

When Munthe and I offered our assistance, Brother Matteo called out, *"Grazie tanto! Non è necessario!"* and continued about his business. While Munthe was briefly locked in bureaucratic conclave with the harbour-master, Brother Matteo appeared on the quayside with a tray of fresh coffee and ham sandwiches.

"He *is* a saint," said Miss Sadler.

Oscar took the refreshments gratefully—it was our first food and drink of the day—and, as Brother Matteo departed, murmured into my ear: "He is so good he really should be our murderer. That's what your readers would expect, Arthur."

On the steamship, while we four sat together on a wooden banquette on the upper deck, sheltered from the ferocious midday sun by a tarpaulin awning, below us, on the cargo deck, Brother Matteo stood, exposed to the elements, keeping vigil by Father Bechetti's coffin. The crossing took two hours. Brother Matteo remained at his post throughout, his left hand resting all the while on the coffin's lid. During the voyage, Oscar dozed and then slept soundly. Munthe leafed idly through Oscar's copy of Butler's *Lives of the Saints* and then fell asleep himself. Miss Sadler and I sat side by side and talked—of her travails and my ambitions. The sea was calm, but in the occasional swell she rested her hand on mine and looked into my eyes for reassurance.

As the steamship neared Capri, Munthe awoke, got to his feet, and called out to us all to stand and admire the island's beauty. We had no difficulty doing so. The island's coastline was wonderfully varied and above the dramatic range of cliffs and crags, creeks and caves, there rose high hills covered in myrtle, cypress, and lemon groves. The Mediterranean light was perfect and the view undeniably enchanting.

"This is where I want to live!" declared Munthe, his arms outstretched towards shore.

"This is where Father Bechetti wanted to be buried," mused Oscar. "I wonder why?"

"Because it is paradise," cried Munthe.

"I'd rather live in paradise than be buried there," said Oscar, quietly.

From the cargo deck, Brother Matteo called up to us: *"Barca a remi!"*

"There's no harbour here," Munthe explained. "The ship can go no further. We must row the coffin ashore."

"How will we get back?" asked Oscar, anxiously.

"The ship will wait for us. We'll row back once we've safely delivered our cargo."

Four of the crew, with ropes, assisted by Brother Matteo, Munthe, and me, lowered Father Bechetti's coffin over the ship's side into the rowing boat. Matteo and I and two boatmen took the oars. The beach was not far off, but the water, though shallow, was choppy and the tide strong. It was hard pounding, made no lighter by Oscar's jocose (and incessant) commentary. As we rowed the boat ashore, my friend thought he would entertain us all by likening our heroic endeavours to those of the Oxford and Cambridge crews in the University Boat Race of 1877, the year in which the race resulted in a dead heat and Oscar composed his "Sonnet on Approaching Italy," which poem, encouraged by Miss Sadler, he proceeded to recite!

As, wearily, we dragged the heavy rowing boat up the pebble beach, Oscar apologised.

"My nerves get the better of me when I am too close to water." His pale and puffy face was awash with perspiration. Shading his eyes with a shaking hand, he looked up into the clear blue sky. A peregrine falcon hovered overhead. "You see, the birds of prey are gathering. My anxiety was perhaps justified."

Irene Sadler and Munthe laughed indulgently, but I was not amused. My arms ached and my head throbbed. "Enough," I snapped. "We have solemn work to do."

Brother Matteo smiled. *"Andiamo in chiesa,"* he said, indicating the donkey-and-cart, waiting at the roadside at the top of the beach.

It was not clear to me at first whether or not we were expected, but two elderly men, unshaven, in ragged trousers and torn shirts, stood by the cart, and, as we came within earshot, one of them called out, *"Capri? Funerale?"*

"Si," responded Brother Matteo. *"Chiesa di Sant'Anna."*

The old men came down the beach to help us carry the coffin to the donkey-cart. I commanded Oscar to assist.

"You've got to face life's harsh realities now and again, old man," I said.

I had noticed that since Brother Matteo and the coffin had first emerged from the railway goods van at the harbour in Naples, Oscar had studiously avoided gazing upon the oak box itself.

"It's not life that I shy away from," said Oscar. "It's death."

Nevertheless, my fine aesthetic friend heaved to and six

of us—the two old men, Brother Matteo, Axel Munthe, Oscar, and I—lifted the coffin out of the rowing boat and up onto our shoulders.

As we carried it, precariously, over the shingle towards the roadway, we were not unattended. Eight or ten young boys—all barefoot, some quite naked—had run along the beach to discover what was going on. Catching sight of the coffin, they had fallen silent and now they stood, wide-eyed and open-mouthed, watching the scene in wonder.

When we had placed the coffin on its simple hearse, we followed it along the roadway and up the hill, our cortège of naked boys in tow.

"I'll not forget this death march," murmured Oscar. "I'm glad I came."

Brother Matteo led the procession, walking alongside the donkey. He and the animal seemed to know the way.

"We are going to the Church of St. Anna," said Axel Munthe. "It is the island's parish church and very old. It's where Father Bechetti was baptised."

"St. Anna is the protectress of women in childbirth," said Oscar.

Munthe pulled Oscar's copy of *Lives of the Saints* from his jacket pocket and handed it back to my friend. "You know all about her, of course."

"I do," said Oscar, taking the book. "I already did. She is the mother of the Virgin Mary. She is Our Lord's *grandmother*. Her story is well known, Doctor."

"Is it?" asked Munthe. "I am a Swedish Protestant and a lapsed one at that."

Oscar laughed and pushed the book into his outside

jacket pocket. To make room for it, he had to transfer his cigarette case to an inside one.

"I suppose I am not allowed to smoke under the present sad circumstances?" he asked, balefully eyeing the box containing the mortal remains of Father Bechetti. "I could use a 'gasper,' as Arthur's ne'er-do-well characters like to call them. In this heat, to be natural is such a very difficult pose to keep up."

As we got close to the village, the naked boys began to fall away. As we entered the old church, there were just the seven of us, the six men carrying the coffin and Irene Sadler following behind. The ancient building—constructed, according to Munthe, in the thirteenth century with materials taken from the ruins of villas dating back to the heyday of Imperial Rome—was deliciously cool. And still. And dark.

Evidently, we were expected, for immediately in front of us, at the head of the nave, just in front of the altar steps, stood a simple wooden bier, with, at its head, a heavy brass candlestick bearing a single burning candle. To the right of the bier, seated alone in the front pew, was a nun dressed in a blue serge habit, her head bowed. From the outline of her form, she might have been a young woman. When we had lowered the coffin onto the bier and I turned towards her, I saw that her face was deeply lined and she had sunken, black-ringed eyes.

As we stepped away from the bier, Brother Matteo whispered to Axel Munthe in Italian. "Sister Anna," Munthe translated, "she does not speak. She weeps. She prays."

Irene Sadler had remained at the back of the church. Axel Munthe, Oscar, and I joined her in her pew. As we sat down, the nun got to her feet and stepped into the nave. She genuflected towards the altar, made the sign of the cross, and went to kneel at the foot of Father Bechetti's coffin. She knelt on the hard stone floor, her back erect, her hands placed together and held up before her face, palms and fingers touching. Brother Matteo stood beyond the candle, on the steps, facing the High Altar. He genuflected slowly and then turned back to lead his little congregation in prayer.

"In nomine Patris, et Filii, et Spiritus Sancti. Amen."

He made the sign of the cross over the coffin, then smiled at the Reverend Sister.

"Requiem æternam dona Joachim Bechetti, Domine; et lux perpetua luceat ei. Requiescat in pace. Amen."

For twenty minutes, we sat at the back of the church listening to Brother Matteo's prayers and the old woman's sobbing.

"Gloria Patri, et Filio, et Spiritui Sancto. Sicut erat in principio, et nunc, et semper, et in saecula saeculorum. Amen."

When Matteo was done, and we had been blessed, the Capuchin friar came down from the altar steps and walked to the foot of the coffin. Gently he placed his hands on the nun's shoulders and raised her up. He turned her towards him and took her in his arms. She lifted up her tear-stained face and rested it against his chest. He embraced her and, with great tenderness, he kissed the top of her coif. As he led her back to her place in the front pew, she whimpered pitifully. He leant over her for a moment and whispered something to her. When she had fallen silent and lowered her head once more, Brother Matteo left her and walked down the nave towards us.

Oscar got to his feet to greet the friar. *"De profundis clamavi ad Te, Domine,"* he said, distinctly. He was visibly moved.

"Domine, exaudi vocem meam," responded the Capuchin, taking Oscar's hands in his.

"'Out of the depths have I cried unto Thee, O Lord,'" said Oscar. "It is my favourite Psalm."

Brother Matteo spoke to Munthe in Italian. Munthe translated: "Sister Anna is all the family Father Bechetti has. She will wait here until the funeral. It will be tomorrow. Then the village will come."

"We cannot stay," said Oscar. "We must return to Rome." He looked at Munthe. "We must return at once."

"That is the plan," said Munthe. "We can go now. Our duty here is done."

"Will Brother Matteo come with us?"

"He will return tomorrow, after the funeral."

"Domani," said Matteo, *"a Dio piacendo."*

"Indeed," muttered Oscar. "Who is safe now, I wonder? We must return to Rome."

"Come, then," said Munthe. "We can go."

As we moved towards the church door, Oscar pulled away from us, saying, "Excuse me for a moment. I will just speak to the Reverend Sister."

"She has taken a vow of silence," said Munthe. "She cannot speak with strangers."

"I will speak to her. Wait here."

Leaving us standing in a pool of sunshine by the church door, Oscar walked down the nave. I stepped out of the light to watch him. When he reached the nun's pew he waited a moment, as if in doubt. He took out his wallet and opened it; then, lightly, he touched the nun on her shoulder. She looked up at him and, not recognising him, turned away at once. He touched her on the shoulder a second time and called her name: "Anna," he said. *"Il sua anello."* He stood looking down at her. From inside his wallet he had taken the little envelope that contained the rose-gold ring and the lock of lamb's wool that he had been carrying with him since we had left Bad Homburg. He gave the envelope to the Reverend Sister, bowed, and stepped away. The old nun took the envelope, uncomprehending.

He came back up the nave towards us. *"Avanti!"* he called. "We must get back to Rome before it's too late. I'll take one of the oars if I must."

Outside the church, when we had bade the Capuchin farewell and promised to meet up with him the moment he returned to Rome—*"Immancabile,"* said Oscar, earnestly, "without fail"—and were walking down the hill towards the beach, I said to my friend: "Well, what was all that about?"

"Don't you see?" he cried. "You must see, Arthur." He stopped in his tracks and looked at me in amazement.

"I'm afraid I don't see," I said.

"I know who she is."

"Sister Anna?"

"Yes. And I know who Agnes was."

"But the nun did not speak."

"There was no need. Some secrets lie too deep for words."

20.

Duty Calls

*I*t should never be forgotten that Oscar Fingal O'Flahertie Wills Wilde was essentially a man of the theatre. His very name has a theatrical flourish to it. His life, by his own admission, was a five-act drama that turned from comedy to tragedy. His literary reputation rests, not on his poetry or his prose, but on his *plays*. The men in whose company he felt most easy were all men of a theatrical disposition; the females he most admired were all actresses—and Queen Victoria. Oscar was essentially a man of the theatre and so, to him, the *effect* was everything.

No doubt, when he declared in the sunlit doorway of the ancient Church of St. Anna that he would "take one of the oars" if he must, he meant it. But when we reached the rowing boat on the shore of Capri, and Munthe and I heaved to, Oscar did nothing but help settle Irene Sadler opposite us and discourse on the beauty of the sunset. He had a playwright's way with words and a showman's instinct for timing. He loved to "hold the moment," as he put it, to keep the audience "in suspense—on the edge of their seats." He resolutely refused to share with us what had been revealed to him in the church that afternoon until he was ready to do so, "and that will be," he announced, "after the interval, when we are safely on board the train to Rome, beakers of champagne in hand."

By the harbour railway station in Naples he found an inn and from the innkeeper he purchased three bottles of French champagne, already iced, four glasses, and a basket of local fruit: grapes, peaches, and strawberries. But even when we were ensconced in our compartment—first-class now, courtesy of Lady Windermere—with beakers at the ready and the train at full speed, he seemed reluctant to speak.

"Are you playing for time, Oscar?" I asked, as he poured the sparkling yellow wine into my glass and it spilt over the rim onto my hand. "Have you lost your nerve, old man? Changed your mind?"

"I am playing with ideas still, certainly. As a detective I am an amateur, but I am a writer by profession, as you are, Arthur. We writers do play with ideas, don't we? Is it not our duty to do so—to take them and toss them into the air—to let them escape, to recapture them, to make them iridescent with fancy and wing them with paradox? I am not plodding the streets of London in muddied boots with your Inspector Lestrade of Scotland Yard; I am barefoot in the hills of Capri pursuing Truth in her wine-stained robe and wreath of ivy—following her where she dances like a Bacchante and mocks the slow Silenus for being sober. Facts spread before her like frightened forest things. Her white feet tread the huge press at which the wise Omar sits, till the seething grape-juice rises round her bare limbs in waves of purple bubbles, or crawls in red foam over the vat's black, dripping, sloping sides."

"Oh for goodness' sake, Oscar," I cried, "who is Sister Anna? If you know, tell us!"

Oscar roared with laughter. "I will tell you," he said. "Sister Anna was the mistress of Father Bechetti, thirty years ago. In her mind's eye, she was his bride. Agnes—Pio Nono's 'little lamb of God'—was the fruit of their illicit union."

Axel Munthe nodded and sipped at his champagne. "I thought that might be the case," he said.

"Poor lady," murmured Irene Sadler.

"It's one thing *thinking* something," I expostulated. "It's quite another *knowing* it. How do you know this, Oscar, *for a fact*?"

"I don't 'know this,' Arthur, 'for a fact,' as you crudely put it. But I believe it."

"You believe it? *Why* do you believe it?"

"Because I am a writer and a writer reads. I knew the old story of St. Anne and her husband—of how he was turned away from the temple because he had no child, and how Anna prayed to God and made sacrifices until an angel came to her and told her that God would grant her and her husband the baby that they longed for—and that the child would be conceived without sin. I knew all that, but until this afternoon, when I was sitting at the back of the church, leafing through my copy of Butler's *Lives of the Saints*, I had forgotten that St. Anne's husband was called St. Joachim."

"This is an ancient legend, Oscar," I protested, "about mythical saints."

"Yes, and Sister Anna of Capri and Father Joachim Bechetti were flesh and blood—and all too human. When they met, thirty years ago or more, and fell in love she was already a nun and he was already a priest. They could not marry, but neither could they deny their love. They conceived a child, and in their hearts they knew—and in the eyes of God they prayed—that it was a child conceived without sin."

I shook my head. "It's just a coincidence of names."

"Indeed," said Oscar, "but *nomen est omen*. It gave them their excuse, their justification."

Irene Sadler, seated next to me, pressed her hand on mine. "Love and religious fervour will make men and women do strange things, Dr. Conan Doyle," she said, softly. "I know."

Oscar reached for his cigarettes and lit one. "Agnes, their little lamb of God, was their secret and their problem: a problem and a secret shared at first, I imagine, with Anna's band of sisters in the monastery on the island—and then a problem solved when Agnes was old enough to be sent to Rome to be brought up as a waif and stray by the Reverend Sisters who work in the Vatican laundry. The little girl never knew who her parents were. She did not need to know: she was always surrounded by love. As a baby, she lived among the nuns on Capri, with her mother keeping a watchful eye over her. As a little girl, she lived among the nuns at the Vatican, with her father keeping a watchful eye over her and His Holiness the Pope, no less, as a kind of honorary grandfather. She was brought up as one conceived in innocence, as a little gift of God. She was brought up almost as a saint—and it seems that she behaved like one."

I smiled as Oscar filled the compartment with a cloud of smoke and poured me more champagne. "It's a charming story, my friend," I said.

"It hangs together," said Munthe.

"It has the ring of truth," said Irene Sadler.

"But is it true?" I asked. "Do you have anything for a man of science to work with? Any *evidence*? Anything beyond your imaginative leap of faith?"

"Her tears were a widow's tears and not of my imagining. And her ring. As she prayed, you saw the ring she wore on her wedding finger."

"All nuns wear a wedding band, don't they, to show that they are brides of Christ?"

"This was no ordinary wedding band, Arthur. This was one of the rose-gold rings . . ."

"It was the missing ring?"

"It was Bechetti's ring, yes. Sister Anna wore it on her wedding finger."

"And the ring that you gave to her was Pio Nono's ring?"

"Yes."

"Will she understand its significance?"

"She will see that it matches the ring that Bechetti gave her years before. She may think that, at the end, her erstwhile lover thought of her and wished her to have the second ring—as a parting gift."

"But he didn't, did he?" I protested.

"No, he didn't," Oscar conceded, "but he might have done. If I'd been him, it's what I'd have done."

Silence fell. The train steamed on. By now it was ten o'clock at night and our compartment was shrouded in smoke and darkness. Oscar drew on his cigarette, the tip of it glowing red and gold in the gloom.

"Is there more champagne?" asked Axel Munthe.

"There is," said Oscar, raising the final bottle.

"I have been wondering . . . ," mused Munthe, holding out his glass as Oscar uncorked the wine. He spoke slowly and deliberately. "I have been wondering . . . Do you think that Father Bechetti could have killed his own daughter to protect his guilty secret?"

Oscar laughed. "I think it more likely that Monsignor Felici ravished the poor child and then murdered her to hide his shame."

I sat forward in amazement. "Is that possible?"

Oscar looked at me. Through the darkness I saw that he was smiling. "Once you read the *Lives of the Saints* anything seems possible!"

He wedged the champagne bottle next to the basket of fruit beside him and pulled the book out of his jacket pocket, holding it up towards Axel Munthe.

"Did you read the story of St. Agnes of Rome—the virgin-martyr, the patron saint of chastity? It's a torrid tale." He flicked through the book and found the page he was looking for, squinting down at it in the dark. "Here it is. St. Agnes died on 21 January in the year 304, during the reign of the Emperor Diocletian. She was only thirteen, poor girl, the same age as our little Agnes at the time of her death."

"What happened to St. Agnes?" asked Munthe. "I did not read it."

"She refused to marry the son of the Roman prefect Sempronius and was sentenced to death for her insubordination.

But as Roman law did not permit the execution of virgins, to make her eligible for the scaffold she was dragged through the streets to a brothel."

"How terrible," murmured Irene Sadler.

"Indeed," said Oscar, closing the book and resting his hand on the cover, "though in her hour of need it seems that Agnes turned to God, and the Almighty, in His infinite mercy, spared her the fate worse than death. While she lost her life, she kept her virtue. Before she was ravished, she was killed."

"How was she killed?" I asked.

Oscar returned the book to his pocket. "The authorities can't agree on that. There are lots of contradictory stories. Some have her burnt at the stake; some have her beheaded; in one she tries to escape and a Roman soldier catches her by the throat and stabs her in the back of the neck."

"How horrible," whispered Miss Sadler.

"Murder is horrible," said Oscar. "And men are not nice."

"Some are, I'm sure, Mr. Wilde," she said, touching my arm in the darkness.

"No," said Oscar. "They are all the same, more or less. It's a matter of degree." His eyes fixed mine. "Men become old, but they never become good."

"Have I heard that before, Oscar?" I asked.

"I hope so," he replied. "It is from my play, *Lady Windermere's Fan.*"

That day, by land and sea, we spent some sixteen hours simply travelling. Long before we reached Rome, we were all too weary for words. For the last hour of the journey,

Oscar and Munthe slept while Irene Sadler and I told one another stories from our childhoods and then lapsed into easy silence. I was very comfortable in her company.

I was less comfortable, to be candid, when we got off the train at Rome station to find her brother, the Reverend Martin Sadler, awaiting us on the platform. I felt that his presence there was a kind of reproof. He was taller than I, more saturnine, and apart from his clerical collar, he was dressed entirely in black. His appearance that night seemed to me malign as well as forbidding.

"We have looked after your sister, I do assure you," I said, stiffly, as Miss Sadler put her cheek up to her brother to be kissed.

He nodded towards me. "I am sure that you have, sir," he answered, quite civilly.

"Dr. Conan Doyle has been assiduous in his gentlemanly duties," added Oscar, with a sly grin.

"Capri is very beautiful, Martin," said Miss Sadler, taking her brother's arm. "I am so glad I went. We saw ilex woods on the hillside and euphorbia all along the coast and there was a peregrine falcon flying overheard when we arrived."

"I am pleased the day went well," he said, smiling down at her.

"Of course, it was sad, too, accompanying Father Bechetti's coffin." She looked up into the clergyman's dark eyes. "Thank you for coming to meet me, Martin. How did you know what train I would be on?"

"This is the last train," he said. "I assumed this would be the one. But the truth is I have not come to meet you, Irene. I have come for Dr. Munthe."

Munthe sighed. "What is it? The boys up the hill?" He shook the clergyman by the hand.

"No," said the Reverend Sadler.

"Is it Monsignor Tuminello?" asked Oscar.

"Yes," said Martin Sadler.

"What has happened?" I asked.

"The papal exorcist is dead, Arthur," said Oscar. He, too, shook the clergyman's hand. "Am I not right, Mr. Sadler?"

"How did you know?" asked Sadler. "Did Felici send you a wire?"

"No," said Oscar, shaking his head despairingly. "I feared this would happen." In anger, he stamped his foot on the cold stone platform. "We are too late. Once he let it be known what he was doing, this was inevitable." He regarded me balefully. "We are to blame for this, Arthur."

"I am lost," I answered. "I don't understand."

Oscar looked directly at Martin Sadler. "How was Tuminello murdered? Was he struck from behind or poisoned?"

Sadler gave a nervous laugh. "Monsignor Tuminello wasn't murdered, Mr. Wilde. It was a heart attack."

"It was poison, then," said Oscar, quietly.

"He collapsed during Mass. He was an old man."

"He was sixty," said Oscar, "and he was murdered. We can be sure of that."

The Reverend Sadler now appeared as bewildered as the rest of us. "As I understand it, Monsignor Tuminello had a heart attack, Mr. Wilde, this afternoon, during Mass. That's all I know. The sacristan sent word to me asking me to fetch Dr. Munthe as soon as possible. That's why I'm here."

"Monsignor Tuminello was taking Mass?" persisted Oscar.

"Yes."

"Alone?"

"I do not know. I presume so. I was not there. It was in the Sistine Chapel. I was at All Saints'."

"And Monsignor Tuminello collapsed, you say, during the service?"

"Yes, according to Verdi."

"Yes, but *when*? Was it before he served the Sacrament or after?"

"I really do not know, Mr. Wilde."

Oscar heaved a heavy sigh. "Of course not," he said. "My apologies, Mr. Sadler. I am angry with myself because I am at fault."

Munthe removed his spectacles and rubbed his eyes. "I'd best go to the Vatican now," he said.

"Yes," said Oscar. "You must. You were his doctor. You should go. We'll share a cab as far as the Piazza del Popolo."

It was after midnight, but we found a solitary coach and two waiting on the cab rank outside the *stazione termini*. We clambered aboard and clattered through the empty Roman streets in silence. When we reached the Anglican church on the Via del Babuino, Irene and Martin Sadler bade us the briefest of good nights. Miss Sadler pressed her hand against my knee as she climbed out of the carriage on her brother's arm.

"Good night, gentlemen," she said, "and thank you for a memorable day."

"Good night."

When we got to our hotel, Oscar gave the coachman money (too much, I am sure: it was his way) and told the man to take his instructions from Dr. Munthe. "Good night, Doctor," he said. "It has been a long day—and for you it's not over yet."

"Duty calls," said Munthe. He held Oscar by the shoulder for a moment. "Thank you for your company today and for the champagne."

"Shall we meet in the morning," asked Oscar, "in the piazza, whenever you wake?"

"Yes," said Munthe. "I will report to you in the morning. I'd better go now."

"It will be murder," said Oscar, stepping out of the carriage. "I have no doubt of that. And a Catholic murder, too."

"What's that supposed to mean?" I asked.

"That it would not have taken place in an Anglican church, that's for sure."

"I don't follow you, Oscar," I muttered, climbing out of the carriage after him.

"You will, Arthur. You will."

"And if it *is* murder," asked Munthe, leaning his head out of the door, "should I call the police?"

"Not yet, Doctor, not tonight . . . if you don't mind."

"I am a physician, not a policeman, and it's very late. I don't mind."

I stood with Oscar on the pavement by the carriage door. Munthe stretched out a hand to shake mine. "You don't have your medical bag with you," I said.

"The patient's dead," said Munthe. "I don't need the bag tonight." With his right hand he patted his jacket pocket. "I have a death certificate with me. I always carry one, just in case."

"Of course you do." Oscar closed the carriage door. "Good night, Dr. Death!"

21.

Mass Murderer

*I*did not wake until almost noon on the following day. It was the hotel chambermaid rattling at my door that roused me from my slumbers, and from a troublesome dream, I recollect, in which Mycroft Holmes and I were engaged in a tussle to the death with a peregrine falcon from Capri and a giant rat from Sumatra! As I have said, I like regularity in my habits and when that regularity is disturbed I suffer in consequence.

Awake, I rose at once, threw on my clothes, and saw immediately that Oscar was not in his room. The hotel porter advised me that my friend had breakfasted long since, collected his post—and mine—and taken himself off to the Piazza del Popolo, where I would find him at his customary watering hole.

I did. Oscar was seated, in the far corner of the grand piazza, outside the café beneath the city gate. In the centre of the square, between the ancient obelisks, a hurdy-gurdy man was playing folk tunes while a little dog danced and the two urchin boys from up the hill stood watching. As I passed them, the boys smiled at me and waved. Uncertain what to do, I paused and walked on—then turned back again. I went up to the boys and, as I approached them, for the first time I looked fully into their young yet grimy faces. They were fifteen years of age at most. They grinned at me with brilliant smiles and dazzling white teeth, but I noticed that their shining eyes were rimmed with yellow pus, with black rings beneath and tear stains on their cheeks. I gave a coin to each of them and muttered, *"Condoglianze,"* awkwardly. They shouted, *"Grazie!"* gaily, pocketed the money, and immediately put out their hands to beg for more. I laughed and said, *"Basta,"* and went on my way.

Oscar did not notice my arrival until I reached his table. He was seated in the sunshine, wearing his green linen suit and my straw hat, absorbed in one of his books. He had the volume propped open in front of him, with a glass of champagne at its side, a cigarette in one hand and a sliver of peach in the other. As I cast a shadow across the table, he looked up at me and smiled.

"Give me books, fruit, French wine, fine weather, and a little music out of doors, played by somebody I do not know . . ."

"A happy sentiment," I said. "Good morning, Oscar."

"Not original, I fear." His face clouded over. "Keats. He always said it first. He always said it better." He put the piece of peach into his mouth and laid down his cigarette. He picked up the book and handed it to me. "Keats's letters, published in the year of Pio Nono's death, as chance would have it, 1878, the year of little Agnes's disappearance."

I drew up a chair and joined my friend. I saw that he had an empty glass waiting for me. He reached beneath the table and from a shaded ice-bucket produced a bottle of champagne. He filled my glass.

"You recall Keats's last words, don't you, Arthur?" he asked.

"I never knew them, Oscar," I said, smiling. "I'm a doctor, not a poet."

"Did they teach you *nothing* at Stonyhurst after Alexander Pope?" he wailed. "John Keats's last words, spoken not a quarter of a mile from where we are seated at this very moment, uttered in the very room Axel Munthe now shares with a dope-fiend of a monkey . . . last words, Arthur, that deserve their immortality."

"Yes," I said, raising my glass to him. "And what are they?"

"'My chest of books divide amongst my friends!'"

"Another fine sentiment," I said, putting down the glass and examining the volume admiringly.

"Books are everything, Arthur. They are our truest friends. When I die, you shall have a share of mine."

"Thank you," I said, touched by the thought.

He picked up the other volumes from the table. "These two will certainly come to you." He brandished the books before me. "Butler's *Lives of the Saints* and Mark Twain's *Innocents Abroad*: they've solved our case between them."

I looked at him and laughed. "You've lost me again, Oscar," I said. "I am still trying to unravel last night's riddle. The unfortunate Monsignor Tuminello dies—collapses at the altar, evidently of a heart attack—and, without a moment's pause, you cry 'Murder!'"

"Of course," he exclaimed. "Murder it must have been. I did not need a book to help me to that conclusion. It is obvious."

"It is not obvious to me, Oscar."

"Come now, Arthur. Tuminello tells us his long-kept secret—that he is to be God's advocate in the cause of the canonisation of little Agnes—and within hours of this revelation, he dies. You and I have not killed him, so who has?"

"Why should anybody kill him?"

"Because his advocacy of Agnes's cause will lead inevitably to a thorough investigation of her death, and whoever killed Pio Nono's little lamb of God all those years ago won't want that . . ."

"In your view whoever killed that poor child on 7 February 1878 also killed Monsignor Tuminello yesterday?"

"Indubitably. Tuminello told us that achieving the canonisation of little Agnes had become his 'life's purpose.' Once known, his determination to uncover the truth about her death ensured his own. On Sunday, he was either seen by someone talking to us, or we were overheard, or perhaps, naïvely, he unburdened himself to one of his colleagues . . . Whatever it was, on Monday he was killed." Oscar raised his glass as if to the late monsignor's memory. "Who's next, I wonder?"

"You think the murderer will not stop at Tuminello?"

"Anyone pursuing the truth about the death of little Agnes represents a threat to her murderer. The man—I *am* assuming it is a man—killed a defenceless child, Arthur. The secret he once thought safe has been disturbed. To safeguard that secret, he will stop at nothing."

I looked around the sun-drenched piazza. The hurdy-gurdy music played on, but I noticed that the feral lads from up the hill had disappeared. In their place, a pair of nuns, in black habits with well-starched white cornettes, stood arm in arm watching the dancing dog running round in circles chasing its own tail.

"So even we are not safe?" I said, surveying the comfortable scene.

Oscar leant across the table towards me. "We're here, engaged on Tuminello's business, at his behest. We *in particular,* Arthur, are not safe. Why else do you think we are drinking French champagne? It's a deuced expensive drink in Italy, but so long as I can see every bottle as it's uncorked and keep it within my sights until it's drained, I can be sure the wine's not been tampered with. It's the only way." He emptied the last of the champagne into my glass. "Peel every peach yourself and make sure you lock your hotel room tonight. We don't want you murdered in your bed. You never know who may not be rattling at the door."

"Shouldn't we inform the police?" I asked.

"The Swiss Guard or the *carabinieri*?"

"Either? Both?"

"According to the natives, neither can be trusted and each is as incompetent as the other. And I don't think they'd be inclined to read Butler's *Lives of the Saints* or Twain's *Innocents Abroad,* do you, even in translation?"

"Be serious, Oscar."

"I am serious. We need to wrap this up ourselves, Arthur. And we shall. Within twenty-four hours, as soon as the Capuchin friar is back from Capri. I have a plan. You'll be back in South Norwood by the end of the week, my friend." He delved into his inside jacket pocket and produced a couple of telegrams, one of which he passed to me. "I opened it inadvertently. I apologise. Your darling wife is missing you."

I took Touie's telegram and opened it to read her brief and loving message.

"She calls you her 'soul's partner,' I see," said Oscar, his head tilted to one side, his eyes appraising me. "Another fine sentiment, but quite a responsibility."

"Yes," I said, pocketing the telegram and turning back to my glass.

"Marriage is quite a responsibility," he said.

"Yes," I said.

"A world of pains and troubles is very necessary to school an intelligence and make it a soul, don't you think?"

"I'm not sure," I replied. "That's rather deep. Is that you and the champagne speaking, Oscar, or John Keats?"

"I don't recall—but it's rather good, isn't it?"

"It is Keats," said Axel Munthe, firmly. "And it was murder, Mr. Wilde. You were right."

The Swedish doctor brought over a chair from an adjacent table and sat down facing us, sitting forward so that my shadow fell on him, shading his eyes. He folded his hands together and rested them on Oscar's pile of books. "Good morning, gentlemen," he said, nodding to each of us in turn.

"Murder, eh?" murmured Oscar. "I am sorry to hear it, but I am delighted, too. It's always charming to be found in the right." He dropped the end of his cigarette into his empty champagne glass. "Monsignor Tuminello was conducting Mass alone?"

"He was."

"With an acolyte or two in attendance, but no other priests?"

"Correct."

"In the Sistine Chapel?"

"Yes."

"At the High Altar, before a small congregation?"

"Yes."

"And at the conclusion of the service, before pronouncing the final blessing, he suffered his 'heart attack'? He arched backwards up onto his heels and fell forward clutching at his chest?"

"By all accounts, exactly so. Who told you?"

"No one told me."

"Then how did you guess?"

"I didn't 'guess,'" declared Oscar, indignantly. "Occasionally, I allow myself an imaginative leap, but I never 'guess.' As Arthur's friend Holmes will tell you, it's a capital mistake to theorise before one has data. Insensibly one begins to twist facts to suit theories, instead of theories to suit facts."

"Then, how did you know?" demanded Munthe.

"My father was a doctor. I was brought up in a household filled with medical textbooks. I like to read. I am familiar with the symptoms of strychnine poisoning. I take it that it was strychnine?"

"I fear that it was," said Munthe.

"Mixed, I suppose, with the Communion wine?"

"Yes. There were still plentiful traces of the poisoned wine at the back of his throat when I examined him."

Oscar turned to me with a look of satisfaction on his wide face and revealed his crooked teeth in a complacent smile. "An ingenious way to kill a Catholic priest, eh, Arthur? Try the same trick in an Anglican church and you'd kill the whole congregation. In the Church of England, when it comes to taking the Holy Sacrament it's liberty hall: every communicant is given the wine as well as the bread at Communion. At a Catholic Mass, the celebrant alone takes the wine. So long as the murderer knows who will be conducting the Mass, he can place his poison in the sacramental wine decanter at any point before the service starts and then be a mile away, or more, by the time his intended victim raises the chalice to his lips and the grisly death occurs . . ."

He looked around for a waiter from whom to order a second bottle of champagne, evidently in a celebratory mood. I turned to Axel Munthe. "I am going to give my character Sherlock Holmes an older brother and model him on Oscar. I shall sit him in a chair in his club from which he'll never stir—"

"Like Diogenes in his tub?" quipped Oscar as he caught the waiter's eye.

"Exactly," I said. "And from there, in his club, in his chair, I will let the sedentary sage solve every crime that comes his way."

"I shall be stirring myself tomorrow," said Oscar, turning his attention back to us. "You will be, too, Arthur. We are going to host an old-fashioned English tea party—in the Capuchin Church of the Immaculate Conception."

"Why there?" I asked.

"Because Mark Twain says it's a 'must see' for all who come to Rome, and because Brother Matteo is a Capuchin and a key player in our unfolding drama."

"Brother Matteo will be there?"

"We need them all there, Arthur: Brother Matteo, the Grand Penitentiary, the Pontifical Master of Ceremonies, the sacristan, the Reverend Sadler and his sister, even the egregious Rennell Rodd. We must despatch the invitations as a matter of urgency."

"Will they come?"

"We shall lure them there with the promise of a reading of your newest Sherlock Holmes mystery . . ."

"I've not written it yet," I protested.

"This isn't until tomorrow, Arthur," he said, playfully, greeting the arrival of the fresh champagne with an elaborate salaam.

Axel Munthe looked at Oscar sternly. "You seem in a remarkably gay mood, given the news I've brought. Monsignor Tuminello has been murdered, Mr. Wilde."

"If he was a good man, he is in heaven already," said Oscar, now eyeing the waiter as he eased open the bottle of champagne. "We are not to mourn for our brother's soul being in heaven, surely?"

The waiter offered Oscar the wine to taste: he sipped it gingerly, then took a mouthful and rolled it around his tongue before swallowing it gratefully and nodding his approval to the waiter.

"And if there was the odd venial sin still outstanding, he will be in purgatory—with his fingers crossed. Either way, he is in a better place than this vale of tears."

The waiter made to charge our glasses; I covered mine with an open palm. "Did Tuminello die instantly?" I asked Axel Munthe.

"From what I gather, within moments of suffering the spasm. It seems that the poor man breathed his last even as he was being carried from the altar to the sacristy."

"Who carried him?" Oscar enquired.

"Cesare Verdi and one of the acolytes."

"It was definitely a lethal dose, then?" I said.

"It was no accident, Dr. Conan Doyle."

"But all present took it to be a heart attack?" asked Oscar, placing a glass of champagne in front of Munthe.

"Yes, that's how it appeared."

"And you did not disabuse them?"

"I followed your instructions."

"And you examined him discreetly?"

"Cesare Verdi had laid him out on the Seat of Tears, but I was on my own when I examined him and I have spoken to no one since."

"Good," said Oscar. "Thank you. That should provide us with the time we need to gather in the final pieces of the puzzle." He sipped at his champagne and, over the rim of his glass, looked beadily into Axel Munthe's blinking eyes. "Do not misunderstand me, Doctor. I do not take Luigi Tuminello's death lightly. I am exhilarated just now because the play is reaching its climax, the curtain is in sight, and I look forward to the audience's applause. But I am stricken, too. My conscience pricks—and so should yours. I've played my part in Tuminello's death. And so have you."

"In any event, he was not long for this world," said Munthe, transferring his gaze from Oscar to the champagne glass before him. "He was not a well man."

"It was you who prescribed him strychnine, Doctor—"

"Yes," answered Munthe, looking up sharply, "but not a lethal dose or anything like one. Very occasionally I gave him a thousandth of a grain, as a stimulant, and I administered it personally."

"Were you in Rome on the day that little Agnes died—on 7 February 1878?"

Munthe looked perplexed. "On the day that Pope Pius IX died? Yes, as it happens, I was. I was a student, aged twenty, on my first trip to Italy."

"And you went to the Vatican that day?"

"I did, out of curiosity. I was not alone. The Pope was dying—all Rome knew that."

"So you were there, *locus in quo*, on the day that little Agnes died."

Munthe laughed. "I was, but I did not kill her. I do assure you of that. And I did not kill Tuminello."

"Do not protest too much, Doctor. Are you not, like Keats, by your own admission, 'half in love with easeful Death'?"

"I did not kill the child Agnes. I did not kill Monsignor Tuminello."

"If you didn't, then who did, I wonder?" Oscar raised his champagne glass to his lips and looked out across the grand piazza.

I smiled. "You believe you know, don't you, Oscar?"

"I believe I do, Arthur. And, God willing, tomorrow afternoon, over tea at the Capuchin church, all will be revealed. And, Arthur, while I explain the mystery, you can serve the cucumber sandwiches."

22.

Old Bones

*T*he austere and elegant church of Santa Maria della Concezione dei Cappuccini was commissioned by Pope Urban VIII in the year 1626 at the instigation of his younger brother, Cardinal Antonio Barberini, who was both powerful and of the Capuchin order. In 1631, on the church's completion, Barberini commanded that the mortal remains of thousands of Capuchin friars be exhumed and transferred from the old Capuchin friary of the Holy Cross nearby to the crypt of the new Church of the Immaculate Conception. There, over time, in five interconnecting subterranean chapels, the bones of more than four thousand Capuchins were laid to rest. They were neither buried nor entombed but displayed: as a celebration of the dead and a reminder to the living. Bones—*thousands of bones*—laid out in extraordinary, elaborate, ornamental patterns, adorn the walls and ceilings of the church crypt. Complete skeletons, some dressed in Franciscan habits, lie or sit or crouch in dark corners and individual niches. A plaque in one of the chapels reads: "What you are now, we once were; what we are now, you shall be."

It was at this bizarre ossuary that Oscar chose to host his

English tea party and bring what he termed "the drama of the Vatican murders" to its climax. It was in this dimly lit gallery of bones and skeletons that he insisted that I hand round cups of Indian tea and plates of cucumber sandwiches (thinly sliced and lightly salted). To my astonishment, the Capuchin church was happy to allow my friend to commandeer the crypt for his divertissement. Indeed, it turned out that the priest in charge had a "set fee" for an afternoon's hire of the crypt and since Brother Matteo, a good Capuchin and friend to the church, was to be of the party, and Oscar was ready to pay four times the going rate, there were no awkward questions asked.

To my delight, Irene Sadler agreed to help me with the refreshments. The sandwiches were not a problem. It turned out that in the larder of her apartment at All Saints' she had a ready supply of bread she had baked in the English manner; I bought fresh cucumbers from the vegetable market on Piazza Barberini, and Darjeeling tea from the English tea rooms by the Spanish Steps. And at the Church of the Immaculate Conception we found a stove, a kettle, and sufficient crockery for our purpose in the pantry adjacent to the crypt.

The guests were invited for four o'clock and all came, in good order and in good humour—in remarkably good humour, I thought, under the circumstances.

"They are excited by the prospect of hearing your story," Oscar whispered to me, teasingly.

"They will be disappointed, then," I said.

"A little disconcerted, perhaps, but when they hear what

I have to offer in its place I believe their attention will be held."

The trio of chaplains-in-residence from the Vatican were the first to arrive. Monsignor Felici, the Pontifical Master of Ceremonies, vast and wheezing, but with a twinkle in his eye, descended the crypt's stone steps, gripping Brother Matteo by the arm. The friar, stalwart, upright, equable as ever, though returned from Capri only that lunchtime, betrayed no sign of weariness. When I asked after Father Bechetti's funeral, he nodded gently and said simply, *"E andato bene, grazie."* Monsignor Breakspear brought up the rear, bubbling with bonhomie.

"I love this church," he declared, to no one in particular. "Urban VIII was brought up by Jesuits, of course. He *was* urbane, arguably the most civilised of all the popes. As we can tell from Caravaggio's portrait, he was wonderfully handsome. He had a brilliant mind and exquisite taste. He got the better of Galileo in debate. He wrote fine poetry and beautiful prose." Breakspear caught my eye and beamed at me. "He would have enjoyed your work, Conan Doyle. If only poor Tuminello were still with us, he might have been able to summon up Urban's ghost to listen to your story this afternoon."

I smiled wanly at the Grand Penitentiary and offered him a cucumber sandwich.

"The Lord be praised," he breathed. "These do look like the real thing." He took a bite of a sandwich and gazed about him. We were standing in the "crypt of the skulls," the empty eye sockets of a legion of dead Capuchins staring down at us. "Perhaps Tuminello *can* hear us," he said, "and Father Bechetti, too. And Pope Urban . . ."

"And Pio Nono?" suggested Oscar, joining the group.

"Pio Nono was very hard of hearing towards the end," said Monsignor Breakspear, beaming at me once more. "Be sure to speak up during your reading, Conan Doyle."

Hurriedly I moved away, mumbling that I had to be about my butler's duties. I took my dish of sandwiches through to the "crypt of the pelvises," where I found the Reverend Martin Sadler, Axel Munthe, and James Rennell Rodd, teacups in hand, standing in a semicircle and peering up at a ceiling rosette formed by seven shoulder blades set in a frame of sacral bones, vertebrae, and feet.

"We don't do this sort of thing in England, do we?" murmured Rennell Rodd. "I'm glad." He looked at my plate of sandwiches. "This is more like it," he said.

Truth to tell, everyone at the gathering seemed more taken with the tea and sandwiches than the extraordinary memento mori all around them. Indeed, everyone, it appeared, apart from Oscar and myself, knew the crypt already.

"It has been a tourist attraction since the eighteenth century," Axel Munthe explained. "The Marquis de Sade, Hans Andersen, Mark Twain: they've all written it up. When you've been to St. Peter's and seen the *Pietà*, this is where you come next."

"The English do come," said Rennell Rodd, "but rarely more than once. It's not terribly jolly, is it?"

"We Swedes come time and time again," replied Axel Munthe, pleasantly. "We find it very soothing."

At half past four, Oscar, checking his watch, called the assembly to order.

"Ladies and gentlemen, there are chairs laid out in the last chapel. Please make your way there now. Miss Sadler and Dr. Conan Doyle will bring through further refreshments. We are nearly all gathered, I think. We're just waiting on Cesare Verdi, then we can begin."

There was no dillydallying. The assembly moved eagerly along the vaulted corridor to the last room, the "crypt of the three skeletons," where Oscar had arranged nine chairs in rows facing the altar.

The four clergymen, without prompting, filled up the front row, with the Capuchin friar at one end, the Anglican chaplain at the other, and the two monsignors in pride of place between. Once Miss Sadler had topped up the teacups and I had finished serving the sandwiches, we took our places in the second row, alongside James Rennell Rodd, who remarked loudly as we joined him, "Don't let Wilde hog the limelight with his preliminaries. It's your story we've come for, Conan Doyle."

"And a tale of Sherlock Holmes is what you are about to receive, James," declared Oscar, standing centre stage before us. "But on this occasion, forgive me, it'll be I who tells the story, not Arthur."

"The man's incorrigible," grumbled Rennell Rodd. "I should not have come."

"I am glad that you did, James," said Oscar, unperturbed. "You have a significant part to play in what's to come."

From the front row Nicholas Breakspear looked up at

Oscar and enquired tartly: "We are getting a Sherlock Holmes story, aren't we, Mr. Wilde? That is what we were promised."

"It all begins with Sherlock Holmes," said Oscar, tantalisingly, checking his watch once more, then looking behind him at the candles flickering on the altar. He glanced at the skeletons, bones, and vertebrae that lay all around. Peering into the enveloping gloom, he smiled as Cesare Verdi—unshaven, dressed in an unseasonable wool suit and holding a brown bowler hat—appeared beneath the archway. "Ah, you've arrived," said Oscar.

Verdi raised a hand as if to speak, but Oscar stopped him.

"Please," said Oscar, "take a seat, then we can begin."

"Yes," muttered Rennell Rodd. "Let's get on with it."

The seating arrangement in the crypt of the three skeletons

ENTRANCE TO CHAPEL

Cesare Verdi

Arthur Conan Doyle   Irene Sadler

Axel Munthe   James Rennell Rodd

Brother Matteo   Monsignor Felici

Monsignor Breakspear   Reverend Martin Sadler

Oscar Wilde (standing)

ALTAR

Verdi took his seat in the half-light in the back row by the doorway. Oscar gazed upon the assembled company with apparent satisfaction. Irene Sadler smiled at me and whispered softly, "This is exciting." She pressed her fingers gently on my sleeve. I looked around at the expectant faces all fixed on Oscar and thought to myself, If there is a murderer in our midst, either he is a mighty cool customer or he has no notion of what Oscar has in store.

"The scene is set," said Oscar. "I will begin."

Oscar Wilde was a seasoned lecturer, veteran of more than three hundred platforms, concert halls, and stages across the whole continent of North America and throughout the British Isles. On that late-July afternoon, in that macabre crypt, he commanded his small audience with effortless authority. He began his story simply, in a conversational tone, without rhetorical flourishes.

"Arthur Conan Doyle and I arrived in Rome a week ago, drawn here by three curious messages, sent care of Number 221B Baker Street, London, to Mr. Sherlock Holmes, the world's foremost consulting detective."

"I'm glad Holmes is getting a look-in," muttered Rennell Rodd.

Oscar smiled. "If it weren't for Holmes, we wouldn't be here, but we are here instead of Holmes, because Holmes, of course, is a fictional creation and these messages were not the stuff of fiction. They were an all too human cry for help and they came, we discovered, from the Vatican City, from one of the chaplains-in-residence to His Holiness the Pope, from the papal exorcist, as it transpired—one Monsignor Luigi Tuminello."

GYLES BRANDRETH

"This is better than fiction," murmured Monsignor Breakspear from the front row.

"And worse," said Oscar, without pause, "because this is real."

My friend turned again towards the candles on the altar. I could tell that he was wondering whether he dare produce his cigarette case. I know that, as a raconteur, he always felt the prop of a lit cigarette added a certain something to his performance. I watched him resist the temptation and, with shining eyes, turn back to survey his audience once more.

"This is a murder mystery," he continued, "and at its heart lies the murder of the young girl called Agnes, a child whom I once heard Pope Pius IX describe as 'pure innocence—a lamb of God.' This child, aged no more than thirteen or fourteen, disappeared on Thursday, 7 February 1878, from the sacristy of the Sistine Chapel at St. Peter's here in Rome. What happened to her? Where did she go? Alas, she was not assumed into heaven as Monsignor Tuminello hoped and prayed. She was murdered—but by whom? And when exactly? And how? And for what reason?"

Oscar held the moment. Had he had a cigarette in hand, this is when he would have drawn upon it languorously and then have lingered to watch the twin plumes of smoke filter slowly from his own nostrils. Instead, the heavy silence was filled by Monsignor Felici remarking wheezily: "If Agnes was murdered, why was her body never found?"

"It was," said Oscar, simply.

"When?" demanded Felici.

"On the night she was killed."

"Where?"

"Where she was murdered—in the sacristy, on the Seat of Tears."

"But then it disappeared," said Nicholas Breakspear, leaning forward in his seat.

"Yes," said Oscar, quietly, "it was brought here."

"Here?" exclaimed Breakspear. "To this church?"

"To this very room," said Oscar.

He turned and with his right hand pointed slowly to a human skeleton seated on the ground immediately to the side of the altar steps. The skull was tipped forward, the arms were folded across the ribcage, the legs extended, the little feet resting on a footstool made of blackened collarbones.

"There she lies," said Oscar. "I believe those are the mortal remains of Pio Nono's little lamb of God."

We sat in silence, all eyes fixed on the skeleton laid out on the floor before us. I half stood in my place to get a better view. "Can you be sure of this, Oscar?" I asked, in a voice barely above a whisper.

"No, Arthur, I cannot be sure," Oscar replied. "All I can tell you is that Mark Twain writes about this chapel in his book *The Innocents Abroad,* published nine years before the death of Agnes. He describes this altar and its surrounds in some detail. This little skeleton—so elegant and slight—does not feature in Twain's description, which makes me think it was not here then. And it *is* a little skeleton, which makes me think it is the skeleton of a child. And its bones are so much paler than the others all around it, which makes me think that it has not lain here many years . . . I cannot be sure that this is Agnes's skeleton, but I feel that it is—in my bones." He smiled. "Perhaps Brother Matteo will tell us if I am right?"

"*Si,*" whispered the Capuchin friar, almost inaudibly. "*Si,*" he repeated, his eyes cast down. "*Mea culpa.*"

"This is a good man," cried Monsignor Felici, turning his huge bulk towards the barefoot monk slumped at his side. "If Matteo killed the child, he had his reasons. Let me plead for him."

Oscar laughed and shook his head. "Brother Matteo did not kill Agnes. He would not hurt a fly—we all know that. Brother Matteo did not kill Agnes—but he believed he knew who had."

Oscar looked down into Francesco Felici's fat red face: beads of perspiration now bespangled the Monsignor's cheeks and brow.

"I take it that all of you in the sacristy knew that Agnes was the child of Father Bechetti. You never spoke of it, but you knew."

"I never believed it," said Breakspear.

"I had almost forgotten," muttered Felici.

"Sometimes that is the best way," said Oscar. "Men forget and women forgive. If it were not so, how could any of us survive? But Brother Matteo did not forget. He knew that Agnes had been conceived on the island of Capri— by a priest and a nun in lust. He knew that Agnes was to Bechetti the living embodiment of his sinfulness. When Brother Matteo discovered Agnes's body lying on the Seat of Tears he assumed that she had been killed by her own father. It was not so, but he believed it—and with you men of God, belief is all."

"*Mea culpa*," repeated the Capuchin friar, now wringing his hands wretchedly, his head swaying from side to side, his eyes tightly shut.

"You might wonder why, in the years that followed, Brother Matteo was so solicitous of Father Bechetti if he believed him to be a murderer? The answer is simple. As Monsignor Tuminello reminded me, 'Brother Matteo is the pattern of earthly goodness. He despises the sin, but goes out of his way to love the sinner.' It was almost as though Brother Matteo felt obliged to love Father Bechetti more because he believed him to be a murderer! Besides, what worthwhile purpose would be served by bringing Joachim Bechetti to civil justice? Ultimately, God would be Bechetti's judge—and a better one than any that the Italian courts could afford. And meanwhile, why bring unnecessary scandal on the office of the chaplains-in-residence and shame on the memory of the innocent Agnes? What good could be served by that? Let the unfortunate Bechetti wrestle with his conscience on the bitter road to redemption and let poor dead Agnes rest in peace."

"*Questo' è quello che è successo,*" muttered Matteo, despairingly.

"On the morning after her death, Brother Matteo brought Agnes's body here. Where he hid it overnight, I do not know: in his cell, perhaps, or behind the altar in the darkness of the Sistine Chapel. What I am sure of is this: in the early hours of Friday morning—8 February 1878—he brought the child's body here, hidden from view, wrapped in the brown habit of a Capuchin friar. I imagine he brought it here by cart, in the cart of the bone man who would come to the kitchens of the Vatican every Friday morning. He brought the body here and hid it until, over time, it turned from flesh to bone, and he could lay it out in a manner that was fitting—in a place fit for the purpose, in a place of prayer, in a chapel of rest."

Nicholas Breakspear moved forward to the very edge of his seat. "I must speak," he said. "I cannot let this pass, Mr. Wilde. Whether or not Agnes was his daughter, Father Bechetti truly loved that child. The portraits he painted of her after her disappearance will show you that. He did not murder her."

"And how do you know that, Monsignor?" asked Oscar.

"I cannot tell you, but I do know," answered Breakspear, solemnly.

"You cannot tell me, Monsignor Breakspear, because to you the secrets of the confessional are sacred. You cannot break the sanctity of the confessional box. Is that not right?"

Breakspear made no response.

"You assert that Father Bechetti did not murder Agnes because you believe you know who did."

Still Breakspear said nothing.

"You believe that it was Luigi Tuminello who killed the girl. You believe it because, in the confessional box, you sensed that the papal exorcist as good as told you so!"

Oscar stood triumphantly, head held high, legs apart, hands on hips. (Oscar confessed that he did sometimes like to "strike a pose.") Breakspear looked up at him and smiled. The Grand Penitentiary's voice was steady as he spoke. "When I take confession, Mr. Wilde, I do so as God's

316

servant. The words I hear are intended for God's ears, not mine. I am merely the conduit. You understand that, I know."

"I do," said Oscar.

"As Grand Penitentiary and as a fellow chaplain, I heard Monsignor Tuminello's confession often. I heard what turned out to be his last confession only a day or two before he died. I cannot tell you what he said to me, but I can tell you this: he did not confess to the murder of little Agnes."

"No," said Oscar, lightly, stepping away from Breakspear's seat and viewing him with half-shut eyes, picking his words carefully as he uttered them. "No, but, nevertheless, you think that he might have killed her . . . because she had told him something that made him think that she, the little innocent, had been defiled."

Breakspear said nothing.

"Agnes spoke to Tuminello of violence and of a secret she had not shared."

I was watching Breakspear from the far end of the second row. Almost imperceptibly, he nodded.

Oscar's oration now gathered momentum: "When Tuminello told you that Agnes had told him of violence and an unspoken secret, you assumed that he was telling you that the poor child had been taken, carnally. When Tuminello told you of the hand at her throat and the single finger pressed against her lips, and, full of passion and distress, spoke of her violent death, you feared the worst . . . Knowing of Tuminello's obsession with Agnes's innocence and purity, you jumped to the conclusion that, once he discovered that her innocence had been violated and her purity defiled, he decided to despatch his angel to heaven before the world could learn of her shame."

Breakspear, his face quite white, gazed up at Oscar in amazement.

"You heard all this from Tuminello only a matter of days ago," Oscar continued, "but tell me this, Monsignor Breakspear: did the papal exorcist tell you when it was that he had his 'conversation' with Agnes, or when exactly it was that she spoke to him of 'violence and of a secret she had not shared'? No? He did not—so you assumed, naturally enough, that it was fourteen or fifteen years ago, not long before the poor child's death."

Oscar leant forward and looked closely into Breakspear's eyes.

"Never make assumptions, Monsignor. As Sherlock Holmes would tell you: it is the golden rule. On Sunday evening last, among the Tombs of the Popes in the crypt of St. Peter's, Monsignor Luigi Tuminello told Arthur Conan Doyle and me of this same conversation with Agnes, and it took place not in 1877 or 1878, but earlier this year—yes, in 1892—on 21 January, to be precise, the feast day of St. Agnes of Rome. Agnes spoke with Tuminello during an exorcism. She identified herself by name. She was much troubled and what she told him caused him much distress. It prompted his cries for help. Indeed, it prompted him to send the first of his messages to Sherlock Holmes on the very next day. But could it be that Monsignor Tuminello had done what we have all done from time to time: could he have broken the golden rule and made a false assumption? No doubt he believed that the voice he heard during that exorcism was the voice of the child Agnes, Pio Nono's lamb of God—but is it not much more likely to have been the voice of St. Agnes of Rome, on her feast day, on the anniversary of her martyrdom, telling of her travails at the hands of vicious and violent men sixteen hundred years ago?"

"Do you believe in angels, Mr. Wilde?" asked the Reverend Martin Sadler, quietly, from his place beside Breakspear in the front row.

"I believe there are many more things in heaven and earth than are dreamt of in my philosophy. I also believe that a grain of strychnine prescribed to a patient to stimulate a sluggish heart is known to have hallucinatory side effects." Oscar's eyes moved from Martin Sadler to Axel Munthe. Munthe did not stir.

"Who killed this girl, then?" Rennell Rodd demanded.

Oscar returned to his central position before the altar. I could see that without the prop of a cigarette he was uncertain what to do with his hands. A little awkwardly, he folded his arms as he resumed his presentation.

"Father Bechetti did not kill his own daughter," he began. "He felt the shame of her existence—but it was his shame, not hers. He would have been more likely to take his own life than his own child's, but he did neither. And Monsignor Tuminello did not kill Agnes, either. Had she been defiled, the fault would not have been hers in any event. Tuminello trusted completely in her goodness and her innocence. He may not have heard her voice, but he understood her spirit and he wanted to discover the truth about her death only in order to advance her towards sanctity."

Nicholas Breakspear nodded emphatically at this last remark. Oscar looked down at him.

"And you did not kill her, either, Monsignor Breakspear-Owen." The Grand Penitentiary tilted his head and gazed up at Oscar with narrowed eyes. "You don't mind if I use your full name, do you?" added Oscar.

"Not in the least," replied Breakspear, without the faintest sign of being discomfited. "It's a bit of a mouthful. I haven't used it for years."

"Not since you came to Rome, in fact."

"I suppose not," said Breakspear, easily. He laughed. "It's not a criminal offence, I trust."

"No, Monsignor. It turns out that you are exactly who and what you claim to be. It's quite disappointing. You are not a fraud at all. Because Conan Doyle couldn't recollect your name, I suggested he make enquiries at your old school. He sent a wire to the bursar asking after 'Nicholas Breakspear.' I sent another on his behalf, supplying your initials: NB-O. I found that you had written them on the flyleaf of your first edition of *A Study in Scarlet*."

Oscar glanced in my direction and pulled a telegram envelope out of his inside jacket pocket.

"This came for you from Stonyhurst yesterday, Arthur. I know I shouldn't have opened it . . ."

I raised my eyebrows, but said nothing.

Oscar turned back to Breakspear and eyed him beadily. "You are a killer, after your fashion, of course."

"Am I?" The Grand Penitentiary appeared unmoved by the assertion.

"You are, and you boast of it. With the help of those scavenging boys who live up on the hillside behind the pyramid, you are eating your way through the animal kingdom. It's not original and it's not nice—but it doesn't make you a murderer in the eyes of the law."

"I am relieved to hear it."

"The worst we can accuse you of, Monsignor, is the sin of pride: dropping the humbler part of your surname for the vanity of being able to give yourself the name of England's only pope."

"I plead guilty to the sin of pride," said Breakspear, quite unabashed. "I am grateful not to be charged with murder."

"Who is to be?" asked Monsignor Felici. "We are all guilty of something, it seems. No doubt, I am guiltier than most. I am fatter than most, I know." He laughed wheezily and glanced over his shoulder towards Axel Munthe.

"We all wrestle with the sins of the flesh—" Oscar began.

"Speak for yourself," muttered Rennell Rodd, from the second row.

Oscar paused. "I stand corrected, James. I am sure that Brother Matteo does not. But Monsignor Felici does."

"Is he your murderer?" demanded Rennell Rodd impatiently.

"No," said Oscar, "he is not. Agnes gave him her ice cream and he accepted it. Monsignor Felici will not become a saint on that account. Canonico del Bufalo, a missionary and a truly holy man, failed when it came to the chocolate cream test."

Oscar considered Felici's ample form: self-consciously the Monsignor smoothed out the purple sash across his chest. Oscar then turned to Axel Munthe and stared fixedly at him as he spoke.

"Francesco Felici looks like a man who struggles with the temptations of the flesh. There is no reason to assume that *invariably* he succumbs to them. The Monsignor was Agnes's confessor. She was a child and she trusted him. I have no reason to doubt that he repaid her trust with his respect."

Oscar appeared suddenly weary. He stepped back towards the altar and, with a profound exhalation of breath and rubbing his eyes with clenched fists, he said slowly: "There is no evidence of any kind to suggest that Monsignor Felici—or anyone else—took an unwholesome interest in Agnes. And there is no evidence of any kind to suggest that Agnes, when she died, was anything but a virgin undefiled. It was only the old exorcist's confusion of one Agnes with another that could have led us down that blind alley."

"So who did kill the wretched girl?" demanded Rennell Rodd.

"The murderer is in this room," said Oscar, quietly. He smiled and looked directly at Irene Sadler. "Yes, it is a man, Miss Sadler. Most murderers are." He took his silver cigarette case from his jacket pocket and held it between his open palms. "And it is not a priest. Outside of novels, very few clergymen commit murder, it seems." He revolved the cigarette case between his fingers. "So the Reverend

Sadler is off the hook as well—at least so far as this charge is concerned." He opened the cigarette case and considered its contents, musing as he did so: "According to an article that I read in the *Daily Chronicle* not long ago, one in a thousand murderers is a man of the cloth, but one in ten is either a diplomat or a civil servant."

"Come on, Wilde," snorted Rennell Rodd, from the second row. "Murder is a capital offence. If you are about to accuse a man of the crime, you can't dress it up as a game of charades. It's a serious business."

"I agree, James. Thank you. And thank you for being here. I need you for the denouement."

"Then get to the point, man, because I am leaving in a moment."

Oscar snapped shut his cigarette case and slipped it into his trouser pocket, looking directly at his audience. The sparkle had returned to his eye. I sensed this was to be his final aria and he gave it to us *con fuoco.*

"Where was she killed? How was she killed? Why was she killed? I will tell you. She was killed on the Seat of Tears in the sacristy of the Sistine Chapel, late on the afternoon of Thursday, 7 February 1878, as Pope Pius IX lay dying. She had gone there to shed her own tears. She loved Pio Nono—as if he were a father and a grandfather. It was there, on the Seat of Tears, that Cesare Verdi, the sacristan, found her, when he came to the sacristy at around five o'clock to collect the little silver hammer that would be required within the hour to prove the death of the old pope.

"Cesare Verdi entered the sacristy, his sacristy, and on the Seat of Tears, the papal Seat of Tears, he saw this wretched child: Pio's Nono's favourite, Pio Nono's little lamb of God, crying her heart out. When Monsignor Tuminello told us that Pio Nono allowed Agnes 'a freedom within the Vatican enjoyed by no one else, no one at all,' I realised how much she might be resented. To Cesare Verdi, Agnes was more than a nuisance: she was a usurper. The sacristy was his domain, his inheritance, and yet this child had the run of the place, she could go where she wanted, she could play as she pleased, she could do no wrong . . .

"As little Agnes lay there, so impertinently, weeping in her sleep, Cesare Verdi decided that her reign should end with Pio Nono's—that the new pope, whoever he might be, would not be subject to the little girl's seductive charms. Verdi took the silver hammer and, with a single blow to the back of her head, he killed her. And to make assurance doubly sure, having struck her with the hammer, he suffocated her with a cushion. When he was certain that she was dead, he straightened her head, closed her eyes, pushed her lips up into a mocking, beatific smile, and laid her feet to rest upon the cushion. Later, he discovered that blood from the wound to her head had left a mark on the velvet. It is still there. It is no larger than a thumbprint. I would not have noticed it, had he not pointed it out to me. He said it was the mark left by past popes who had shed tears of blood upon the Seat of Tears. He called it a 'stigmata.'

"Cesare Verdi left the dead child where he had found her and went back, with his little silver hammer wiped clean, to the bedside of the dying pope. How he would have disposed of the child's body, I do not know, but the dilemma was solved for him, inadvertently, by the intervention of

Brother Matteo. Agnes's body—left for dead by Verdi, seen briefly by Monsignor Breakspear on his way to Compline—was stolen away in the darkness, wrapped in a Capuchin's habit, and brought here before daybreak, where it has rested, undisturbed, ever since.

"Within the world drama of a pope's death, the disappearance from the Vatican of a little girl, a waif and stray, did not count for very much. Searches were mounted, enquiries were made, but nothing was found. The child was not forgotten by those who had known and loved her, but the issue of her 'disappearance' disappeared, for years . . . until Monsignor Tuminello conceived his madcap notion of making Agnes a saint!

"On Sunday of this week, Cesare Verdi discovered that Monsignor Tuminello had set his heart upon unearthing the truth, the whole truth, about the death of little Agnes. Tuminello had to be stopped, so on Monday Verdi murdered him, using strychnine stolen from Dr. Munthe's medical bag. Dr. Munthe is not careful with his bag: I saw him leave it, unlocked and unattended, by the sideboard in the sacristy dining room. Poisoning the Communion wine presented no challenge to Cesare Verdi. He is sacristan. He is the guardian of the Communion wine at the Sistine Chapel. With the murders of both Agnes and Monsignor Tuminello, the only man with the motive, the means, and the opportunity in each case is Cesare Verdi. He is our murderer."

Oscar ran his hands down the front of his green linen suit and adjusted the pale-yellow cottage-rose in his buttonhole. He cast his eyes down and paused, almost as if he might have been expecting a round of applause. None came. The silence in the room was broken only by Monsignor Felici's heavy breathing. Felici, Breakspear, and Matteo stared fixedly in front of them. Martin Sadler and his sister, Munthe, Rennell Rodd, and I all turned towards Verdi. He was seated alone in the corner of the chapel, quite still, erect, his unshaven face clouded and perplexed.

Oscar looked up and addressed Rennell Rodd.

"James, I asked you here for a purpose. Cesare Verdi is half British; his mother is a cockney. He was born by London Bridge. I don't know my way around the Italian judicial system, and I don't want to, but I know British justice, and I respect it, and I know you. I trust that, as First Secretary at the British Embassy here, you will have the authority to arrest the man."

Rennell Rodd got to his feet and turned towards Verdi. "Don't move, sir," he said.

"I've no intention of moving," replied the man, getting to his feet defiantly. He looked beyond Rennell Rodd towards Oscar and, scratching his head with one hand while holding his bowler hat to his chest with the other, enquired: "What's all this about, Mr. Wilde? I'm one hundred per cent British. Don't you remember me? I'm Gus Green— from Willis's Rooms in St. James's. I am not my brother, nor my brother's keeper. I came only because I got your telegram, telling me Cesare was dead. I got to the Vatican just now and they sent me down here. Where is he? What's going on?"

Oscar blanched.

"I sent you no telegram, Mr. Green." He swayed and

closed his eyes. "I have been outwitted," he whispered, almost to himself, "outfoxed."

And then he laughed. It was a bitter, barking laugh, not like Oscar's laugh at all. Finally, slowly, he opened his eyes and, looking down towards the little skeleton that lay at the side of the altar, said quietly: "I apologise to each of you but most especially to the spirit of Agnes, Pio Nono's little lamb of God. She was pure innocence." He gazed around the gloomy chapel. "Her murderer will be halfway to Istanbul by now. We shall never see Cesare Verdi again."

We never did.

Aftermath

We never saw Cesare Verdi again, though sometimes, in later years, in London, dining with Oscar at Willis's restaurant in King Street, St. James's, I would look across the crowded room and catch sight of the maître d'hôtel standing at his desk and ask myself: is that Gus Green or is it Verdi?

Oscar said: "I wondered briefly whether they were the one and the same person, but I know that they were not because, back in the 'eighties, I saw them in the restaurant once, standing side by side. Together they appeared quite different and one was taller than the other, though I can't remember which. They were not close, except to their mother. I imagine on that fateful Sunday in July 1892, when Verdi saw us hugger-mugger with Tuminello on our way to the Tombs of the Popes, he realised that the game was up. He decided to silence Tuminello and then disappear, taking with him from the sacristy enough papal treasure to live in comfort for the rest of his days, but not so much that the Vatican would feel the need to send the Swiss Guard in hot pursuit of him. I suppose he sent that telegram from me to his brother announcing his 'death' for sentimental reasons. He wanted his brother to come to Rome to fetch home his personal belongings, as a souvenir for Mama. You know how Italians are about their mothers . . ."

We left Rome within twenty-four hours of concluding the case. The portmanteau of correspondence that I had taken with me to Bad Homburg ten days earlier returned with me to South Norwood, still requiring my attention! Though pressed to do so by Felici and Breakspear, we did not stay for Monsignor Tuminello's funeral. Dr. Axel Munthe kindly agreed to represent us.

"I'm not a great one for obsequies," said Oscar. "Death is more in Munthe's line than mine."

Over the next few years, the Swedish doctor and I corresponded occasionally—on literary matters mainly: we shared the same publisher—but we never met again. Oscar, I believe, last saw Munthe at his house on the island of Capri in the late summer of 1897, not long after Oscar's release from Reading Gaol. They talked, so Oscar told me, about death and Keats and monkeys—and the price of love.

On the day of our departure, Munthe had said he would see us off from Rome's railway station, but, in the event, he was instead called away to meet a new patient. She was Crown Princess Victoria of Sweden and I understand that she became his mistress and remained his mistress for many years. Axel Munthe was not regular in his habits but he was a good man. On the morning of our return to London, as we were saying good-bye, I mentioned to him that I had noticed the gum around the eyes of the two boys who lived in the woods up on the hill. He told me that he had noticed it, also; that the boys were both suffering from trachoma; and that they would soon be having treatment—paid for by James Rennell Rodd.

Rodd, I learnt, also paid for the funeral of the boys'

father and arranged, with Martin Sadler, for the poor man's ashes to be dispersed in the Protestant Cemetery adjacent to the pyramid, as his sons had wanted.

"Rodd's a bit stiff," I said to Oscar. "*Nomen est omen* and all that, but I like him. And you like him, too, really, don't you? It's a pity he doesn't like you."

"He doesn't like me because he is frightened of what he sees of me in himself. Nothing must be allowed to get in the way of James's career."

Nothing did. James Rennell Rodd's rise through the diplomatic service was meteoric. He served in Rome, Berlin, Athens, Cairo, and Paris, and did the Swedes such service that King Oscar II—the son of Oscar Wilde's godfather, the father-in-law of Axel Munthe's mistress—awarded him the Grand Cross of the Order of the Polar Star. He returned to Rome as British Ambassador in 1908. As I write this (in the winter of 1928) he has just become the Member of Parliament for St. Marylebone. I have no doubt that Oscar was right and that it is only a matter of time before he receives a baron's coronet.

Nicholas Breakspear did not secure a cardinal's hat. Shortly after our visit to Rome, he wrote to me, telling me of his intention to apply for the post of head of languages at our old school, Stonyhurst College. He asked me whether I would be one of his referees. I said I should be honoured. As you may know, under the name Nicholas Breakspear-Owen he went on to write what many regard as the definitive biography of Cardinal Newman. He died at Stonyhurst, aged seventy-four, in the spring of this year.

Monsignor Felici lived into his midseventies as well,

despite his girth, his concupiscence, and his appetite for ice cream. He had a good physician in Axel Munthe, who, no doubt, eased him towards a good end. When and how Brother Matteo died I do not know, but I imagine it was many years ago. The last I heard of him was from Breakspear-Owen, who travelled to Rome for the funeral of Pope Leo XIII in July 1903 and, for old times' sake, visited the Capuchin Church of the Immaculate Conception. There he found the aged friar, less upright but still barefoot and sweet-natured, tending the bones of little Agnes in the crypt of the three skeletons.

And what of Irene and the Reverend Martin Sadler? He served as Anglican chaplain in Rome for thirty-three years. According to a journalist of my acquaintance—the Rome correspondent of the London *Times*—Sadler, "though you could never fault him, never entirely settled in." The last time that I saw Irene Sadler was on the platform at Rome's station on the day of our departure. She came to see us off, looking very lovely in her pink summer frock and her wide-brimmed straw hat. We stood together, she on the platform looking up, me at the window of my compartment looking down, as we waited for the train to depart. As the guard's whistle blew, she pushed her face up towards mine and I caught the scent of lily of the valley in her hair. She whispered some words to me and kissed me farewell.

When I settled back into my seat and the train had begun to gather speed, Oscar said to me: "Arthur, are you quite well? You look as white as a sheet."

"I am puzzled by something that Miss Sadler has just said," I replied.

"And what was that?" he enquired.

"She said that I must go back to my wife and love her truly, just as she must go back to her husband and love him. She is *married*, Oscar."

"Ah," he said gently, studying the burning tip of his cigarette. "She admitted it, did she? The Reverend Sadler is her husband, not her brother, but as the post of Anglican chaplain in Rome is open only to unmarried clergy, they have opted for a life of deception. He called it 'a life of discretion' when he told me. He said he knew that he could rely on mine."

"A life of deception." I repeated the phrase.

"Yes. And it might work for them. Who knows? They are in a foreign country, far away from home, after all. Don't forget, when I first saw them I assumed they were brother and sister. This whole case has been riddled with false assumptions." He flicked some ash from his cigarette into his cupped hand. "I observed 'Miss' Sadler, as I thought her, making overtures towards you—coming on that balloon trip, inviting herself on our expedition to Capri—and I encouraged the friendship, thinking a little holiday romance would put some colour in your cheeks, but I did wrong. Martin Sadler is a weak man married to a strong and wicked woman, who appears to be neither because she is beautiful."

"She lied to me?" I said, shaking my head in disbelief.

"I fear she did, from start to finish. It's not impossible to live a lie and it does have its advantages. How much money did you give her?"

"I gave her one hundred pounds in all."

Oscar smiled. "I think you got off quite lightly. And it's a lesson learnt. One should always be suspicious of a woman who tells you that her past was burnt in the flames of a schoolhouse in Peshawar." He drew contentedly on his cigarette and observed me with kindly eyes. "You sent another telegram to Touie, I trust? Will your darling wife be waiting for you at the station in London?"

"I hope so," I said. "I don't deserve her, Oscar. I really don't."

Oscar laughed. "If we men married the women we deserved, we should have a very bad time of it." He leant across the railway carriage and tapped me on the knee. "In this world, Arthur, there are only two tragedies. One is not getting what one wants, and the other is getting it."

"Who said that?" I asked.

He smiled. "It wasn't Keats."

Chronology

1821: Death of John Keats in Rome, Italy, at the age of twenty-five

1846: Accession of Pope Pius IX, aged fifty-four

1854: Birth of Oscar Wilde in Dublin, Ireland

1857: Birth of Axel Munthe in Oskarshamn, Sweden

1859: Birth of Arthur Conan Doyle in Edinburgh, Scotland

1875: Axel Munthe's first visit to Rome and the island of Capri

1877: Oscar Wilde's audience with Pope Pius IX in Rome

1878: Death of Pope Pius IX, aged eighty-five, and accession of Pope Leo XIII, aged sixty-seven

1879: John Henry Newman becomes cardinal deacon of San Giorgio in Velabro, Rome

1882: Publication of *Rose Leaf and Apple Leaf,* verses by James Rennell Rodd, aged twenty-four, with an introduction by Oscar Wilde

1884: Oscar Wilde marries Constance Lloyd

1885: Arthur Conan Doyle marries Louisa "Touie" Hawkins

1887: Publication of *A Study in Scarlet,* the first appearance of Sherlock Holmes

1889: First meeting of Oscar Wilde and Arthur Conan Doyle

1889: Stories by Axel Munthe and Arthur Conan Doyle appear in *Blackwood's Magazine*

1890: Publication of *The Sign of Four*, the second appearance of Sherlock Holmes

1890: Publication of *The Picture of Dorian Gray*

1890: Axel Munthe opens his medical practice in Rome

1892: First performance of *Lady Windermere's Fan* in London

1892: Publication of *The Adventures of Sherlock Holmes*

1893: Publication of "The Greek Interpreter," featuring the first appearance of Mycroft Holmes

1893: "Death" of Sherlock Holmes in "The Final Problem"

1895: First performance of *The Importance of Being Earnest* and the arrest and imprisonment of Oscar Wilde

1897: Oscar Wilde, released from prison, visits Axel Munthe in Capri

1897: Arthur Conan Doyle meets Jean Leckie, who becomes his second wife following the death of Touie from tuberculosis in 1906

1900: Death of Oscar Wilde, aged forty-six

1901: Return of Sherlock Holmes in *The Hound of the Baskervilles*

1903: Death of Pope Leo XIII, aged ninety-three

1908: James Rennell Rodd appointed British ambassador to Rome

1924: Publication of *Memories and Adventures* by Arthur Conan Doyle, featuring the first account of his friendship with Oscar Wilde

1929: Publication of *The Story of San Michele* by Axel Munthe

1930: Death of Sir Arthur Conan Doyle, aged seventy-one

1933: Sir James Rennell Rodd GCB, GCMG, GCVO, PC, elevated to the House of Lords as 1st Baron Rennell

1938: Publication of *Two Englishwomen in Rome 1871–1900* by Matilda Lucas, featuring incidents touched on in *Oscar Wilde and the Vatican Murders*

1941: Death of Baron Rennell, aged eighty-two

1949: Death of Axel Munthe, aged ninety-one

2000: Beatification of Pope Pius IX

2010: Gyles Brandreth unveils the plaque commemorating the first meeting of Oscar Wilde and Arthur Conan Doyle at the Langham Hotel, London

For further historical information and for details of the other and forthcoming titles in the series, for reviews, interviews, and material of particular interest to reading groups, etc., see:

www.oscarwildemurdermysteries.com

Oscar Wilde and the Vatican Murders

Arthur Conan Doyle, exhausted from the wild success of his Sherlock Holmes mystery series, retreats to Germany to relax and respond to a large quantity of fan mail. Moments after arriving at his hotel, he meets his friend Oscar Wilde. As the two sort Sherlock Holmes fan mail, they come across a mysterious package, postmarked Rome, containing a mummified human hand. Another package contains a lock of hair or wool, and a third contains a human finger with a distinctive ring. Wilde and Conan Doyle head to Rome immediately to investigate the mystery, where they meet a cast of characters ranging from "Dr. Death," a Swedish euthanasia enthusiast, to a Jesuit Monsignor who is attempting to eat his way through the entire animal kingdom. When a fifteen-year-old murder mystery overshadows the mummified body parts, Wilde and Conan Doyle put the clues together to solve the Vatican murders.

For Discussion

1. In the first pages, Wilde exclaims to Conan Doyle, "You cannot deny your destiny. No man can" (page 8). Do you agree?

2. Throughout the novel, Oscar Wilde refers to his fondness and admiration for John Keats and his poetry. What is it about Keats's life, work, and death that connects Wilde to him in such an important way?

3. Oscar Wilde is described several times throughout the novel as an *aesthete,* defined as a person who has or affects to have a special appreciation of art and beauty. Is this a compliment coming from Conan Doyle?

4. As a scientist, Conan Doyle is observant and factual in his descriptions, while Oscar Wilde takes leaps of faith based on hunches. How would the story be different if Wilde narrated rather than Conan Doyle?

5. What modern day celebrities or artists remind you of Conan Doyle and Wilde? If you were casting this movie, whom would you choose for these roles?

6. When the two men open the mysterious packages addressed to Sherlock Holmes, how do each of their reactions reflect their personalities?

7. On the train to Rome, readers are introduced to Irene and Martin Sadler. What are your initial impressions of the two? Do you think Oscar Wilde's deductions are far-fetched or accurate?

8. The details about the papacy in this book are historically accurate. Does learning about specific eras while reading novels enrich your reading experience? Did reading about the inner workings of the Catholic church add a level of interest and mystery?

9. Do you think that Dr. Axel Munthe's mysterious companion, dark designs, and enthusiasm for euthanasia make him an untrustworthy character?

10. Conan Doyle finds himself attracted to Irene Sadler, but it is important to him to remain faithful to his wife. Were you pleased that he honored his vows, or were you, like Wilde, rooting for him to live in the moment and pursue the romance?

11. Why do you think Sir Rennell Rodd seemed so put out by Wilde? Do Wilde's affectations make him likable or obnoxious?

12. One of the Monsignors describes Agnes as "the personification of innocence" (page 207). Why was Agnes so precious to the Monsignors and Pope Pius IX?

13. There are a great many coincidences that tie this story together, one being that Oscar Wilde met several principal characters fifteen years previously. Another is the Cesare Verdi/Gus Greene connection. In your opinion, do these coincidences add to or detract from the excitement of the mystery?

14. When the killer is revealed, were you surprised? Who had been your primary suspect or suspects?

What is it about Wilde's life and the papacy that compelled you to write this novel?

Oscar Wilde's life is extraordinary—so much happened to him and he knew so many remarkable people. He knew actors and artists, politicians and poets. He mixed with all conditions and types of men and women—from princes to street prostitutes. But when I discovered that as a young Oxford student he had been given a private audience with the Pope at the Vatican, I thought immediately, I must—I simply must—make that the starting point for one of my Oscar Wilde murder mysteries. Eat your heart out, Dan Brown. Oscar got there first!

The novel is rich with historical facts about Wilde, Conan Doyle, Rome and the Vatican, and the papacy of Pope Pius IX and Pope Leo XIII. What research techniques did you use?

Everything in the novel that you would expect to be factually correct is so—I hope. I have been diligent in my research and for this book I travelled to Rome and stayed in the Hôtel de Russie, where Wilde stays in the story; visited Keats's apartment, where Dr. Axel Munthe lived; spent time in the Anglican church; and secured a privileged and remarkable tour behind the scenes at the Vatican. The sacristy in the novel is as I found it when I visited it. I have been privileged to sit on the Seat of Tears. I have done my utmost to ensure that the details of life at St. Peter's in the 1890s are all correct. (If you happen to be a cardinal and spot a mistake, do be sure to let me know. I don't claim to be infallible.)

Wilde wrote several essays about the work and life of John Keats. What did Wilde find so magnetic about Keats? Do you have a favorite Keats poem?

Wilde admired youth and beauty—and Keats had both. Wilde loved the quality of Keats's poetry and was moved by his personal history and the tragedy of his early death. In putting words into Wilde's mouth for my novel, I have borrowed from Wilde himself. One of my favourite books is *The Complete Letters of Oscar Wilde,* edited by Merlin Holland and Rupert Hart-Davis, and I recommend the letters in the collection where Wilde writes about his love for Keats. I am not ashamed to admit that my favourite Keats poem is "Ode to a Nightingale."

Of the characters in the book, quite a few are historical figures including the popes, Sir James Rennell Rodd, Axel Munthe, and of course Oscar Wilde and Arthur Conan Doyle. What different techniques do you use when writing about a historical figure versus a character you are inventing?

None at all. They are all real to me. With the characters who happen to be historical figures I try to get the facts right: I do my research in the library and on the internet. I read "around" them; I read biographies of them; I try to find copies of their correspondence, to help hear their voice; and I get pictures of them to keep on my desk as I write. With those I have invented, I still do the research, but it's a little easier. I just have to look into my head.

Wilde criticises Nicholas Breakspear for being an unoriginal thinker. What do you, and what does Wilde, see as the harm in unoriginal thought?

Wilde was not an intellectual snob. He did not set himself up as someone superior to others. But he found originality exciting and more interesting than predictability. Breakspear in the novel wants to be someone special, he wants to appear as an original. He sets himself up as someone out of the ordinary. Oscar sees at once that Breakspear is not as original as he pretends to be. That arouses suspicion in Oscar but not contempt.

When you began this novel, did you have a great deal of familiarity with the Catholic church, including the differences between the Jesuits and Capuchins?

I am an Anglican by upbringing—like Oscar Wilde. My wife is a Catholic—like Arthur Conan Doyle. I have been a churchgoer, off and on, all my life. I know a lot of priests and I am intrigued by their vocation—and by the rites and rituals of the church. I am also fascinated by the heritage of the Anglican communion and the Catholic church, so part of the pleasure of writing the book has been delving into this world and trying to understand the mind-set of those who dwell there.

Does it get easier or more difficult to channel Wilde's distinctive voice and personality in your novels as the series continues?

It gets easier. I have been fascinated by Wilde since I was a child. My father was a friend and colleague of H. Montgomery Hyde, who published the first full account of the trials of Oscar Wilde in 1948, the year I was born. As a boy, I lived in London in the street Oscar Wilde's mother lived in; I lived around the corner from the Wildes' home in Tite Street. Later I lived in Sloane Street, near the Cadogan Hotel, where Wilde was arrested in 1895. At my boarding school, Bedales in Hampshire, I got to know the school's founder, John Badley (1863–1965), who had been a friend to Oscar and Constance. The Wildes' elder son, Cyril, was a pupil at Bedales. I have been soaking up the words and world of Oscar Wilde all my life. I am a friend of Merlin Holland, Oscar's only grandchild, who generously reads my books—and does his best to put me right when I go wrong. In the 1970s I produced a stage version of *The Trials of Oscar Wilde*. In 2010, as an actor, I appeared as Lady Bracknell in a musical version of *The Importance of Being Earnest*. In writing these mystery stories about Oscar and his circle, I have spent months—no, years—studying the man from every angle. I feel I know him quite well now. Not completely, of course. And the more I know him, the more intrigued I become.

Do you see yourself as more like Oscar Wilde or Arthur Conan Doyle in personality and working style?

I would love to have Oscar's genius and wit; I would love to have Arthur's fundamental decency. They were two remarkable men. They were very different as people, but each was a man of ambition and extraordinary achievement. Oscar was the more flawed of the two, of course, and that may make him more interesting as a hero in a series of murder mysteries—in the way that Sherlock Holmes is more charismatic than Dr. Watson. I fear I am not very like either of them. I am more in the mold of Robert Sherard, the poet, journalist, and serial biographer of Wilde, who is the narrator in several of the novels—and may be again in the next: *Oscar Wilde and the Murders at Reading Gaol.*

Enhance Your Book Club

1. The Italian Monsignors have a tradition of gathering together to speak English, read Sherlock Holmes, and enjoy English tea. Serve a proper English tea at your book club, complete with, of course, cucumber sandwiches.

2. The Monsignors have an inside joke that they encompass the seven deadly sins. Go around the room and figure out which sin each book club member personifies.

3. Several of Rome's landmarks are described in the novel, including the ancient Colosseum and the pyramid tomb of Gaius Cestius. Research and discuss how the landmarks and terrain have changed over the last century.

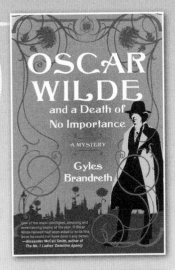
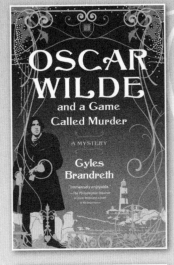
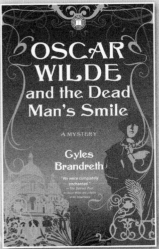
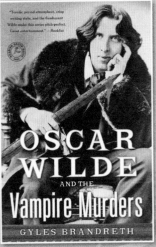